BLOODSTAINED
Wings

FEATHERS AND THORNE SERIES
BOOK 2

IVY BLACK
AND
RAVEN SCOTT

YOUR EXCLUSIVE ACCESS

From the bottom of our hearts, thank you so much for your support.

To show our appreciation, we've created an exclusive VIP newsletter just for you. When you join, you'll immediately receive a free prequel for another dark mafia romance series, that you won't find anywhere else!

You will also receive bonus chapters, notifications of future releases, future discounts, and many more surprises!

Download the prequel for The Umarova Crime Family Series, receive future discounts and other bonuses by visiting: https://BookHip.com/JAJXVPR

See you on the inside,
Ivy Black and Raven Scott

CHAPTER ONE

Isabella

The realtor raves over the recessed lighting, the stunning marble floors, and the copper tub in the ensuite upstairs that is perfect for date night. I hardly hear a word she says, instead staying focused on how often she leans into my lover when she talks. She takes every opportunity to brush Carter's arm casually, laughing through her words when nothing funny is said and giving me a rather dismissive look whenever he takes my hips in his hands.

I stray from her guided tour, poking my head around the corner into the wide office space with built-in cabinets and storage under the bench by the large front window. It's not a bad house by any means, but every time I turn around, I catch the petite realtor in her thin heels hitting on the man who hasn't just saved my life but saved the entire Blackthorne legacy.

Carter catches my eyes for a moment, not even giving this needy woman the time of day. I appreciate his attentiveness in coming to my side in long strides, his black hair tamed with just the right amount of gel. He adjusts the cufflinks on his crisp white shirt, the typical black roses I've grown so used to finding lying around the penthouse.

"So, what do you think, Mr. Blackthorne?" the realtor asks, following him as he joins me at my side. She makes no effort to step back a few feet, instead grazing his forearm with her overly manicured nails. "It's the most luxurious home on the market right now in Manhattan. Fit for a king."

He looks at me, one of his brows cocked. "You hear that, Bella? Fit for a king. I guess that means this is a decision to be made by a queen, wouldn't you agree?"

I shrug, exhausted from house hunting and never finding the one that feels *right*.

"I don't know, it's not really something that I—"

"It's the hottest home on the market. You won't find a better deal," the woman chimes in.

Carter flicks an unimpressed look over his broad shoulder. "You know what? I think we're done looking for a home with you."

She perks up, her grin lopsided and hopeful. "So, are you putting in an offer?"

"No," he responds, speaking through his taut jaw. "I'm going to find a different realtor. One that doesn't act like a bitch in heat whenever someone with money walks through her office doors."

Her mouth parts in a rather unflattering shape, her eyes searing with hate and heat, both fueling her frustration as it caresses her posture. She slouches, storming out of the house at once. When we can no longer hear the clicks of her heels, he pulls me in closer to his firm body.

"Now that we've settled that," he purrs, his lips caressing my exposed throat. "What do you really think about the place?"

I hesitate, not saying anything.

"Talk," he says against my throat. "Say whatever you want, dove."

"It's just… this house is so… and we're just—"

"If you don't get those words out faster, I'm going to be forced to find a bed in this damn place."

I snicker under my breath, feeling weightless, like I may float away. He holds me in a way that would prevent that from happening, the sensation of his tongue and teeth trailing against my skin keeping me in place. His hands skim down my sides and settle on the curve of my ass, kneading my backside until there's a sharp press of his erection pushing through his slacks.

It's enough to shift my focus from this house to pleasing Carter, but he never makes it easy on me.

"Decide," he says, speaking through his teeth. "Do you want this house?"

It's impossible to think straight with his mouth nipping at me like this. I need to focus, to make a definitive decision on this matter, but how can I? He pulls one hand away, bringing it sharply against my ass. It's enough to make me yelp, my answer pushing through my lips.

"No, I don't want this house," I gasp.

He steps back, his thumb stroking the sore spot on my neck. "Alright, then, I guess we should get going."

My brows pinch in desperate angst. "Wait, that's it?"

He straightens out his coat, buttoning it up in the middle so it covers the bulge in his pants. I'm happy to see he's just as on edge, but I hoped to get a little bit friskier before watching him pull away. He hardly seems worried by my question, taking my hand in his as we walk out of the mansion.

The realtor is outside, tapping her foot with moderate impatience. Carter doesn't even look in her general direction, opening the back door to our waiting SUV and urging me inside. I fall over the seats, but Carter doesn't mention it, climbing in next before he yanks me upright and plants me right onto his lap.

Ernesto gives us a hopeful look through the rearview mirror. "Well, was that the winner?"

"Not by a long shot," Carter replies, spreading his legs and, in turn, doing the same to mine. "Take us to my club, Ernesto. We have some business to attend to."

He nods, pulling the car toward the bustle of downtown. "You're still planning on going to the election party tonight, right? Everyone has already said they're coming to support you. It's a big deal, Carter."

"Yeah, yeah," he growls, his hands skating over the tops of my thighs and caressing the insides. He pulls my legs apart further, exposing me to the back of the seat in front of us. Thankfully, Ernesto can't see anything of my vulnerable position, but Carter loves riding the line of almost making that happen. "We will be at the gala on time and dressed to the nines."

I lay my head back on his shoulder, already throbbing with the heat that shoots down my stomach and settles in my pussy. Carter knows it, too, just like he knows everything else about my body. He drags his hands up the back of my shirt next, undoing my bra clasp by clasp.

His teeth pull at my ear, his voice deepening in tone. "Take it off. Now."

I manage to slip my bra off through my shirt, pulling it out through one of my sleeves. He looks over the expensive pink lace before tossing it onto the backseat beside us.

"Good, dove."

I practically purr against him, my ass writhing against his erect cock. I can almost feel the taut tip of his dick when I inch my ass back, grinding into his lap until it's clear that he's going to erupt. His hands snatch my hands, stilling me until the car comes to a screeching halt.

"Stay out here," Carter sighs, nudging me out the door while he speaks to Ernesto. "We won't be gone too long."

"You got it," he replies with a tilt of his head.

My arms cling over my thin shirt, the freezing fall breeze pushing past us both while we scale the sidewalk and duck into the Blackthorne Lifestyle Club. I used to make up excuses in my head to not meet Carter here, but now it's my favorite place to play.

He ushers me into our room and shuts the door, making sure it's securely locked before turning to face me. Carter is all but salivating at the sight of my body, even while wearing simple denim jeans and an oversized white blouse. Still, he begs to be turned on, and I'm the fix he's looking for.

All that matters now is what toy to use. The wall is filled with them, including a few that are laid in baskets around the room. There's also a wardrobe near the back, filled to the brim with lingerie that I couldn't fit in the closet at his penthouse. He could have me do anything right now, and I gladly would, my panties damp and getting damn near soaked quickly.

"Go to the pole," he demands, dragging a chair to the edge of the stage.

I try not to give away my true feelings about the stripper's pole in the middle of the room. It's never my first choice, or even close to my favorite, but I think that's why he likes to use it every so often. He is addicted to making me feel flustered, begging for me to blush and delve back into my shyness.

But, of course, I don't argue with Carter Blackthorne.

I step onto the platform and wait for further instructions. He falls back into the chair, legs outstretched with the material of his pants tight against his crouch. He leans his chin into his palm, his elbow bent against the armrest of his chair.

"Take it all off, dove."

I slide out of my shirt first, my nipples erect from the cold Manhattan air outside. He looks rather amused by the sight of my chill, my arms delicately trying to cover myself up as I slowly step out of my pants and panties.

Kicking everything off the side of the stage, Carter watches me like a hawk.

"Grab the pole, Bella, and put your back against it."

My brows knit at his command. "Okay..."

I do as he says, standing right against the pole, at least happy that I don't have to spin around it like an exotic dancer. I certainly don't have the skills to perform like that, so this is much easier. He sits up straighter, leaning forward while his eyes draw over every inch of my body.

"Cross your wrists behind you," he adds. "Behind your back and behind the pole, too."

Again, I follow his instructions, unsure of what he's planning.

"Kneel," he adds in a heavy exhale.

I have to be very careful with my movements, making sure my hands stay right where they are and keeping my back pressed to the pole. I kneel, the cold bar pushed against the seam of my ass, only adding to the chill that ignites over my heated skin.

While I'm propped up on my knees, Carter finally stands, walking to the front of the platform until he is just an inch or two away from me. I stare up at the tall posture of the man I love, wishing he would just get naked already and put my trembling desire to bed.

If there's anything Carter Blackthorne is good at, it's making my body pulsate with constant sexual need.

He strips out of his coat as if on cue and tosses it to the floor with my clothes. His shirt comes off next, his perfectly carved abdomen taut from the restraint he's displaying right now.

Instead of reaching for his pants, he strokes my face, tipping my head back against the pole and yanking my chin up as high as it will go. I strain all over, fighting to stay put, but he's making it damn near impossible!

"Tell me something, dove," he says in a deep exhale. "Where do you want to live?"

I'm taken aback by his question. "You're going to ask me that right now?"

"I want an answer, dove," he growls, shooting me an unkind look of warning. "Do you even want to move in with me full time? Is it me you despise, not the houses we've toured the past three weeks?"

"It's not that at all," I pant. "I want to be with you forever, Carter. I do! It's just…" I hang my head, his fingertips drawing through my scalp. I lean my forehead onto his inner thigh, desperately wanting to pull at his zipper with my teeth, but his treacherous belt still stands in my way. "I don't know, Carter. None of those houses felt right to me."

"Why not?"

Swallowing hard, I subdue a tremble in my exposed posture. "Because it's just... I don't know, really."

"You do know," he contradicts. "Say it, dove."

When I finally muster enough courage to say something, it floods out of my mouth like a cracked dam. "I'm just scared, Carter."

"Scared about what?"

"About *us*."

He grips my scalp in his hand, pulling my head back up. Somehow, with my head down and my eyes darted away, he's managed to undo the clasp on his belt. I take it as a warning, a negative threat, and I hope I didn't just earn a punishment. Then again, he hasn't done that since the finality of the Lacey incident.

I've gotten better over the last few weeks, including the two weeks Carter spent getting interrogated by every law enforcement agency in the country. Once Frances Johnson, the disgraced ex-mayor, was indicted with enough charges to land him life in prison, they gave Carter back to me, and we healed—physically and emotionally—together. It could be better, though. Even after Frances pled guilty and was sent to Sing Sing to enjoy a four-by-four cell with murderers, I still feel like he's nearby, his spirit looming through the state.

I guess that doesn't ensure that Carter won't use his belt on me, but I'm hoping it's enough to deter a hearty spanking with it.

"You have nothing to worry about with us," he says, speaking smoothly. "It's not much different from you coming to stay at my penthouse every day. Or like when we stay at Anita's. It's just expansion."

"Exactly," I breathe. "I don't know if I want a big house."

He cocks his head sideways, watching me closely while his hand pets the top of my head methodically. "Elaborate, dove. What are you saying?"

"If we get a big house, I don't know if I can handle it. I'll be there alone, without you, during the day, and I don't want to be that lonely. I want somewhere that keeps you close to me when you're home. I don't like the space between us. Unless, of course, while you're at work, then maybe I could find something to do, too."

He bites his lower lip, a familiar rage rising in his darkened eyes.

"Is this about you having a job again, Isabella?"

I swallow, hating when he uses my full name.

"Sort of…"

He flicks his belt off, undoing it from the loops on his pants. I push back against the bar as much as possible, already preparing for what's coming. He nearly lost me before, and I know that asking for independence right now, so soon after I was almost ruined by his rival, isn't the best idea. I just want to remind him that whatever house we pick is the house I'll be trapped in all day.

I don't like being alone without him, and he doesn't like me being in public without protection.

But even in public, where do I go? My father is in the hospital, and while he has stabilized, his mind has worsened. I have tried reaching out to Sam but to no avail. At least with Jacob Lacey, I had a purpose. I had a job to do and bills to take care of. With Carter, I feel myself slowly growing roots in a place he won't be near. If I stay stagnant in life, and he keeps moving forward, then won't that tear us apart?

Bracing myself for the worst, he stalks behind me and slaps the looped belt against his open palm.

"We're not talking about this anymore," he growls. "I've told you enough times before, Isabella. I'm not losing you. I let you stray too far before, and it got you kidnapped and wounded. If you think I'm going to overlook that and let you wander Manhattan alone for the sake of some frivolous income, then you're wrong. I'll give you something to do."

I hang my head slightly, bracing for the imminent impact against my ass.

CHAPTER TWO

Isabella

The hit against my skin never comes.

Instead, Carter wraps the belt around my wrists and then loops the leather around my crossed ankles. I am forced into a tight spot, pinning all my limbs together behind the pole while Carter slips out of the rest of his clothes. He strokes my hair, pulling it off my face and over my shoulders. It gives him the perfect view of my bare chest, leading down to my throbbing, soaking wet sex below.

He takes a short stroll along the nearby wall, glancing up at the options available. When he finds the one fitting his needs, he comes back to where I'm tied, leaning forward and taunting me by pressing his lips into mine. I fight the restraints just to be closer to him, just so maybe my lips can graze his.

He smiles at my desperation. "Easy, dove. All in good time."

"I want you," I beg. "Whether we're in a mansion uptown or a small apartment by the docks—I don't care, Carter. I just want to be with you."

His face falls slightly, keeping his toy of choice behind his back in secrecy. "I know you do, but for now, we will focus on the elections. After that's over tonight, we can see what to do with your desire to have another job, okay? But it's out in the open now, Bella. This world knows I'm dangerous. The only way to take down a powerful man is to go for the heart."

I wilt ever so slightly, knowing that ordeal has been proven a few times already. Truthfully, even with the Lacey family taken down and the Phillips family not far behind them, he still feels like there's a looming threat out there somewhere. I can't be sure where he's getting these inclinations, and I don't care.

All I want is to please Carter in this moment, and he wants the same for me.

The rivals, the election—everything that went down just a handful of months ago. It led us to a very dark place, one that I'm not sure that we're out of yet.

He finally exposes his hidden hand, reaching down suddenly and flicking his thumb against the cold, hard dildo. It strokes my clit carefully, using my already plentiful juices to slide slowly into my folds, filling me completely. I nearly slam my head back into the metal pole, fighting the urge to scream in pain and pleasure.

Once it's all the way inside, I begin to notice its vibration. It must have been doing it the whole time, but my senses are so numbed that it didn't click at first. Carter straightens up, flicking my lower lip with his index finger. He watches me squirm for a long minute, delighted with the sight.

"There you go, dove. Enjoy that for a while," he hums, bringing his fist to the base of his stiff cock.

He strokes himself slowly at first, increasing his speed while my desire triples before his eyes. The vibration is hard enough and deep enough, to the point that I shiver with my first orgasm not long after he inserted it into my core.

I chew on my lip, leaning forward to push my lips onto the very tip of his erection, but he snarls and steps back, preventing me from letting that happen.

"Not until I say," he snaps. "I want to watch you come for me, dove."

It doesn't take much longer for his wish to be granted. Fire brushes through my chest, settling in the base of my throat. The saturation between my thighs licks my skin with fire. I lean forward, exhausted and weary. I'm unable to make sense of anything while the orgasm overwhelms my naked body.

"Oh, Bella. Tell me something. Are you ready for this?"

I couldn't nod my head faster if I tried.

He leans in closer, his hips grazing my body as he says, "Are you my submissive dove?"

"Yes," I pant. "Yes, sir."

"Good. We don't stop until I'm finished."

I rattle with excitement. "I don't want to stop, either."

He doesn't waste another minute, pushing against my lips with the head of his erection. It slowly crawls into my throat, the tightness of my lips around his thick base making his head fall back. He gently thrusts into my mouth, methodically moving his hips like they're the waves in the ocean. He doesn't pause, hardly looking at the erotic sight of my mouth stroking his length.

Instead, he grips the pole with his fists, pumping into me while he rests his forehead on the steel bar. I can see the angst pulling at his features, his entire body carved deeper with more muscles than I've ever seen before. He doesn't stop pushing, diving into the depths of my mouth until I have no choice but to choke.

The sound, the feeling of my mouth tightening on his manhood, is enough to send us both spiraling. He doesn't come until I do, the vibrator between my legs finally dropping to the floor from the sheer slickness of my pussy.

The device rattles on the floor, and his cock jerks against the roof of my mouth.

He strokes the back of my head, gasping for each breath. He didn't even need to spank me this time, but the fact that I'm still tied up does worry me.

Being at the behest of Carter Blackthorne is a scary place to be at times.

He doesn't make me wait long to be untied, pulling his belt back through his pants that he hikes up over his hips. I collapse onto the floor, numb and exhausted. The last thing I want to do tonight is go to this election party, but it's the biggest event of the year.

We will see if Carter will be the next mayor or if his challenger, the same man who took on running against Frances Johnson, will be the new man in charge. The election had to obviously be postponed for a while due to Frances being sent to Sing Sing. Carter leveraged just enough power, and probably a little sprinkle of money, into making sure the mayor got what he deserved, even after his confession and guilty plea.

Meanwhile, my brute lover hasn't spent a day in jail.

The only thing more fucked up than the ordeal we had with the Lacey family is the dismissive attitude of the city when they found out Carter was the mayor's hitman for a long, long time.

He pulls me to a sitting position on the floor, forcing my shirt over my head. My arms are like noodles hanging at my sides, his hands brushing my thick, brunette hair back over my shoulders. I dare to yawn, the lasting taste of his ejaculation still coating the back of my throat.

It doesn't bother him, his lips still teasing my own with a gentle kiss.

"We have to settle this, dove," he mutters, kneeling on the platform with me. "I am just cautious about letting you out into the world, Bella. After everything that happened, I just need to confirm our enemies have been stifled."

"Jacob is dead," I mutter. "So is his father. Why are you so scared that something will happen to me?"

He pauses, his heavy palm raking through my untamed hair. "Because if I let you out into the streets of Manhattan, and anyone was to use you to get to me, it would work. If I didn't make it in time to stop Jacob and his father, well—"

"I know," I cut in, not needing him to recap that treacherous event. "He came close, but I was fine. I fought back, too."

"Yes, you did," he adds with a gentle smile. "I just need time, okay? Give me time. For now, we have an election party to attend. No matter the outcome, we will be going to Aunt Anita's tonight to be with the family, okay? Maybe after that, we can talk about your job search."

I sit up straighter—hopeful he's actually going to give me a chance to gain back some independence. Granted, I love being with Carter as much as possible, even when we're just doing nothing. But there's a certain aspect of my life that still beckons for my attention.

Jacob Lacey was a horrid boss with ill intentions toward me and my body, but that job gave me a sense of purpose. My father's bills have been paid off and paid ahead of time, so the money isn't really the issue anymore. I just don't want to be overly dependent on this remarkable man and force tensions to rise.

I want to appease him as much as possible right now, so I ignore my tumbling thoughts and reach for my pants. He clutches the hem of my jeans before I can pull them up, his hand gripping the vibrating toy from before. He presses it back into my core, my body wilting and shuddering while I grab at his wrist and take the pressure in stride.

He leans into my shoulder, nibbling on my earlobe in a way that makes my skin spark with chills.

"You're so tight after you come."

"It's your fault," I reply, feeling him release the toy as it's securely inside of me.

Carter takes over the task of zipping up my jeans and buttoning them up securely.

"It's always my fault," he whispers, his palm grabbing at my ass. "But let's see if this remote still works."

"Wait, remote?"

He clicks a little device in his two fingers, the pressure in my pussy suddenly starting to vibrate. I nearly fall forward, clinging to his chest while the sensation practically pushes me to the ground. He keeps me upright, though, snickering into my hair while his tongue drags across my exposed shoulder through the collar of my shirt.

"There you go, dove. Keep coming for me tonight, okay?"

"Y-yes, sir."

"Good," he pants, grasping my hand and whisking me out of the club.

I hardly make it back into the SUV before I double over, butterflies releasing through my stomach relentlessly until a slight *click* comes from his fingertips. The rattling ceases for now, but the looming threat of it is enough for my body to grow tight with anticipation.

He pulls me to his side, and Ernesto veers the SUV into the dense Manhattan traffic.

When I'm nearly passed out with exhaustion, draining away the feeling of being overwhelmed with orgasm, a soft voice catches my attention.

"What were the last polls showing?"

Ernesto clears his throat to reply to Carter in a whisper, "Wasn't looking good. Behind by eight percent."

Carter growls, a noise I can feel with my shoulder tucked into his chest. "This is going to be fun. If Killian wins, we're all doomed."

"He's an ex-cop," Ernesto sighs casually. "He isn't the end-all to our operation. We still have backup plans in case things go in his favor. We will shut down the docks projects you acquired from auction after the Laceys were obliterated as a family. Nothing is in our names downtown, not even the spot we took from the Lacey family. What was it again? Gambling or—"

"Guns," Carter cuts in. "They were about to barge into my market with the Laceys desire for exporting guns, but their fearless leaders all caught a bullet."

"Funny how that happens." Ernesto's attempt to soften the taut aura of the car doesn't work. "Listen, boss. It's going to be okay. The dust is still settling after the Frances issue. Killian can't do a thing to you if he wins the election. You made a deal to give up all the information in exchange for Frances going to prison, right?"

"That may be true, but I didn't tell them *everything*. I had to shift accounts into different names in the family. Any business, contact, purchase—everything in my name is being tracked right now. I don't need the heat on me, and…"

He pauses, his fingertips stroking my cheek so my hair is pushed back behind my ear.

"Do you ever just consider leaving everything, Ernesto?" he asks in a hushed tone. "Perhaps it's just me that they want to take down. If I gave them that, would she finally be safe?"

"She is safe," he mutters. "I'm confused, Carter. I've never heard you so unsure of anything in your life."

"Walking in on your rival getting ready to ravage the woman you love will do that to you," he replies. "Let's just pretend I never said anything about this at all, okay?"

"Of course."

"Good. I have a fucking election to win."

Chapter Three

Carter

I sit back on the foot of my bed, watching Isabella Julis getting dressed for the event. The button in my hand is heavy, tempting me to send her to her knees, but I refrain for now. I want her to forget it's there and go on about her night as normal until I can punish her through the hours as they come.

She stalks out in a long, shimmery white dress, something reminiscent of a roaring twenties outfit or maybe even something for a new-age wedding. Either way, she looks too stunning to take into public. If I could have her all to myself, right here and right now, then I would.

But we are nearly late for my own party.

"What do you think?" she asks, giving me a twirl of the fabric. "Do you like it?"

"I'd like it better on the floor, around your ankles."

She frowns like I've insulted her.

"Dove, when will you learn?" I make my way toward her, brushing her cheek with my fingertips and igniting a shudder down her delicate spine. "You will never find a piece of clothing worthy of your body."

She blushes, leaning in to kiss my cheek. I take that delicacy for now, knowing that if I dare pursue more with her, that dress will end up in a puddle on the floor. She takes her little purse with her, hiding a cell phone that I got for her. She checks it once in the hallway, then again in the lobby.

"Expecting something?"

"I was texting Sam a while ago. I asked if she would be at the party with Tristan."

"And?" I ask.

She shakes her head. "I haven't heard from her much since…" She hangs her head, refusing to continue with that somber thought.

Ernesto opens the door for us, and I help her inside the backseat first, holding my finger up before I join her.

"One minute, dove. Work call."

She nods, and I shut the door, pulling my phone out of my pocket, dialing a familiar number, and pressing it to my ear. It rings once, then twice, before a gravelly voice picks up on the other side.

"What's up, boss?"

"Hey, Tristan. Have you spoken to Sam lately?"

He clears his throat, and I hear rustling through the phone line as if Tristan's moving rooms. "I was just in bed with her, actually. She's asleep. What's up?"

"Nothing. Isabella was just concerned. She said she hadn't heard from her in a while."

He hesitates, and I can already tell something is off. "Well, yeah. You're partially right about that."

"What's going on then?"

"She's just a little cautious, that's all."

"She was about ready to kick my ass when she found out I used a belt on her favorite neighbor. Now she's cautious?" I roll my eyes, no longer finding the energy to deal with this. "What's really happening?"

He swallows so hard that I can hear the *gulp* through the call. "Look, cuz. You kind of took down the mayor by exposing that you killed a few people for him in the past. The FBI and ATF know about some of the drugs and guns shit, maybe even the nightclubs we run by the docks. But admitting that you've killed people is hard for people to swallow. Sam is just a little leery of you right now."

I try not to get pissed off too quickly. I want to be upset, but not because it's some sort of insult to not be liked. I've been hated, feared, and damn near killed all my life. Her opinion doesn't hurt my feelings.

But it does hurt Isabella if Sam doesn't want to be around her because of me.

"Well, thanks for being honest, I guess," I growl. "Why the fuck are you sleeping, anyway? Don't you have to be downtown at the gala hall soon?"

He pauses as if checking the time. "Fuck, you're right. I'll get dressed and be there soon."

I dare to hang up, but I can see Isabella in the backseat of the car, staring at her phone that doesn't ring. She's already feeling so trapped with me, which is understandable. Some hint of normality might do her well.

"Hey, Tristan."

"Yeah, man?"

"If you could convince Sam to come, I would owe you one."

He exhales lightly. "Yeah, of course. I'll see what I can do."

I tuck my phone into my pocket and find the button for Isabella's toy. Sliding into the car beside her, she looks downtrodden but covers it semi-well. Her smile is enough to melt my heart, though I can't wait to see the look on her face when it changes.

Ernesto takes us down the main road, spotlights shining into the cloudy skies overhead. It beckons to the people, letting them know something big is going to be happening soon. It's only a matter of time before we arrive at the venue, but I can already feel the excitement in the air.

"You're going to win," she whispers, clinging to my arm.

I rest my arm in her lap for control. "I've already won once with you."

She hides her blush and moves in close to my side. She's so sure that she loves me, something I never thought would come true for me, but it's

18

been nice. It's also been interesting. I've gotten to know her so well these last few months, seeing her fear that I'd be arrested and never make it out of my prison cell.

I've also seen her hopeful for a fresh start, wanting to create a normal life with me, something that just isn't possible. I can only predict that's why she hasn't liked any of the homes we've been looking at. They're huge, they create space between us, and they're nothing like what she's used to.

I hold her tight while we get out of the car and make it to the red velvet carpet on the stairs. I picked the venue where Frances Johnson held his little election party before. I thought it would be ironic, perhaps even hilarious to some, to keep this place as my election party venue.

Isabella goes stoic at the sight of this place again, recalling the last time I brought her to a party there. She grazes the scar on her wrist methodically, thinking about the moment when Jacob and Frances tormented her just to get at me. It worked, but I tried very hard to not let it show.

She makes her way through the doors first, leaving me for a moment to find the bar. I don't stop her, nodding for Ernesto to keep a close eye on my dove. He understands my intent and follows her like a faithful guard dog. I spot a few familiar faces in the crowd, with Nicolas and Lorenzo finding me instantly.

"If it isn't the future mayor," Nicolas taunts, his boyish face smiling ear to ear.

Lorenzo chuckles as well, elbowing him in the side. "Who knows, maybe one day we can say we're related to the president."

"Shut up," I groan, rolling my eyes. "I don't have high hopes for tonight. Killian is still ahead in the polls."

"It will work out," Nicolas says. "Don't fret. The Blackthorne family will prevail either way."

"I'm inclined to agree," I add, scoping out the bar area again.

Isabella is a vision in her long, white gown. She sits on the barstool but keeps an eye on the front doors, waiting for Sam, I assume. She crosses her legs, still holding a martini glass in her hand. When she sets it down, I reach into my pocket, far too tempted to watch her squirm.

I push the switch into the *on* position, watching her snap upright with a wild streak in her eyes. She practically falls backward off the chair, catching herself against the edge of the bar. She adjusts, plays it cool, and tries to catch her heavy breath.

"Stunning date. Carter." Lorenzo pops up beside me, watching my darling dove struggle to keep her composure. "Is she alright? She looks uncomfortable in the dress."

"It's not the dress," I admit. "But don't worry about her. She won't be in it long."

"Is that why you've been ditching the downtown project lately?" Nicolas asks.

I swivel around, letting my focus fall off the sight of Isabella at the bar. He sips on a beer that he's taken from a passing waiter, almost oblivious to the insult he's just lashed me with.

"What the fuck did you just say?"

Nicolas looks perplexed. "What?" He shrugs, taking another gulp. "I'm just pointing out the obvious, Carter. You haven't been at work lately. It wasn't a dig."

"Bullshit, it wasn't," I reply. "I've been working my ass off these last few months to make sure the entire family doesn't fall through the cracks that led to Frances Johnson getting his ass locked in a four-by-four cell at Sing Sing. I don't need you to tell me I haven't been at work."

"The office," Lorenzo mutters. "That's all he meant. You haven't been to the office. We've been at the job site you bought off the Laceys after their unfortunate demise. The downtown building. That's just the place you haven't been around; that's it."

I trade a look between them both. "The day you get to run things is the day I give a shit about what you both have to say about my whereabouts."

Nicolas looks offended, but I don't give a damn, even if I try.

"Carter, please," a demure voice cracks behind me.

I turn, taking Isabella in my arms. She leans against my chest hopelessly, panting while it's clear she's already suffered through an orgasm or two.

I flick the switch in my pocket, but her knees still tremble underneath her.

"I'll be back," I sigh, looking at the guys. "I need to handle something first."

My cock is begging to break out of these pants just to drag up her silky wetness, but something stops me. The music in the venue is loud, making the chatter among the guests even louder, but I still catch a few words I don't think I was supposed to hear.

"Yeah, just like always. Tend to her instead of the business on hand."

Even Isabella looks perplexed, forcing herself out of my arms. She hangs her head slightly, pushing her fingertips into my chest.

"I'll go back to the bar. I just... I didn't mean to interrupt."

"You're not going anywhere," I bite.

I hold my finger up, signaling her to give me a minute. Turning back around, Lorenzo takes a long stride backward, trying to make himself invisible. Nicolas clearly regrets his choice of words by now, holding his hand out in surrender while the other clings to his beer.

"I'd like to know where you get the balls to tell me how to run this family," I snarl.

Nicolas swallows before speaking. "I was just being an asshole. Sorry, Carter. I wasn't trying to be rude, but come on, even you can admit that things have been different since she came along."

"Different doesn't matter," I bite. "What I say, goes. That's final. I'm still in charge, even without you keeping tabs on my whereabouts."

He looks as if he's realized my looming ferocity, but he speaks again, proving his idiocy is far from over. "I don't need to keep tabs, Carter. I know where you've been. Besides, I'm not saying you can't play with your woman; it's not about her."

"Then what the hell is this about?"

He hesitates, tripping over his words at first. "Well, I guess it's about——"

"Don't fucking say it," Lorenzo cuts in.

I trade an irritated look between them both. "Don't say what, exactly?"

Nicolas chugs the rest of his beer and sighs. "The fact that you swing your weight around in this family, but you're not even a real Blackthorne."

Whether it's true or not, I can't be sure, but the room goes absolutely silent. I step forward, standing against Nicolas while he rattles slightly. He is afraid, as he should be, but I can't make a scene here. It's the election party, after all. I have to uphold some level of decorum.

Instead, I flick a look toward the exit, and he takes it without pause.

Ernesto presses his hand to my chest, muttering something about taking a seat. I acquiesce to his suggestion, finding a table off to the side of the party commotion. Isabella lingers a few paces behind as if trying to stay out of the way. Lorenzo shoves past her and Ernesto, coming to sit down beside me.

"He didn't mean that; he's just frustrated," Lorenzo pleads, trying to cover the tracks of what that asshole just said to my face. "Don't do anything stupid, okay? That was his fifth beer tonight. Wait for him to sober up before you do anything."

My eyes lift only to see Isabella coming forward, her hand grazing my shoulder. I snatch her wrist rather abruptly, pulling her around to my lap. She squirms in my arms, my hands digging into her thighs and her ass, needing her to stay planted firmly against my body.

She leans into my chest, her delicate hand pressing to my chest. "Carter, your pulse."

"It's fast," I snarl. "I'm pissed off."

Lorenzo looks worried, which he should be. His best friend in this family might lose his throat over what he just said to me. But there's too much going on right now for me to handle. I have to worry about the election, not about some frivolous rumors spreading through the family about how I'm not a blood member of the Blackthorne gene pool.

Isabella strokes the side of my face, bringing her lips to mine. It's enough to steal the heat from my chest, but it sends rivers of fire straight to my cock. With her pressed up against me like this, her ass on my lap, it's hard to not imagine plucking that toy out of her pussy and taking her right here, right now, on this table.

Public sex isn't really her favorite thing to do lately, which is understandable.

Tristan's face weaves through the crowd, and while I'm happy to see my right-hand man, seeing him come alone has me even more irritated. Isabella notices it, too, climbing off my lap so she can leave this meeting to the boys.

She doesn't make it far, my fist finding her dress.

"Where are you going?"

She swallows at my stern tone. I don't mean to be strict with her, but she's not leaving my sight tonight. "The bathroom, Carter. Just to fix my makeup."

"Your makeup is fine, dove. Sit down."

She looks at Tristan once more, seemingly so uneasy around him still. He wasn't the nicest to her before, especially after that shit he said about her being Brooke's replacement. I beat his ass for it, though, and he's aware that he made a tragic mistake.

Still, she's been uneasy around him these last few months.

I'd still rather rip her panties off with my teeth right here in front of everyone than let her leave my sight. I bring my hand against her ass, swatting at the spot I know is probably the most sensitive. It's close to her thigh, making her jump slightly, and I give her a very clear warning to get back into her spot before I make her.

She finally surrenders, digging her backside into my crotch while she sits back onto my lap. Tristan brushes past her, which is his best move yet, and trades a tense look with Lorenzo and Ernesto.

"What's going on here? Feels like I just walked into a freezer. What's with the cold shoulder?"

I sneer at his attempt to be casual. "I'm not in the mood for this bullshit right now. Would someone tell me what's going on with the poll closings?"

"Last one just closed," Ernesto sighs, scrolling through his phone. "We should get a phone call in about thirty minutes or so."

Lorenzo stands from his seat, speaking briefly into Tristan's ear before stalking for the exit. My most trusted cousin falls into the chair once occupied by Lorenzo. He looks at me with a hopeful look, like he's waiting for the bad news to start pouring in.

"What's the plan with Nicolas then?" Tristan asks while shaking his head. "That wasn't the wisest move on his part, but if he's drunk, then it should be excused."

"Bullshit," I bite. "He knew what he was saying when he spoke. The alcohol just helped him say it."

"Carter," Isabella mumbles, shifting uncomfortably against my cock. "I should go. This talk doesn't really concern me, and I don't want to be in the way."

She slides down my leg like she's going to defy me a second time.

"You move another fucking inch, and I'll bend you over my knee, dove."

She pauses with a tranquil look of panic lightly kissing her features. She moves back up my leg, readjusting herself while I lean back into my chair. She doesn't move very much, still keeping her eyes on the floor. I would like to enjoy myself tonight at some point, but everyone is trying to piss me off.

As much as I would hate to take it out on her ass later with my belt, I fear that's where we're headed.

"Let's all just calm down tonight," Ernesto sighs, patting my shoulder. "Enjoy the drinks, the snacks, and maybe even go take a spin on the dance floor."

Isabella winces at that last suggestion, something about that offer making her deflate.

"I agree," Tristan adds. "We should just reconvene later about the Nicolas issue. Let's worry about the election tonight, okay?"

I finally agree, whisking Isabella onto the dance floor, where we sway to the light music. She doesn't like the attention it brings her, but I remain firm with her in my arms. She tips her head onto my shoulder, letting my hand on her hip slide over to cover her lower back.

"Sorry I snapped," I whisper into her hair. "That remark he made about family set me off more than it should have."

"I don't like it when you're upset," she mutters under the sound of the music. "I just want us to be happy, Carter. No more fighting."

I force her chin up in the middle of our casual stroll of a dance. "There's no such thing as peace in this family. There never will be, either."

She doesn't act surprised, but she does look wounded.

I keep her in my arms as long as possible, holding her tighter while the time passes by us. Eventually, Tristan pulls me toward the stage. I make sure Isabella knows to stay put, leaving with a kiss while I make it to the microphone stand in front of the large, live band. Everyone claps, and I try to remain charming with a smile, but I'm far too pissed off for that right now.

The media is off to the side, snapping photos and trying to get their angle for the announcement. Tristan hands me his phone first, his eyes downcast as I take it into my palm. A headline reads in bold font across his screen.

Killian Hughes is the winner of the mayoral campaign in New York City.

I prepare my concession speech in my head while also trying to think of the damage this will do to the Blackthorne enterprise. Everything I've been avoiding for the last eight months is about to go down the drain for good.

Mr. Tough on Crime is moving into my domain, and I'm the epitome of a lawbreaker.

Chapter Four

Isabella

Carter begins his speech, and I can already tell it's not good. He thanks everyone for their support and then breaks the news that he won't be the mayor we all were hoping he would be. Instead, he thanks his opponent and wishes him the best of luck, the cameras snapping their photos while it's clear that Carter Blackthorne has finally lost something.

He's had everything in life he needed to be successful, so I know this isn't a fair battle. Everyone was raving about Carter before when he took down Frances and exposed the ugly face of politics around here, but it's over now. He's not the mayor, and his days at work are probably going to decrease even more.

The cameras battle to get a glimpse of him walking off the stage. He doesn't spot me in the crowd, instead giving in to talk to the media. I try to get to him, but someone else catches his attention, and he turns his back toward me before I can even get close.

I bail for now, stalking outside for some fresh air.

It's not the night to be selfish, I know that, but part of me is a little happy he didn't win the mayoral election. I have been afraid of the repercussions of his actions for a while. Even if he says that he can't be charged with anything, he has already told the police just enough to pin Frances down. There's no doubt that he's safe from those actions.

So, what about the new ones? If he gets caught doing half the stuff he shares with me at home in his penthouse, then I fear what will happen when Killian takes over.

Taking a seat on the steps, I couldn't care much less about the white of my dress getting dirty. I hug my knees to my stomach and exhale, wondering if it's too late in the evening to visit my father. He would be happy to see me, even though his health has been in steady decline for weeks.

His mind is still wandering elsewhere, but his body has reached its final stop.

I think about him, about Sam, too, and wonder if either of them misses me right now.

A cold brush of fingertips pulls my hair aside. I glance back to see Carter behind me, his eyes glazed over with too many emotions to count. He ushers me to stand up, and I do, taking his hand while he whisks me away to the SUV on the street. I didn't even notice Ernesto come outside before, but there he waits with the door open, waving us inside.

I only get one foot in before I realize that Carter is on the edge of the curb, staring at the mass of media flooding down the steps. They surround him at once, but something else catches his focus. He stares at the top of the stairs, a single reporter standing with her back straight and her eyes piercing through me. Carter doesn't move for a minute, looking right back at the reporter.

A cryptic expression passes between them, one that I'm not sure if Carter recognizes, but it's enough that he stops to exchange a passing glance with her at all. I shouldn't be concerned. I know Carter has his demons, but he very rarely looks at them with such uncertainty as this one.

I want to ask him what he's doing, but he pushes his way into the car, pinning me to his lap before he slams the door shut. His hand rips through the short slit of my dress, finding the toy that rests under my thin panties. He yanks it out in a single swipe, causing me to arch and writhe with shock, pleasure, and a bit of pain.

"Ouch, Carter!"

"Shh," he snarls, hooking his arm around my stomach so I can't move off his legs. "Be silent, dove."

I retreat back into myself for now, watching the city pass by as we drive to the penthouse. Ernesto doesn't speak, which is abnormal for him. We all just sit in stunned silence until the car pulls into the garage. I spy my little red sports car, the sight of it under the penthouse almost comforting.

The door swings open, and Carter hikes me over his shoulder, carrying me to the elevator. I thrash in his grip, unsure why he won't just let me walk, but every push away leads to a harsh slap against my ass cheek. He doesn't say anything or give me a playful warning.

We make it upstairs without a word said.

He drops me into our shared bed, my back hitting the mattress rather abruptly. While Carter waltzes into the bathroom, I hesitate to stand up, to move an inch, unsure what's going on in his head right now.

"I thought... I thought we were going to Anita's tonight," I whisper at last.

He comes back, wearing nothing but his pants while his midsection is bare, exposing the muscles that create his finely toned body. He grips his leather belt in his hand, his other shaking furiously at his side.

"Why were you outside?" he shouts, changing subjects rather abruptly. "I was looking for you for ten minutes, Bella. Why did you go outside alone?"

Swallowing hard, I sit up on the bed. I want to appear innocent in this situation, though I know it won't matter—he's too pissed off to negotiate with.

"Sorry, Carter. I was just—"

"No," he bites, his teeth grit. "Try that again."

I swallow, seeing where this is leading. "I'm sorry, sir. I just wanted a breath of fresh air, that's all."

"You remember what happened last time we were there, don't you? Did that slip your mind, dove? You can't just be lounging around the sidewalks of Manhattan, not after I've lost the election."

My brows furrow with the fear that grazes his tone. "I thought you said if you lost, it would be okay."

"I lied," he bites. "It's not okay. It's not good, Isabella. That prick Killian Hughes is going to try and drown me now. I can't let that happen. I have to be careful now and not ruffle any feathers, but how can I do that when my own family is questioning my place?"

I inch back slightly. It's not about me; I can see that, but his anger has no other place to escape right now. Pushing off the bed, I kick my heels off and stand before him. He watches my every move, the belt trembling in his palm.

Steering clear of that threat, I let my fingernails drag over the bumpy surface of his abdominal muscles.

"Everything will be fine," I say at last. "It's going to work out. We just have to adjust."

He looks skeptical. "Adjust. How do you suggest we do that, dove? I already work in the shadows. I can't hide it any more than I already have."

"Maybe you should work in the open, then," I suggest.

His face turns hesitantly curious. "Keep talking."

"You have that downtown project, right? The stripped building that Jacob was going to use. Move your office there and work right across the street from the mayor's place. Rub his nose in it. You said it yourself, Carter. Most of the things that the FBI wanted to pin on you can't be charged now. You gave it up to put Frances in prison."

"If I do anything stupid, I'm next," he snarls.

I nod slowly. "I understand that. That's why you won't be doing the dirty work. Sit in his face, move across the street from his new office, and be the best citizen of Manhattan possible. Let your family handle the shady shit for a while. Killian will be so focused on you that he won't see what's going on behind you."

For the first time tonight, Carter seems to relax. "That's not a bad idea, actually. The only thing is that I have to get my family back in line. After what Nicolas spouted off about, I'll need to be a bit more tactical in how I handle it. I just need his words to keep from spreading poison in the family."

I stand on the tips of my toes just to get a better angle to kiss his cheek. "You can handle anything, Carter."

"I can handle everything except for the fact that you're still in that dress."

"Are you saying I should take it off?"

His hand tightens around the belt. "If you don't, I'll cut it off of you, dove."

My throat closes, and I strip out of my dress, watching him circle back into the bathroom. I make sure to take everything off, waiting for him to return. I can hear him rustling through a few boxes in the closet, waiting for him to return with a toy or two in his hand.

Instead, my mouth blurts out a random question that's probably better left in the back of my throat.

"Who was that reporter you were looking at earlier?"

The rustling stops. He leans on the doorframe of the closet, his head cocked to the side. "What did you just ask me?"

Swallowing hard, I repeat the question with a change or two. "Well, when you were getting into the car, you stopped. Like you knew that woman."

His eyes narrow, and I can already see that I've crossed a line.

But why?

He throws his belt aside, steps out of the closet, and circles past me. I wait for him to lay my stomach on his lap so he can swat at my ass, but instead, he turns on the faucet. Hot water fills the tub, and steam clouds the room. He doesn't say anything; he just climbs into the running water after stripping naked.

When he's settled, he uses one finger to signal me to come forward. His hands catch my hips while I climb into the tub, setting me down between his legs so he can hold me against his chest. I lean back, nearly comfortable enough to sleep, while the blanket of warm water covers us both.

He runs his fingertips through my hair, the feeling sparking chills down my shoulders.

"I'm going to tell you one time, dove," he whispers into my ear. "You won't be taking little field trips alone again. I don't care if you need to go out for fresh air, you tell Ernesto to go with you, or Tristan, if you can't bring me along. Okay?"

I nod, though he still hasn't mentioned the woman I just brought up. "Okay, Carter. But I want to know who that was. Why won't you just tell me?"

"Because if it was important, then I would tell you whatever there is that you need to know. We're going to stay right here, though. You're going to relax with me."

I pull my lips to the side, unsure if I can do that.

"It's a good idea," he mumbles. "The thing about putting my office right under Killian's nose. It's a good idea, dove. I like that."

I sit up straighter, clinging to his arms that wrap around me. "Really?"

"Yes, but there's one issue."

Trying not to feel disheartened already, I keep my upbeat tone. "What's the problem?"

"Well, the building isn't done being constructed. It's just exterior bones. I need someone who knows architecture to draw me up a few samples for the construction company to work off of." He brushes a hand down my shoulder, running it down my stomach before stopping at the slit between my thighs. "Think you can do that for me?"

"Yes, of course," I exclaim, excited by his offer and by his fingers that slowly begin to swirl around my swollen clit. He pinches it a bit harder, making me twitch. "Ah!"

"There you go," he says into my hair. "Just part your legs for me, Bella. I may have lost the election, but we're still going to celebrate tonight."

"What is there to celebrate?"

"For starters, you just got a job as the designer of my new office building."

My face ignites with heat. "Thank you, Carter."

"Anything for you, dove. Now, relax. I'm going to make you come before we go to Anita's."

I gladly do as he says.

CHAPTER FIVE

Isabella

It's well past midnight by the time we make it to Carter's family home. Everyone is spread out in the living room, still in their nice clothes, as they opted to stay there and watch the election results at the house. I stretch and yawn while I follow him into the kitchen, wearing a loose set of shorts meant for bed, while my top is something I stole out of Carter's closet.

Anita greets me with a tight embrace, the greetings going down the line of the entire Italian family. There are too many people here to count, but I know most of them, if not all of them, already. Carter pulls a barstool out for me, and I jump into the seat, my legs still numb after our stint in the bathtub.

It didn't take me long to come once, but the next four times made me weak.

Anita pulls out a pan, even though the house is stocked with snacks from the watch party. "Well, Isabella, what are you hungry for?"

"I'm fine with whatever you want to make," I reply.

"Careful now," Carter pants into my exposed shoulder. "She'll spend four hours making pasta if you let her." He tips his head when Anita swats at him with a spatula. He scurries off into the living room, greeting everyone one by one. "Come here. I want to talk to you."

I catch a glimpse of him pulling Nicolas into the nearest room on the first floor. My stomach drops, and I dare to jump out of my chair, but Anita pulls my focus.

"Don't worry about them," she sighs. "Nicolas shouldn't have said what he did."

"You know about that?"

She gives me a pitiful look. "Yeah, nothing gets said in this family without everyone hearing about it. That's why I'm surprised most of my boys in that living room haven't ended up in prison yet. But we don't rat on one another. We also don't hold anyone's past against them."

I sip a glass of iced tea that she sets down before me, the cold liquid sliding down my throat.

"How is Carter being adopted fair game for that remark? It's his past, sure, but it's not like he chose to be adopted. It's not a bad thing. I'm just confused about what would make Nicolas say that in the first place."

Her features droop with her reply, "Yeah, it wasn't wise of him to stoop to that level, but he was drunk. He's also frustrated. Carter hasn't been around as much as before. I think some of the guys are just aggravated that he's been distant, that's all."

"*Some?*" I reply. "It's more than just Nicolas?"

She gives me a demure nod and goes about cooking something, but my appetite is gone. It's not necessarily my fault that Carter has been away from the family business. He isn't the type of man to be controlled by me and my whims. It's nearly impossible for me to convince him to do anything at all.

Still, this could have all been avoided somehow.

Even though I know I shouldn't, I kick out of my seat and hurry to the room, around the corner from the busy common space. The door is cracked open enough for me to hear Carter's voice, something solid about his tone and unwavering in his movements.

He strikes Nicolas right across the cheek, his cousin falling to the floor at once.

I press my fingers over my lips, gasping lightly. Carter swings the door open at the sound of my exhale, leaning on the doorframe while Nicolas tries to make it to his feet behind his back.

"Dove, go to the kitchen."

I swallow but can't seem to move. "I don't want you to hurt him," I mutter. "It's not his fault."

His brow rises. "Really? So, whose fault is it?"

"Mine," I admit. "You've been with me since the entire Lacey thing went down. You wouldn't have been in that mess if not for... for me."

"I will not go through the semantics of that war with you again," he says. "I'm done letting you take the fall for things around here. Jacob Lacey would have met his fate one way or another. It had nothing to do with you. Believe me. He was as dirty as a rat and wouldn't have lasted long with me anyway."

I can only nod, Nicolas storming past us both. I manage to make it out of his way, but not before he throws the front door open. He retreats into the night, not uttering a word to any of the onlookers in the living room. Carter comes up behind me, his hand slipping down my spine while he watches the people gathered in the house.

Everyone is still, silent, and unwavering through the tension.

"Killian Hughes is going to come after me," Carter says, his voice no longer his own. "We're going to have to tighten up around here. If anyone has anything to say about my role in this family, then let's talk."

No one moves an inch.

"Good," Carter adds. "Everyone working with guns, drugs, and clubs can meet me in the office. We're going to talk over a few things." He leans sideways while everyone moves toward the office. He kisses my temple, his lips coming down to my ear. "Go eat dinner and then go to our bedroom in the tower. I'll be there eventually."

I want to protest, but I can't. He leaves my side and wanders into the office, the door shutting me out. It's the first time he's been so geared up for work, especially after the trouble we just went through with Jacob and William Lacey. I don't want to interrupt now, not after the issues with Nicolas have risen to a breaking point.

Falling back into my chair in the kitchen, Anita gives me a woeful look.

"What's wrong, dear?"

I shrug, not wanting to hurl my issues at Carter's aunt, but given I don't have anyone else to confide in right now, I don't really have much of a choice.

"It's just been hard trying to find our new normal, that's all."

She nods knowingly. "Yeah, there's no normal after what happened to you and Carter. Everything that went down was unfortunate, but you made it through."

Swallowing hard, I speak lower in volume. "I just… I can't fight the feeling that something else is coming."

"What do you mean?"

"Well, there's the new mayor. Killian Hughes. I haven't seen enough about him to know what his plan is, but Carter is going to go head to head with him through the streets rather than the election."

She seems to follow so far. "Okay, I can see that happening. But it's nothing he hasn't handled before."

"True, but that doesn't make it right."

She pauses over the stove, the food bubbling before her. "And what is your definition of *right*? The Blackthorne family has never been a clean penny. We've had our bad side for generations. Carter was just the first one to pull us all together to profit from it collectively."

"I'm not saying I would be upset if he got a parking ticket or something, but they interrogated him for two weeks, Anita. What if he never came back from that?" I hang my head lower than before. "What if everything catches up to us, and we fall?"

She comes closer to the kitchen island, her light brown eyes sinking deep into my soul. "If there's one thing we don't do in this family, it's give up on one another. We don't run from trouble. We handle it. Carter is the best at that, dear. You have nothing to worry about."

I can only nod, making sure to never mention this out loud again.

The only person really concerned here, apparently, is me.

I turn over in bed, feeling the spot beside me is still empty. My eyelids are weary and tired, but they crease open enough to see a dim light in the corner of the bedroom. Sitting up, I cling to the blanket that still offers me a hint of warmth.

Carter is clicking around his laptop on the desk; his back is turned toward me while the screen nearly lights up the room. I almost ask him to come over to the bed, but I can see he's far too invested in his work right now. I lie back down, watch him work, and wait for him to join me.

When he finally closes his laptop, he stands and turns, his eyes catching mine.

For a second, he doesn't move.

He doesn't say anything either, tucking his hands into the pockets of his sweatpants. I sit up straighter, admiring the swell of his erection that pushes against the fabric of his pants. He must see me focusing on it as well, the sight of his arousal only growing while I chew on my bottom lip.

"Why are you up?" he asks, catching me off guard.

I swallow, turning the question around on him. "Why are you up?"

He shrugs. "Just checking on a few things. I have to be at the old office in an hour. I figured I'd brush up on a few details before heading in."

I nod along to his explanation. "Okay. Can I come with you?"

"No," he replies, almost a little too fast. "I have a special job for you tomorrow."

My senses perk. "Really? Does it have to do with the new office design?"

"No, I bought a house."

I try not to sound as shocked as I feel. "Really? When?"

"A few hours ago. I wired the money to the owners and bought them out of their house. They were selling, no realtors, and it's over now. We have somewhere to move to, somewhere new. The place has been vacant a while, and I've already emailed the movers to bring our things there."

It's been his goal to have a fresh start since everything happened with the Laceys and Frances. As much as I would have preferred to be in that decision making, it's obvious that Carter is on a rampage right now for control. He can't grapple it from Nicolas or anyone else whispering behind his back, and he just lost the election.

He needs to feel in power again, or he will crumble. I'm okay with that, too. I just want us to be together, maybe somewhere simple and cozy, but I'm fine with whatever he chooses. He is finally letting me work on a project that actually has to do with my passion for architecture.

"Okay, so where are we moving?"

He points out the tower window to the street below. "Next door."

My heart leaps out of my chest. "Really? You bought the house beside Anita's?"

He nods. "Yes, I did. She mentioned that it was vacant and that the owners didn't trust the banks. I bought it as-is, so it might have some issues. But it's something near family, so I figured it would be worth a shot. How does that sound to you, dove?"

For once, being deep in the veins of the Blackthorne family actually sounds good. "I can't wait."

He leans over the edge of the bed with a sly smile. "Good. When I come home tomorrow after work, we can unpack. Or undress. Whichever comes first."

I kiss his lips deeply, giddy over the option I know Carter is going to choose in the end. I look forward to that and being near the rest of the family. Everyone sees Aunt Anita's place as a safe haven, as a fortress, and being right next door is going to help Carter gain his sense of security back.

Maybe this move will be really good for us. After all, nothing can break us apart now.

Chapter Six

Carter

I leave the house while Isabella is still asleep. It took some time for her to fall back asleep, but the news of our new house was good enough for her to relax. She went back to sleep in my arms, and I held her for as long as possible. Now it's Ernesto and I fighting morning traffic, but there's too much on my mind right now. He gives me a knowing look from the driver's seat, watching as I meander through my thoughts in the seat beside him.

"What's going on?" he asks at last. "Is this silence about the election loss?"

"No," I say. "Well, not really. I will find a new way to handle Killian Hughes. There's just something that happened after the election party. It has my mind in a frenzy."

"What was it?"

"There was a woman, a journalist. She didn't even ask me anything, but there was a look in her eyes. Something that told me that I'd seen her before. I don't know, Ernesto. It's odd, but I think I know her."

He shrugs it off. "Okay, so what's the issue? You know a woman in Manhattan. What else is new?"

I lean on the door, thinking about her dark hair and her curvy, short posture. "It's weird, but I can't shake this bad feeling now. Even Isabella noticed her."

"Did she bring it up?"

"She did, but I didn't know what to say. I can't just say I *think* I know who she is. I can't even recall her name, let alone who she was to me. It was just a feeling I got. Isabella asked who she was, but I didn't say anything about it. I just dropped it. She wants to focus on her new project, and I just want her to get into some kind of new rhythm."

He pulls the car against the sidewalk of my building, but I don't move yet. I'm still perturbed over what I saw on the steps of the venue. Somehow, I know that woman. I just can't pin down how or from when.

"You need to chill out more," Ernesto groans. "You're so stingy lately. Go get some work done. I'll hang out in the city, check on the movers at the penthouse, and then come back and get you in a few hours."

I nod at his plan of action. "Yeah, I guess that's a good idea. I want to help her navigate the new house, make sure she's happy with it."

"And if she isn't?"

"Then I'll buy all of Manhattan and let her pick one that she does like."

He chuckles with that response, and I duck out onto the pedestrian-filled sidewalk. I'm antsy to get back to work, to get into the running of operations on the ground floor again, but it's weird not having Isabella by my side. She's been with me through everything, good and bad, and I feel a strangle of knots in my heart that makes me feel like I should still be with her right now.

I push through my hesitations, walking into my office to see someone already sitting on my couch. I'm slightly peeved that security let this woman by, but given her appearance, they probably figured it was another fling for me to use and toss aside.

I toss my things on the desk and lean back against it. The woman from the gala is laid out on my couch with her feet propped up on the table nearby. She wears cheap heels and dark stockings that don't go all the way up her thighs, exposing her tanned skin before her skirt attempts to take over the job of keeping her half-decent.

She matches it all with a top that exposes her deep cleavage, the sight of her bra almost showing, more desperate than attractive. She's in a place of business dressed as if she works on the corner, but that's hardly my concern right now.

Being this close to her, rather than the distance from where I saw her last night, I can finally trace her features and match them to my memory. Nothing huge calls out to me, but a small beauty mark above the side of her lips is familiar, one I know I've kissed in the past.

"Lilian?"

She sits up straight, pushing her chest out more obnoxiously than before. "Aww, I'm flattered, Carter. You acted like you saw a stranger last night."

"I'm just confused about what you're doing here," I sigh, seeing where this is going already. "I haven't seen you in years. What do you want now?"

"Oh, I should have mentioned it before," she adds, pulling a notepad out of her large purse and matching it with a ballpoint pen. "I'm a journalist."

"I'm not interested in giving you a story," I snip, coming around my desk and falling into the chair. "You can let yourself out now."

She gives a pathetic pout. "Don't be silly, baby. I already have the story. In fact, I brought you a little sample."

As much as I'd like to scold her for that attempt of endearment, I let it slide, watching as she takes a massive file out of her purse and tosses it onto the desk between us.

"Give it a read, Carter."

Unimpressed already, I flip the file open, first finding a picture that makes my blood boil. The rest doesn't get much better, either. There are easily two hundred photos in here, nearly all of them taken from a distance, though a few are up close and personal.

My jaw locks as I realize what this tramp is trying to do. "Why do you have all these?"

"I've been busy since you fucked me over, Carter," she sings.

She takes a seat and kicks her heels up on the edge of my desk. I'm tempted to push them off, but my eyes fall back to the stack of photos. When those run dry, it's a couple thick packets of handwritten notes that I read to myself. She continues chatting in the meantime.

"Now, if you keep digging through those pages, you'll find the exact time and place of your indiscretions. Not only does it have to do with your salacious history with the women of this city but also your tendencies to be a bit on the *rougher* side of things."

I push the file away when I've heard enough. "Whore."

"I wouldn't say that," she replies. "I'm the one dangling proof that you've slept with almost every brunette in Manhattan, baby."

Shaking my head, I try to appear unbothered. It doesn't work. "So what? I'm a man. I like sex. What do you have here but a history of failed dates and meaningless flings?"

Her thin lips curl upright slyly. "It's just a little bit of defamatory proof, Carter. I know you have a longstanding flavor of the week. What would she think if she saw all these details?"

My heart skips a beat. "She knows my past."

"Does she really?" She takes the file, flicking it over to the middle so she can pull out a sheet and read from the notes. "He undressed me in his penthouse, threw my back onto the bed, and fucked me for hours on end. I got up in the morning, and he told me to be back that night, but when I came back, he already had a different woman in bed with him."

I look elsewhere, trying to forget the pain of my past. I'm not proud of my behavior, but I can't be held hostage by it because I met Isabella, and I love her. She's the one I want to be around every night, and from the minute I claimed her as mine, I stopped finding relief elsewhere.

"There's also this fun piece that says some woman was in this office, actually, on her knees while she was sucking your cock, Carter. This was after you first met Isabella Julis, right?"

My brows furrow, worried this witch can read my mind. "Excuse me?"

"What do you need the excuse for? This proves nothing, right, Carter? You said so yourself."

"I hadn't made my move on Isabella yet, so that moment isn't important."

"It's *very* important. When she sees this, she will—"

"You're fucking dead," I breathe. "You try to show her a thing or come near her, and I'll slit your throat."

She hardly seems fazed by my threat. "Hey, that's almost like how you used to grab my throat in bed, right?" She stands from her seat, hikes her skirt up even further, and stalks around to my side of the desk. I get ready to push her away, but she falls to her knees, licking her lips while she stares at me from the floor. "Remember when you had me suck your dick, Carter? I came over every day for three weeks. I was the first one that you had seen more than once."

I lean forward, smiling back at her wickedly. "That doesn't mean I enjoyed your company, Lilian. You were just cheaper than the hookers uptown."

I can see my words wound her. It gives me hope that this ordeal will end soon enough. "I might have been cheap, but I was good to you. I did everything you asked, and I took that belt like it was my job, baby. And what did you do to me?"

I lean back, recalling our history from forever ago. "I don't actually remember."

She looks more insulted by that than anything else. "I came over to find you fucking my sister in your shower."

It all comes flooding back to me, the memory of her sister bumping into me in passing, joking about how she's heard about me from Lilian, and then practically begging to try some of my length for herself. I agreed to it, of course, because I wasn't looking for feelings and emotions.

I was looking to heal the wound where Brooke's legacy has scarred me for life.

"So, this is what, exactly? You're going to hand my sex life to Isabella and then do what? She knows who I used to be. I'm hardly afraid of what you have in those files. I never cared about you or any of the others. But I care about her. That's what matters."

She inches forward on her knees, her eyes drifting over me stealthily. "Carter Blackthorne, you think I'm just going to show Isabella and leave it at that? How about I show the whole city... hell, the whole state? I can make this world a living hell for you both. She wouldn't be able to walk down the sidewalk without everyone knowing that she's the whore of the month."

"She isn't a whore," I yell, speaking directly into her face. "She's nothing like you."

Her head tilts. "Well, if you say so. I can release these details online, and we can both watch and wait for how she reacts. Maybe there are some moments in those letters where you've done the same thing to her. I bet it would make her feel violated, don't you think?"

"Fuck you."

"Exactly," she gasps. "That's all I need to make this all go away."

I push my chair back nearly a foot. "What the hell are you talking about?"

"Fuck me, Carter, and I'll ditch the story. I will give you every copy and every photo down to the originals. I'll give you everything you want, and all I need is for you to fuck me one more time."

"Get the fuck out of here," I say through my locked jaw. "If I see you again, it's going to be very, very bad, Lilian."

She leans forward, her skirt coming up more while she throws her ass into the air. I look away, the sight of her thong coming into view. She pushes her arms together, making her breasts look bigger than ever, and I can only move my focus along the far wall, uninterested in her attempts to bait me into trouble.

The door flies open, and I nearly jump out of my seat in a panic. For some reason, I expected Isabella, but instead, it's Tristan holding a coffee cup. He gives me a concerned look before backing out of the office slowly. He disappears from the glass walls, and I walk to the other end of the office.

"Get out of here before I throw you out the window," I warn.

She finally gives in, gathering her things before she saunters from my office. "I'll be back, Carter Blackthorne. This isn't over."

When she's gone, Tristan barges into the room. I don't have the energy to face him right now, instead opting to lean my forehead on the bookshelf.

"I've pinned you for some pretty bad shit, boss, but I didn't see you ever cheating on Isabella."

"Did you see my dick out?" I snap.

He holds his hands up in surrender. "No, that's fair. But that woman was—"

"She was blackmailing me, dammit."

"With what, exactly? A blowjob?"

"She's an old fling I scorned. She wants to do it again, no doubt to ruin things with Isabella. I didn't partake, of course, but she's going to write something online about it if I don't."

He gives me a blank stare. "So, what are you going to do?"

"The only thing there is to do, Tristan. I'm going to take her down… and not in the way she wants."

CHAPTER SEVEN

Isabella

Anita is a godsend. She barks at the movers as they come into the vast mansion. I'm already thankful to have her living so close by. It gives me time to explore, the owners hardly waiting to drop off the key and get the hell out of there. I pace through the large, open foyer, the even larger living room, and the massive, dark marble kitchen. The tile and countertop are nearly black.

It's an interesting look, one that I oddly know Carter will enjoy. The living room has two fireplaces and enough space to heat up a football stadium with both. I poke my head into the spare rooms downstairs before making my way to the next floor.

The master bedroom is nearly the size of the living room on the first floor. It has a large fireplace on one wall, with another near the bathtub in the attached ensuite. My stomach growls for something to eat while I've only made it halfway through the house, finding a spa, a movie theatre, and another spare kitchen. There are almost a million other bedrooms, but I don't concern myself with having to fill all this space.

Carter can focus on that. I just want to get our bed set up so we can be together properly tonight.

Coming downstairs, I see Anita has been joined by some company that doesn't consist of the movers. It's a few women, the group adorned with tall heels and full faces of makeup. I didn't bring anything to change into or spare mascara to at least make myself look presentable. I was just coming over to stay the night and catch up with family.

Now, I feel overwhelmingly underdressed in my new home.

Still, I greet the women with polite nods while they comb over the sight of me. They all have perfectly curled hair, flawless skin, and long, unmanageable nails that are covered in extensive designs. I hide my hands in my pockets after a moment, feeling even more pathetic than before.

"Everyone, this is Isabella Julis. She's the new neighbor. Isabella, these are the ladies of the block. They're all housewives as well," Anita says.

I nearly choke, wanting to correct her title for me. I keep it to myself, though. "Hello, everyone. It's great to meet you. I wish I had worn something better, but this is all a shock to me."

The woman in the front steps forward, her hair bright red like fire. "It's okay, dear. We tend to pop by unexpectedly. We didn't anticipate that you would be ready for us."

"Oh, I meant the house, too," I say. "I didn't know that we were moving until this morning. Carter told me he bought this place, and now—"

"Anita," the woman gushes, looking at Carter's aunt like I insulted her. "You didn't tell me this was Carter's new girl. Ugh, I swear. You should have just started with that." She turns her button nose back toward me for now. "You're a lucky gal. I tried setting my niece up with him ages ago, but he turned her down. Something about blondes, I think."

My stomach cramps more with her attempt at small talk.

"Yes, well. Thank you all for coming, but I should get back to getting things set up."

The woman cackles with laughter, the sound echoing through the empty house. "Oh, dear. You have movers to do that. Why would you want to worry yourself with it."

I stammer to reply, my words stuck in my throat. "I just

want… Everything needs to be organized, and…"

Anita steps in to save my life. "She just wants to get settled, Rebecca. That's all."

Her smile goes from friendly to downright disgusted in a matter of milliseconds. "I see. I was just hoping to grab lunch together with the new lady on the block, but I can see you're both busy. Besides, I doubt you'd be interested in going out to Gianni's dressed like that."

My throat closes, and I wince.

The women behind her find the remark funny and chuckle under their breaths.

When it's clear that I've been somewhat slighted by her barging in and passing judgment, she smiles and waves her hand through the air between us. "Don't be upset, dear. It's just a joke. Lighten up. I'm sure you have a lot to work with under those sweats. It landed you a billionaire, right?"

She turns on her heels before I can even comprehend what she just said. Her posse follows, and Anita balls her fists like she's going to throw down at any second. I lean on the kitchen island for a moment, needing to catch my breath. The world stops turning long enough for me to realize two things.

First, people in this neighborhood already think I'm a worthless, penniless gold digger. And secondly, I apparently can't wear these shorts ever again, not without that insult ringing through my mind.

Anita gives me a deep look of pity, but I brush it off.

"They seem nice."

She shakes her head. "I'm sorry about that, dear. I didn't think she would be so snobbish and insulting. They're really nice women, I promise. You just need to get to know them better."

Tucking my hair behind my ear, I try to agree for now. "Okay, I trust you. Maybe we can meet up with them another day."

"Sounds good to me," she sighs. "Now, let's get these movers in here. I already know where I want the couch and the coffee table."

"Good," I reply simply, still feeling overwhelmed by that simple interaction. "I'm going to give you the floor to boss everyone around. I think I just need a break for now."

Her smile turns sympathetic. "Oh, Isabella. It's going to be okay. Go back to my place and take some time for yourself. I can handle everything here."

"It's fine, really. I'm okay. I'm just going to be in the master suite upstairs, that's all."

I leave her before she can talk me out of it. I just want to take a breathing break so my heart doesn't feel like it's in my stomach. Without anywhere to sit in the main bedroom, I round the corner and walk into the vast bathroom. The shower wall is covered in jets, but it's not as stunning as the bathtub that stands alone in the middle of the floor.

Climbing inside the space, I feel so small in this tub. I curl my legs into my stomach, hold my knees tight, and feel the tears brim against my eyelids. The last thing I wanted by being with Carter was for everyone to think I was just his live-in prostitute.

We've been to hell and back, and people still consider us to just be lousy roommates who fuck, while apparently, I spend his money. I don't need to be looked at as a pathetic slut in a big house, but how can I convince the neighbors that's not what I am?

I'm wearing baggy sweats, for crying out loud!

I push their comments aside, but I can't force myself to get out of the tub. I want to disappear for a while, drowning in the spitefulness of their judgment and just basking in the reality of their words. I'm going to be a feckless housewife for the rest of my life.

They will be my only friends, mostly because Sam refuses to take my calls, and my father thinks the nurses are neighbors. Carter is the only life jacket I have these days, and I just advocated for him to go back to work to give me a bit of independence.

I miss him dearly, but I can't bother him while he's working. I just hope he's starting to get back into his old groove again.

Light steps ring out against the tile after some time has passed. I peer up over the edge of the tub, tears sliding down my flushed cheeks while my itchy and wet eyes weep relentlessly. Carter circles the wall, his bright, cyan irises colder than ice as they fall over me.

"Dove, what's going on?"

I open my mouth to speak, but nothing really comes out that's comprehensible. He takes off his jacket and lays it on the countertop nearby, coming over to the edge of the tub.

"You don't look so good," he mentions.

"I'm fine, Carter."

Coming closer to my lips, his eyes flush with ferocity. "Tell me who hurt you, and I'll end them."

Swallowing hard, I shake my head. "No, it's fine. It's just... nevermind."

"Don't lie to me, Bella."

Tucking my hair behind my ear, I ask, "Did you talk to Anita?"

He gives me a look that I can read all too well. "I may have. She mentioned a few pretentious hags from down the street stopped by. I didn't think it would impact you like this, though."

Wiping my cheeks, I sit up straighter, feeling slightly pathetic by my position in the bathtub. "It didn't, but there was nowhere to sit down. The movers weren't done yet, and I just needed somewhere to relax."

His eyes swirl with sadness. He reaches forward and caresses my cheek, a distant and faraway feeling to his touch. I move forward, pressing my lips to his in an effort to make tonight be what he wanted it to be earlier. Still, even in intimacy like this, he feels different.

Pulling away first, my eyes meet his.

"What's wrong with you?"

"Nothing, dove. I'm just concerned about your well-being."

He's lying, and I can see it. His face is so stoically firm, his lips hardly moving when he speaks, and he anxiously taps his fingers along the ridge of the bathtub. He's antsy and cold. Something is wrong with him, but as long as I'm upset, he's not going to open up to me about it.

"We should get downstairs," he hums. "I have business later. A few people are coming by to talk about... well, a lot. I just want you and I to have dinner first, okay?"

Wiping my cheeks, my brows pinch. "It's already dinner time?"

"It's three o'clock in the afternoon, Bella. Close enough. Why?"

I hang my head, looking at the pale color of my hands. I didn't realize I had sat there for so long, but the sore and stiff aches in my body prove that to be correct. I must have partially fallen asleep or drifted so far into my own mind that I didn't realize it.

Composing myself, I step out of the tub. My walk is rigid and uneasy, but I'm happy to see the bedroom furnishings have been moved into the house. Part of me is perplexed, though.

"Hey, this isn't the bed from the penthouse."

He nods rather dismissively as we move past the room.

"Um, none of this is from the penthouse, Carter. I saw it on the truck. What happened?"

"I called the guys this morning to toss that stuff. I bought all new things and had them expedited here. Luckily, I know a guy who owns the best furniture store in the state. He made sure to only send us the best products."

I glance over the new things with a weird sense of abandonment. Why would Carter replace all his things at the last minute? I know he's been wanting to move on from the Lacey issues we faced in the past, as well as forget the Lacey troubles we defeated, but new furniture?

He leads me to a small space off the main bedroom and swings the door open. My stomach fills with butterflies, seeing a full-sized desk in the middle of the room. It's surrounded by art supplies, special lamps, and tons of blueprint paper just waiting to be sketched on. I can already see that this is a setup meant for me.

I rattle with excitement at the opportunity he's offering now.

"The builders need a mockup of a design plan soon for my office building, dove," he says, his words caught in a heavy sigh. "Give them a few options to work off of, and I'll relay the message. The dimensions are on the laptop on the desk already, as well as some kind of software that sets up the 3D model for viewing."

"How… how did you do this?"

"That would be me," a familiar voice says.

I turn to see Sam in the hallway nearby with her hands pressed into her front pockets. Tristan stands behind her, almost protectively, but I want to run up and hug her. She beats me to it, throwing her arms around my shoulders and clinging to me for dear life.

Carter is careful to move away from us, leading Tristan down to the main floor.

"I've missed you, friend," I cry.

She holds me tighter. "I've missed you, too."

"Then why have you been so distant with me?"

"Because of *him*," she replies, not skipping a beat. "You're dating a sadistic villain, Isabella."

Whether Manhattan sees Carter as a villain or not isn't my issue. All that matters is that he's my villain, and I love him enough to be thankful for his effort to help mold our lives into something spectacular. When I pull away from Sam, she smiles softly, but I can see Carter is the point of contention between us.

He's my world, but without a confidant in this new life, I don't know how I'll survive.

Chapter Eight

Isabella

Sam doesn't say much, and I can't really pull it out of her.

I lean forward on the desk where we sit down, something I thought would involve us talking, but everything is off. She hasn't liked Carter from the start, so it's hard to be upset with her saying that she wants distance. I'm just shocked that her distance involved ignoring all my phone calls and texts. Yet, she's been cuddling up close with Tristan Blackthorne.

I don't want to come across as rude, especially with her finally just coming back to my side, so I drop it.

"How have things been?" I stammer, opening the door to our friendship again.

She seems receptive so far, offering a smile in return. "It's been okay. I moved into Tristan's apartment."

"Oh, that's good. I bet it's a lot better than our last place."

Her eyes flash at the memories of where we first ran into one another. "Oh, yeah. It's certainly a step up. The Magnolia apartments have washing machines inside the apartments. They don't take quarters."

"Oh, yeah, that's a step up," I breathe. "So glad we're out of there."

She looks around the office. It's not yet put together all the way, and it's basic in the fact that it's just been thrown together in less than a day, but it's stunning and perfectly put together for the effort. I'm thankful for

Carter's attention to detail in times like this. Besides that, it feels like we've compromised for once. I wanted a job, and he wanted a home for us to share.

Now we have both, and he doesn't have to worry about me walking aimlessly through Manhattan.

"This is a beautiful house, Isabella," she says, breaking the second dose of heavy silence between us. "I'm really happy for you."

Biting my tongue, I only nod.

Sam must sense my apprehension. She shifts in her chair, throwing daggers with just a look. "I didn't mean to call him a villain, Isabella. I didn't intend it like that."

"It's okay, Sam. It's fine. Just… you don't have to talk about it if you don't want to. I don't want you to stop being my friend over this."

She nods slowly, leaning into her palm with her elbow on the desk. "I'm not going to say Tristan is any better. I just have a *feeling*."

My senses perk at her claim. "A feeling about Carter?"

She nods slowly. I keep a close eye on the door, my stomach sinking.

"I've had a bad feeling, too," I admit.

Her eyes narrow. "Why is that, Isabella?"

I hesitate to say anything about it out loud, mostly because it will seem more real if I do. Eventually, I garner the courage to bring it up, even if my heart aches with the thought.

"Okay," I mutter. "At the election party, after Carter found out that he lost, there was this woman. They didn't speak or anything, but there was this weird eye-contact thing that threw me off. I wasn't really bothered when I saw it, but he got really short with me after that. Then, when I asked about it later, he blew me off like it was nothing."

Her lips curl into a ribboned bunch on one side of her face. "Okay, so what does that mean? You think he's cheating on you or—"

"No, never," I cut in, not even willing to consider that.

"Isabella, if he is, then you need to know now before you get deeper with Carter."

"I'm already in too deep. I love him. He would never cheat on me."

"What're we talking about in here?" Carter turns the corner slowly. His glare pulls through me slowly before slicing in Sam's direction shortly after. "Sam, I think Tristan is downstairs waiting for you. You should go."

I stand and give my dear friend a hug, watching her scurry out of the room. When I try to leave, Carter stops me, his hand resting firmly on the front of my sweats. I freeze like he's pinned me to the floor, but having his fist dig into the mound of my sex is daring enough.

"What were you speculating with your friend about, dove?"

"Nothing," I pant, feeling like a filthy liar. "We were just catching up."

His eyes glower with rage. "You think I'm unfaithful to you?"

"No, sir. Not at all."

He leans in close, his lips brushing the shell of my ear as he whispers, "Do you think I could fuck another woman like I fuck you, dove?"

I shake my head in refusal. "No, sir."

"Good," he breathes. "Go bend over onto your desk, then."

My heart falls into my stomach. "What?"

His hand rips my sweats down, leaving me in a tiny pair of lace panties. I hug my sweatshirt a little tighter, knowing that it's the next article of clothing to go. Sure enough, he pushes me to turn around and pulls the back of my sweatshirt up and over my head before throwing it on the floor.

"Desk, now."

My breath hitches while I walk toward my new desk, wishing I didn't have to break it in so soon. Thankfully, there's not much on it yet, so when I lay forward against it, I don't have to clear a space. I shut my eyes, hearing his belt slide through the loops of his pants.

"I don't get it, dove."

"Don't get what?"

His voice turns into a rumbling snarl. "Why you would think my cock would rise for anyone else."

"I know who you are," I admit. "I know who you used to be. I'm not accusing you of being unfaithful. I just know that your needs are—"

My words are stopped short when the belt cuts through the air, smacking my ass with perfect precision. I cough a cry, fighting back from jumping right off this desk and breaking into hysterical pleas. But Carter needs this more than I do sometimes. So, despite my terrible pain intolerance, I accept it.

He hits me two more times before my knees can no longer refrain from trembling.

"Go to the bedroom," he snarls, still out of breath. "Get out of here."

I finally stand and turn, my body shivering while he looks over my exposed chest and my tearful eyes. Carter isn't one to feel much sympathy, but lately, I've seen that change in him. He grabs my arm when I try to move past him, pulling me into his warm, familiar chest, where he pins me in his embrace.

"I don't want us to go down *that* path again, dove."

I don't need him to elaborate. The scars on my ass will probably never heal fully. He sees them every time he's behind me, and even with my tight panties on, he can probably still see the marks. I've never seen him so untamed, so vicious, and I don't need him being that man anymore.

I need to tame him before everything falls apart, but how do I tame a man who was born to be reckless?

He nudges me into the hall, signaling that it's time to go to the bedroom, but I need to entice my furious lover. I take his hand, walking toward the other end of the hall and then downstairs. Thankfully, Tristan and Sam left without needing to be shown out the door.

It's also good that the movers have taken the rest of the afternoon off, guaranteeing that our home full of boxes is left for us to play in for the night. I open the basement door and scurry down the stairs, Carter most likely considering throwing me over his shoulder and taking me to the bedroom anyway.

I flick on the light downstairs, exposing a steaming hot tub with an attached pool separated by a waterfall barrier. His eyes light up with enticement, and I strip out of the rest of my underwear before I walk along the barrier between the pool and the hot tub.

"Alright, dove," he hums. "I'll play with you."

He strips out of his clothes slowly, thankfully not bringing the belt with him. He tosses it aside, but I reach over and grab it. His eyes glimmer with curiosity, and his cock is already erect when he steps out of his pants. He takes the steps down into the hot tub, and I loop the belt around my neck, pushing the metal clip into the hollow of my throat.

It's not the best sex leash I've ever seen, and it's nowhere near the level of quality that he has hung on the walls at the lifestyle club, but it's enough for him to lean back where he sits and give me a firm nod.

I walk into the warm, bubbling water to meet him where he sits. His hands slide up my slick, wet sides, his fingers clutching the belt suddenly and yanking it down. The leather grows tight around my throat while I lean forward, his lips dangerously teasing my own.

"You're getting clever," he whispers, his teeth taking a little bite of my bottom lip while I pant to breathe with the belt strung firmly around my neck. "But you know you're not in charge, right?"

"Yes, sir," I manage to pant out. "Not in… control…"

"Good, girl."

He pulls tighter, forcing me onto my knees where he can loosen the strap on my neck. He doesn't remove it, though, adjusting his knees to further spread my thighs. I'm fully vulnerable now, his erection brushing the entrance of my pussy.

"I'm going to enjoy you for a long time, dove. You know that, right?"

"Yes, sir."

"And you know your job is to come for me over and over again, right?"

Again, I nod. "Yes, sir."

"So, why aren't you straddling my cock yet with your tight, throbbing pussy?"

I lean forward, my chest brushing his so I can distract him from punishing me again. I line little kisses across his shoulder, settling on one spot near the center of his neck where I can kiss, bite, and suck as needed. He pushes his fingertips down the small of my back, his index finger adding pressure to my tight little asshole.

It's enough to make me release the skin of his neck, my pussy desperately crawling over his daunting length. I don't care how many times we're together. I'm always as apprehensive of his size like it's the first time he's ever entered me.

I try to manage a steady pace through the water, feeling the hot temperature crawl up my back while I create a new wave of movement under the harsh jets coming from the walls of the space. He doesn't let up on his finger, pushing into my ass, daring to enter my anus with one knuckle, then two, causing an eruption of pressure in the small orifice.

I can hardly hold it anymore, running through my first orgasm at a fast pace, the next quickly following.

Before that can happen, though, he flips me around, his fist curling into the belt around my throat. He slams my ass into the wall, the pressure from a single jet punching the hole he was just fingering and adding to a new, harsh spike of pain and pleasure. His hips still thrust into mine, splashing water all over the floor, but it doesn't matter.

Nothing else matters right now.

My ass is going through pleasing pain, my pussy is filled with my lover's cock, and my neck is slowly being teased with pressure as he fights to yank every emotion out of me at once. I scream when I come, and he muffles it with his lips, accepting my groaning pants as part of our deepening kiss.

I lay my head back, forcing my legs as wide as possible while unsure whether to cry from joyous pleasure or overwhelming pain.

"Come, dammit," he snarls. "I want another from you."

I squeak through the pressure of the belt, breaking into another round of speckled vision and dizzy senses. My fingernails dig into the back of his shoulders, most likely drawing blood. He doesn't care, gripping the belt in one hand while holding onto the edge of the hot tub for dear life with the other.

"Do you think any other woman could make me feel this way, dove?"

His voice echoes off the walls, surrounding me with his authority.

"No, sir."

"Are you going to accuse me of cheating again?"

I shake my head, daring to fall into another deep swell of pleasure. He waits for it to pass, hitting his own edge of orgasmic relief. We end up falling together, and the tightening pull of the belt on my neck doesn't help. It's so savagely dominant that it makes everything so much more intense.

When the smoke settles, he undoes the belt and throws it across the floor. I gasp, working to catch my breath and clinging to his body in the hot tub just so the harsh jet can finally stop hitting my asshole with such precision. He laughs as he stands up from the water, working hard to keep me upright and against his chest.

"Good, dove," he whispers, kissing my cheek. "Now, let's go to bed. I'm not nearly done with you yet."

He sets me down and finds a spare towel in a moving box down here, wrapping me inside of it. He doesn't care to do the same, pushing me to walk up the steps while he slides into his pants, still soaking wet. He doesn't bother fighting with his shirt, and I'm happy about that, his chiseled physique driving me crazy.

We're halfway through the living room when there's a light knock on the door. Carter kisses my temple, points to the stairs to signal our bedroom, and makes his way to the front door. For some reason, perhaps due to my constant desire to defy him and be punished over it later, I hesitate to leave, keeping him in my sight.

He swings the door open, and an unfamiliar man stands on the doorstep.

"Who the fuck are you?" Carter asks.

The man slides his hands into his front pockets and looks at me through the clearest eyes I've ever seen in my life. Like glass, I can sense the resemblance in his features already, and it makes me far too afraid to move.

"You look just like—"

"Like Jacob Lacey?" the man interrupts, finishing my sentence. "He was my twin brother."

CHAPTER NINE

Carter

I grab the stranger by the collar of his shirt, pushing his back against the foyer wall and pinning him there for safekeeping. Isabella is frozen in a panic on the stairs, watching the scene unfold.

"Dove, get my phone off the kitchen island and call Anita."

She works quick to do as I say, this man's eyes darting sideways while he watches her move. She's wearing nothing but a towel, and it doesn't do much to hide her stunning body. Her ass is nearly out when she reaches to grab my phone, and I move into his line of sight to prevent him from getting a glimpse.

His smile turns innocent. "Relax, Carter. I come in peace. Check me if you'd like. No weapons, wires, or otherwise."

"I don't need to check you," I bite. "I'll just have you killed for coming over here, whether you're related to Lacey or not. You better hope you're not. It won't end well for you."

Isabella speaks in a panicked whisper, my eyes catching the sight of my family spilling out of Anita's house and crossing the lawn to get here. I'm even more thankful that I bought this house so close to my family's hub, meaning that backup is only a few yards away.

I throw the stranger into Lorenzo's chest, purely because he makes it through the front door first. A few other people manage to pin him down on the foyer floor, meaning I can shift my attention to Isabella in the kitchen. I take my phone from her, cradling the back of her head so I can let her lean forward into me.

I kiss her forehead, feeling her racing pulse, either from our sex downstairs or the new fear lacing through her body now. I want to calm her down, but my first concern is getting her out of sight… and fully dressed.

"Go upstairs and change. Don't come down here, dove." I release her, and she nods, but I take her arm and meet her eyes one last time. "I mean it. Stay up there, or we're going to have a problem."

She gives a more believable nod this time.

It's not as though I don't trust my little dove or that I enjoy punishing her more times in a day than I should in a week, but she's very curious. She likes to be involved, and until she knows how to work a pistol and deal with some of these sadistic pricks in my line of work, then I need her to stay back.

Losing Isabella Julis would ruin me.

When she's through the hall upstairs, and I'm sure she can't hear the scuffle down here, I stand over the wiggling rat on my foyer floor. He is the spitting image of Jacob Lacey, which just makes my trigger finger too damn happy.

Lorenzo hands me his gun, and I'm thankful that he can read my mind, the barrel lining up to this prick's chest while I consider how fast I want him to bleed out compared to how fast I want him to die.

"Give me a moment to explain," he says, oddly calm for a dead man. "I'm not here to cause problems. I came alone and unarmed. Just give me the opportunity to explain."

"A Lacey doesn't get to explain," I snarl. "You're lucky you still have a tongue right now."

He nods as if agreeing with me. His fucking gall is unbelievable, I'll give him that, but it's also increasingly annoying.

"What the fuck do you want, then?" I snap, needing to know what he's thinking.

"Can I get off the floor to explain, at least?"

I give Lorenzo a careful nod, and he lets the man up off the ground. When he's standing, I have someone check his pockets and look for a weapon, wire—anything to give me an excuse to stain my new tile floors. He comes out clean, though, so I tuck my gun into my waistband, and he sheds his jacket casually.

"Let me just say, I'm not a Lacey," he says first, following me to the kitchen, where I pour myself a whiskey. Giving him a skeptical look, he continues in his explanation. "I'm actually a Donahue. Rich Donahue."

"Rich," I repeat between gulps of bitter liquor. "No doubt named by a Lacey, that's for sure."

"My father was William," he explains. "I believe you two met."

I give my family a careful look, and they make a short trip to the door. Lorenzo stays. Aunt Anita rushes inside the house with a curling iron in her hand. I roll my eyes at her determination, making her reputation as a firecracker in this family a bit comical. Her hair is half undone, but she looks at me like she's carrying a shotgun, ready to go to war.

"Isabella is upstairs," I say. "Do you mind?"

She hurries up the stairs, and I'm at least happy that Anita will keep my lover occupied. I'm a bit surprised that my meek aunt was ready to fight with a hot, unplugged curling iron, but I give her credit all the same. Blackthornes are resourceful, after all.

"You have a very peculiar family," Rich says, watching everyone but Lorenzo leave my new, now-nearly empty home. "How'd they get here so fast?"

"Don't worry about it. Just tell me why you're here."

"I just want to talk."

"Then fucking talk," I say. I empty my first glass and consider having another. "Why are you wasting my time, prick?"

He runs his fingers backward through his brown, short hair. "I've come to make amends for my family. Well, I guess that's a bit complicated to understand. I'm a Donahue, my mother's son. Jacob Lacey, he was my father's son. They took us separately at birth. My mother decided to divorce William in the middle of her pregnancy, and she chose me. Jacob left with my father."

"And now you're on my porch with a death wish," I hum. "Get to the point quickly, or I'll have to christen this new house sooner than I anticipated."

He waves his hands between us, a little boyish in his movements, like he's not nearly out of his adolescence yet. "I don't need you to baptize your home in my blood. It wouldn't be that fun; trust me, I'm anemic. You'll just end up with a watery version of red on your floors. Horrible for the grout."

"Get to the fucking point!"

His eyes widen. "I can see the bridge between our families has certainly been burned. I didn't know about that at all. I'm here as an ally, or a prospective one, at that. My brother and father died, which means everything in their name funnels to my mother. She's sick right now, terminally, and I'm her power of attorney now. Everything she has comes to me now. Hence—"

"You're the new Lacey boss," I cut in.

"Exactly."

My fingers stroke the handle of my pistol. "Not looking good for you, Rich."

His eyes follow my movements with precision. "Look, if you kill me, you'll just end up with my third cousin Bernie. He's a dumbass. Trust me, you're better off dealing with me. I don't want anything to do with guns, drugs, casinos, or strippers. I don't care what you're working with, Carter. I just want to make things right between our families."

My brows hike, and I look to Lorenzo to make sure I'm not going crazy. "He wants to be friends."

"I don't think he knows what he's in for," Lorenzo taunts.

"Certainly not."

"Listen, I understand the hilarity in this moment. I do," Rich says, begging for the benefit of the doubt. "I'm not trying to be difficult. I'm trying to offer you an opportunity here." He straightens out his shirt before methodically rubbing the wrinkles out of his coat that lies on the back of the chair. "I have a piece of property that might interest you."

"I already have the downtown development," I snarl. "Bought it cheap in an auction after the owners mysteriously wound up dead in their mansion."

"Funny how that happens," Rich adds, still trying to break the tension here.

"Well, congratulations on that property. It's a hotspot, for sure. But it's not the one that I'm referring to. This is one that was passed down from William's name to my mother's—and it has inevitably fallen into my lap. It's a section of the docks."

I pour myself another crystal glass of whiskey. "Go on."

"It's a building my brother was going to dedicate to international trade. It includes four docks, each of them large enough for freight liners. I'd like to offer you the chance to lease the place out while still providing funding to complete the project with our crews."

It takes everything in my fucking willpower not to burst out in hysterical laughter right now. "Okay. Let me clear this up right now," I snicker. "You want my family to pay your broken, scattered little remains of a family that you claim no loyalty to as a Donahue to fix a project that Jacob was working on and then make me pay to lease the property after just paying to build it?"

He looks up through his eyelashes as if tracing the plans in the air. "Yes, that's right."

"This guy is a joke," Lorenzo groans, leaning on the kitchen island. "Want me to take him out of here, boss?"

"No," I say, sipping on my whiskey, the heat of the alcohol starting to burn the base of my throat. "I'm actually enjoying the entertainment. I wish I had popcorn."

Rich chuckles lightly, his smile crooked just like his filthy brother's. It brings me back to the moment I saw Jacob Lacey pinning Isabella against his desk. It was the first time I had met either of them, and she looked so terrified while he was smiling.

Planning on ravaging my precious dove, he was fucking smiling at the prospect of her fear and pain.

I pull my pistol out, my trigger finger twitching. Everyone notices it, and it brings a stiffness to Rich's back. He holds his hands up near his shoulders, watching my gun while I rest it sideways on my kitchen island. When it looks like he's finally serious about talking again, I give him the opportunity.

"I'm not here to offend," Rich reassures. "I'm here to offer you a business opportunity. That's all. I would pay to have the project completed and just sell it myself, but I'm reaching out in an act of peace here. Besides, most of the money that came from my brother and my father is going to my mother's debts and her medical expenses."

"Surely they had a few million," I counter.

"Not even close. Most of the money went to trying to pay off everyone they owed money to. That included taxes that they had been avoiding for years. I ended up paying the government more money than my mother will ever see."

"Okay, so I pay to have the project finished. Your family of construction crooks finishes the job, and then you lease the building and the docks to me?" I shake my head, wishing I knew how this man had enough guts to come to this horrible idea. "It's not that I'm saying you're a jackass, but you're acting like one."

"Totally understandable," he says.

Why does it seem like for everything I fire at him, he has a way of deflecting the bullet and letting the shell casing roll off his shoulder? I can't pin his charm on work now, but it's so odd, and weirdly enough, he's confident about it.

"If you lease the property, then you'll have full access to the docks. With those, I'm sure you can take your operation to the next level. You ship things in all the time, right? And don't you ship out goods for guns and whatnot?"

"Perhaps," I say coyly enough. "What do you want out of it, though?"

"I just need the lease money to keep my mother on treatments as long as possible. The construction fees are to help my family finish the project. If it falls through, a lot of my distant relatives will be stranded without a paycheck."

"This is the same family that attacked me and my family, right?"

He nods solemnly. "If it makes any difference, I did get rid of those who were closest to Jacob Lacey."

"The Donahue and Lacey clans are coming clean? Doubtful."

"If it helps, I'll show you receipts for where the money would be going. My mother, she's my everything. I'm trying to keep her well enough to watch the Donahue name rise to some level of respect. Being associated with the Lacey family has ended with us dragged through the mud enough."

"You also put my family through hell," I snarl, the gun feeling heavy in my hand, even with it resting on the counter in front of me. "Why would I want to work with you?"

His eyes flicker to the stairs, something small catching my eye as well. I turn enough to see Isabella nearing the top of the stairs as Anita tries to pull her back, but she's unsuccessful. I growl slightly, slipping my gun into the back of my waistband. She hurries down the stairs, stopping a few feet away from Rich.

Her eyes trail over his features, the same ones that resemble Jacob's far too closely for comfort. Anita isn't far behind, giving me a pleading look. She heads for the front door, leaving this meeting with a slam of the front door.

"Bella," I breathe, watching her snap out of the trance that she's in. "Go upstairs, dove. Please."

She gives me a pleading look, eventually stepping around Rich so she can come to my side. "I got scared," she whispers, kissing my cheek. "I didn't hear a gunshot."

"He's trying to convince me to spare him."

"Are you going to?"

I bring my lips to her ear, her body twitching when my bare chest hits her loose blouse and tight shorts. "If you don't go upstairs right now, I'm going to take you back down to that hot tub, dove."

I can hear her swallow. "I want to help."

Her hands run over the impressions of my abdomen. She's trying to soften me up, and weirdly enough, it's working. I kiss the tip of her ear and wrap my arm firmly around her waistline. After the conversation she was having with Sam earlier, the one that accused me of being a cheater, I suppose she just needs to feel involved and not in the dark.

I'm happy to accept that for now.

"He wants the Blackthorne family to pay for the completion of a dock project for the Laceys," I explain. "If we pay for the job to be done and then lease the building, we can use the docks, which means we might be able to skate around marina fees and having to bribe the inventory police."

Her lips pull to the side. "The dock project where we met?"

My stomach aches with that unfortunate realization. "Oh, I suppose so, dove. That is the one you were working on before, wasn't it?"

She nods slowly, and I take her mind off the trouble of it all. I tuck her hair back behind her ear, and she leans into my warmth.

"What do you think, Ms. Architect?"

"I didn't finish my degree, Carter. I'm not an architect."

"I still trust your judgment, dove."

She stands a bit taller with that assurance. "It's a nice piece of property. There's nothing like it on the docks. There's even a basement in the project. It's pretty deep, lots of storage."

"Sounds like you're on board."

Her eyes flicker to Rich, a certain unease on her precious features. I aim to relax her, but the best way I know how to do that is better suited when not so many people are around. For now, I pull her closer and let my hand take hold of her ass. She goes tight, her cheeks striking red.

"I think you might have a deal then, Donahue," I breathe. "I need to go out there to see how much needs to be done to it first, just for my own curiosity."

"That's fine. All the equipment and workers have been sidelined for now, so you'll be alone out there if you want to give yourself a tour. It's still pretty rough, so I wouldn't go to the top floor, but the others will be fine to climb and explore."

I lean forward, my seductive growl purring in Isabella's ear. "Go get some shoes on, dove. I'll be upstairs soon to grab a shirt."

She hesitates, obviously not keen on leaving my side. I knew she was stubborn before, but the chaos with Jacob Lacey has only exacerbated that. I can't be sure why she thinks that she is going to protect me from Rich or the Donahue and Lacey families or what she's even trying to prevent in the first place.

It could be her lack of trust in me when it came to Lilian, but she doesn't know that whore yet. I'm just thankful that I've managed to postpone that trouble for a while. She will be back, though.

I have to protect Isabella at all costs.

"Fine." I surrender, kissing her forehead. "Lorenzo, show Mr. Donahue out, please. And get Ernesto to bring the car around. We're going out tonight to check out this project."

"You got it, boss."

Rich stops, taking a long step forward with his hand outstretched. I take it as a courtesy, and he leaves his hand out, motioning toward Isabella next. She stares at him tentatively, unsure what she wants to do with his hand right now. He's the spitting image of Jacob Lacey, and she's hardly over that ordeal.

"I'm so sorry for the pain my father and brother have caused you, ma'am," he says, his smile innocent enough, even for someone related to a Lacey rat. "If you'd accept this as a peace offering, it will mean the world to me and my family."

"I just don't want any more trouble," she whispers. "I don't want anyone to get hurt."

His smile sprouts even more than before. "We have the same goals."

"Good," she says at last, taking his hand gently.

Something passes between them, and I don't know if it's his bloodline being so close to a Lacey that it just makes me uncomfortable or if it's the simple fact that they have this wordless, gentle passing of emotion right in front of me. Either way, it's frustrating.

I pull Isabella back, and she sinks into my chest, both of us watching Rich leave with Lorenzo. When we're alone, I spin her around to face me, my fingers pinching her chin.

"Let's go see what this project is all about, dove."

Her eyes light up with familiar fires. "Together, right?"

"Always."

Chapter Ten

Isabella

We stop at the hospital on the way to the docks. My father doesn't get to see me as often as before, but that's not his fault, obviously. It's been hard to come around him now that he's in this state. The treatment was supposed to help his body function better, but it's taken a further toll on his mind.

As much as I'd like to think he can bounce back from this unconscious state, it's not likely. I sit down by his bed, working through the emotions that race through my hectic mind. I want him to get better, come home, and live life normally, but it's slowly becoming clear that it won't happen. Still, I try to keep my hopes up, watching Carter pace the hallway on a phone call.

I finally muster the courage to leave my father's side for the night, not wanting to be at those chilly docks for too long. Coming out of the room, Carter is already outside, his conversation growing more hectic as time passes. I stop in the lobby break room, making myself a small cup of coffee, when a light tap on my shoulder nearly startles the cup out of my hands.

"Wow, I'm sorry. Didn't mean to frighten you," the light voice says.

I turn, seeing a bright smile offered by a woman with long, curly brown hair. She's dressed in a suit, the style befitting for a newscaster or a lawyer. Either way, I smile and make room so she can fix herself a cup.

"I love your shoes," she hums.

I look down at my clean sneakers, their pink shade a bit childish in hindsight, but they're comfortable. Carter gave them to me as a gift, but I'm sure he was more interested in just getting me into another fitting room than he worried about what I checked out with.

"Thank you," I reply. "Your suit is so nice. It's so edgy and cute."

"Thanks," she says with a growing grin. "You look so familiar. I hope that's not weird of me to say."

I shake my head slightly, realizing that she looks just as familiar. "Oh, you know what… I think I've seen you before too. Were you at the Blackthorne election gala?"

She lights up with realization. "Oh, yeah. That's right. I'm a journalist, so I was there to get a comment on Carter's infamous loss against Killian Hughes. You're the girlfriend of Carter Blackthorne, right?"

"Yeah, he's just outside," I breathe.

"I would go say my *hellos*, but I have to get back to work."

My brows furrow while she mixes her coffee with a thin straw. "What do you mean, work? You work here at the hospital?"

"Oh, no. My journalistic duties include digging up some feel-good stories and whatnot. I caught wind that Carter Blackthorne has made a sizable donation to the hospital in the past. I'm looking for some records of that transaction just to back up his generous image."

"Huh," I sigh, slightly confused. "That's nice of you, I guess. I didn't know stuff like that was in high demand right now."

"Oh, for sure. Anything that upholds the values of Manhattan within certain public figures is always news to the public. They'll be happy to see this side of Carter, considering the smear campaign that is still making the rounds in the background."

I set down my cup, my stomach aching with her every word. "Smear campaign? What are you talking about?"

Her face falls suddenly. "You didn't know?" She shakes her head slowly, taking a long sip of her coffee. "I think I have a copy of the file at my house. I can show you if you'd like. Maybe we can meet over coffee."

"Okay," I reply, feeling a pit deepen in my stomach. "Sounds good."

She takes a small notepad out of her purse and scribbles on the face of it with her pen before handing me the sheet of paper. It has her phone number and her name written in beautiful cursive.

"Lilian McCoy," I hum. "Nice to meet you."

"Same to you," she says with a smile. "I've got to get going. Tell Carter I said *hello*, okay?"

I nod while she walks away, stuffing the paper into my pocket before making my way outside. I take a gulp of coffee and offer Carter a sip, watching him dismiss his phone call before taking the cup and giving me an exasperated sigh.

"I'm sorry, dove. Dealing with a workplace crisis. Nicolas is still being an asshole after everything that happened. I'm getting exhausted dealing with it. How is your father, Bella?"

"He's the same still," I whisper. "I ran into a friend of yours, though."

He lights up with bewilderment. "Really, who?"

"Lilian McCoy. She said she's investigating some kind of donation you made to the hospital or something."

His body goes rigid, and the light in his eyes darkens enough to notice. He drops my coffee into the trash can and takes my elbow in his grip, yanking me toward the parking lot. I hiss slightly, trying to squirm out of his harsh hold, but when he opens the back door to the SUV, he tries to throw me inside like I'm a rag doll. I fight him ever so slightly, needing to understand why he's become so cold so suddenly.

"What are you doing?" I cry, fighting his hand off my arm. "What's wrong, Carter?"

His hand shoots out to hold my chin, steadying my face to stare up at his dominating height over me. "Tell me what that bitch said to you,

Isabella. Right now."

My breath catches in horrid shock. "She didn't say anything, really. I swear. Why are you being like this?"

"Tell me the truth!"

I wince, his voice echoing through the parking lot. His anger is so hot that it's palpable, and I lurch my arms out, shoving him back a step or two. He staggers upright, still seething. His hand rests casually on his belt, but I'm not going to take his threat kindly.

He's furious at the situation, not at me, and I need to know why that is.

Maybe what Sam and I were talking about is coming true.

"Carter, you're scaring me," I whisper. "What's the problem? She came up to me and started talking to me. It's not like I met her behind your back or something."

"You won't do that," he bites, as if I was threatening him with that insulation. He steps forward again, growling in a low hum into my ear. "I'll tie you to the bedpost if I have to. You don't go behind my back with anything."

"Isn't that what's going on here?" I ask.

"What did you just say?"

"You're doing something behind my back, aren't you?"

He shakes his head, tucking his lips into his mouth while trying to calm down. It's not working. He's more furious than ever, but I don't care. I won't let him get angry and pushy with me. It's not my fault he doesn't want me to know what's going on with Lilian McCoy. It's something he needs to work out and bring to my attention rather than be surprised when it comes up to me in a business suit and a smile.

"I told you before, dove," he snaps, his voice unkind while he fights himself to calm down. "I am with you, and you alone. I have been for a long time. I won't sit here and field accusations that are saying otherwise. I want you. I *only* want you."

"Then tell me how you know her."

He flicks his focus elsewhere, and I can see the avoidance in his eyes yet again. I climb into the car and sit furthest away from Carter. He eventually gets inside; Ernesto nervously looks between us.

"Take me home, please."

Carter sits up straight. "We're going to the docks, dove."

"You can go alone. I want to go home. Please, Ernesto. Take me home."

"Fuck," he breathes, flicking his hand in the air between us. "I'm trying to protect you, Isabella. I don't need you hanging out with shady journalists that have it in their best interest to ruin my fucking life."

"Then just be honest with me," I plead. "Why is she trying to ruin your life? What did you have with that woman?" My stomach knots tighter than ever before, and I swallow the building lump in my throat. "Is she someone that you used to be with, Carter?"

He looks at me thoughtfully, his entire demeanor unfamiliar to me. "No, dove. She's not. She's just someone in the media that I fear has it out for the both of us, okay? I want you to be careful."

I look at the man I love, the man I've spent every day with for nearly six months, and I break.

He's lying to me.

If there was ever a woman who looked more like Brooke Blackthorne than me, it was Lilian McCoy.

"Take me home, Ernesto. Please," I pant.

The Blackthorne chauffeur nods glumly, headed back onto the highway toward the heart of Manhattan.

I wake up too early in the morning, feeling the missing indention of the mattress. Carter must not be back home yet, perhaps still touring the dock property. I wipe my wet eyes, realizing that I'd fallen asleep mid-sob, and stand up out of bed to stretch my body.

When I make it downstairs, my mouth desperately dry, I see a pacing figure on the doorstep. My heart slams in my chest when I walk up to the doorway, looking through the peephole to see Rich hanging out casually on the porch, hands in his pockets while he looks at the empty street.

It's bad enough the women in this neighborhood already think I'm a gold digger.

It would be much worse if they get the impression that mysterious men are lined up at the door while Carter is away. I could be overthinking it all, but I make the reckless decision to unlock the door and open it up.

Rich's face softens when he sees me, his entire demeanor harmless and relaxed. "Hey, Isabella. I'm looking for Carter. He wanted to meet up right after he took a look at the docks. Is he awake yet? If not, I can wait here until he does."

"No, he's back yet. Come on inside, though," I sigh. "We can wait together."

He stares up at the dauntingly tall foyer as if looking for laser beams that are going to zap him into oblivion if he steps inside. "Do you think he'd be okay with that, ma'am?" he asks cautiously. "I'm trying to stay on his good side. Is this a trap or…"

"No, it's not," I assure him. "Come on in. I'll make some tea, and we can wait for him in the living room."

He shrugs at his defeat, coming inside the house and taking a look around. There's hardly much furniture set up in the living room, and it's not exactly a cozy feeling, given that this house takes up the same space as the entire apartment building where I just moved from. It's a massive space with so little inside of it. I decide not to bring the issue up to Carter.

I'm sure, with all his daunting, overbearingness lately, that he will go ahead and fill this place with new furniture without checking in with me first.

Just like how he bought this place without telling me his idea, but I digress.

Rich sits down on the couch, and I go to the kitchen to heat some water. I return and choose the chair, waiting for the water to boil so I can steep the tea into the kettle. I sink into the chair and pull my legs to my chest, sulking over the reason I had fallen asleep in tears. Carter is nearly more unhinged than I've ever seen before.

But I don't understand why.

William and Jacob were the reason he was so afraid for me before, but they're gone now.

How is one journalist making him more chaotic than the threat against our lives every day?

"I love this house," Rich says, attempting to make small talk. "It's lovely."

"It's okay," I sigh.

His eyes narrow. "You don't like it?"

"I do. I just didn't have a hand in picking it. Carter can be a bit trigger-happy at times. If I don't make a decision quick enough, he will."

"He probably just has your better interest in mind," he replies.

I can't help but shake my head at his stance. "So, you agree with Carter? You think this was a good idea?"

"Well, I can't say something like that or not. I don't know either of you very well. I do know that Carter is a smart businessman. He's very determined to grow his empire in Manhattan. I doubt he makes moves to hurt you, seeing that you're his family, and he doesn't want to hurt his family."

"We aren't married or anything."

"Yeah, but everyone can see that he cares for you. He's protective, and for a good reason. I know better than anyone that Jacob and William were not to be crossed without repercussions. Their behavior took a toll on you, I'm sure of that. Everyone knows about my brother's obsession with you."

I swallow hard, recalling the memory. "You knew about that?"

"Only after the fact," he admits. "I've been taking care of my sick mother for years. It wasn't until someone on the Lacey side of the family reached out and spilled all the gossip. My brother has a history of wanting things he can't have. I don't doubt that he tried to get too close, and it wound up getting him killed. It doesn't concern me too much. I'd been at my mother's bedside for too long to even maintain a relationship with him or my father."

Hugging my legs tighter to my chest, I see a glint of pain in his eyes; I know the feeling too well. "Your mother is sick?"

"Terminally," he replies. "I've been with her through it all, but it's not getting much better. She's slipping away slowly. It's hard to watch, but it's better that I'm there."

"I understand that feeling," I admit. "My father has been sick for a long time. I quit college and moved back to the city to be near him."

"I'm so sorry to hear that. It's hard, isn't it? Feels like you have no choice but to watch them deteriorate. You can't help them or stop the sickness, so you feel helpless."

I inch to the edge of my seat. "Yeah, you're right. It's like you can help them with anything else in the whole world, but you can't take their pain away. You just sit there, powerless."

He offers a sincere grin. "It's nice to know someone going through the same thing as me," he admits. "I do enjoy that. It's nice to know we're not totally alone."

"I agree."

The kettle screams on the stove, and I pop out of my chair hurriedly. Rushing to the stovetop, I pull the kettle aside and release the lid, steam filling the air like a hot cloud. The burner is still on, and I tinker with the knob slightly, trying to figure out how to turn it off.

The flame is exposed through the metal grate, something I've never had to work with before. I turn the knob sideways, thinking it's going to turn off, only to watch the flames overtake the grate and lick the air recklessly.

"Ah!"

I back up instantly, the burn already marking its path around my wrist. Stiff hands keep me from falling. Rich manages to flick the stove off with ease before turning the water on in the sink. He yanks my wrist under the water, fighting me while I scream and sob through the hot agony.

He manages to keep me standing, his arm securely wrapped around my side while I struggle to stay upright through the shock and pain of the burn.

It doesn't last long.

The front door is nearly slammed shut, Carter's furious features kissing the sight of Rich and me in the kitchen, side by side. Rich finds out a second later that Carter is back, looking up just in time to see Carter's wrist cocked back over his shoulder, his knuckles as pale as possible while they sweep through the air, headed right for Rich's face.

I could step back and let Carter be his furious, overly protective self.

Or I could stand up and show him that I have a backbone in me that won't be ignored. I could prove that I have enough sense to never cross him and that he can trust me as I trust him. We should be a team that no one questions, and yet I don't know how much I can trust him now, and he obviously doesn't trust me.

I step forward, pushing his fist aside, and stand between Carter Blackthorne and Jacob Lacey's twin brother.

CHAPTER ELEVEN

Isabella

Carter grits his teeth when his punch doesn't land. "Move, dove."

"No," I bite. "You're not going to freak out over nothing."

"He had his hands on you. That's enough to die."

"It was harmless."

He stands over me now, his irises burning through me. "The only harm that will come out of this will be us in the bedroom when this asshole leaves. Move, Bella. Right now."

I stand firm, my arms hiked over my chest. "Please, Carter. Just be rational. I burned my wrist on this damn stove, and he helped me. I was making tea, and we were waiting for you to come back, that's it. We talked about our parents. Nothing more. He didn't touch me or do anything terrible; I swear."

Carter looks past me, darting his deathly glare through Rich. "Alright. Go upstairs, then. I'm going to talk to Donahue."

"No, I'm staying," I say again, pushing back even more than before. "I want to be involved."

Carter's glare grows more and more impatient with me. "Dove, why are you being like this?"

"Because you can't just shut me out to protect me anymore. I want to help, but you being coy with that Lilian woman worries me."

He looks between Rich and me like he just caught us in bed together, and I'm the one accusing him of being unfaithful. He rolls his eyes and leans in, kissing my forehead lazily. I take it for now, watching him trot past Rich without so much as a lingering look. He strips off his coat and retreats to the living room, working on taking off his tie while he sits on the couch.

"Sorry about that," Rich mutters. "I wasn't trying to cause any problems."

"You're not, trust me. We already have problems."

"Don't sweat it, Isabella. You're the power couple of Manhattan. I wouldn't worry about it too much."

"Thanks," I groan. "I just have a feeling that it's going to get worse."

His brows furrow. "Worse? How so?"

I can only shrug for now, looking over the wound on my wrist. It's an open sore, burned, and pink, but it's not bleeding, and it doesn't feel like it's on fire anymore. I pour a few cups of hot water into some mugs and hand them out with separate teabags.

Carter tips his head in thanks and then pulls me into his lap. I lay against his chest casually, trying to feel how we once were, but it's different. There's mistrust, secrets, and so much stacked against us that it nearly feels impossible to face anymore.

"How did you like the property?" Rich asks, steeping his teabag into his mug. "It's a big place, right? Lots of options for you to tinker with."

"Yeah, I suppose so," Carter admits. "I'm just wary."

"About what?"

"Going into business with you," I whisper, reading the hesitation on Carter's handsome features.

My lover nods in agreement. "It's too close to the business we tried to strike with Lacey. I just needed a simple money launderer into the campaign. Now I've got an ex-cop as mayor and a twin brother to my rival coming in here at six in the morning to be alone with the woman I love. Don't take it personally that I don't trust you, Donahue. But I don't."

"Understandable," Rich says, not showing an ounce of being offended. "I sincerely have no ill will toward anyone here. I'm trying to fund my mother's treatment, that's all. My other option is to sell it to the city and have them auction it for pennies. This way, we can work with one another, Carter. If you need something, then me and my resources can step in, and vice versa."

Carter holds me tighter, his once furious demeanor now softened in his light touch. "I'm not sure about this. I'd like to say I agree, but I think I need to run it past the rest of my family." He hesitates, looking deeply into my eyes. "What do you say, dove?"

I swallow hard. "What?"

"I want you to tell me what you think. Should we take this deal?"

I look at Rich, seeing a person that is in a position too similar to mine. He wants to care for his mother, just like I did everything in my power to look after my father. If I needed something to help fund treatment, I would have sought help from wherever possible.

"I think you should," I mutter. "He doesn't seem like he has bad intentions. Plus, with Killian taking office this week, we will need someone on our side who understands the business."

Carter's features are sad, but he nods and presses a kiss into my cheek anyway. "Alright, then it's settled. Looks like we're in business, Rich."

"So great to hear," Donahue breathes. "I'm very happy to hear this. We can have the construction crews out there by this weekend."

"I'll write you a check," Carter replies. "But that will be in a day or two. I haven't slept in nearly two days, and I need to retire for the rest of the day."

"I'll show you out," I hum.

Rich sets his teacup in the sink on the way out, tipping his head toward me while I hike the front door open to the blue sky outside. There are a couple joggers on the sidewalks already, waking up to the morning, and they look to be Anita's friends in tight pants and tall ponytails. They give me the look I was hoping to avoid by letting Rich inside earlier, and it looks like I avoided it for nothing.

"Thank you for this," Rich says, lingering on the front porch. "I think going into business together will be the best thing possible for both families."

"I hope so," I whisper. "Hey, good luck with your mother. I hope she gets better."

His smile grows. "Thank you, Isabella. Good luck with your father. I hope the same."

"Me too."

I shut the door softly, biting down a warm grin as I turn and meet Carter's eyes from the stairs. It's clear that his ferocity was bedded down for the sake of our company, but it's clear now that he's not too happy with how I stepped in to defend Rich Donahue.

He holds onto the banister halfway up the stairs, giving me a look that I know all too well.

"Come on, dove. Let's sort this out," he says.

I hesitate to move from the foyer, not sure if my ass is ready to be greeted by that damn belt. "I don't want to be punished, Carter. I've done nothing wrong."

"He had his hand nearly on your ass, Bella. I walk in here before sunrise to see you in our kitchen with another man. How is that fair?"

"Tell me about Lilian," I fire back. "Since we're striving to talk about what's *fair*."

He comes down a few steps, looking through me like I'm glass. "Dove, what are you implying."

"She looks like Brooke," I bite. "So I just want to know the truth. Is she someone that you slept with?"

"I told you that already," he groans. "We talked about this at the hospital, and I told you the truth."

"No, you didn't!"

My voice echoes through the nearly empty house.

Carter goes taut. "I hope you're not being serious, dove. If you want me to lie to you, then I will, but I'm not going to bullshit my way through this disagreement and pretend that your best friend isn't feeding lies into your ear about cheating."

My heart drops suddenly into my stomach. "Don't bring Sam into this."

"Why not? You brought her into this relationship, dove. She thinks I'm a lousy cheat now, and you were going to believe it, too. I could see it in your eyes. You don't believe me in the slightest, and I can't do anything to change that!"

I step back, tears pushing to the rim of my eyelids. "That's not fair," I whisper. "I don't know what to believe, Carter. You can't sit here and deny your past. I already know about it. I know that if you and I weren't together, you would be in bed with someone just like Lilian."

"No, I wouldn't!"

"Yes, you would! It's so obvious, Carter! You would still be working past your trauma with Brooke, the family, me, the world, your own fucking heart—all of it! You just want to deny the past ever happened, but I know that if Lilian was in your life before, then you did something with her. The resemblance is uncanny. I just don't see why you can't admit that you—"

"That I did what?" he roars, his voice the most ungodly sound I've ever heard in my life. I back down, watching him race to the foyer, where I'm frozen in place. "So, what if I fucked her? I fucked a lot of people, Isabella. It's sex. It didn't mean anything until I started doing it with you!"

My back presses flush with the wall, and his arm caves me into his domain by resting on the wall over my head. He's massive in muscle but throbbing with anger. I can't help but feel trapped and secure in the same breath, something so unnerving about that realization.

"I want you," he breathes. "That's why I don't think it matters what

I've done in the past. It was all before I met you, okay? So, why can't you just be on my side about this? I'm not hiding anything, Bella. I'm trying to keep you safe and keep you in my realm. Seeing Rich with his arm around you when I come home after a fight with you isn't what I need to see."

"I understand that, but it was innocent. I burned my wrist. He was just trying to help."

"I don't want him to help you," he adds.

I swallow hard, wishing I could understand his reasoning here, but I can't. Still, I have to give in. Arguing with Carter is the last thing I need right now, and it's the worst way to spend our time together. I give in at last, leaning against his fiery hot chest and kissing the hollow of his throat. He purrs with delight, the tension withering out of his body at last.

"Okay, then," he whispers. "Let's go upstairs. I need to shower and catch up on sleep."

My brows furrow. "That's all?"

He rests his hand on the top of his pants, toying with the buckle of his belt. "No, that's not all."

"I figured as much."

I kiss him on the lips once, then slide out of his possession before making my way to the stairs. He follows closely, watching his feet rather than me. He's wounded, and that's clear, but why should we be arguing? The worst we could ever go through is finally over. We should be happy.

When we make it to the doorway of the bedroom, he pulls me back by my arm, tucking me into his side.

"I love you, dove. We have to stop being like this."

"I know that we do," I admit. "I don't want to argue, either. I love you, Carter."

"Then let's take a break. Once this morning is over, and I get some rest, then I think we should go shopping, okay? Maybe find some things to fill this house with."

I nod, hopeful. "I'll wait in bed then."

He yanks me back when I nearly walk away. "Go kneel first."

I swallow hard, knowing it's coming but still hopeful my wide eyes will get me out of this punishment. He doesn't care, nudging me toward the bed. I garner the courage to shimmy out of my shorts so I can kneel. He flicks my shirt off my back while I do so, tossing it aside so I'm left only in my panties.

I keep my head down, pressed into the side of the bed, while I hear his belt slide through the loops on his pants.

I hate that damn belt, and he knows it.

"Sit up straight, dove."

My body moves with rigid action, managing to sit up straight while he comes around to sit on the edge of the bed where my face was just resting. He spreads his legs out past my shoulders, caging me in his thighs and leaning forward so I can feel the belt lick gently against the plane of my ass.

"When we're done here, you can come shower with me, dove."

"I know," I sigh, a bit fearful of the belt that casually strokes my lower back. "I'm just tired and worn out, Carter. It's been a bit hectic lately. I need a break."

"I understand," he sighs, his free hand tucking my hair back behind my ears. "Are you ready?"

He lifts the belt, waiting for my permission. I act quick, undoing his zipper and freeing the erection I know is there. He growls, his fist in my hair as though to pull me back, but it's too late. I run my tongue under the length of his shaft before swallowing his girth into my throat.

I nearly choke on the feeling, and it turns him on more. His fist in my hair loosens to the point of guiding my cheek to take the brunt of his throbbing cock, pushing me as deep, or as shallow, as he sees fit. His growl is enough to know that I've distracted him well enough, but it doesn't last long.

He throws the folded belt out, landing a stinging slap against the top of my ass. I choke, more in shock than in pain, gagging against the tip of his dick and feeling him fight back the urge to shoot his sweet cum down the back of my throat.

"Goddammit, dove," he whimpers, thrusting slightly as he fills my lips with every inch he was blessed with. "You're trying to get out of punishment. I'm just mad that it's working."

I release him from my lips long enough to catch a breath, his hand finding my throat and lifting my face to his. He makes out with my tongue, tasting the corners of my mouth while I lose track of his hand wielding that evil belt.

It cracks through the air, whipping my ass again and making me whine into his mouth.

His smile deepens while he releases my chin, watching me scatter to get back to his daunting erection. I take him in both hands, working the base with the precum that covers my mouth again. He drops the belt at last, using both hands to hold my head in his grasp so he can thrust appropriately into my throat.

"Damn," he growls. "You're fucking perfect."

It's not long before I feel him twitch and come, tasting it as it settles on my tongue. He yanks his hips back, pulling my bottom lip down enough to see the product of his relief still settled on my teeth and tongue. Shaking his head, he redoes the zipper on his pants.

"That was a good move, dove," he whispers, speaking directly into the frame of my ear. "But I still owe you a real punishment. Looks like we'll have to do it while shopping later."

A pit builds in my gut. "Oh, no."

"Yes," he says with a grin. "Lay down and get some rest. You'll need it for when we go shopping."

I crawl into bed, feeling his lips press against my forehead. My body is exhausted, and I consider sleeping, but hearing him start the shower nearby just makes me miss him more. He has the door shut, and I hate that there's so much unsettled between us right now.

Eventually, I climb out of bed and lean on the door, opening it slowly. I expected to see him in the shower, where he would convince me to join him. Instead, I watch Carter lean against the countertop by the sink, his body bent forward while he's stark naked, his arms folded around his face. I recognize the position well.

He's deep in thought, too much to move or react. His eyes are shut, his breathing shallow, as he fights through the demons in his mind while refusing to stand up straight again.

I dare to leave, catching a glimpse of his phone on the edge of the counter. I know I shouldn't, but I can't help myself. While he's going through his many thoughts, I take his phone and shut the door as softly as I had opened it.

I consider putting it back the moment it's in my hands. I'm tempted to forget about it, to simply trust the man who says he loves me, but my nerves are shot through after this entire ordeal. We have too many enemies closing in, ones that might be worse than Jacob and William combined.

If he doesn't let me in, we will fall together.

I open up his phone, coming to the screen where Tristan and Carter have been texting religiously over the last twelve hours. Scrolling up a little, I start from the point where Carter left work, even though he wasn't there for more than a handful of hours to begin with.

Tristan starts the conversation:

Did you find out what you're going to do about Lilian? What are you going to tell Isabella?

My heart already aches. Carter is pretending she's not an issue, but she apparently is if Tristan knows about her, too. Now I wonder what else Tristan knows that I don't.

I'm going to end things soon. Don't worry about that.

I hope you make it fast. Don't hurt her too badly.

It'll be quick, but I won't let her stand in my way anymore. She's nothing to me, brother.

If you say so. Just be careful. Isabella will be upset if she finds out before you say anything to her.

I slowly wipe my rising tears away, feeling warm pain spread throughout my chest.

Carter's going to break up with me, or in his words, *end it*, and it's all for this stupid woman I hardly know anything about. I set his phone down on the nightstand and lay in bed with my back to the bathroom. I hold my stomach and hug myself, praying not to throw up in utter shame and guilt. Instead, I press my tear-soaked face into the pillow and hope to fall asleep fast.

We haven't been in this house long, but I've already cried myself to sleep twice.

I'd hate for that to be the new normal, but I doubt this will be my life much longer. I have a lingering feeling through those text exchanges that Carter's going to make quick work of leaving me, and it will all be for the woman who surpasses my similarity to Brooke Blackthorne.

I thought I proved myself before, but it's clear now that it will never be enough for him.

CHAPTER TWELVE

Carter

Isabella is abnormally standoffish tonight. She doesn't want to look at me or talk to me, and I chalk it up to the fact that I promised punishment while we're shopping. I know she hates that belt, but watching her squirm with the idea only turns me on more. She gets so wet when she's hit with the belt, the feeling of her pussy tightening around my cock whenever I bring it into her sight adding to my pleasure.

I miss that feeling already, but as we peruse the furniture shop, she does everything in her power to avoid me like the plague. She turns into one room full of couches, the entire upper level nothing but living room furniture that she looks over without interest.

I've managed to keep this place open an extra hour or two so we can look through this stuff alone, but her diminished interest in anything has put a damper on our evening. She didn't look at me in the car, and she hurries away from my side whenever she gets the chance.

I hold my hand out, catching the youthful man who holds out his clipboard, checking off every item that I want to be delivered. I've made a few offhand choices already, but Isabella hasn't picked a single thing out. He stops with me, watching her walk around in a tight little skirt and a loose blouse without a bra. I know for a fact that she's not wearing panties under that skirt, either.

I made sure she was well aware of what to put on when we left the house. Given her desire to be nowhere around me right now, I'd like to assume that she's just uninterested in sex with me or receiving her punishment for earlier. I can't pin down why that is.

She sucked my cock without needing to be prompted earlier. Now she's acting like the mere thought of being near me is sickening.

"Give us this space," I say, nudging the young man away.

His eyes crane up at me in bewilderment. "Sir?"

"I want to discuss a few things with my companion," I breathe. "I need you to go."

Eventually, he gets the point and walks away.

The entire room of couches is left for us now, and I intend to fuck her on every single one of them until she'll look me in the eyes and tell me what's wrong.

"Dove," I call, watching her stagger to a standstill.

Coming up beside her, I drag my hand across the sore, red spot on her ass where my belt licked her backside this morning. She sinks into the massaging touch, but her eyes are still elsewhere while I walk around to face her fully.

"What's going on?" I ask.

She shakes her head vehemently. "Nothing, Carter. Just looking at the—"

"Don't lie to me. You've been avoiding me since this morning, and I want to know why."

"No reason," she assures me, though it's hardly convincing. "I'm tired, Carter. I just don't want to be here right now, that's all."

I nod slowly, my hand gnawing at her bare ass cheek under her flimsy skirt. "Fine. Pick a couch right now, and we can go."

Her eyes light up. "Really? Just like that?"

"Yeah, just like that. Pick one."

She looks around quickly, pointing to a black leather couch across the floor. I snatch her body into my arms, throwing her waist over my shoulder and carrying her to that couch. She elbows my spine, trying to steady herself, but it's too late. As I walk, I draw her skirt over her ass, exposing her tight pussy to the cold air.

"What are you—"

"Shh," I bite, shutting her up with two fingers that slide into her damp core.

"Ahh!"

"That's not being quiet, dove."

I drop her onto the couch, watching her turn over suddenly. It's the perfect position, too, making it easy for me to place her ass in the air. I steady her hips in that position, moving one of my knees over the backs of her legs so she can stay propped up for my vanity.

"Carter, what are you—"

I bring my hand over the helm of her pussy, slapping that spot just hard enough to watch her writhe with pleasure and pain. She groans out loud, fighting to get up, but it only drives me further to subdue her. Keeping her ass in the air, I wet my index finger and slide it into her sweet sex, maneuvering it in and out carefully.

She's still so tight, shivering with delight while I add another finger to the mix.

Her legs naturally want to spread, but I refuse to let them do so. I add another finger, bringing the tension between her thighs to an all-time high. She gasps and writhes beneath me. Eventually, I stop moving my fingers inside her sweet pussy. She tries pushing back and fucking my hand with ultimate need.

"Good girl," I pant, giving her all the pressure she needs to come beautifully for me.

"Carter," she pants, her ass rocking back over my knuckles. "P-please!"

I can't help but snicker under my breath. "Please, what?"

"Give me… everything."

For a woman who wanted nothing to do with me a few minutes ago, she's certainly making a full turnaround now. I can't help but fuck her like she wants, my cock practically begging for the same. But I hesitate, pulling my fingers back to watch her juices drip down the insides of her glistening thighs.

"Alright, dove," I whisper. "But first, I need you to answer me something."

"What?"

"Why are you upset with me?"

She doesn't reply, which only feeds into the idea that she is indeed upset with me. I use the only tool left at my disposal, reddening her ass with another strike of my palm. Her body cringes and tightens, her knees shifting while she fights to not come or cry—perhaps both at the same time.

"Nothing is wrong," she assures me. "I'm just… I don't know what…"

"Tell me," I bite.

Her head drops. "Carter, I know about Lilian."

"What about her?"

"You're going to leave me for her."

I pause, unsure how to even address that remark. Isabella's the best thing that's ever happened to me, and she still thinks I want nothing to do with her. She's tremendously better than Lilian ever was, but I don't want Bella to know that I've fucked that journalist a few times.

It was the past, for crying out loud. Why does that matter now?

"Why would you ever think that, dove?"

She hangs her head lower, resting her forehead on the couch with her bare ass and pussy still in the air near me. "Because I read what you and Tristin were texting about. You want to end it with me, and he asked you to make it quick."

Rage boils inside of me, but also shame.

Even in text, how could she believe something so false unless she got the feeling elsewhere that led to her picking up my phone in the first place? If she thinks I want to leave her or that I'm cheating, then she won't listen to reason first. She will find claims to back up her suspicions, and it's obvious that she's done that here.

My stomach aches with her admission and the fact that I can't just spank this out of her.

"Come here, dammit."

I lift her off the couch and sit down, forcing her to straddle my lap. I spread my knees out, making her legs push outward more. She's bent forward against my chest, sniffling lightly into my shirt. I run my hands over her hair in a soothing manner.

Whispering into her ear, she shivers as I speak. "I wasn't ending things with you," I say. "I would never do that, dove. You're mind, forever, and I won't sit here and let you think that any longer. If I didn't want you, would I be here?"

She shrugs lightly. "I don't know."

I rip my zipper down, the tip of my cock springing upright and brushing her soaked folds. "If I didn't want you, and I wanted to fuck that whore instead, would I be like this, dove?"

Finally, she shakes her head in refusal.

I press her hips down, watching her face while I fill her to the hilt with pressure. She tips her head back, nearly looking to the ceiling, but I latch my palm onto her throat and pull her focus back.

"No, you watch me, and watch me only."

She swallows hard and nods, slowly bouncing on the base of my erection. I admire her ability to take charge at times and her ability to follow my orders during sex. Her eyes don't leave mine, just like I said, and she chews on her bottom lip while flicking her hips up and down slowly.

"You love me, right?"

She nods with such assurance. "I love you, Carter. So much."

"You know I love you, right?"

"I do, but I'm just scared of losing you forever."

I can feel her gasp against the palm of my hand that is still wrapped around her throat. I bring her forward, my tongue tasting the depths of her mouth, only feeling her pussy get slicker with desire. I inch forward, letting her have more room to ride my dick while she takes my tongue without hesitation.

"You're mine, Isabella Julis. All mine. If I wanted someone else, I would have her, but you're the only woman in my eyes and the only one on my lap."

Her eyes narrow as she gets ready to come all over my cock. "You only want me, Carter? Forever?"

"Forever," I affirm. "Now, are you going to take punishment once and for all, or am I going to have to take my belt off again?"

"No belt, sir. Punish me."

"That's my precious dove."

I hold down her hips, burying myself into the depths of her core. She gasps aloud and leans into my chest, fighting back a scream of delight. I get so furious, feeling her hold back, that the idea of her punishment comes to mind just in time.

I thrust upward into her with such power that she has no other choice but to scream. She takes every inch of pressure, and I fill her with everything I have and then some. I'm balls-deep by the time she finally lets go and submits to me fully.

"Scream for me, dove."

Her head tilts back, her nipples pressed to the edge of her blouse, while she bellows a yelp of orgasmic pleasure. She's panting and sweaty, filled with so much cum that I can feel it pushing against the tip of my dick. It's enough to send me into my own frenzy.

I give her one last thrust, filling her tight little core with every drop of sexual delight possible.

She's still relatively loud while still calming down from the explosive orgasm, and I catch a glimpse of the salesman coming back into the room with a curious look on her face. I growl, biting into her shoulder just to hear her pants fill the showroom. He doesn't spend much time watching, ducking out of the room seconds later.

I grab her ass methodically, chewing and kissing her throat while she settles into a whimpering, panting state.

"If you ever suspect that I'm going to leave you, ask me first," I snarl against her neck. "Don't you ever go snooping for clues again. Do you understand me?"

"Yes, sir," she whispers.

"Good. Now, let's buy this fucking couch and get home. We have some business to handle."

Sitting up straighter, her eyes widen. "Business?"

"I need to meet with the family over the Donahue pact we have in place. And you have a building to help design downtown. I want those renderings soon so we can get my office ready."

She gleams again at the mention of getting back to work. "Okay, Carter. Thank you."

I stop her from climbing off me first, rolling her nipples through my fingers just to further the tease of punishment.

"Make sure you include a storage cabinet of toys in my office. The minute it's time to put that desk in there, I'm going to bend you over the side of it and fill you with my cum once more. Capiche?"

"Yes, sir."

Chapter Thirteen

Isabella

I never used to be a night owl, but hanging around Carter and his family has drawn it out of me. I watch him stalk to Anita's house in the dead of the night, alone and leaning into his long, determined steps. He's called everyone over for a meeting, and while I'm not allowed to sit in and hear the semantics of this war, I was allowed to go to Anita's and hang out with her in the kitchen.

He didn't specify the kitchen in his offer, of course, but I know that's where she spends her time.

Instead, I've opted to stay in my new office, my fingers running over the contact paper by the window overlooking the street. The homes are lit up in the night, beautifully done, but the women in those homes still writhe with spite toward me.

I ponder briefly if I'll ever be accepted anywhere—by anyone.

Instead of dwelling on that thought, I sink into my desk chair and look over the stale blueprints of the office building downtown. I tap my pen against the blank sheet I've set up beside it, but nothing comes to mind. I may not have finished school, but I did learn a lot. Besides that, I have every topic pertaining to architecture drilled into my head with news articles and inspirational photos sent to my phone so I can stay up to date with the newest fads in the industry.

Even scrolling through that back catalog, I'm lost.

There's just too much in my head right now for me to know what I should do. And it's not just about the building design.

Pulling out my phone, I dial Sam's number and hope she answers.

It rings twice before the call clicks through. "Hello?"

I sink at the deep voice that answers. "Tristan?"

"Yeah, what's up, Isabella?"

Swallowing hard, I toy with the corner of the blueprint in a fidgety manner. "I was just calling to speak with Sam, that's all."

There's a brief pause before his tired exhale can be heard through the line. "I'm sorry. I must have grabbed her phone when I left the apartment instead of mine. I'm so tired I didn't even notice it was her phone, not mine."

I hide my relief slightly. I was worried she didn't want to talk to me after everything that happened, and instead, was having Tristan field her calls so she didn't have to speak to me.

"Oh, okay. That's fine. Just… Just tell her I called, okay?"

"Yeah, of course. Is something wrong? Do you need anything?"

I hesitate, unsure if I should lie to him. Everything isn't okay, and I really need to speak with Sam, but I can't get ahold of her. Besides that, I'm not sure if I should ask Tristan about the Lilian thing. Is he at the meeting with Carter already? I don't want Carter to realize I'm talking to Tristan, as it would just further the strain between him and me?

"Hey, where are you?"

"I'm going to the docks. Carter said he wanted me to check out the spot Rich is building up. Why?"

I nod and sink back into a place of ease. "Oh, I just didn't know if you were a part of the meeting at Anita's place, that's all."

"There's a meeting at Anita's?"

The confusion in his tone is obvious.

"Yeah, Carter just called everyone over there a few hours ago. He actually just got there himself. I didn't know if you were there already or on your way."

"He never mentioned it to me."

We let an awkward moment pass between us as the line goes silent.

"Listen, Isabella. Let me be honest with you, seeing as Carter is trying to be dodgy with me, okay?"

"Yeah, what is it?"

He clears his throat, but the spite is still clear in his tone, "You need to be careful. There's going to be a lot of stuff coming out about the election, and it's not going to be pretty. Killian Hughes isn't the nice cop of a mayor that everyone thinks he is. His history with Carter runs deeper than some office uptown, okay?"

"What are you saying?"

I lean forward in my seat, needing to know what to expect. It's obvious that Tristan knows more than what he's saying to me, but I can't decipher what it means. Is it bad? Should I prepare for another war that no one is telling me about?

"Just keep an eye on the news, okay?"

I nod against the warm screen of my phone as if he can see that motion. "Yeah, yeah. Of course." Before he can hang up, I blurt on impulse, "Does this have to do with Lilian?"

"Excuse me? Isabella, you know I can't talk about certain things if Carter isn't—"

"I know, I know. But I have a feeling this is more about Carter and me and not the Blackthorne trouble. Am I at least right about that?"

He clears his throat like he's fighting the words that dare to come tumbling out. "Well, yeah, it is. But I didn't say that to you, okay? Lilian is troublesome, Isabella. You need to be careful when it comes to her. Just be careful what you do, okay? The election is still a firestorm in the news, and it's not going away anytime soon. They will use any bit of information possible to bring Carter down. That includes going through you."

"Yeah, thank you, Tristan. If you could just tell Sam I called, that would help." I brush my hair back, tapping my fingers along the desk while an idea comes to mind. "I'm going to be at the coffee shop by the hospital, the one across the street from where my dad is. If you could ask her to meet me there in the morning, I would owe you one."

"Of course. I can tell her, but I can't be sure she's going to show up."

"I know. Just tell her that I miss my friend. Okay?"

"Can do. I'll talk to you later, okay? Call me if you need anything."

I hang up, feeling more defeated than I did before. What does it mean when Carter doesn't let his right-hand man into a big family meeting? I know Tristan and I have a rocky past, and he made a pretty huge mistake that he's paid for a few times over, but I now feel like he's being more upfront than Carter is.

Even though the boss of the Blackthorne family told me to stop digging for answers behind his back, he never said I couldn't ask Tristan about a few things. He's his nearest confidant, and Carter isn't here to field my questions. He has to deal with small divides in his family next door, and I have to figure out how to design an office building when my prior job was taking calls and ordering inventory off a list.

Either way, I want to do the job well, so I draft a few throwaway options before really digging deep into the meat of this project. It's pretty simple. Most of the sleek design is a modified rendering of the office building they use currently, but it's fun to get to use my new tools and create something malleable for the future.

I just hope Carter likes it.

My fingers eventually become sore, and my palms are red and sweaty as I turn them over in front of me. It's exhausting to do this much work in one sitting, and I only have two floors done in my third draft before I decide it's time to take a break. I'm nowhere near completion today, and I need to get another few drafts down before letting Carter see any of the designs.

I make a pot of tea, break out a bag of chips, and pull myself up onto the edge of the kitchen counter while waiting for the water to boil. My limbs are sore, and my ass is still a bit raw from my earlier punishment with Carter. He grabbed me so hard while I rode his lap that I was sure he would rip me in half.

He looked furious enough to do so, that's for sure.

When the tea is done, I stay in my spot, eating my chips while I take in the vast size of this home. It's still pretty empty, and I'm too indifferent to the idea to fill it with furniture that I just don't care what it looks like anymore. It's Carter's doing—his vision—and I'll let him have it.

Truthfully, if I had my way, I would pick out a modest, cozy apartment downtown for us. He's the one with a history of large homes and a lavish upbringing.

I came from the working class, which betrayed me the minute my father fell sick.

Being from opposite worlds has never brought us apart before.

The front door swings open, and my thought process is stifled seeing Carter storm into the foyer. He throws his coat on the railing to the stairs, storming over to me so fast that I nearly flinch. I don't think he'd ever hurt me, but the icy glare and the stoic look on his face are too impossible to ignore.

He brings his hands to my hips and yanks me forward, my arms curling around the back of his shoulders while I take his embrace in cold silence. His breathing is shallow, his body taut, and he doesn't move or speak for what feels like ages.

"Is everything okay?" I ask.

He shakes his head. "I think I'm losing control of this family, and I don't know how to fix it."

It's the first time he's been so forthright with me in a while. It should relax me, but it doesn't.

"I'm sorry, Carter. I wish I could help somehow."

"You can help, dove. Just be here with me. I needed a break from all the bickering over there, and I wanted to see if you were sleeping yet."

"No, I don't think I can," I admit. The mere thought of sleeping after everything Tristan just told me is impossible to comprehend, as well. "I wanted to know what you were doing tomorrow, though."

"I have to go to the downtown building most of the day. Seems that's the hot-button issue with everyone. I haven't been making my presence known at all places, at all times. I'm spread so thin with everything that it's not easy trying to show up at every project. Still, it would appease the Nicolas situation, so I should start there."

"The election, the Lacey thing, the Frances problem. It's a lot, Carter. You've been doing really well juggling it all."

He shrugs, his arms around my back, squeezing me to his chest tighter. "I guess so. Just do me a favor, okay?"

"Anything to help."

"Don't take it personally when I'm not home as often. I will try, dove. But it's not looking good. I have a lot of work coming up this week and more people to keep an eye on that could shatter this family in a second. I have an obligation to protect everyone and be everywhere just in case."

I should tell him about meeting with Sam, but I don't want to add stress to his situation. It's an easy thing to go get coffee downtown and meet with my best friend. I shouldn't have to make a big deal about it when Carter is literally holding the foundation of his family on his shoulders.

I do what I should do in this moment and let it rest. I kiss his cheek and let him know I'm here for him when he needs me to be. I don't want to make things worse, so I simply just let things be.

Chapter Fourteen

Isabella

I turn the coffee cup around in my hands constantly, my palms warmed from the paper cup that never ceases to spin. It's hard not to feel anxious, like I'm waiting for a blind date to show up, but the longer the morning passes, the more I think Sam plans to blow me off. I don't blame her; she's worried about me and not a fan of Carter in the slightest, but it's not like he's here breathing down my neck.

In fact, he doesn't know I'm here at all. He went to work after his long overnight meeting with the family, and he won't be back until the late afternoon. I grabbed my laptop on the way out of the house, borrowed Anita's car on the sworn secrecy of me leaving the house, and have been waiting here ever since.

Aunt Anita was kind enough to lend the car to Carter and me for practice, and while driving through the city is terrifying, it does offer a smidge of freedom.

Carter took my cherry red sports car after the Lacey incident. Driving alone isn't allowed anymore, not until things *cool down*, but I know that may never happen.

It's raining in Manhattan, the hospital eyeing me from across the street. My father is probably in bed, watching the water trickle down his window. I need to go check on him, but it won't make much of a difference to him. He's always sleepier on rainy days, which means the confusion is more severe than normal.

I would only upset myself if I visited him today.

But it might be better than nothing.

Eventually, I push my screen down on my laptop, tired of browsing through the news articles that are trending through the city today. I haven't read anything too terrible yet. Most of the news about the election is starting to veer into Killian Hughes and his band of campaign brothers, but even then, it's nothing that would shock anyone.

The news about Carter isn't great, but I have yet to see anything truly damning.

Whatever Tristan was worried about might just turn out to be nothing.

"Hey, familiar face," a voice hums from beside my table. I didn't even notice them before, but looking up now, I see Rich Donahue standing by my chair, a coffee clutched in his hand. "You like the coffee here, too?"

"Oh, yeah, I guess so. It's next to the hospital where my dad is, so I always just come here. What are you doing downtown?"

He shrugs, pointing to the chair across the table from me. "Mind if I sit?"

"Go ahead."

Once he's settled in and done taking a long drink of his warm coffee, he rests his elbows on the table casually. "I was going to the docks to check on the building. They can't do too much in the rain; it's a lightning risk right now, but I like to keep an eye on it. Seems like Carter's family is doing the same."

I shiver slightly. "Yeah, he has been having his guys go look at it every so often. Tristan went last night, but I don't know what for." I have the sudden urge to stop talking, my mind hazy with the idea that maybe I shouldn't share this with Rich. But he doesn't seem to care, his focus more on the coffee than it is on the looming eyes of Carter's family. "How is that place, by the way? I haven't been there since..."

He gives me a knowing look. "Yeah, it's alright. You don't have to talk about it if you don't want to. I know the history involved. I do want to apologize for it, though."

"It's not your fault. You weren't even associated with your brother at the time."

"True, but it doesn't mean I can't feel bad about it. My family has always been a tough subject for me to talk about. I'm sure it's been worse for you to have to live through it all. It sounded horrific."

"It was hard," I mutter. "I didn't know if I would make it out alive or not. Carter saved me, he really did."

Smiling softly, he leans forward over the table ever so gently. "He's a good guy, Isabella."

"I know that."

"You don't seem to believe it right now. I can tell by the way you look away. Your eyes. They look sad. You seem to be withdrawn, too, and I can only imagine it has to do with my last visit."

I look over the soft burn on my skin that has healed since that incident. "No, of course not. Carter isn't upset about that anymore. It was a misunderstanding, nothing more. He just likes to think that I'm always in harm's way. He wouldn't be wrong sometimes, but with the Laceys gone, I think I'm as safe as ever."

He grins with such assurance. "I agree completely. It's a nicer city with my brother and father out of it. They were always into something they couldn't handle. They even dragged my sister into it. She's been missing for a while, but that's a story for another day."

"Oh, I'm so sorry." My brows pinch. "So, can you handle it?"

"What do you mean?"

"You've gained their messes. Is it too much for you to handle, or not?"

He thinks over my question for a long, quiet moment. I can't help but see Jacob in his face, the resemblance threatening a tremor down my back that normally would send my alarm bells off. But I don't let it show. There are no real red flags with Rich Donahue other than his lineage, and he's told me that he's rejected them as a family already.

He's harmless, and being handed a horrible family aftermath of a mess isn't his fault.

"I think I'm doing okay," he says at last, sipping his coffee in short spurts. "It's been a challenge at times. I never thought Carter would agree to work with me, and I was certain he would have killed me instead, but he seems okay with it now. You know him best, Isabella. How does he seem?"

I play with the cold surface of my laptop in front of me, my coffee empty and useless for me to fidget with at this point. "I don't actually know. He is okay with you and your family now, I guess. It's not the same as when we were under attack, and they were trying to hurt me or kill Carter. It's just been different, I guess. We have other problems on the horizon."

He looks perplexed. "Really, like what?"

I stifle and inhale, knowing for sure that I can't divulge any of that. He seems to understand my tensile body language because he holds his hands up in mock surrender, shaking his head.

"No, no, forget I asked that. I shouldn't be probing. Carter wouldn't appreciate that, so maybe it can be our secret."

I toy with my fingers now, running out of physical distractions that can help me distance myself from this talk. "He doesn't know I'm here, actually. I won't tell him about it or that I saw you; don't worry."

He tips his head sideways. "Is everything okay?"

His question has me confused. "Yeah, everything is fine."

"I meant, are *you* okay?"

Twiddling my thumbs, I want to nod and say I'm fine, but I'm not. I can't even pinpoint why that is, either. It seems petulant, trying to act like everything is fine and nothing is looming through my mind at all hours, but that's a lie. I have a lot of reasons to be worried about the future, about what's coming for my new family, and I'm too scared to even ask Carter about it all.

He wants to shield me as always, but that's not the best idea right now. We can walk around this city and not fear Jacob Lacey, and that's a huge step in the right direction, but that doesn't mean we are in the clear. We have a lot to deal with now—things that I don't even have a full grasp of yet—and it's not going well.

It's like Jacob Lacey was the gatekeeper to the plethora of problems behind him. Now, we have opened the can of worms, and dirt is everywhere. I can't clean it up fast enough. Carter won't tell me where they all are, and Tristan is trying to warn me of the impending mess.

It's not good enough. I don't know enough.

I don't think I'm enough to stop it all, either.

I blink back tears that are already rolling down my cheeks, and Rich looks shocked by the sight. He grabs a few napkins and hands them over, his eyes wide while I try to compose myself as quickly as I had unraveled.

"I'm sorry, I just—"

"No, don't apologize," he breathes.

"I'm a little stressed out, that's all. I feel like something bad is going to happen, but I don't know what it is yet. It's annoying, and it's constant, but no one will clue me in. It's like knowing a storm is coming but not knowing what kind. Should I take cover or find high ground? I just don't know."

"I'm sorry, I had no idea it was that bad, Isabella. I shouldn't have brought any of this up to begin with."

"It's fine. It's just Carter," I say, shaking all over like I'm drenched in cold rainwater outside. "He acts so furtive these days and demands to know everything, but he's not giving me an ounce of information. I don't know what to think when he shuts down, but it's happening more and more lately. I'm scared it's going to affect us if something bad happens, and we aren't strong enough to withstand it."

"You are, I'm sure of it."

"How are you so sure? You don't know us?"

He nods slightly, pushing his coffee aside as an afterthought. "I know you. You and I are alike in a lot of ways. I was tormented by my brother for years growing up, and when I stopped communicating with him, it was like peace again. I also have a lot on my plate with my mother being sick, like your father, and I have to deal with Carter, too. He's not an easy man to read, and sometimes I think he'd rather shoot me than work with me."

I wave him off, trying to change the subject.

Not because it's hard to talk about, but because he's right.

"It's nothing," I admit. "I'm sorry I mentioned any of this. I'm just a little emotional today. It's been difficult bottling everything up from Carter, and I was going to tell my best friend Sam, but I guess she decided to bail today. I asked her to meet me here hours ago."

"She didn't show?"

"No, and I don't think she ever will. She's distant because of Carter. I can't blame her, but I feel more alone than ever. I have new neighbors I could talk to, but they think I'm a gold digger and nothing but a poor woman sleeping her way into a wealthy relationship. They wouldn't welcome me as a friend, and the only friend I thought I had isn't even willing to meet for coffee."

He bows his head in similar defeat. "That's a lot to deal with, Isabella. I'm sorry everything is turning out this way. I wish I could help more, but I can offer to take you home if you want."

"I have a car in the lot down the street, actually, but thank you for the offer, Rich."

He holds up his umbrella, something I didn't even think to grab on my way out the door this morning. "Can I walk you to your car, then?"

I stare at the rain that has picked up in pace. It's pouring buckets outside, and I'll be soaking wet by the time I get to Anita's car in the back lot. Rich has been pleasant enough and seems normal to the point of trusting. He's not like his brother at all, even if the resemblance is uncanny. But his demeanor is nothing like Jacob's. Maybe that's why I'm drawn to opening up to him so easily. Even if he was only an unexpected fill-in for Sam, I have found a bit of relief talking to him today.

"Yeah, that would be nice. Thank you."

He opens the umbrella at the front door and holds it over us both, but I notice his shoulder gets drenched when we step out into the downpour. He ignores the water flicking onto his neck and keeps it over my head mostly, taking the direction where I'm parked with ease.

"Over there," I breathe, turning the corner to point at the borrowed car, only to see Lorenzo and Tristan leaning against the soaking wet car. They both lack umbrellas, their eyes finding mine in an instant. They hardly look pleased, either. "Wait," I say, stopping short.

They both cross the lot and sprint toward us, Tristan's fists grabbing Rich's shirt while Lorenzo rips me away from the Donahue boss. He's pinned to the nearest brick wall, and any effort to be dry has gone to the wayside. The umbrella falls from Rich's hands and floats down the sidewalk canal of flooding, my heart punching into my throat at the cold rush that the rain brings with it.

My laptop falls to the ground, ruined in the rain while I try to break this fight up, but it's met with fierce opposition from Rich, who tells me to back up.

It doesn't stop Tristan and Lorenzo from cornering him, though.

An opposing force of men comes rushing forward to break up the fight, and Rich tries to calm them down throughout the confrontation, but it's not helping. The impression of pistols on hips and tucked into waistbands of every guy in this fight now is evident.

Tristan and Lorenzo are not just outmanned—they're outgunned.

"Wait, can everyone calm down?" I shout, speaking over the splashing of tires in the street nearby. "What is going on here? Guys, I'm fine. Why did you just come up and push him like that?"

Lorenzo looks less than pleased as he replies, "Tristan wanted to see if Sam was coming to meet you. We drove by, saw Anita's car here, and thought maybe she was nearby. Seeing you with him just triggered our concern, that's all."

"I'm fine," I say, blinking back the rain that hits my eyes. "Rich, who are these guys?"

"They're my family. I told them to pick me up on the way home so I'd have a ride from the coffee shop. They dropped me off down the street, and I got my coffee. They must have seen the fight and jumped in."

"Sorry, boss," one of the guys says, agreeing to that alibi. "It looked like they were going to rough you up. We had to step in."

I run my hands through my hair, exhausted from this trouble already. "Okay, let's just separate and forget this happened, please. We need to be working together, right? Not fighting in the parking lot like a bunch of heathens. Let's just break it up before anyone sees and blows this out of proportion."

"Too late," Tristan says, staring across the street at a woman in heels with a large camera mounted before her eyes. She walks briskly away into the crowd before Lorenzo and one of Rich's guys can even get across the street. But it's clear that Tristan is right.

It's too late.

"Fuck," I say, looking at Rich. "Carter's going to be pissed if he hears about this."

CHAPTER FIFTEEN

Carter

The new office building is nothing but bones and bad memories. I hate anything having to do with Lacey, and this place still reeks of his scent. Having Nicolas here to oversee the build of it isn't helping. I decide to take a break, just to keep my cool, and hurry across town to get to my main office. It's quiet here, less hectic and messy due to the lack of construction going on.

My office is warm, and I strip out of my wet coat, finding a large envelope on my desk before I can even sit down and catch up on emails. I turn it over, the sides of it damp, but nothing is written on the outside like it was sent in haste. It's not even postmarked or addressed, so whoever brought it here clearly wanted it here pretty quickly.

I sit down and tear open the top, finding a few glossy pictures stuffed inside. They're warm to the touch, hot off the presses, but not as hot as I am when I turn them over to see what's in the images. Everything about these photos makes my pulse spike.

The first is of Isabella wearing the same clothes I saw her in this morning. She's at some coffee shop downtown, the fuzzy haze of the photos clearing as the shot becomes more and more obvious.

She's not alone at the table.

I squint, making out Rich's familiar hair and his Lacey resemblance with surprising ease. He sits across from her and even reaches over in one of the photos, handing her something that I can only guess is a napkin. It's hard to tell with the quality of the pictures, obviously taken from a distance, and the way the window is angled where she sits at the table, the reflection of the city faint on her gentle cheeks.

"What the..." I sigh, flipping through the stack with heavy determination.

I slip from my calmness more and more as I look further into the fresh stack of photos, one of them smearing as my thumb crosses the image in heated shock. She's practically leaning against Donahue now, his hand over her shoulder with an umbrella while she smiles kindly at the gesture.

I toss the rest away at that, uninterested in seeing anything else.

That is until a little note flies out of the stack, separated from the last photos, where I catch a glimpse of some other people making their appearance, but it's not that concerning. I can make out Tristan's face briefly, and I trust he got this meeting—or whatever it was—taken care of.

It's the note that has me heating up now, reading the cursive handwriting with a bit of skepticism about the intentions.

> *Hey, baby. Gave it some thought. Maybe handing out those sexual photos and stories isn't my best move. If anything, it would just let Isabella know how much you've changed. But that doesn't mean I can't make you feel pain where it hurts the most.*
>
> *Keep an eye out for your girl. Looks like she's up to no good, just like you.*
>
> *Something tells me you and she are just perfect for each other, after all.*

I crumble the sheet, throw it away, and then kick my trash can over for good measure. "Fuck!"

As soon as I throw my fit, my phone rings with a notification. I take it out, seeing a news article flagged with the only keyword I am monitoring the internet for right now: *Isabella Julis.*

I skim the article, seeing the same photos plastered online with nothing but venom attached to the words that preceded them. It's a gossip column, and it's already doing its job. There are twenty comments when I first open it and another fifteen when I refresh the page.

I shouldn't read them, but I do, so fucking troubled by Lilian's obvious scam to smear the woman I love with this bullshit. I know she's not seeing Rich—or any man, for that matter—behind my back, but that doesn't excuse why she's out with him in the first place.

She didn't even tell me she was leaving the house today. If she had, she would have someone with her to prevent this shit, but it's too late to get that done now.

The commenters show no semblance of control in the comments, hell-bent on smearing my dove's reputation without considering her feelings. What angers me the most is the amount of vitriol these people spew while hiding behind the anonymity available online.

"She's nothing but a gold digger, and she's found a new bank to break into," I say, reading one of many scornful comments on the gossip column. "I don't see how Carter Blackthorne could fall for this scam! So happy he's not the mayor. Just wait; we will hear about the many indiscretions of this woman in no time. He should dodge a bullet and ditch her."

I have to put my phone away to try to keep calm. It's no use, though, and I gather the photos I've tossed around, shove them into the envelope again, and head for the lobby downstairs. When I get past the security desk, Ernesto is already at the doors, storming inside the office building.

"Did you see it?"

I don't need him to elaborate on what *it* is. "Yeah, I have. We need to get home and deal with this. Now."

He nods, and we get into the SUV in a hurry to avoid the rain, but that's not all we end up dodging. There are photographers everywhere, swarming the sidewalks with or without umbrellas. I hope Ernesto drenches their lenses as he speeds away, but I can't even get the satisfaction of that.

Long brown hair catches my peripheral, and I tense, seeing Lilian on the outskirts of the mayhem. She doesn't have a camera, but she does wear a satisfied smirk on her face. I nearly tell Ernesto to stop so I can wring her neck, but I know better than to do that.

There are too many cameras watching right now.

We lose them all on the way home, and my body fills with fury while I try to make sense of this sudden turn of events today.

"What are you thinking about?" he asks, filling the void of silence with his voice.

"Nothing, I'm just pissed off," I gripe.

"I know that, but what are you going to do about it."

My belt comes to mind first, but I think better of that after a moment. "I don't know yet."

"Try talking to the girl, Carter."

"Why? So, she can tell me it's nothing? She will talk this Rich Donahue thing away without trouble, and I know that. But it's not even about that now. I mean, it kind of is. She shouldn't be meeting with him in coffee shops behind my back, but she can't see this news article, Ernesto. She's already so…"

He pulls the SUV down our dead-end street. "So?"

"Fragile."

He parks in silence, and I jump out of the car with the envelope in hand. Anita's car is parked in my driveway, so I head for our house first, finding company already lingering in my kitchen when I do so. Lorenzo looks elsewhere, shirtless, while his shoulders spot a well-used towel. His pants are soaked, though, and I'm happy he's decided to keep them on.

Tristan comes forward in the same drenched state. I shove the envelope into his chest, and he takes it at once, opening it and thumbing through the photos quickly before tossing everything in the kitchen trashcan nearby.

"Fuck those photos," Tristan says.

"They were on my desk today. Right before the article went live."

"Not just live. It's going fucking viral now, boss," Lorenzo chimes in.

Tristan nods solemnly. "Around thirty thousand people have viewed it in the last thirty minutes since it came up, Carter. They know you're still reeling after the election, and punishing this just feeds the sharks wanting to see you fall."

"Well, it's not me they're attacking now. They're calling Isabella the worst kinds of names in the comments. The article was just as scathing, too, and I didn't need to look at the writer's name to know who is doing this."

Tristan gives me a knowing nod. "She's gunning for you both."

"Where is Isabella?"

He looks up the stairs and then shakes his head. "She's been terrified all day."

My brows crease. "About what?"

"You, Carter. She didn't want you to find out about what happened, but Lorenzo and I got there and escalated things. Then Lilian came by and took those damn photos. I don't think she's seen them yet. Her phone and computer are down here, both ruined from the rain and the scuffle. She left them with me and hurried upstairs. Won't talk to anyone, not even Anita."

I hate to ask, but I do, anyway. "Has Sam come by?"

He looks uncomfortable with that question. Sam is her best friend, and while it wasn't anything I could have seen coming, she's now very close to my cousin. They've been together so much lately that I haven't been bugging him about some stuff having to do with the family. I sent him to the docks on easy work that could have been done later rather than to the meeting with everyone else that lasted all damn night.

I haven't talked with him since I asked him to check out the dock project, so I guess it went well.

But now isn't the time to bring it up.

"Sam was supposed to meet Isabella for coffee this morning, but she didn't go. I texted Sam, but she said she didn't want to see Isabella right now. I'll talk to her tonight. I just didn't want to leave Isabella here alone. Not with the article coming out so damn fast."

I don't even mention the scathing article again, trying to block it from my mind before I go to Isabella. I will deal with Lilian personally and swiftly, but I need to check on my dove first. I don't need her to be afraid of me. She loves me, and I love her. I can handle this without rage.

I can handle this without rage.

I can... *Bullshit.*

I hope that I can handle this without rage.

Chapter Sixteen

Isabella

I lie in the shower, the warm water drenching me endlessly. It's nearly impossible not to feel guilty for what happened, and I know I should have done things differently. But now I feel like a dog in the pound. Carter's going to find out from Tristan, and he's going to be furious with me. Then there's that wretched woman who took photos.

I don't understand it, but I know it's not good for me. In fact, it feels personal, but that's what I deserve for being in love with the ex-mayor-in-running for the city. He told me countless times that the cameras would be on us, and if he won the election, it would be our new normal, but this doesn't feel normal.

It feels like the world is slowly cracking under my feet, and there's nowhere else to run.

I glance up, catching a shadowy silhouette in the doorway. I don't need to look closer to know that it's Carter. I can tell by his lean stance, his hands hidden in his pockets, and the strict flat line of his lips that he constantly displays when he's not happy about something…anything. It almost makes him look like he's always mad, which isn't too far from the truth, but it's not what I'm used to.

I like the dominant, protective man who would burn the world down for me.

This man is similar. He holds a match and all the spite possibly necessary to bring the world to its knees, but I'm included in that. I'm no one to him in this version, and I bow to the entity above me, just hoping they don't flick me with a flame in their mission to create fire.

I'm kindling in his world of heat, and I'm not helping calm things down in the slightest.

Slowly, I watch him get undressed, dropping an article of clothing with every step. He comes forward purposefully and starkly naked, standing in the hot water with me curled on the floor before him. I have to prepare myself for punishment, an explanation, and sex, which always comes with a mix of pain and pleasure.

Instead, he kneels under the spray of the shower and sits on the cold tile beside me. I don't look at him; I only feel his arm snake behind my back and yank me sideways. I'm perfectly placed under his arm now, all comfy, without a hint of ill intent in his touch.

My ass is thankful for this temporary mercy.

"Did Tristan tell you?"

He nods slowly, staring into the darkness of the bathroom. I didn't turn on any lights. The shower is mounted with an LED strip that casts blue hues over both of us, but it doesn't offer much light in the grand scheme. Even with the shadows eating his features alive, he still holds the flat line of his lips. It's not a grin, and it's certainly not a frown.

It's contentment. It's not like Carter.

"What did he say?"

"He told me everything, dove. Everything. Besides that, there was…" He stops himself short, the words muttering out of him too fast for him to control, I guess. When he does speak again, he says it slowly and carefully, like he's tiptoeing around something else. "There's an article online about it. A few pictures."

I swallow those words carefully. "The ones from today? How is that possible? It just happened a few hours ago."

"It was enough time for someone to throw together a stupid smear campaign against *you*."

My stomach drops. I've heard that phrase before and recently, but not from Carter.

"Lilian."

This time, Carter perks upright. "What did you just say?"

"I said Lilian," I repeat. "At the hospital, she told me there was a smear campaign against you."

He's silent for a long minute. I don't blame him, either. What is there to say about that woman? He could tell me the truth, something already telling me that he's been involved with her in the past, but that's as much as I can assume at this point.

And I don't want to assume, but he leaves me such little choice in the matter.

"Please, Carter. Just be honest with me."

"Honest about what, dove?"

"Everything."

He shakes his head, unwilling to budge on some things. "I can't tell you everything. There is nothing to say, Bella. I'm sorry this happened today, and I need to talk to Tristan and Lorenzo more about handling these issues in the future, but it doesn't excuse you."

I let my head fall further.

"Dove, why were you out with Rich Donahue?"

Running my hands up and down my wet legs, I try to settle my nerves for now. Punishment is on the horizon, and I know I can't avoid it. Still, I want to lessen the severity of it if possible.

I'm not sure if it's possible, but I can *hope*.

"I was waiting for Sam. I called last night, practically this morning, and Tristan picked up the phone. I asked if he would tell Sam I'd like to meet with her for coffee, and he said he would tell her. I went after you left for work, but she never showed up."

His hand on my side tenses slightly, squeezing my hip in his long fingers. "Go on."

"Rich showed up, and he just sat down to talk, Carter. He could tell I was upset, so I talked to him a little bit. It wasn't anything serious, I swear, but it was personal. He just seemed like he would listen to me, and I needed that so badly because—"

"Because I don't listen to you?" he bites off.

I shrink in size, feeling that I've angered him even more. I didn't mean for this to happen, and it's not to say that Carter doesn't hear me, but sometimes I need someone else to hear me, not just the man who loves me and says he listens. He listens to everyone else, too, and sometimes it overshadows what I have to say.

With the election failure, the family drama, and the tension between the two of us, I know I'm making it worse by pointing out the obvious; at least, I thought it was obvious to him, too.

"You've been so wrapped up with everything lately that I just needed someone to—"

"What did you tell him, dove?"

"Nothing too personal, Carter. We talked about Sam, about the Lacey family."

He nods like it's appeasing the anger inside him, but his lips have started falling into a deep frown, one that I won't be able to bring back up into a grin anytime soon.

"Please, Carter. Trust me for once."

"I do. It's him I don't trust, dove. I want to make things right, for argument's sake, because the Lacey trouble was woven through the city and stirred up far too much attention for the family. But that's not to say I trust this guy. I don't. He's still a Lacey, no matter what he claims. And having you around him, alone, it's like you've learned nothing, Bella."

"*Learned?* What the hell was I supposed to learn, Carter?"

I shouldn't raise my temper here, but it's only natural since I feel I'm under attack for not doing anything.

The thought of him telling me that I should have learned something after what Jacob Lacey did is a little bit hypocritical, and I won't stand for it.

He brought half of that trouble onto me, and I won't be blamed for the war that preceded it.

I shove his arm off my shoulder and stand at once. Storming out of the shower is my attempt, but I don't make it to the glass door, a set of very hungry hands finding my hips. Carter moves me like a rag doll, lifting my feet off the floor and pinning my back to the wall just under the blue lights and the hot water. I choke on the heat from both the shower and his touch.

It's a lot to handle at once.

He stands against me, naked and fuming, his hands squeezed into my sides without an inch of mercy. I can't help but suffocate from the pressure, from the intensity, and I can hardly inhale through the proximity of his lips against mine.

We're not kissing, though, he's just…

Breathing.

"You want to walk away from me, dove? Just like that. You act like I don't listen, but you don't talk, Bella. You keep shit from me, from the man you claim to love, and then you tell me that some Donahue-Lacey fucker is a better listener?"

"I never said that, Carter."

"You might as well have."

He stands straighter and taller, but his pressure-heavy position against me hasn't changed at all. Looking down the bridge of his nose, his frown is nothing but a gritted expression, full of spite and ire that can't be tamed. I don't attempt to, either. It would only set him off more.

If that's possible right now.

"You are mine, Isabella. Right?"

I swallow my hesitation and nod. "Of course, Carter. I love you."

"And you want me forever, don't you?"

"More than anything."

"So why do you make these careless remarks and think I won't be jealous? You think you can parade around with the brother of my enemy, and I won't find out about it? The election may be over, but this is my city, dove. If I want to burn this city down, I will."

"I know that," I say sadly. "Everyone knows that, Carter."

"And you? What would you do, Isabella, if I took this city and flipped it inside out? Would you listen to me then? Would you see the monsters I'm trying to obliterate from your eyes, or would you still trust that there's nothing wrong if that's what I told you?"

My brows pinch. "Are there monsters I don't know about?"

"More than you could ever fucking imagine. I promised to protect you from them, but if you think the lesson you should have learned before isn't something that matters, then I will show you the repercussions of what can happen to you."

I stare up at the shell of a man I thought I loved.

He's not the same man right now, and it's terrifying to see.

"What are you talking about?"

"Meet me in my office down the hall in five minutes, Isabella. I'll show you who you can trust and who you should never believe is just being kind enough to lend an ear."

He walks away from me quickly, and I have to stand straight against the wall to catch my breath. He's naked still as he stalks into the bedroom, and I wonder briefly if he's going to grab a towel or get dressed, but it doesn't matter. I flip off the shower and hurry after him, naked and vulnerable.

I trust Carter more than I trust myself at times, but the thought of him exposing monsters does frighten me.

What is he talking about?

What have I sparked in the man I love to feel this passionately angry with me, a man who doesn't yell, get his belt, and spank my ass before sending my body into wonderful waves of pleasure? No, this man is different.

He's dangerously reserved, and I have a feeling that's my fault.

Lesson learned.

CHAPTER SEVENTEEN

Isabella

I wrap my wet, bare arms over my breasts and follow Carter's wet steps into the office next door. I didn't notice this stuff in here before, but it's a nice office. It's not finished and organized like mine is, but it has a big, sturdy desk and some file cabinets in the corner in case he wants to work.

For now, he stands naked behind the desk, clicking rapidly around the keyboard of his laptop that he has yawned open. Water gets on the screen, and some seeps through the keys, making me wonder if it will short out like mine had earlier today. But that's the least of his problems, apparently. He clicks around the keys for a long time and then turns the computer to face me.

I can already sense the tone of the article before I get halfway through the first paragraph.

Thankfully, there is somewhere to sit because I melt into the chair slowly, covering my shivering frame with my hands that seem warm with humiliation—same as my warm and flushed face.

My eyes skim over the words typed out alongside every photo, portraying a scene that didn't actually happen with how the writer spun it. Then comes the comments at the bottom of the page, filled with personal ridicule against me. They don't even know who I am personally, but the worst accusations and assumptions are made about me.

It's hard to keep track of them all.

There are new comments about every ten seconds, and they're far from kind.

"What is this—"

"That's what you get for seeking out a good listener," Carter spits. He slams the screen down, but the damage is done. "Rich is no better than a Lacey, and I wouldn't be surprised if he set you up, dove. You fell for it, too. You let that man set you up to look like a slut searching for a rich guy and betraying the man you love."

"I would never."

I'm whimpering now, the tears pouring from my eyes, sliding down to the sides of my jaw and continuing down my neck. I hope they are masked with the shower water, but I don't think they are. If anything, they feel like they are laced with highlighter ink, making noticeable streaks down my pale skin to show how weak and gullible I am.

And gullible I will forever be.

"How would he even... He couldn't have known that I... If this was his plan, why would he come after me, Carter? What I have done to..."

"You are the reason the war with Jacob Lacey started. Sure, Jacob had it coming, but if he hadn't expressed such outright interest in you from the start, and I didn't have to step in to save you, he would have lived a lot longer. Maybe that's what Rich wants. Maybe he is punishing you for the start of the domino falling that caused this chain reaction."

I cry harder, my body shaking in angst. "I thought you said this wasn't my fault, Carter. You've always said it's not my fault, and now this is retaliation. But for what, exactly? I've done nothing but love and trust you. Do you not trust me?"

His eyes widen with every accusation.

I don't stop there, though.

"Do you feel jealous of Rich, Carter?"

He picks up his laptop in a single swoop, throwing it against the nearest wall. It rattles the house, and it doesn't stop there. He grabs at his desk, his fingernails digging into the wood as he leans forward, absolutely seething beyond sexual measure now.

"I am not jealous, dammit! I am trying to protect you! Why are you making that so *fucking* hard?"

"Because I don't need to be protected, Carter. I can handle my own problems!"

"Bullshit. If I let that happen, Jacob and William would have had their way with you, Bella. You know that. You're just trying to hurt me."

I flinch, unsure where this is even coming from.

He's never accused me like this, and I can't help but wonder if the riffs in his family are sending him on a rampage to find the loyal and pick out the ones who aren't being exactly like he wants them to be. Loyal, blindly in line, and on his team one hundred and ten percent.

I thought I was being loyal to Carter.

"Do you think I'm not loyal, then?"

He stiffens in posture, his fingertips reddened, and his face flushed in the coldest shade of ivory I've ever seen. He's like a ghost now, too far gone to save, his life withered away into nothing but smoke and mirrors. He's an enigma and an illusion, and there's no catching him now.

"Tell me the truth," I whisper. "Do you think I am not loyal to you, Carter?"

"I think you are loyal, dove. I do. But this can't be overlooked. Whether you knew it at the moment or not, you had to have known that hanging out with Rich was going to get back to me."

"I wasn't trying to *hang out* with Rich, he just—"

"Silence," Carter orders, slamming his fist into the wood and breaking the skin on his knuckles.

I bite my bottom lip, his command too harsh to ignore.

Brushing his hands through his hair, blood dribbles from his hairline and mixes with the water on his face like a watercolor painting. It's disturbing, but it's Carter Blackthorne in his element. Pain doesn't hurt him like it hurts everyone else.

Sometimes, I wonder if he's inhuman because of the way he can switch emotions with such ease.

He only does it when he's threatened with pain that could touch his heart, and I see those walls building right before my eyes. He's going to leave me out here in the cold, outside the dark shadow of the walls he's creating in front of his soul, and it's going to be hell to get those down again.

After this hell of a fight, I don't know if I'll get the chance to take them down.

"I'm sorry," I finally offer, not sure what else to say at the moment. "It was a coincidence that he was there. Or at least that's what I thought it was. If you think he's out to get me, to get *us*, then I won't ever speak to him again, okay? I'll stay in this house, wait day and night for you to come home, and won't do anything that makes you question my loyalty again."

For the first time tonight, his features soften. "I didn't say I wanted that, Isabella."

"You don't sound like you know what you want, Carter. And I'll do anything to help you. If it means staying safe, learning my lesson, and keeping out of trouble, then I'll do that. I don't want you to not trust me. I love you more than I love anyone else in this world. You are my life now. I will change everything to appease you and make you feel safe with me."

He fully breaks now, slowly sitting in the chair behind the desk. He rests his elbows on the edge of the polished wood and presses his tired face into his palms. He looks rough and beaten, and I can see this argument has bested the man I love.

It's not what I wanted to happen, but at the same time, I can't ignore the irony of it all.

He has secrets that he's not telling me, ones I have to look out for, and now he's accusing me of the same indiscretions. As if I have a history with Rich Donahue. As though I have any other man out there on the streets of Manhattan with a past that connects to mine in a salacious manner.

Whatever he had with Lilian, I know it exists without knowing exactly what it was or what happened between them. I'm not stupid.

But to be accused of lying and hiding things with another man by a man who's doing the same to me—it's funny to see. It's not humorous to laugh at, but it's funny in a way that hurts my chest. It's a joke that hits home, one that incites pain, but the only way to get through it is to grin and play like it's nothing. Like the sting of it doesn't exist.

Like he isn't projecting his worries onto me because that's exactly what he's doing.

He's hiding something that I can't know about, and he's very purposeful in his attempt to keep whatever happened between him and Lilian in the shadows. Well, I'm in those shadows now, and I need to find out what happened, but not like this.

Not with the accusations multiplying between us.

I love Carter, and he saved my life in many different forms when we first met, and I will never be able to give him that back. But I can give him peace of mind, at least for a little while. When his family trouble stops boiling over, maybe this will change, but I'll tie myself to the bedpost in the morning and not move until he gets home at night if that's what he wants from me.

I'll tell him he's the best listener in the world, that I can tell him anything without fear of backfire because of how understanding and subjective he can be, even if it's a lie.

And it is a lie.

I think our conversation has proven that, but he won't listen to reason now.

Instead, I move across the office, push him to sit up, and lay back into his lap and his cradling arms. We kiss briefly out of formality and fall back into place as usual. He's the one who needs support right now, and even if I'm dying for a little bit of support, I'll let it go if it means he gets what he needs.

I owe him that much... right?

CHAPTER EIGHTEEN

Carter

It's a week of nothing.

No word from the witch Lilian, not a peep out of Donahue, who received a pretty harsh tongue lashing from me over the phone a few days ago, and certainly nothing ill-intended from Isabella, who has been rather reserved since our argument.

It was unlike anything I'd ever had with her before, and it hurt tremendously.

While I usually like the aftereffects of such a high-energy, intense moment where we both scream our feelings out and then have amazing sex to redo the bond between us, it never happened.

And it hasn't happened since.

My body is rigid with the thought of what I've done. I can't reverse what I said or accused her of doing, and at that moment, it felt like I was fighting the good fight. I was fighting for her, for us, but the longer I waste away at my desk, in my head until sunset, I realize it wasn't about her at all.

It was about me.

I don't want to lose the woman I love to anything, especially not my own mistakes. I think I've made the mistake of being too harsh about the Rich Donahue situation known now. She shouldn't have sat down and talked to him long enough for a handful of photos to be taken, and she gets that, but to accuse her of doing more than that was a bit of a stretch.

She wouldn't leave me, and she wouldn't fuck another man. I think it was stupidly immature of me to think otherwise. I should have controlled myself better.

I need to do better in the future, or I'll drive her away more than I already have.

Gathering my things, a little buzz pops up on my phone from an unknown number. Isabella's phone was ruined in the rainy altercation, and I know Anita loaned her one of the family burner phones until she could take Isabella to get a new one. Unfortunately, I forgot to get the number from Anita. Seeing this text does have me excited, though. It has to be Isabella.

Meet me at the Blackthorne Club. I'll be wearing my best outfit for you.

My blood runs hot as I hurry downstairs and find Ernesto outside the SUV, ready to usher me into the backseat as soon as the shuttering noise of the cameras begins. The paparazzi hasn't let up since the article about Isabella and Rich came out, and I can't wait for this to blow over, but it's going to take time.

"Where to, boss?"

"The club," I say, my leg bouncing in excited anticipation.

He gives me a weary look through the rearview mirror. "Going out for a drink or something?"

"No, I'm meeting Isabella. I think she's finally ready for us to get back to normal. I fucking hope she is. We've been so silent and cold to one another since our fight. I'm trying to make things right, but she hasn't been too receptive. Maybe this is her attempt at making it right for us."

He shrugs but hardly looks convinced. "Alright, if you say so, boss. Just be easy with our girl. She has a fragile heart, and you have hands

133

of stone."

I wave him off, practically jumping out of the moving car and into the club when it gets near. The place is loud tonight, the sun setting and the rich of this city coming out to play. The club is alive, and the smell of liquor makes my mouth dry. I stop by the bar, down a few fingers of bourbon, and then head to my room in the hallway of many playrooms.

Opening the door, the lights are dimmed, and a curvy brunette stands at the pole in a leather bustier. Isabella is wearing a matching black thong, the choice a bit unusual for her style. She has paired the daring outfit with a black lace mask that nearly covers all her face except her lips.

I don't like the mask, and I never have made her wear one because it hides the look on her face when I fuck her just right. She knows that, but she's put it on anyway. Maybe it's to defy me a bit more than usual or keep me from seeing what she's really feeling. But I let it slide, pushing the door shut and stripping out of my coat.

"Dove, what are you doing up there?"

She doesn't reply, just continues to turn around the tall, metal pole with her black patent leather heels on to display her strong, toned legs. She does another spin, hanging onto the pole with a bit more skill than normal.

She hates being up there because it puts her on display, and that unease only adds to the fact that I find the woman I love even more attractive. She's so hot when she's unsure about herself because the minute I part her legs and please her body, she relaxes like she was never embarrassed at all. It's endearing and sweet, and I don't see any of that here.

I walk closer, watching her put on a little performance on the pole that I know she's not accustomed to doing. I stare at her carefully, watching every twirl, flick of her ass, and press of her breasts against her inner arms as she tries to seduce me—but it's not working.

My cock isn't cooperating, and after a week without her precious pussy wrapped around it, I think I'd be a bit more ecstatic to see her like this. But it's not the case at all. She does another turn, her back against the pole with her ass facing me while she slides down with her knees out toward the back wall. It's a sexy move, but something isn't right.

Her ass is in full view as I come closer for a better look, and the marks I've made with my belt aren't there. Not only are they not there, but a tattoo of sorts flashes into view, and I instantly feel sick to my stomach. Kicking the speaker nearby, I listen to the music spit and stutter in static. It's enough to make the witch stand abruptly, peeking over her shoulder through the thin slits in her mask.

"You whore," I bite, shaking in rage. "Lilian. Get down from there."

She smiles as she undoes the mask, taking it in her hand as she slowly comes off the stage to stand before me. The outfit is one I don't recall her having before, which worries me that she found it in here out of the many things I've given Isabella. Unless Lilian's income has really increased, then she's taken it from that array. It would make her intent even more sickening.

"You think I'd fuck you and not know the difference between trash and quality?"

Her face turns sour, a sight to see. "You seemed to like it before you thought I was some meek slut, Carter. What's the matter? You can admit you wanted to watch more. I won't tell Isabella."

She leans forward, her lips nearing my neck while her hands slip down my arms. She doesn't make it close enough on either to be successful, and I act on blind rage and impulse. My hand takes her neck, and my other palm finds the top of her shoulder. I swing her around sideways and pin her chest to the wall.

Right now, she should fear me, but she instead laughs at the position we're in. "Oh, Carter. You always did like it *from behind*."

She purposefully rolls her hips backward, propping her ass against my hips like she's got a chance of my dick falling out of my zipper and coming anywhere near her. Even with the façade she's put on, it hasn't made my cock twitch. If anything, it may not get hard for weeks on end after this ordeal.

I press her chest harder into the wall, enough to hear her groan in discomfort. "Now that I have your attention, Lilian. We should talk about that envelope you sent me last week."

"What about it?"

"Did you set up Rich to get those pictures of her and him together?"

She stifles a laugh, playing a risky game with her safety right now. "Carter Blackthorne doesn't know something for once. This is interesting, actually. You are the man who knows everything, right? You're the guy with all the answers. What do you think happened?"

I bite my tongue, refraining from lashing her with useless threats right now. It won't scare her, and given the insanity of this woman, she might actually enjoy the prospect of being threatened by me. Anything to dig herself further under my skin like a burrowing tick.

I want to rip her away from the wall and toss her over a cliff, but I'm worried it still wouldn't do the trick.

"Just tell me, Lilian."

"What do I get in return?"

I release her at once, watching as she turns against the wall, her breasts out but still hidden through the outfit enough to not be too revealing. She bites on her thumb, trying to be sexy in her smeared red lipstick, but it's pointless. She's not fooling me or anyone else with this innocent act.

She's far from innocent, and sexy isn't even a town on her map.

"I want a kiss," she says at last. "One kiss… on the lips, and then I'll tell you about Rich."

I hesitate before replying, "Fine. But you tell me first."

She lets out a laugh that signals she's either drunk or just outright crazy. I had my suspicions about the second one all along, but the first one is starting to shine through a bit. Maybe it's how she got ballsy enough to get me down here and put on that little dance, but it's going to take a lot more than a sip of liquor to make me attracted to this slut ever again.

"Rich Donahue had nothing to do with it," she says, leaning forward. When her lips get close to mine, she pauses and adds, "It was all your girl, Carter. She met with Donahue, opened up her weeping little playbook of pity, and paid for it. I just did my job and reported the news, Carter. I can't help it if the woman doesn't know any better."

"Know any better?"

"Yeah. She thinks you and her are nothing, but I would value being with a man like you again. I always knew you were loyal deep down, and you were almost loyal to me before. If you would just let me prove how worthy I am, I could show you how being loyal to me would never result in a mistake like that."

She leans in, nearly about to kiss me, but I stop her just in time. I shove her into the wall and take a few long steps back, watching the betrayal spit on her face. She looks furious and wounded, and I almost savor the sight of it before shaking my head, grabbing my coat, and heading outside.

She doesn't follow.

Maybe she isn't as completely stupid as I think she is.

Ernesto picks me up with a confused look in his eye, but he doesn't mention it. We drive home in downtown traffic without a word shared between us again. I prefer it that way. I need the time to think, to consider what Lilian said. She has no reason to lie when she thinks she's getting something out of the truth being told.

Maybe Rich Donahue and Isabella meeting up was just an unfortunate happenstance. It does worry me to think about Lilian following the woman I love around aimlessly, with a camera aimed at the ready to ruin her, but I have to be realistic at the same time.

Isabella wouldn't be caught dead in a similar predicament like that again, not after the words we threw at each other almost a week ago. Lorenzo has been watching her during the day, sometimes Tristan taking over the task just to make sure she doesn't sneak out again and stays safe at home. From what I've heard, she hasn't tried to go out on her own lately.

She did promise to do better, but that may have been overkill. She was already perfect, and knowing that it was just supposed to be a harmless coffee date with her best friend that turned into an online frenzy of harsh critiques makes me feel worse and worse as we get closer to home. I laid into her when she was already fresh off the fire, and I shoved her right back into the hot coals.

Earlier, Ernesto mentioned the family waiting for me at Anita's place for another meeting about the progress at the docks and downtown, but I head home instead. The door opens and shuts, the sound the only thing filling this large, echoing house.

I check the bedroom first, then her office, but I don't find her anywhere. It makes me a little worried to think she's tried to leave because of the unease between us lately, but it's not fucking possible. She knows better now.

I know she does.

I open the door to the basement and hear the hot tub running its bubbly cycle. I shut the door behind me as I descend the stairs, seeing Isabella in the pool, her lightly tanned figure passing under the surface with nothing on but a tiny bikini.

There's not much I'm thankful for, but I can at least be mighty grateful for the invention of a string bikini on a woman's body that absolutely wears it right.

She comes up for air, holding onto the edge of the pool opposite from me. Without noticing I'm on the stairs, she gets out of the water and crawls over the barrier into the hot tub. She whines at the sudden shift in temperature, and her face is bright pink by the time her eyes meet mine.

"Carter, when did you—"

I hold up my hand, silencing her without anything but a simple notion. She recedes into herself, guarded and understandably so. I come to the edge of the hot tub and look down at her. The glimmer in her eyes is stunning, and the purse of her perfect lips is everything I need to see today.

They probably feel even better, too.

"Stand up, dove."

She does so without a moment to waste, and I point at the bikini next, flicking my hand sideways. She reads my movements with her wide eyes and undoes the strap to the top, then the two ties to the bottoms. She tosses them both aside, and I finally get what I want.

She stands in the water, exposed and vulnerable, and tries to hide her assets with her arms and hands coyly enough to be the cute, meek woman I know she is.

Swallowing the sight, my dick is so stiff it fucking hurts, but I don't care. It doesn't hinder me from undoing my belt and waving her forward. She looks uneasy at first. I take her hands in mine and wrap the belt around her wrists to make her more comfortable.

We were pretty vicious in our fight last week, and we haven't really been physical since then. She might be expecting punishment, and she might even *deserve* a little bit of it, too, but I don't want to take it to that extreme. Instead, I undo my pants and kick them off with my shoes and socks. She holds out her tied wrists as an offering and melts back into the water, her chin resting on the edge of the hot tub for now.

I undo my shirt, standing naked and stroking myself wildly over her head.

Her eyes never leave mine, and the smile on her lips almost looks familiar.

She's missed me as much as I have missed her.

"What do you want me to do, Carter?"

I step into the hot water, sit down across from where she's perched, and wave to the walkway behind the hot tub. "Get out of the water."

Her brows furrow, but she gets out of the water, dripping wet and naked with her wrists bound. "N-now what?"

"Dance for me, dove."

It's the sight I wanted to see when I thought she texted me, and I'll be damned if the lasting memory of a salacious dance in my head isn't by her body and her wonderful figure. I want what I want, and it used to be for the sake of plugging up the past where it bled out.

But things are different now. This is the woman I want, the one I deserve, and even if she doesn't believe it, I trust her more than anyone else in my world right now. Rich Donahue is a blip on my radar, a source of contention I know I'm not done dealing with yet, but if that means more time spent with my dove, hashing things out just to rebound from them stronger than ever—then so be it.

I enjoy her dance as she moves her hips, and I count the ways I'm going to make her scream in ecstasy tonight all inside my head. She doesn't know it yet, but I'm going to fuck her like I should have been fucking her all week long. If that means cramming it into one night together, I'll do just that.

I'll have the woman I love, the woman who loves me, and no one will come between that. No one.

Chapter Nineteen

Isabella

I don't know what's gotten into Carter, but I hope it doesn't disappear.

He has been watching me attempt to dance for what feels like an eternity, and just when I think my legs are going to give out, he stands up. He leans back, his cock harder than ever, and he stares me down like a hungry lion would a gazelle.

"Go upstairs, dove."

His voice is like ice on my clit, and I shudder with both shock and delight at the roughness of his new demeanor. As my hands are bound in front of me, I carefully move to grab a towel, feeling his hand swing against the plane of my ass when I do so. The towel goes flying as I recoil from the instant pain, and his hand finds the back of my hair.

He tips my head up, my back and my sore, hot ass now pressed to his chest and his hips. He keeps me pinned there, too, his lips moving to my ear closest to the center of his chest where he has me hostage.

"Did I say you could cover up, dove?"

I shake my head in shame. "You want me to walk up there naked?"

He nods slowly, his hand tightening on my scalp. It's not enough to hurt, but it is enough to know that he's taking control back, and the week we spent without sex wasn't spent in vain. "You will do everything I say to the word, or you'll be punished, dove."

Given all this time I've spent with Carter, I thought I knew all his antics by now, but I don't. He places my focus back on the stairs leading to the main floor, and I pray when he came home that he sent anyone in the living room to Anita's.

I walk up the stairs, naked, with his hands crawling over my sore ass. He rubs the spot he spanked over and over again until the searing pain is nothing but a distant memory against my skin. I plan to keep it that way, stopping in the living room while I wait for my next instructions.

"Go to the kitchen island, dove. Put your back on the countertop."

I do as he instructs, but the dark marble slab is so cold that I hiss and step forward, bumping right into Carter as he comes around me. He gives me a warning look, and I wait for his hand to swing sideways against my backside. He's lenient, which is new for him, and I'm happy about it.

However, his hands grab at my sides, and he lifts me off the floor with such ease. I mutter under my breath about the coldness against my ass, and he smiles wider at my discomfort over it. Tapping the edge of the countertop where my legs are parted, he gives me a narrow look.

"Lay down on your back, with your head off the edge of the countertop right here."

My eyes widen. I'm already soaking wet and slipping around. Now I have to manage this position with my hands bound and my body covered in chills? It's been a week of us tiptoeing around one another, and I figured it would be another few days before we would talk about what was said. Then maybe, and only then, would we reconnect sexually and fall into our old ways.

Half of my excitement is encouraged by the fact that I wasn't expecting this at all. It's even more driven by the thrill of what is to come and what this dynamic and sensual man has planned for us next. I could never keep track of his ideas before.

This only leads to a steeper edge of possibilities, and I'm excited about every single part of that.

I do as he wants, laying on my back with the back of my head hanging off the edge of the countertop. My back is frozen on the cold marble, my legs shivering and shaking, but I hope he just takes that as my enthusiasm and nervousness about what's coming next.

He grabs my wrists, his hands stroking up my bare stomach and then between my breasts. When my hands are over my head, he looks slightly satisfied, letting them hang off the edge and below my head that's already hanging off the side.

Blood rushes to my fingertips while some goes to my head, but I ignore it for now. This is worth it.

He stalks along the side of the kitchen island, his eyes sinking into my skin at every possible opportunity. It's a little overwhelming to be like a meal for this powerful man, but that's how I feel right now. He makes it known, too, that he can have what he wants when he wants it.

While the option to call for mercy is always present, I don't do it. I've used it once when Carter got out of hand, but this isn't the same. He might still harbor some anger, but it could be his normal amount. He's typically an irate man anyway, so it's hard to tell the distinction these days, but I know his breaking point.

It was last week in our argument.

As long as that side of him is held in check, then I think I'll be just fine in this odd position. He walks away without a word, leaving the kitchen for the spare bathroom in the foyer. I get a bit antsy, worried someone will barge in and see me strewn naked over the kitchen countertop.

The family would have *plenty* to talk about then.

But Carter returns and puts those fears aside, holding a plastic bottle. He kneels on the edge of the countertop by my ankles, climbing onto the kitchen counter with more grace than I had. His mouth is full, his cheeks puffed out from their usual chiseled state. I glance up slightly, watching him settle between my legs like he's got his tongue out, but he doesn't.

He leans sideways and spits a mouthful of something into the sink. I watch with intense curiosity as he slides the bottle off to the side. There is just enough light in here for me to read the label.

Minty mouthwash.

I nearly jump out of my skin as he leans forward, his breath trailing across my parted, wet pussy. He exhales on purpose, the tingly sensation of the minty mouthwash brushing my aching clit and needy folds. I bite back a scream, ready to throw myself onto the floor, but it's too late.

He brings his dripping wet lips down against my silky sex, his mouth moving in rhythm to every shiver, shake, and writhe of my body against the marble. He makes no effort to slow down while I moan and groan, sometimes in intense pleasure but also in frightening cold surprise. It's like nothing I've ever felt before, and it doesn't stop.

The more I ebb with delight, the more wet I become, and the more the warm aftermath of my pleasure is met with a freezing cold sensation that stings in more ways than one. It's not just shockingly delightful, but it's also incredibly hot.

My head hangs off the edge of the countertop in shock, and I fight the urge to scream to the ceiling while he threads his tongue in and out of my pussy. The temperature seems impossibly real the whole time, and just when I think he's found his own time to declare mercy for me, it intensifies.

He takes another swig, freshening the sting against my clit before working me through yet another orgasm.

"Ah!"

He chuckles against my pussy as I call out in desperation—in tentative astonishment. "Go on, dove. Scream."

My breath hitches, and my body does the same physically, flinching under his weight as his hands pin my hips down firmly. It's just the leverage I need to lift my back off the cold countertop, the aching spike of pleasure and pain in my core just about pushing me to my max.

"You're not screaming, dove."

I don't have to look up to know he's sucking on his fingers. The mouthwash is transferred on purpose, his knuckles slipping into my core deeper and deeper until I feel the base of his hand. He can't go any deeper, and I'm happy about that a little bit, but the icy shock of the solution now lining the inside of my pussy isn't cold anymore.

It's burning hot, and it's delicious.

"Carter!" I scream, his name a hearty moan in many ways. He snickers more at my delightful coo of orgasm than he had at my shocking realization of what he was up to down there. It's like ice against my sex—ice that turns into warmth at the flick of his fingers.

And he flicks his fingers very well.

He works me through another orgasm, then one more, the back-to-back stimulation rocking my body to the very center. I break and rebuild myself again and again. I have to stay focused, seeing stars while my head hangs limply off the edge of the countertop.

When he finally pulls his fingers free, he sucks them into his mouth and climbs down. I pray for some leniency now, needing a moment to adjust back to Earth while my head was just in Pluto and my body thrust even further into the weightless space beyond that!

I watch him come around the countertop, still sucking his fingers like a popsicle in the summer. He stands over me, his cock jerking naturally while he keeps his focus on my eyes. Removing his fingers from his soft lips, he slides them into my mouth. I can see him positioning himself just right to enter my lips with something else after his knuckles.

It's a genius plan, really, and the height of the countertop is perfect for his cock to slip in through my mouth and align down my throat, all while I'm left vulnerable on the countertop for his pleasure.

"Relax, dove. This is going to be good for us both."

I've never believed anything more than that phrase coming from Carter's lips right now.

CHAPTER TWENTY

Isabella

Carter doesn't waste any more time. I'm lined up perfectly, and he's been saving up for seven long, treacherous nights. The anger between us has fizzled, but I can't help but think he's not over that spat yet. His movements are brash and slightly brutal, his hips rapidly moving against my face.

His cock fills my throat in a heartbeat, and he grabs the side of the kitchen countertop to thrust into my mouth. He is fluid in his movements, his threatening patience almost a record for him, but his speed doesn't stay moderate for long. It gets brutal again, his intentions clear as he fucks my face without relenting.

I keep the back of my head pinned against the side of the island to keep it from banging too hard and knocking me unconscious. At this point, I don't think he would notice, his hands kneading at my breasts and flicking my erect nipples before he leans in to choke me with his dick as his hands find my parted legs.

He massages my clit while he humps my mouth, fucking me like it's the first time we're meeting, and we're just trying to get a good come out of it. It's so dirty—no, it's *filthy*.

But I fucking love it.

His knee pins my bound wrists to the side of the cabinets, rendering me useless and at his will entirely.

He doesn't slow down on either action, treating my clit like my tongue and applying pressure to it with a back-and-forth rubbing movement. His dick is as deep as possible, the feeling of his testicles fully pressed against me something that I never thought would be so possible, but also so damn delicious.

He's using me as his outlet, and he's not taking any survivors. He's going to fuck me mercilessly, endlessly, and I can only part my legs to make sure I get another few orgasms out of it.

And I do.

But still, he has yet to come. It's weird for him to last this long, especially given how we haven't had sex all week. I can't imagine he hasn't touched himself in seven days just to appease the needs in his body. If it were any different between us, and he didn't claim to love me, then maybe I would worry.

I trust Carter more than I trust myself, though. He wouldn't cheat on me for some cheap, quick sex.

Yet the possibility remains in the back of my head while he flinches, his hands coming to my throat where he applies just enough pressure to choke me. I cough and gag, the back of my neck tightening to the point that I can feel my throat close against the slick edge of his dick.

He did it on purpose.

I try to swallow some of the warm cum that covers my throat, and I choke on the taste while he pulls out of my lips with a harsh twitch. His hands tug at my hair, forcing me to sit up suddenly on the edge of the countertop, just in time for me to cough and drool, his cum finding its way out of my throat.

He keeps one hand in my hair, gently keeping me upright, while the other squeezes my chin, pushing against either of my cheeks. My lips part on impulse, his eyes scanning the sight of my mouth drenched in his cum. He pins my jaw shut with his hand, forcing me to breathe through my nose.

"Drink it all, dove. Right now."

I gag to myself, still trying to fight the sensation of his cock in the furthest depths of my throat just seconds ago, but I aim to appease the man I love. I swallow down a large gulp, fight back a coughing fit, and nod with my eyes peeled against his.

He looks surprised at my speed, letting go of my mouth and pinching my cheeks once more. I can feel the slimy, warm aftermath of his cum against my tongue still, but it's all gone. When he sees it, too, he lets me go, backing away to catch his own haggard breath.

I lean sideways, needing to rest, but it doesn't work out well. The darkness has mixed with the spots forming over my tired, wide eyes, and my palm misses the countertop outright. I whine in shock, knowing it's too late to catch myself, but Carter is there as always.

He catches me in time for us to hit the floor a little lighter than anticipated. I'm strewn out over his lap, naked, wet from the hot tub, and still bound by the belt on my wrists. He undoes the belt eventually, curling me into his lap like I was the night after our last fight. I snuggle into his warm chest, my head tucked against his shoulder, and we breathe together in a stifled silence.

"Easy, dove," he says, his voice coming down to normal again. It was rough and demanding minutes ago, more than it typically is, but now he's the Carter Blackthorne I know and love. The giving, caring gentleman that I fell for. He tucks my hair back and kisses my temple as he holds me. "You're perfect, Isabella. You know that?"

My brows pinch. "Why do you say that, Carter?"

"You and I have had a rough week. You could have called mercy and ended it downstairs, but you were more than willing to play along. You and I may fight and have a rift here and there every so often, but I know it won't last forever. We will always find our way back to one another, right?"

I nod slowly, comfortably sandwiched against this chest. "Yeah, you're right, Carter."

"You want that, don't you? You want me forever?"

"How could you ask that? If I didn't want to be here, I wouldn't be. I would have called mercy. I would have left you. I am here because I love you, and I believe in us. I just…" I shake my head, aware I've said too damn much, as usual.

"What is it, dove? Speak up."

"I'll just ruin it again. Like always. I just need to keep my mouth shut before I make things worse."

"You aren't doing any such thing, Isabella. Talk to me."

Still, I'm hesitant. "No, I just can't. It's not worth the trouble."

"What do you mean? Why won't you just tell me what you're thinking, dove?"

I find his eyes, unsure how to explain his without starting another fight with the man I adore. "Because it's just going to cause you to be mad, Carter. I love you, and I believe in us, but yeah, I'm afraid. I'm afraid we will break."

His eyes turn cold, and his hands hold me tighter to his chest while we sit on the floor. "Why do you think we will break?"

"Because you don't trust me."

His head falls slightly. "I do trust you. I really do. I was mad about the Rich thing because I thought you had snuck out to meet him or were sneaking behind my back. I didn't think it was as harmless as you insisted it was because I was afraid of finding out later that it was something bigger than how you explained it. I don't want to lose you, and I don't want to be lied to, either."

I hesitate to ask, but the words tumble out of me without hesitation. "What made you change your mind over the last few days? You thought it was personal before—that I was hiding something or even had some affection for Rich Donahue. Now you're saying you trust me fully. What changed?"

He pauses for a long, pondering moment, and I can see the gears in his head turning as usual. He doesn't answer right away, and I take that as my sign to shut this down. I bring my fingers to his lips, press down to signal his silence is okay, and then peel myself off his lap.

We both stretch before his arms link around my hips, yanking me to his warm, naked physique. He kisses my temple, and I settle back into our usual closeness.

But it's not normal. It's anything but normal.

I can feel it in the way he touches me that something has changed in his mind, but I don't know what it is yet. He asked me not to snoop around his back for answers, but it's easier than trying to get an answer directly from him. So, while he gets ready to go to the meeting next door, I plot my plan to find out the truth.

What has changed with Carter Blackthorne? Why has he suddenly given in to the truth that I would never leave him for another man or even want to meet another guy behind his back? To me, it's an obvious answer. I love him with everything in my body.

But for Carter, it's not that simple.

It never is.

CHAPTER TWENTY-ONE

Carter

The family looks pissed off when I make it to Anita's, but I don't care. She's serving heaping bowls of Italian wedding soup, and I even try to snag one before the pot is empty, but my aunt isn't in the charitable mood with me right now. She sets down an empty bowl before me, a sign that means she would kill me if we were back in the motherland, but thankfully, here in Manhattan, it just means I'm in for a well-earned scolding.

"I'm sorry I was late," I say, kissing her cheek for forgiveness.

She doesn't budge. The ladle in her hand looks more like a club, threatening to crash against the back of my head if I'm not careful and observant while in her kitchen. "You're late, Carter. I didn't sign up to be the hostess every night for these powwows. I'm getting tired of having everyone barge in here at night."

"I'm sorry, Anita. It wasn't my intention to be late. I had to fix things with Isabella first."

She seems to relax with that assurance. "How is she doing? I haven't seen her since the article came out, and even then, she didn't seem too talkative with me."

"She's okay. A little shaken up and despondent over the ordeal, but I promise she's okay, Anita. She just needed to see me for a bit before coming over."

"So, she was home the whole time?"

I swivel around, seeing Ernesto clutching a can of beer. He leans against the back door, a few people outside sucking on cigars under the faint stars in the dark skies above. I give him a cautious look, one he should heed right now, but it's not looking good.

Ernesto doesn't drink often, but when he does, it's easy to unravel any truth in that man's body. "You said you were meeting Isabella at the club earlier this evening. Now she's at home, where she's been all along? How is that possible? I doubt she drove from the lifestyle club and beat us to the house."

Anita doesn't hesitate, a large, heavy ladle coming down over the back of my head. She gets about three good *whacks* in before I catch the arm of the utensil and get her to cease fire for a moment. A welt has probably already formed on my neck from one of her stray hits, and I'm damp with wedding soup broth now as well, a stray noodle caught in the back of my coat while I release the ladle in surrender.

"You have it all wrong," I say, trying to calm my feisty aunt. "I didn't cheat on Isabella."

She crosses her arms over her chest. For a small, portly woman with cooking as her love language, she sure can knock the sense into someone in a heartbeat. It's too bad Ernesto is wrong about his assumption. I never told him what happened at the lifestyle club—just like how I left that out from Isabella's knowledge as well.

"I didn't cheat," I reaffirm. "Give me some credit, Anita."

"Then explain yourself."

"I got a text that I thought was from Isabella's new number. It happened to be an old fling, and I went up to her, told her to stop trying to get with me, and left. That's it."

She cocks a single brow, watching me like I'm about to grow a four-foot-long wooden nose. "You know if you hurt that young girl, I'll hurt you. Right?"

"I would hope so. I don't want to hurt Isabella. I promise, Anita." I turn toward Ernesto next, hoping he remembers this in the morning because when he's sober, I'm going to lay into him for starting this shit. "It was Lilian, dammit."

His eyes widen, and the snarky "I caught you in a lie" façade falls with his cocky grin. "Fuck. She was there? Did she say anything about the photos of Rich and Isabella?"

"Yeah, but I sent her away before she could say too much. I didn't do anything with her, but she wanted me to. She's just trying to get me to go back to her. I can't imagine why after what I did to her in the past."

He gives me an unsteady look. "Wait, what did you do to her?"

I realize now that the only person I told that to was Tristan, and he doesn't look to be here right now. I know I've been giving him quick jobs at some of the job sites and not having him around all that much, but I could have sworn I told him to be here tonight. He's typically pretty dutiful about being on time, too, better than I am, but still, I can't make out his face in the kitchen or outside on the back porch.

"Nothing," I tell Ernesto, waving the topic off in an attempt to drop the subject for the night. "It's nothing. Hey, have you seen Tristan?"

"He called, and I told him everyone was here," Anita cuts in.

Ernesto only shrugs. "I haven't heard anything from him. He would be here by now if he knew it was going on. You did tell him, right."

I can only bury my face into my hands, the smell of Italian soup lingering all over my skin and in my hair. "Fuck if I know. I'm losing my damn mind."

"Been there," Anita chirps.

"Let's just get this meeting going."

Ernesto waves the guys inside from the back porch, and I track who all is here, but it doesn't seem right. Not only is Tristan not here, but Nicolas isn't either. I have to force myself to be calm, to remain levelheaded so I can get through this talk. But seeing him blatantly ignore my order to be here is a little frustrating.

It's more than frustrating, actually, but I have to bury it for now.

I nab Tristan's younger brother, Paul. It's weird to see him here without his twin sister, Luce, but I try to keep the women out of this family dynamic as much as possible. It's not in my nature to put them in immediate danger, but I know Paul would rather his other half be here than his older brother.

"Have you talked to Tristan much?" I ask, pulling him off to the side while everyone settles in the living room.

His boyish features soften slightly, like he thinks he is in trouble or something. "No, not really. I called him earlier today, but he just talked about Sam and Isabella. Not you."

I nod, letting him walk away when his words finally breach my brain. I grab him by the shoulder and yank him back into the spot he was just in.

"What did he say about Isabella, exactly?"

He looks nervous as hell, which is pretty understandable. I've been on a rampage lately, and most of the family has taken the brunt of it. It hasn't been without warrant, of course, but watching me strike Nicolas in retaliation to his smart-ass behavior lately wouldn't go over well.

"Hey, relax, kid. You're not in trouble. Just tell me what he said about Isabella."

After a brief pause, he catches his breath and says, "He talked about Isabella and Rich Donahue. He said she was upset because everyone thought she was cheating but that he was actually really nice to her. She's been talking to Tristan a lot, too. He drove her to the phone store today, and she vented about the situation with Lilian and—"

I step forward, knowing I need to get my temper under control, but it's becoming impossible. His eyes widen in horror, waiting for something terrible to happen, but I keep my tone and volume down to a manageable, semi-calm level.

"What did he say about Lilian, Paul?"

He swallows so hard that I can hear the *gulp* of his throat. "I shouldn't have said anything about it, Carter."

"TELL ME!"

Any semblance of me trying to be calm is thrown out the window. Not just that, but it's thrown out the window, tumbled down the hill in the backyard, and then kicked down every door from here to fucking Boston. Even while I try to maintain my sanity, I want to rip my way through this family and leave nothing in my trace.

I want revenge and control again.

How to do that, I'm not so sure, but I have to figure it out before it's too late.

I pat Paul on the shoulder, ushering him to sit down. Anita clutches her ladle in the kitchen like it's a warning she'll slap me if I get close, but she gives in eventually and sets it down in the pot of soup. I wait for her to scurry off to bed and for Paul to settle after my outburst, and I face the onlookers in the living room.

"I'm fucking done with this shit," I bite.

I storm to the middle of the group, looking at these men I have had as a family ever since I was young. They have seen me through my life and loss and picked me up off the floor more times than I can count. In return, I've tripled our wealth and quadrupled our power, so I'm not sure how it's for any of them to spread such bullshit through the gossip mill.

I'm going to shut it down.

"The first person who can get Lilian McCoy to give up this attack against me gets a raise and a promotion. I don't care how it happens or what is done to get her to back off. I just need results, dammit."

"Is this about your sex life again?" Lorenzo asks, giving me a snide look alongside the inappropriate question. "We are crime lords in this city, boss. What's the big deal about this journalist?"

A few people nod their heads in agreement, while the other half of the room is just as offended as I am. The divide in the family is becoming clearer every day. While I know that everyone here is loyal to me, I don't think it's for the right reasons anymore.

I change gears for a moment. "Who here thinks I should have control of this family?"

Slowly, hands raise into the air, and even though the majority hangs with me, there are a few stragglers. A couple of distant bloodlines, a particular cousin, and a family friend or two who have been introduced into the Blackthorne lineage one way or another.

It's not something I want to see—this outright mutiny—but at least I know for sure it exists.

"Fine. I see how this is going to go. If you didn't raise your hand, I want you to stand up."

There are a couple of passing glances, but the handful of hands that didn't rise all get to their feet one after another. Some of them are bloodline, purebred from the fucking motherland. I need them in this organization to keep it family-oriented, but I won't be second-guessed.

"If you think I'm not a *real* Blackthorne and that I have no right to run this family as I see fit, then you can get the fuck out of this house and leave the business for good."

A humming mutter crosses the room as soon as the words leave my lips. Everyone looks around in shock, a few of the people who are singled out already trying to take back their answer and sit down, but I won't have it. I point them out and motion to the door, unwilling to budge on this matter.

"Boss, what are you doing?" Lorenzo asks.

"I'm taking control back. It's time this family recognizes what I've done, and if you think I haven't pushed the Blackthorne name to the echelon of respect in the city, then I won't tolerate you being in my camp. You will fuck off, or I'll drag you outside myself and *handle it.*"

The people who naysay my reign all get up one by one, leaving the house with their heads down. I don't meet their eyes when they look at me, unwilling to budge an inch on my ruling. I have to be the iron fist, the sturdy post, and I'm not going to let the poison that Nicolas spewed out first spread like a disease through this bloodline.

I'm a fucking Blackthorne, and whoever says otherwise will pay.

But they're not the only ones who need to watch their mouths.

I'm going to double my efforts to stop Lilian McCoy from ruining the love of my life and tearing me away from her precious heart and her perfect body. Isabella is the full package that Lilian could never be, and she's just the right amount of normal to tolerate my family.

I'll protect her to the end, and I'm not going to let anything bad happen to her again. If it does, there will be hell to pay.

And it won't fucking matter if you're family or not, either.

CHAPTER TWENTY-TWO

Isabella

I wake up to the sounds of furious yelling downstairs.

Glancing at the clock on the nightstand, it's only a few minutes before sunrise, and I can see that the spot in bed beside me hasn't been touched. I grab my pajamas and throw them on, hurrying down the hall to the top of the stairs.

Carter is in the living room, pacing and on a rampage. He is throwing his hands into the air, his voice rattling off the vaulted ceilings, and I wince at the sound of his familiar spite.

He has softened lately—for reasons I don't fully understand—but I can see how he got his sternness back. Tristan, Lorenzo, and Nicolas are all lined up in the living room, where Carter yells at them like a damn drill sergeant.

I shiver at the sound and emit a slight gasp, and Carter's eyes find me like magic.

"Dove, go back to bed."

I dare to turn, to walk away, but my feet don't want to move! "Carter, you're yelling."

"Then shut the door. I need to handle this, Bella. Please, just go back to bed."

I don't know why, but I look at Tristan and meet his gaze from my spot on the stairs. He gives me a short nod like he's granting me permission to let him get his ass chewed out from the man I love, but as soon as the look passes between us, Carter has already tracked it.

The burning temper of this wildfire man isn't done with any of us yet, including me.

"What the fuck is going on here?" Carter steps forward, his hand curling into Tristan's shirt to yank his attention back to him, but Tristan wiggles out of it quickly. Carter's rampage is far from over. "Who the fuck is in charge of this family again?"

"You are, Carter," Tristan replies a bit begrudgingly. He gives me another glance. "Everything is fine, Isabella. We'll try to keep it down for you, okay?"

I can see this exchange is only pushing Carter further and further down a deep hole, and I can't leave them in the aftermath. Not like this. Things with Nicolas have already been rough for Carter, and there's no saving Tristan from the mounting blame that Carter has been throwing his way lately.

They have been so close, so trusting of one another for so long that I don't understand why they are being so hostile now. There's a cold, taut thread between them that's ready to snap at any moment.

Lorenzo is in the group, too, which is what I don't understand. Last I knew, things were fine with him, but I've come to learn that the Blackthorne loyalty line can change at any given moment. Whatever happened tonight—or was said among these men—is now trickling into our living room.

And it's not going away anytime soon.

I descend the staircase and come to Carter's side. He looks unapproachable to most, especially with this stern scowl on his face, but it's nothing I haven't faced from him before. He stands straighter, like he's trying to ignore me, but he crumbles and falls after a moment.

He melts after a quick press of my lips onto the hollow of his throat where I can reach. His arm crawls around my back, and I sink seamlessly into his side. His scent is strong, like his voice that woke me up, but he holds me loosely, kindly, and I know I've calmed him down by now.

"What is going on here, Carter? Why are you upset?"

He flicks his wrist, the men scattering to the kitchen—keeping their heads down in the process. "This isn't a conversation for you to concern yourself with, dove. It's complicated and stressful. I don't want to bother you with it, okay?"

I can't help but look back at the three men who once had a strong bond with my lover. Looking back at Carter, it's clear that he's not the same. His demeanor is cold, his face is rung with exhaustion, and I can see that his posture has changed significantly.

He's bent forward just enough for me to notice, his arm around me tighter than it should be in a relaxed setting. It's as though he's on edge constantly, and it doesn't bode well for his mind... or his body. To be precise, I can't recall the last time he's slept over four hours in a night, and it shows.

"Carter," I say, pressing my hand to his taut chest. "You need to drop this for the night."

"What do you mean, dove?"

"You need to set this aside for the night. Did you eat at Anita's?"

"Yeah, I had soup. What are you talking about?"

"I think you need rest." I lean into his chest, his arm around my back, ready to snap my spine if I'm not careful around this topic. "Carter, I'm worried about you. You're not on good terms with your closest family members anymore. Tristan gives me a look, and you get all fired up about it. And then there is Lilian…"

His fingers pinch my chin, pulling my face up and extending my throat against his chest. The coldness in his grip is enough to make me worried, to make me sick, and I can't help but want to wiggle out of his grasp, but it doesn't help.

He's frozen in time, his eyes glazed over in wrath that even the most volatile volcano doesn't compare with.

"Carter," I lead.

"Tell me what he said about Lilian today."

It takes me a moment to understand what he's talking about. I did happen to go to the phone store with Tristan this morning, and he helped me pick out a few electronics for the house that I knew Carter would appreciate. We got some minor security pieces, a cell phone, and a new laptop after mine got drenched.

The conversation between us was relatively light, and while Tristan has felt a cold shoulder from his boss lately, it wasn't like we were bashing Carter. It's obvious in his eyes that he doesn't seem to agree with that assumption, and it's as if he is accusing me of doing something worse than just asking a few questions.

"Carter, I just told him about her giving me her number, that's it."

"You still have it? You didn't call it, did you?"

My brows crease with dismay. "What? Why would I call her, Carter?"

"Bring it to me. Right now. I'm burning that note."

"Carter, I need you to calm down, I don't understand why you're so—"

A deafening *crash* interrupts our conversation immediately. It sounds like glass and metal, the noise catching everyone off guard, from the current to the most recent recipients of Carter's scolding. I sink into his side, Tristan and Lorenzo already drawing their weapons while Nicolas pauses to load his.

I don't like the sight of guns, not after being taken by Jacob Lacey, and the presence of so many in an already tough situation is terrifying. Carter pulls a pistol out of his back holster, his finger lining the side of the barrel while we all stare at the staircase, waiting for the culprit of the noise.

After a hefty *thump*, I shiver and press harder into his hip.

"Easy, dove. You'll be okay."

I nod, trembling in angst. "What is it?"

"Someone has broken in," Tristan hums in a steadfast whisper. "I can hear them walking around upstairs."

My eyes fill with tears. We've just gone through a war with Lacey, but we've made amends with Donahue! I can't imagine who else is here to harm us at this hour, and I'm hugely relieved that I defied Carter and stayed down here instead of heading back upstairs when he ordered me to.

If I was in bed right now, I don't know what I'd do.

"Nicolas, Lorenzo, go check it out. Tristan, you stay with us," Carter says.

Both men don't hesitate, which is a testament to their family ties. Things might be off-kilter right now, but they are getting better. At least, they seem to be when Carter isn't screaming at them. Maybe that will change when this ordeal is over, but that moment can't come soon enough.

Lorenzo and Nicolas both disappear and return almost thirty seconds later, a bleeding, limping man in all dark clothes being held between them. The injured man falls down the last few steps, leaving a trail of blood behind him that smears across the stairs. I cover my mouth with my hand, trying not to scream.

"He was in the office upstairs," Lorenzo grunts, his pistol lined to the back of his head. "He cut himself on the glass breaking in. There's a large piece stuck in his side. He's going to bleed out."

Carter nudges me into Tristan's care before walking toward the man.

It's hard to miss that his finger is now on the trigger of the gun.

"Who do you work for?"

The man looks tainted with defeat, his hands covered in blood against his side, where it's clear his plan didn't go as he thought it would. Carter stands over the wounded man, uncaring of the puddle of blood pooling beneath his body.

"Did you come alone?"

"Yes," the man replies with a hearty groan.

"We checked upstairs. Didn't see any signs of anyone else," Lorenzo adds.

Carter seems satisfied with that. "Are you going to tell me who you work for, or am I going to have to kill you and find out later for myself?"

The man shudders slightly. "I... I don't—"

"Tell me," Carter says, his pistol raising in height. "Or die."

For some reason, the man looks at me. I can't help but find his beady black eyes through the chaos of this moment. It doesn't make any sense why he would look at me! I can't help him, and I certainly can't stop Carter from making his mind up on what to do with this intruder.

"Three."

Carter's counting terrifies me, and I look away on instinct.

"Two."

The tension rises in the room. I feel suffocated underneath it.

"One."

"Wait!" Before another word can be spoken, the man panics and spills his words like they're his last. "I was hired by Killian," the man blurts. "I... I didn't even come armed. He just wanted me to break in. That's all I know."

"He's not armed," Lorenzo adds. "We searched him when we got to him on the floor upstairs."

Carter lowers his pistol slightly, but the man sneaks another look in my direction, and the tension refuses to ease. "Why do you keep looking at Isabella?"

"I'm sorry," he says simply, letting his head fall. "I just... Killian had..."

"I don't understand," I whisper to Tristan. "Why would the mayor want someone to break in?"

"I don't know, Isabella. He has a vendetta against Carter, that's clear. But why he would send him in here unarmed is not normal."

I shake my head, my heart in my throat. "I don't know, but I don't like this. We can't have another war. We're still picking up the pieces from the last one."

"It will be okay," Tristan assures me, but I can hear the doubt in his tone still. He doesn't even believe it. "Maybe you should go upstairs before anything else—"

"He wants *her*."

The intruder's words ring through the foyer.

Carter becomes rigid again, disjointed from empathy and reality at the same time, and he pulls his pistol up and doesn't waste another second. The gun fires, the shot sending the man to his back while the life drains out of the new wound.

I harbor a scream into my hands, Tristan catching me as I turn and trip over my feet. It's nearly too overwhelming to see, but it's not over yet. Carter barks orders to have the body *taken care of*, but before anyone can move, there's a flicking taunt of blue and red lights.

"Fuck," Carter snaps. "Give him a gun."

I don't comprehend his words fast enough or decipher his meaning before the front door is kicked open in violent haste. We are all swarmed with the full force of men wearing body armor and flashing badges. Voices rise through the house, screaming for guns to be dropped, for everyone to get on the ground, and it feels like the world slows down while every new order is shouted to the rooftops.

Someone presses a knee into my back, and I hiss, my arms yanked behind me until a thunderous voice roars through the room, silencing the commotion.

"Get your *fucking* hands off her!"

CHAPTER TWENTY-THREE

Isabella

Wrapped in a fleece blanket, curled on a bench in a stuffy interrogation room, I take the coffee cup from the brute detective. I don't want to drink it as I'm already wired with adrenaline over the last handful of hours and what happened, but it keeps my palms warm. I bring it to my chin and let the steam invade my cold, pallid face.

The detective sits down across from me in the small space, his knees crossed. He's in a suit with his badge hanging around his neck and swinging like a pendulum as he moves. I can't help but watch him settle in with his notepad; the cycle of this ongoing interview starting to drain my ability to be friendly.

"I don't have anything else to say," I mutter, my throat raw. "I've already told you everything. Twice."

"I know, ma'am. We're just following up on some routine questions."

"For what reason, exactly?"

"To line up stories and look for any discrepancies, ma'am."

"I'm not lying."

He gives me a curious look, and I settle on sipping my coffee to fill the silent void for now. He glances up at the camera in the middle of the ceiling, the one I've been tracking for hours, as I feel them watching me, judging my every word. I can't help but notice how intently he stares at it, too.

After a long moment, he jots something down on his clipboard, holds up a finger, and leaves the room. Before he goes, he tosses his files on the seat beside me and then shuts the door on his way out. I swallow, wondering what ploy he's initiating now. Still, I'm surprised to see his notes face-up and turned toward me with specific intent.

I have orders from the mayor to seek Blackthorne's guilt. I will see what I can do. Tell them you're hurt, and I can get you out of here and to a hospital. The questioning will be over.

A knot forms in my throat as the detective returns with a cold soda in his hand. He takes the notes and clipboard back into his lap as he sits across the room, and I plot my escape.

Pressing a hand to my shoulder, I readjust my position on the bench. "When will this be over?"

"Just a few more questions, okay?"

I nod but instantly lean forward, trying to stretch my back. It is sore after the officers pinned me to the ground at home, but not enough for me to claim I need to go to the hospital. Then again, if I need to lie to get out of here and this hellish nightmare, then I'll do it.

I need to know Carter is safe, and given that the cop is trying to help me out, I'm sure he has answers to give when we're not being watched.

Holding my coffee in one hand, I let my free hand flex and unflex methodically, groaning under my breath between questions and answers. It's all been asked before, and I won't change my story at all. There's no need. Everything I tell them is the truth.

There was an intruder. Carter handled it because we feared for our lives.

The rest I just didn't get to see.

"I…" I say at last, my head tipping back while I try to adjust my stiff body. "I don't feel so great right now. My back is in pain, and my arm…"

"You did sustain a pretty big cut there before, correct?"

I nod at the memory—not something I like to recall, though. I made a mess of my hands and arms when I destroyed Jacob Lacey's wine cellar, but it was worth it. Now, the light pink marks seem to prove helpful as another thing to add to my list.

"I… I don't feel good," I whimper, wafting the air toward my face.

The officer tidies up his documents into a single stack before knocking on the door. He mutters a few things to the people on the other side of the doorway, and I struggle to listen, but I fail. He eventually comes back into the room, his hand on my arm while he lifts me from my spot on the bench. He lets me keep the cup of coffee, drops the blanket off my shoulders, and draws me out into the hallway.

My body is numb, my eyes searching through every individual window and pane of glass to look for Carter. The officer notices, waving goodbye to some of his coworkers while bringing me down the hallway that led us inside. His eyes flick to the left, into a narrow window beside a steel door, and my heart sinks.

I almost drop my coffee all over the floor and hit the glass, my hand on the cold, streaked plastic that gives me a clear view of Carter. He's still handcuffed, fuming, and unkempt. His shirt is torn down the middle, his face sporting a short dribble of blood while a bruise shimmers on his jawline.

Whatever the police did to him isn't nearly as bad as what he did to them.

I watched his fury at the house as they arrested us all, his eyes glued to me then like they still are at this moment. He's fuming, his body rigid with every inhale.

"Dove," he says, his words hard to decipher through the hard plastic window between us. "Dove, are you okay?"

I nod in haste, wishing I could break through and get to his side once more. "I'm fine, Carter. I'm okay. He's taking me to the hospital. I'll be okay."

Carter is alone in the room, so it makes no difference when he stands up and kicks his chair out from behind him. It goes flying, denting the wall, and I hiccup at his anger even though I know he's not mad at me. He wants to protect me.

He comes to the glass, his chest showing a few stray drops of blood from the rip that exposes his muscles. I want to tame him, to calm his raging nerves, but I know I can't do that right now.

"I'm sorry," I whisper, blinking back tears. "I'll be back, okay? I'll be safe."

He nods once before looking at the officer beside me. They share a short, secretive look that almost seems trustworthy in some ways. I lean once more on the window before being pulled away from it, Carter's eyes following me down the hallway until we hit the cool air outside that's ushering in the sunrise.

I have to blink a few times to adjust. The fluorescent lighting inside is nowhere as bright as the yellow and orange on the horizon. "Where are we—"

"This way," the detective says, guiding me to a blacked-out SUV in the corner of the lot. He opens my door, and I collapse into the passenger seat, more exhausted now than I was last night before the incident occurred. "Are you hungry? I can stop and get some food. I need to take you to the hospital, though. Just to get checked out and support that I had to end the interview early."

"So, I won't have to come back here?"

"No, you're safe now, Isabella."

I nod but can't help but replay those words over and over again in my head. When the weight of those words becomes too much, I have to ask him to clarify them.

"What did you mean by that?"

He perks up, pulling us onto the main road. "Mean by what? Something to eat?"

"No, I'm not hungry," I lie. "I'm just curious why you're saying I'm safe now. I was just in a police station. Am I not safe in there?"

His narrow glare comes with a hefty reply. "No, you're not safe there. Killian Hughes has officially taken office now. Anything Carter does or the people he keeps around him does, everything is tracked."

"Tracked how?"

"Well, for starters, you're being watched. Studied. Researched. Everything imaginable that the mayor could get his hands on, he already has. And he doesn't like Carter Blackthorne. So, you know what that makes you? A fucking easy target."

I sink into the seat, my stomach cramping with that admission. I know it's bad, and I don't want to be put in the firing line anymore, but it just seems to be how it's going. Anytime I'm tucked into Carter's side, I'm a target that can be used to take him down.

It makes me weak.

"I don't like this," I say, my chest rising and falling rapidly.

I begin to hyperventilate, realizing I've just jumped into the car with a cop and didn't even think about how the mayor—an ex-cop—hates Carter. This detective could be driving me to my death! Why wouldn't he just call an ambulance? I shouldn't have gotten in here with him. I need to get out.

"Pull over, please," I beg, my hands reaching for the door handle.

"No, Isabella. What are you doing? You're okay. I swear I'm not going to…" He slows down enough to stop at the red light in the intersection. It's just enough of a stop for me to jump out of the car and bolt down the sidewalk.

I don't care that he chases after me—I need to get away from him and every other cop in this city!

I turn a few corners, but I can still hear him stomping on the sidewalk after me, nearing my shoulder with his hand so close that I can almost feel him reach for me! I hiccup in shock, my stomach turning while I force myself faster down the city streets.

"Whoa!"

I slam directly into a solid wall, my body tumbling sideways off the sidewalk, where I land with a hard, overwhelming *thud*. I break into a fit of tears, my back sore as I try to sit up, only to see through blurry vision. A familiar face kneels before me, and I can't help but throw myself into his arms in exhaustion and gratefulness.

"Thank you, thank you," I pant between heavy, suffocating gasps for air.

Rich Donahue pulls me upright, his arms taking my weight out of courtesy, but I can tell he's uncomfortable. "What's going on, Isabella? Where's Carter? And who is this guy?"

The detective looks at the hoard of men that surround me and Rich now. I've never been so happy to see members of the Lacey family before, but I'm certainly thrilled with it now. The detective gives up, holding his hands up while he backs away and retraces his steps along the sidewalk.

When he's out of sight and behind the building nearby, Rich pushes my brunette hair back and runs a thumb under my nostrils, coming up with a hint of crimson. I realize now that whoever I ran into was hard enough for my face to slam into their shoulder, my nose bleeding and pained.

How ironic that I really might need to go to the hospital now…

"What is happening, Isabella? Are you okay? Where is Carter?"

I field his questions one by one, trying to catch him up about the intruder, the murder, the arrest, and the cop, who I can't determine is a good guy or not. When I'm done, he shushes me to stop and slow down, but it's not possible right now. I wipe my face clean of the blood that stains my shirt, and Rich gives me a pitiful look.

"You need help, Isabella. How can I help?"

I look at him, fighting back tears. "I don't… I don't know."

He nods briefly and helps me stand up, his hands holding mine while I try to steady myself on shaky legs. I wipe my cheeks, needing the tears to disappear. They don't. I'm too damn freaked out to catch my own breath, and I can hardly make sense of if we were even headed for the hospital.

I just know I can't trust anyone.

Well, maybe I can trust one person who's not a Blackthorne.

"Get my car back here," Rich says, waving to one of his guys.

The man gives him an unsure look. "Boss, we have to get to this meeting, it's very—"

"I need to make sure she's safe first. Get me my damn car. We can stop by my place uptown and keep her there. Call Yuri and have him meet us at the penthouse instead, okay? We can just move the meeting there."

Still, the man hesitates. "It's not ideal."

Rich looks annoyed, his hands balled into fists while he stares through his men. "I don't give a damn. We have a duty to work with the Blackthornes now. They are our allies. I have to protect one of them the same as they would protect one of mine. Understood?"

His team nods.

One of them pulls out his phone, and another offers me an old-style handkerchief pulled from his breast pocket. I thank the man and dab at my cheeks and upper lip, trying to remove the blood and tears that stain my flustered appearance. I wipe my brow and watch as a car pulls up to the curb nearby.

I'm hesitant, but Rich gets in first, and I follow his lead for now. Sinking into the leather seat, I feel a million times safer, even if he is Jacob Lacey's brother. At least he's not trying to kill me or pin me to his desk. I have to be thankful for that much.

I bury my face in my hands with Rich and me alone in the backseat while the driver takes off down the road. I miss my car right now, still parked in hiding after the ordeal that resulted from the Lacey war. Carter doesn't like me leaving alone, and I can't imagine he would be okay with me just up and driving off into trouble.

"Are you okay, Isabella?"

"I still don't know how to answer that. I just… I don't know who to trust anymore." I press my hands harder against my eyes, waiting until I see bright spots in the darkness behind my shut eyelids. "I feel so out of the loop right now. I don't know who is on Carter's side anymore."

"It's not about Carter right now. It's who is on your side, Isabella."

I shake my head. "It's the same answer. We're one and the same."

"Are you sure about that, Isabella?"

"Of course, I am. Carter is the love of my life, and he loves me, too. If someone is against him, they're against me. Same either way you look at it."

I lean back, noticing his stiff posture.

"I don't believe that for a moment," he sighs.

"Don't believe what exactly? I do love him and—"

"No, not that, Isabella. I mean that your enemies are his. You don't have any enemies. You're just a side effect of the plague that runs this city. Not to say that the Blackthorne family is a virus."

"It's not a virus," I whisper, mostly to myself. "It's a poison."

He doesn't reply, and I know why he doesn't. He agrees.

I love Carter, but even I know the truth when it's staring me in the face. The Blackthorne family and its twisted reality are nothing like a virus. Viruses spread—they infect and multiply. The family that once ran this city unchallenged isn't something that spreads and defeats.

It works from the inner circle, and it weakens until one day, it'll be nothing but a limp body.

I love Carter, but I hate the Blackthorne curse.

Chapter Twenty-Four

Carter

I hate handcuffs when they're not on Isabella.

They're pinching my wrists behind my body, and my face is bruised and bleeding. I stare straight ahead at the blank wall just to satiate my fury, but it's pointless. When I get out of this fucking police department, out of this interrogation room, I will burn this damn place to the ground.

My body shivers as the door opens, a cold breeze pouring in from the hallway into this little space. The hallway is still laced with Isabella's perfume, and it accompanies the cooler air. I inhale her scent, needing to have her in my arms so I can breathe in her smell and hold her body. I want her all to myself.

The detective coming in is familiar, a man I had on the payroll at some point. He turned a blind eye to my corruption, but the rules have changed, and their boss is a prick who won't be stopped when it comes to taking me down. Still, I recognize him as the one who took Isabella away.

I trust that he got her out of the precinct safely, but I can tell by his flat, pursed expression that that isn't the case.

"Where is she?" I bite right off the bat. "Where is Isabella?"

"I told her I could get her out of here if I took her to the hospital. But for some reason, she panicked and ran from me, Carter," he says, speaking low as if the cameras are still on. He glances up for a minute, and the red light on the dome of a camera flicks off. "There, we have the room for a few minutes to ourselves."

"Where the fuck is she?"

He shakes his head at first, his eyes distant and glassy. "Lacey."

I nearly jump out of my chair that I managed to kick back into place after my outburst earlier, but he pins me back to sit down, giving me a warning of a look that—if not for these fucking handcuffs on my wrists—I would wipe right off his face with my fist.

"Who? What Lacey took my dove?"

"No, she ran into one. I don't know his name, just that he looked like Jacob."

I swallow the fire that lurches up my throat. "Not a Lacey. It's a fucking Donahue. Rich Donahue, to be exact."

He waves me off, uncaring of the semantics. "She jumped out of my car, dammit. I tried getting her to the hospital, but she freaked out and bolted. I couldn't take on any Laceys, so I left her with them. They seemed friendly enough with her."

"You made her uncomfortable. This is your doing."

"No, that's not it. She's spooked easily, okay? I didn't have anything to do with that."

I grit my teeth so hard that it hurts. "Get her back."

"I can't. You know I can't, dammit. I did the best I could with her before she ran off. I don't work for you anymore, Carter. None of us do. They hired a new damn fleet of officers, too. They're young, and they want to please the mayor like he's some damn general in war. They won't sway to your money. And I can't do it, either. I'm sorry, okay? I have to fall back in line."

I snort back a chuckle that he doesn't appreciate. "You're going to *fall in line*, huh? I gave these crooked cops mountains of money to do one damn thing. Look the other fucking way. And here you are now, telling me that it can't be done. You have to clean up the city. Well, start with Killian

Hughes. He's the one trying to frame me for murder."

"Not murder. We're going to assume it's self-defense at this time, okay? He had an unregistered gun in his coat. It was obvious that he broke in and was going to harm you or Isabella... or both. But we can't spin shit in your favor again, okay? We're going to let you go and keep this information under wraps. It might be used in the future against you, Carter. I'm trying to be helpful here."

At last, I relax with a slight edge of ease. "Fine. No arrest. I won't slit your throats today, then."

His eyes widen. He knows I would do it, too.

Everyone in this city knows what I'm capable of by now.

I took out an entire crooked family for trying to lay a hand on Isabella.

"Let me out of these damn cuffs. I have to go find out where my girl went. No thanks to you."

"We're letting the other three guys free as well. You'll be last, so just give me a minute to get everything in order, okay?" He stands but pauses, looking at the camera overhead. "But first, the only way I was allowed to have the camera skip on tape is I told them I was going to rough you up a little bit."

I grit my teeth. "I'll rip your tongue out of your mouth if you try."

"I'm sorry, man. I'm trying to help you. Just remember that."

Before I can threaten him further, his closed fist meets my cheek, and blood flies from my bottom lip. I feel it dripping down my neck, savagely crimson and hot. I'm searing in anger and fury, but I have to hold back. The camera light comes back on while the detective shakes his hand in pain and rushes out of the room.

I keep calm long enough to feel the blood finally stop flowing down my chin. My lip should start swelling soon, but I couldn't care less about any of it if I tried. Right now, I'm focused on one thing that keeps my mind occupied. I count the minutes until the officer enters the room to undo my cuffs.

I jerk myself free and hurry out of the building, not needing a damn escort. I have to sign for the shit they confiscated from me, and thankfully Lorenzo has my gun when I get outside. I reposition my watch on my wrist and look at him, Nicolas, and Tristan.

"Where is Isabella?" Tristan asks.

I don't know why he has to ask about her, out of everyone here. "She ran off from the detective. She's with the Donahue bunch. I need to get a hold of them."

Tristan pulls out his wallet, still taped as property of the *New York City Police Department*. He hands me a crisp business card. "That's his number. Give Rich a call. I bet he's with her."

"Why do you guess that exactly?"

He shrugs. "He knows her. It's not like she's met any other Donahues or Laceys since the fallout."

I tend to my pulsing, bloody lip. "I don't want to talk about them anymore. I'm fucking done with this Lacey shit. Once I get my dove back, I'm cutting ties with the Donahue prick, too."

Lorenzo furrows his brows, edging into the conversation now. "Why? That docks property is what we need to operate, boss. It's going to help shipments. We have property out there, but none of that size."

"I know what we have."

"Then why are you blowing this?" Nicolas bites, spitting his words out as he says them. "I'm so over this shit, Carter. You're running this family business into the ground over trying to keep that woman as your sex toy. I'm over it."

He throws his hands up and storms off.

I'm not done with him yet, not after that uncalled-for outburst.

Marching up behind him, I grab him by the collar and spin him around to face me. My blood is hot, hotter than hot, and I'm too damn furious to swallow the flames that lick the back of my tongue. I'm done trying to appease this cockroach of a cousin.

If he thinks I'm doing a shit job, then he can choke on my words once and for all and then promptly fuck off.

"I built the business, dammit. I am the reason we are here. The Blackthornes had money before me, sure, but never to this degree. If you want me to send you off like the others, then so be it, but you'll be a rogue pony out there looking for a damn dime because if you turn your back on me, you're turning your back on this empire."

He swallows slightly, taken aback by the hostility I want him to feel.

I *need* him to feel.

"What is it, then? Are you loyal or not?"

He gives me a brief glance before looking to Tristan and Lorenze next. When no one bails him out, he finally drops his head in defeat. I let go of his shirt and nudge him back a step, catching my breath as I relish in my victory.

I'm not four steps away from him when he announces, "I'm out."

I try not to react, but in some ways, it is a bitter admission. "Alright. Then you're out."

I hear Nicolas walk away, Tristan and Lorenzo exchanging similar looks. They watch me, waiting for me to follow and beg him to stay, but we all know that's never going to happen. I'm done being pushed around in this family, and I won't let some punk tell me how to run the empire I built.

And it's a fucking empire all the same.

"I'm calling Rich. You two go get a damn car or call Ernesto."

They disperse, and I catch my breath after that encounter. I didn't think he'd actually quit, but I'll never beg anyone to stay. They can leave as they wish. It's not my problem anymore.

The phone rings twice before it picks up. "Hello?"

"It's Carter."

There's a shuffling noise and what sounds like a door closing through the line. "Carter? You alright? Isabella is here. She's safe, and she told me everything that happened."

I bite my already bloodied tongue. She doesn't need to be telling this prick anything, but I'll punish her later for it. She learned last time that she's mine, but maybe this is a lesson that needs to be retaught a few times until it's drilled in.

"I'm coming to get her now. Where the fuck are you?"

He clears his throat slightly. "Tell me something first."

"Where is she, Rich? I'll burn this city down until I find her."

"I'm not keeping her from you, dammit. I just have a question, Carter."

Maybe it's my furious stubbornness or the way I can't live without her beside me, but I choke on my reply and spit a bit of blood onto the sidewalk. "What is your question?"

"Did Killian actually set you up?"

"It seems that way. Cops have turned on me. I can no longer expect the police department to turn a blind eye when it comes to me. They'll be looking for a reason to book me that isn't self-defense. Why?"

"Would they come after Isabella to do that? I mean, Jacob knew your weak spot. Now, everyone else does, too. Killian might not be a murderer, but he's dangerous, Carter. He could get her in trouble for something of your doing, and she'd be thrown in jail."

I am angrier than ever before. "You trying to tell me how to protect her?"

"No, never, Carter. I'm trying to help you."

Ernesto's SUV pulls up, and I'm thankful he must have been nearby, waiting for our release. I climb into the front seat, the other guys in the back, and he waits to hear an address for me to give.

I just don't know where I'm going yet.

"I will protect her just fine."

"Carter, those cops are still dirty. Killian might… I don't know. I don't want to say it. But it's clear she needs help. You might consider having her stay in one of my safehouses."

"She's not staying with you. She's coming home with me, dammit!"

He clears his throat. "We need to talk, Carter."

"About what, exactly?"

"About me working with Killian Hughes."

I practically crush my phone into my flexing palm. "Tell me where you are right now."

The line goes silent, and I think of my next move if he decides to keep her away from me again.

I'm going to hurt Lilian, and I'll go after mayor-dearest, and then I'll save Rich Donahue for last.

Just so he knows I'm coming, there's no running from me.

CHAPTER TWENTY-FIVE

Isabella

Rich's penthouse is quiet, brightly lit, and has a wonderful view of the harbor. He's offered me one of the extra rooms to freshen up in. The bed sits near the window, and the shower runs hot water like rain in a thunderstorm. I know I'm bruised from the collision on the sidewalk, and Carter won't be pleased with that, but otherwise, I'm unharmed.

I'm just utterly and entirely exhausted.

I curl into the bed, tracing the lines of the sun that reflect and bounce off the windows of the buildings in the city. It's like a prism of sorts, and I can't watch it enough. The knock on the door does steal my focus, though, and I turn over to see Rich holding a bowl of fruit and something to drink.

"Here, I figured you'd need this," he sighs.

I down the water almost instantly, tasting the fizzy, seltzer-like texture of the liquid. It's a bit bitter, but it's cold, so I ignore the taste long enough to pick at the fruit he's offered.

"Thank you," I reply.

"You're welcome, Isabella. Do you feel better after your shower and everything?"

"Yeah, I do. Thank you for offering me this room until Carter gets here. I appreciate it a lot, Rich."

"Oh, don't mention it. I actually just spoke to Carter."

My back straightens with his claim. "Really? Is he okay? Did they release him, or is she getting booked?"

He shakes his head, sitting on the edge of the bed where I can almost make out the green of his eyes. He looks just like Jacob Lacey but softer around the edges. Maybe a bit heavier, but definitely with more muscle. Jacob was scrawnier, and while Rich Donahue isn't exactly a muscleman, he's lean and built well enough to protect himself.

After seeing his men on the sidewalk earlier, I doubt he needs to protect himself that often.

"I wanted to talk to you about something, Isabella."

My eyes nearly cross, sweat building on the back of my neck. "What is it?"

And why didn't he answer anything about Carter?

"It's about Lilian. You know about her, right?"

"The journalist," I sigh, shaking my head in disgust. "It's a sore subject in our house still. He doesn't tell me much, but I have a hunch. Why? What do you know about her?"

"I know she's got dirt on Carter."

"Well, that's not important. He's not running against Killian, Rich. He lost the election. Who cares what she digs up on, Carter? She doesn't seem to want to hurt his reputation. She was just at the hospital trying to get a story on his contributions to the city. The only disparaging thing she's written is probably that article about you and me."

He bows his head slightly. "Yeah, that's right, Isabella. She's not going after Carter, exactly. She's going after *you*."

I hold back a snicker, the task in itself a little tiring, while my eyelids feel like bricks. I fight to keep them open, though, knowing my exhaustion is due to the events last night.

"She's trying to hurt me. Over what, then?"

"She wants Carter."

I should be jealous, but I tamp any sign of jealousy down. "Yeah, who doesn't? He's rich and handsome. I know he's had his past and all, but it's nothing he can't get over. He wants me, and he has made that explicitly clear."

He shakes his head, handing me a small tablet with the screen dimmed. I wonder how I didn't notice this in his pocket before, the screen a little bigger than a phone but still capable of being stowed away in a pocket. Still, the screen brightens to display a photo of sorts.

It's grainy and taken from a distance, but I can make out three very explicit silhouettes in the picture.

Carter. His hands are in his pockets as he stands in our room at the lifestyle club.

A woman. She's wearing my lingerie, but I know my body, and that one in the photo isn't mine.

A stripper pole. The one I've danced on for Carter in the sanctity of our room.

My breath hitches, and I push the tablet away, fighting back an uncontrollable shudder down my spine. "That could be an old photo, Rich. He... he's had a sordid past, okay? I don't need a reminder."

"It's time-stamped, Isabella," he whispers, pushing the photo back into my lap.

My breath is hitched now as I weep, reading the photo almost as clear as day. It's not like this was taken a week ago or two.

It was yesterday.

"Wait... what? I don't understand this. He was... he was *with* me last night and... When he got home, he was... I don't... Rich, I don't understand."

He gives me a pitying look that I know reads like I'm some poor, hapless woman being cheated on. But I'm not. Carter wouldn't cheat on me! I don't understand why he would even watch a woman dance on the pole I've been on before, but my thoughts are running too fast for me to make sense of them.

The timestamp is correct because he came home right after this, and he fucked me until I couldn't take it anymore. Is this why? Did he just go see a stripper and get horny to take it out on me? Or is Rich trying to say that he was turned on by some woman and had a piece of us both?

I lurch forward slightly, feeling sick.

Suddenly, though, my mind clicks on something. The woman looks like me. It couldn't be, could it? I grab the tablet from Rich's hand and stare closely at the picture.

"It's... oh God, it's her, isn't it? It's that journalist?"

Rich pushes my shoulders down into the soft, white bedding. "Relax, Isabella. I'm going to handle this."

I shake my head, not sure what the hell he's talking about. But I can't argue. I can't even if I want to because my wet, leaking eyelids begin to shut softly. I hiss an inhale, choke on the exhale, and cry myself into the deepest sleep imaginable.

Part of me wants to stay here forever just so I don't have to go back home with the man who's been lying to me. The man who has been hurting me.

And why? For what purpose? He could let me go and find another lookalike in an hour.

He's done it before.

Carter

I pound on the door so hard I think I may send my fist through it.

It flies open at last, and Rich Donahue stands before me with a scolding frown and furrow on his Jacob-like face. I barge in, uncaring, and Tristan follows. I have Ernesto taking Lorenzo home to Anita's for now just so he can update everyone on our new policy.

We have to behave ourselves, or the dirty cops that once shielded us from shit are going to arrest us. I have the mayor to thank for that, but I'll deal with him later.

Right now, I need two things. Isabella is the first, and the second is an explanation from Donahue.

He ushers me to a table, but I keep walking, even at the behest of his guys, who try and stop me. There are a few bedroom doors open, a long den area near the end of the hall, and a door that's shut and locked when I try to jiggle the handle.

"Carter, we should talk first," Rich barks.

"What's behind this door?"

"It's a bedroom, alright? Just come talk to me first, and we can—"

I ignore him, sending my boot through the door and watching the thing splinter as it flies open. My eyes find the bed against the large window that overlooks Manhattan, and the outline of a body in the sheets makes my heart pound into my ears.

"Dove."

Walking to her slowly, I watch her little inhales and exhales through her nap. She's tired; that's proved by how she looked a few hours ago when she pressed herself to the window to say goodbye to me. I wanted to headbutt the glass and get her attention, but I couldn't get to her fast enough.

She was gone, and now she's here, sleeping soundly in clothes that I know aren't hers. It's a T-shirt—a man's shirt, specifically—and I don't pull down the covers to see what she has on underneath. I don't need to know that yet because if it's nothing, I'll have a lot of Donahues to murder.

And I'd be slow with my work, too.

I brush my hand over her hair, taking in her pouting, frowning lips. She looks so peaceful, but the light yellow bruise that forms under her right nostril gives me the opposite emotion. I know it wasn't there before, and the idea that someone laid their hands on her in such a disrespectful manner makes my mind wander further on how I'll dismember the Donahues one by one.

I'll make their last moments hell and remind them once more before they find the merciless release of death that they should have never touched a hair on her head.

Before I can sate my temper, Rich comes up beside the bed, his filthy eyes on my precious dove.

"Relax, Carter. She ran into one of my guys as she was running from the detective. She got a few painkillers for the bruising."

I try to relax with that explanation. "How long has she been sleeping?"

"About an hour. Ever since you called, really."

It's impossible to miss the red, puffy swells of her eyes. Tears have dried on her flawless skin, while some are still trying to trickle off the bridge of her nose. "What happened?"

"She was crying, Carter. She got ahold of my phone and saw a news article. It's not looking good, either. She started freaking out and panicking, then fell asleep in the middle of her sobs."

I grab his arm and push him from the room. When we're in the hall, and I have the broken door somewhat shut between us, I ask, "What fucking article is it now?"

My fear is it's *the* article.

Lilian wants to expose every single sexual encounter I've ever had in this city, and I can't let that taint the way Isabella would see me. She would be devastated to know the circumstances of my healing over Brooke but also to see how, at first, she wasn't special.

She was another conquest. But that changed when I spoke to her, got to be around her, and especially fucked her. She was everything to me from that moment on, and I haven't glanced at another woman the same way ever since.

Rich pulls out his phone, a large screen with a dim overcast that shows an article and a photo attached. I scroll past the words to find the pathetic image at the bottom of the rambling article. It's a horrible shot, taken from the ground in a dark room, but I recognize it right away.

"Fuck, fuck, fuck… She saw this?"

"Yeah, I tried to get it away, but it was too late. She saw the picture."

I hand his phone back, liable to crack the damn thing in half. I swipe my hands over my face, Tristan coming to my aid, but it's not going to help. She will never forgive me after this shit has spread. I can just hope she knows I didn't touch that witch.

I don't want Lilian. I want Bella, but this pesky journalist doesn't care about anything except ruining my life. I won't stand for it. Maybe it's time I upped the ante against taking her down, but I can't focus on that right now.

"What do you want me to do, boss?"

"Nothing, Tristan. We will handle Lilian later. I just need to get things in my head cleared. I have to get Isabella home."

"That's what I wanted to talk about," Rich interjects.

"You aren't taking my girl."

"I didn't say I'd take her. I just want to protect her."

I fight against every instinct to beat this man until he's limp, but I can't worry about kicking his teeth in right now. I need to prioritize Isabella and this Killian matter. It seems Rich has ideas for both, and I may as well listen to them. She's asleep right now, too tired and worn to be moved. I'll get her home later. Right now, it is time for business.

And for plotting how to get away with killing a journalist and not looking like a suspect to the mayor.

We all move down the hall to the main room, a white room with tile floors and tall, vaulted ceilings. The table is near the window, and I face it head-on while I sit down, not sure if I can contain myself much longer if I have to sit and stare at Jacob Lacey's lookalike.

"Carter, I wanted to talk about Killian because I had a meeting today with his second-in-command, Yuri."

"Yuri Natori," I mutter. "I know the bastard. He works with the Russians downtown. They're a little group, nothing like ours, and they're not very friendly. He likes to branch out, though. Can't say I'm surprised he is looking in unlikely places for help."

"He wanted me to join them and bring the Donahue name over to his jurisdiction of power. They're coming for you, especially. The Phillips family, too. You know them?"

I can't help but laugh at Rich's question. "Yeah, I know the Phillips family. Why?"

"They have a few stragglers from the motherland. They sent a few men over to restart production and ship out guns. They aren't anywhere near where they used to be, but they're recruiting outsiders. They want to come after you. Made them perfect for Killian's work."

"So, what's new? I gain another enemy every day."

"I can see why," Rich sighs. "But these little groups are going to be a big problem, eventually. I want to help keep the main names intact."

I look away from the city, surprised he thinks the Donahue name has any weight in this town. "Really now? And who is going to help do that? You have no power in New York."

"I agree, Carter. But if we cut through the weeds and worked together to do that, we could come out victorious against the mayor."

"He's going to pin everything and anything on my back."

"Yes, he will try. But he's not coming after me and my family."

"Why do you think that?"

"I'm working with him as of today."

My fists ball on the table, and he holds his hands up in surrender like there's a gun pointed at him under the tabletop. He's wise to do so, too. I may be empty-handed with my gun strapped behind me, but Tristan always wears his pistol in the front.

If he tries anything funny, I trust my righthand man enough to take care of it, even though we aren't on the best terms either.

"So, you want to double-cross the mayor, is that right?"

He nods vehemently. "I think we can, Carter."

"And do what?"

"Same shit he's trying to pin on us. We need to catch him in the act. That journalist of yours is doing a good job undercutting Isabella and your relations with her. I don't see why we can't do the same to the mayor's political face. He would look like a bad leader if we managed to get some dirt on him."

I relax, finally seeing where this is going. "Okay, so you're going to work on the inside and gather dirt. I'll throw it in his face, and we can discredit him when he tries to come after me."

"Precisely."

But still, one thing haunts me. "So, what does any of this have to do with Isabella?"

He inhales slowly, his voice quiet as he replies, "It has everything to do with her. She's the key to this operation, Carter. The only thing I ask of you is to trust me."

"You're not taking her."

"No, but we should get her somewhere safe. Somewhere better to watch her."

My brows furrow. "Safe from what? A rogue journalist trying to ruin my life?"

"She's going to publish something much worse one day, Carter. Something you can't come back from, and I don't just mean with Isabella. I mean with everyone. You need to heed this warning. That woman is dirty as they come, and this vendetta against you isn't reserved for just her. She's working with Killian. She's not a good example of the press, but she gets the word around."

I bury my face in my hands for a minute, knowing that Isabella is going to hate me when she wakes up. "Yeah, yeah. She's going to be dealt with somehow. I have my family already on it. I just need some time. Some place where we can rest and recoup from this. Somewhere that Killian can't fuck with us for a few nights."

He nods. "I have a safehouse upstate if you're interested."

Swallowing hard, I shake my head. "No. I have just the place. We can continue discussions there. Tristan, call Ernesto."

"Back to the old Blackthorne estate, boss?"

I can only nod.

Isabella and I mended our problems there once before. Maybe we can do that again.

If there's anything left to mend, of course.

CHAPTER TWENTY-SIX

Isabella

My sleep is peaceful, almost alarmingly so, but I still wake up in a frenzied panic. My heart is in my throat, the same place I left it when I fell asleep. I can't help but feel my wrists heavier than usual, a hot pressure burning on my wrists where I realize rope tangles my arms.

I pull at it gently, finding the rope connected to the other wrist and then tied to the golden headboard of the bed frame. My body aches in a sluggish pile, and I stifle a breath, trying to pull free until I realize I've been here before.

The ornate wall mounts, the large window with a bay seat that overlooks the woods outside. There's a city in the distance, far, far away from here. I have woken up here once before, and not in much better condition than I am now.

"Carter?" I ask, my throat sore and my voice raw. "Carter!"

His name echoes through the mansion, and the door to the bathroom squeals open. Carter is wearing nothing but ripped white-washed jeans. There's something about the expression on his cold features that I recognize right away, and it steals focus from his perfect, shirtless body.

"Dove, you and I are going to talk."

I shake my head, wincing as that picture returns to my scattered memory. "I don't want to talk to you, Carter. I saw the picture. You... It was… It was *her*, wasn't it?"

"Dove, you will let me talk."

"I won't listen."

I shimmy backward, resting my arms against the headboard where I can turn my face away from him for good. I shut my eyes tight and ignore anything that comes out of his mouth, but this isn't the kinder version of Carter Blackthorne that I'd come to know.

He's back in his element again, the house we fled to so we could escape Jacob Lacey.

He is ruthless again.

His hand crawls up the back of my head and into my now-dry hair. He clenches a fist and yanks my head sideways, my eyes flying open in shock. I stare up at him, the fingertips on his free hand circling under my chin and stroking down to the base of my neck. He tugs at the shirt slightly as if wondering how to rip it off of me.

"Who gave you this shirt?"

"Rich did," I whisper.

He shakes his head in disapproval. "Wearing another man's shirt?"

"Better than watching another woman give you a pole dance," I bite in bitter anguish. "How could you, Carter? Why would you ever—"

"Ssshh," he says, his fingertips pinching my lips together. I wince slightly, the forming bruise still sore where he touches my mouth, but it's not too painful to make me fight him. "You need to listen to me, Bella. These new enemies are not Jacob Lacey. They don't fight with their guns or their cocks."

I inhale sharply through my nose, my lips still preoccupied.

"You're going to learn things, dove. Things that I'm trying to protect you from. And if you're going to react this way for all of them, then you'll be sequestered until this battle is over. I don't want that, and I know you don't, either."

I nod in agreement. I don't want to be set off to the side. I just want

Carter and I to be happy.

That doesn't seem like it's going to be the case anytime soon, though.

"You love me, don't you?"

I hesitate. Of course, I love him, but if he did cheat on me, does that mean he really loves me? Could I love a man who tosses me to the side so carelessly? I can only imagine what he would do if I were found giving a pole dance to another man, let alone in the lingerie Carter bought me!

A searing heat fills my chest, and I feel sick with the pressure.

Constant, never-ending pressure.

He doesn't move his fingers off my lips yet. "You know I wouldn't cheat on you. They're going to try to prove otherwise or angle a sting operation on me to make it look like I'm cheating or that you're having a fling with my once-rival."

He leans forward, his lips nearly touching mine, still pinched between his fine grip. "You can tell me the truth, dove. Do you think I did something to hurt you? Do you think I cheated?"

While the photo was a daunting thing to see, I doubt Carter would have the ability to cheat on me and then come home and fill me with cum as he had. He's got excellent rigor, but he's not Superman. He needs a break, too, no matter what he may say during sex.

I shake my head in finality.

"Good girl," he praises, kissing my forehead. "I didn't want to punish you. Not after everything that has happened the last few days. But this doesn't excuse you from wearing another man's shirt. We will handle that later, though."

He releases my lips and stalks to the end of the bed toward the bathroom.

My lips purse on their own before I blurt, "What? You get to see another woman half-naked, but I can't wear Rich's T-shirt to be modest?"

He stops, the muscles in his back flexed and unkind. "Repeat that, dove."

"I could have walked around his penthouse naked. There was blood on my shirt, Carter. There was blood on everything I was wearing. I ran from the detective. I was arrested in our living room, and I was scared, okay? I wanted something to wear, and he offered it."

He turns slowly, hands gripping the footboard of the bed. "I didn't appreciate that slut giving me a dance. Whatever camera she hid didn't show how I figured out it wasn't you and how I threatened her life if she tried something like that again. I fought her off because I don't find her the least bit appealing."

"But you did at some point, right?"

His nostrils flare. "What the hell are you talking about."

"She looks like Brooke!"

We both shiver, and I can't believe I have to bring her up again, but it's the truth. Carter was using my likeness to get over Brooke, and even though that wasn't the case when we fell in love, it was the original purpose of his interest in me.

It's the same as every long-haired, petite brunette in the city with a curvy figure. He wanted to get what he could never have, and I'm not going to pretend that this slandering journalist doesn't look just like Brooke Blackthorne.

When his teeth finally unclench, his eyes dart through me. "You want the truth?"

I nod steadily. "Tell me what I already know, Carter. You've fucked her before, haven't you? And now what? Do you want her again? Is that it?"

"Goddammit, I don't want anyone but you. I'm not making that clear again."

"Then explain it to me, Carter. Please. I want to understand why she's trying to do this. She's trying to get under my skin, telling everyone I'm cheating on you, and you're cheating on me. For what purpose?"

"She wants me to pay."

"Pay for what?"

He opens his mouth to speak, but something cold flashes in his eyes instead. He shuts his mouth and shakes his head at last. "I won't say."

I swallow hard. "What did you do?"

"Why are you assuming that I did anything, dove?"

"Because if you scorned her, she's not going to stop until we're just as miserable as you made her."

He stands up, his hands sliding around the belt loops of his jeans. I'm happy to see that his belt is missing; part of me worried I'm tied up to take punishment. Which does remind me, why the hell am I tied up? I ignore it, though.

"I want to know, Carter," I plead, fighting back heavy tears. "Why can't you be honest."

"Because I don't want to hurt you, dammit. We're here to regroup, and I have a Donahue huddle downstairs waiting for me to come and find a way to take down the mayor and this woman trying to hurt us, but I needed to be sure of something first."

"Sure of what, exactly?"

"Sure that you love me, Isabella. And that you know I wouldn't cheat."

As much as the memory of that photo does ache, I know the truth.

"You wouldn't cheat. We don't have to keep coming back to this, Carter. It just… looks bad, that's all."

He nods slowly. "I understand how it looks. I'm not happy that she managed to trick me into that situation, but it happened. I love you, Bella. I love you more than I've ever loved any woman before. I just want to drop her as a topic for now."

"And what about the next article?"

He looks uneasy with that question, asking instantly, "What next article?"

I can only shrug, my hands uncomfortable behind me. "I don't know, but we do know she isn't going to stop. There might be another one in the future. She might go for something more personal, too."

"We will deal with it when it comes. If it comes."

He looks relaxed at last as if I had some information on her that he didn't want me to know. Either way, he wipes his face and looks toward the window at the setting sun. I know the Blackthornes operate like nocturnals, which means he will work something out with the Donahue family downstairs. However, this doesn't explain my last searing question.

"Why am I tied up, exactly?"

He tips his head sideways and stalks to the bathroom, only to return with a little suitcase. I can't imagine what could be inside of it other than clothes, and I know he's probably upset to see me in Rich's shirt, but it was this or my bloodstained garments.

He would probably prefer the latter, but it wasn't ideal at the time. Besides, I'm wearing a thong. That counts as something when I'm covered up with the bed blankets, where I fell asleep pretty fast.

He undoes the suitcase, exposing a couple of toys I've never seen before.

My stomach falls like it's tied with concrete bags and tossed into the harbor.

He looks up at me through dark, long lashes, and I can't subdue my tremble.

"Dove, you'll learn the same lesson again, but I'll have to make it more *memorable.*"

I gulp hard. "Yeah? How are you going to do that exactly?"

"Spread your legs."

CHAPTER TWENTY-SEVEN

Isabella

I press my lips together and do as I'm told.

I know how much Carter needs this to give him back some semblance of control, but a part of me is weary.

How much more of this can the two of us take before we shatter? How much can we take before we crumble into dust and ashes?

Once the thought leaves my mind, I realize that Carter is standing at the foot of the bed, a strange twinkle in his eyes. Wordlessly, he leans forward, a small vibrator in his hands, and pauses when he's inches away from my already wet sex. Then he uses two fingers to spread my folds apart and places the device there. I swallow, and my shoulders square together.

"I am not going to cheat on you, dove," Carter purrs, his voice low and thick with emotion. "Nor do I have any interest in anyone who isn't you. When are you going to see that?"

I swallow. "Carter, I—"

He steps back and holds a hand up. "I'm not done talking. I can't control how she looks or the way that I've behaved in the past, but when I tell you that it's over, I fucking mean it. Is that understood?"

I nod. "Yes."

"Yes, what?"

I lift my chin up and hold his gaze. "Yes, sir."

Carter nods, and a shadow falls over his face. "Good girl."

With that, he reaches into the pocket of his pants and pulls out a remote that shines in the semi-darkness of the room. Without looking away from me, he pushes the button, and small vibrations begin between my legs, little bursts at first that shoot pinpricks of desire through my veins. I twist, my mouth parts, and just as I'm about to find a more comfortable angle, Carter powers the device off.

The whimper falls from my lips before I know what I'm doing.

"You're mine, dove," Carter says in a low voice. "And I'm fucking yours. Am I making myself clear?"

"Yes, sir." I breathe, unable to look away from his cold yet handsome face. I suck in another breath when the device comes back on, and rivulets of sweat form on the back of my neck and forehead. Steadily, they drip as I squirm against my constraints and wonder what's going to happen next.

Is Carter going to keep torturing me when there's company downstairs? Is he making it a point to do this so Donahue can hear?

I know the kind of man Carter is and how possessive he can be. Yet, the thought of being marked, of being branded with his signature in the form of his teeth marks and scratches, seared into my very soul, doesn't scare me as much as it should. Instead, it fills me with a strange surge of power and a sense of recklessness.

Like I'm not the only one headed straight for a cliff.

Carter presses another button, and the pressure increases. I throw my head back, squeeze my eyes shut, and moan. Suddenly, he is on top of me, one hand clamped over my mouth and the other splayed over my mound, the heat from his proximity making me feel like I'm going to combust.

And I can't even bring myself to care.

Not as long as Carter burns with me.

Slowly, he withdraws his hand and replaces it with his lips, hot and demanding against my own. When he bites down on my lower lip, my mouth parts, and his tongue darts in. Like Carter, his tongue is harsh and unforgiving, sweeping and claiming every inch of me until I pant and writhe underneath him. All too quickly, my body jerks, and the force of my orgasm rips through me, making spots dance in my field of vision while I struggle to breathe.

My lungs are burning as I struggle to focus and realize Carter is on his feet and peeling off his clothes. He leaves them in a heap on the floor, and I can barely make out the muscles of his lean, taut body as the bed dips and creaks underneath his weight. Without warning, he nudges my legs apart and settles between them. He positions himself at my entrance, braces his arms on either side of me, and pauses.

I blink, my vision clearing, as I try not to clench my legs in anticipation.

"Fuck, dove, you smell amazing. I can't wait to bury myself inside of you." In one quick move, Carter thrusts inside me, filling me to the hilt. He keeps one arm on the headboard, and the other tugs on my restraints, winding them tighter. Tears prick the back of my eyes, but I ignore them.

All I can focus on is how Carter feels buried inside me, filling me completely.

Not a single inch of space exists between us.

I shudder as he throws my legs over his shoulders and eases further in. Using my legs, I nudge him closer before sliding them down to lock around his waist. Carter pinches the skin of my legs and buries his face in the crook of my neck. Another wave of pleasure washes over me, and I gasp, his name a chant on my lips. Then Carter flips me over so I'm on my knees, my arms still held above my head. His fingers are feather light and cool against my flushed skin.

When the slap comes, I'm expecting it, and it sends dual waves of pain and pleasure ricocheting through me. Carter grips my hips with both hands and then gives me another firm slap, which reverberates inside my head. I press my lips together and swallow back the whimper. A heartbeat later,

Carter slams into me from behind, and I cry out, my vision going completely dark.

I can smell him on me and feel him invading every inch of me.

And it still doesn't feel like enough.

I want to climb inside of his skin and stay there, where nothing and no one can hurt us.

Carter makes low growling sounds into the back of my neck, prompting another release. I am gasping for breath when Carter gives a few more thrusts, and warmth pools between my legs. Abruptly, he unties my hands, and I collapse face first onto the mattress. Slowly, I flip onto my back, stare at the ceiling, and wait for my vision to adjust.

Out of the corner of my eye, I see a flash of movement as Carter pulls his clothes back on. "Take a shower and get dressed, dove. We've got work to do."

I lift the sheets up to my chin and gingerly sit up. "We?"

Carter's lips lift into a grim, half-smile. "Our time away from the city is over. We need to head back and show the new mayor how much we appreciate the gift he sent us."

My throat tightens. "Carter, are you sure that's a good idea? He sent that man to set you up. He's dangerous, a lot more dangerous than we gave him credit for."

Carter crosses over to me in two strides, and his features are harsh, the earlier emotion in his eyes stamped out. "Are you questioning my ability to protect you, dove?"

I shake my head. "No, of course not."

But I do know that Carter can't be everywhere at once. He can't run a business and rub elbows with the new mayor, especially not one who is an ex-cop.

Carter is sinking himself further and further into quicksand, and with each passing day, the number of people willing to pull him out shrinks.

I can't save Carter from himself, not on my own, at least.

The thought leaves a bad taste in the back of my mouth as Carter twists on the knob, the blinding white light of the hallway temporarily blinding me. When the door clicks shut behind him, I scramble out of bed and feel around in the dark. My fingers close around an unfamiliar fabric as I stagger into the bathroom. There, I pause to flick the lights on and wait for my vision to adjust. Then I glance down at the clothes and frown.

If I have Carter's clothes, what did he wear downstairs?

With a slight shake of my head, I pad across the tile floors and switch on the water. I scrub every inch of my skin twice and try to escape the images lingering in the shadows. Every time I close my eyes, I see the mayor's man, upright and resolute one second and the next, lying at my feet in a pool of his own blood. The sight stays with me as I step out of the shower, wrap a towel around my waist, and use my hand to clear away the fog.

I meet my own gaze in the mirror and try not to flinch.

My entire body feels like a battlefield, marred with scars of every kind. When I twist and turn to study myself in the mirror, I can't help but compare my skin to Lilian's.

The curvy brunette might not have Carter, but at least she's in shape.

Frowning, I turn away from the mirror, let the towel flutter to the floor, and pull Carter's clothes on. They smell like him, like leather and cigarettes, making butterflies form in the center of my stomach. Once I step out of the bathroom, I see a pair of socks and shoes laid out at the foot of the bed. I pull them on, tie a sweater around my waist, and make my way downstairs.

The first thing I see is Carter on the other side of the kitchen counter, with Tristan a few feet away, wearing an identical somber expression. Tristan's gaze flicks over to me, and he gives a slight shake of his head. I look away and back toward Carter, who is gripping the counter like his life depends on it.

As if it's the only thing keeping him from doing something

stupid. Like launching himself across the room and tackling Rich Donahue to the ground.

I take the last few steps and ignore the warning look Carter gives me. With my heart hammering unsteadily against my chest, I come to a stop next to Carter and brush my hand against his. He laces his fingers through mine, some of the tension easing from his shoulders. Rich glances between us and says nothing. Without saying anything else, Carter pushes himself off the counter, dragging me behind him.

Before I can thank Rich for saving me, I am thrown into the back of Tristan's car, and the door slams shut in my face. I twist to see Carter and Rich exchange a quick look before Rich retreats into his own car. Moments later, the passenger door is wrenched open, and Carter gets in, the door slamming shut behind him.

I fold my hands in my lap and clear my throat. "He did save my life, Carter."

Carter's jaw tightens. "I don't need you reminding me why I couldn't come after you, dove."

"It wasn't your fault." I lean forward and place a hand on his shoulders. "You were being detained by the police. Hughes made sure of it."

Carter shakes my hand off and says nothing.

In silence, Tristan drives back to the penthouse, where several of Carter's men are already waiting for us outside, their guns barely concealed underneath their shirts and jackets. I lower my head, dig my nails into my palms, and hurry into the penthouse, which looks untouched and exactly the same way we left it. After changing into my own clothes, I crawl into the large king-sized bed and wait for Carter.

My eyelids grow heavy as I stare at the door and fight back my yawns.

When I drift off, there is a low murmur of voices outside the door and then silence. I struggle to make out Carter's voice before I drift off. Sometime later, in the thick of sleep, I feel the bed dip and creak, and

Carter's body curls against mine. He presses a kiss to the back of my neck, mutters something into my skin, and exhales.

That night, I toss and turn, trying to figure out how to bridge the wide chasm between us.

Chapter Twenty-Eight

Carter

"Taking your sweet ass time to get ready isn't going to make the event go by any faster, dove." I adjust my tie in the mirror and run a hand over my face. "I don't want us to be late."

The door to the bathroom clicks, and Bella steps out, dressed in a floor-length shimmering silver gown with a plunging neckline. Her hair is left in loose waves around her delicate face, and she has some color on her cheeks and eyelids, making her look more alluring than ever. I twist to face her, and a shiver races up my spine, my fingers itching at my sides.

I want to lay her out on the mattress, rip off the dress, and spend hours on end losing myself in her body.

When she bridges the distance between us and offers me a bright smile, I have to clench my hands into fists. Not only would ravaging her make us late for the gala, but I also know it'll leave Tristan and the other men accompanying us tonight in a bad mood.

I'm well aware of what's at stake when it comes to Mayor Hughes.

And all too aware of how important it is for me to put on a calm and unaffected demeanor, to make sure the prick doesn't know how badly he's rattled us.

Or how badly I want to put his face through a wall.

All I need is to get close enough, and I'll teach Killian Hughes that there is a price to be paid for crossing a man like me. For now, though, I need to put on a smile and my best suit and pretend like nothing bothers me. Straightening my back, I hold my arm out to Isabella, who tucks her hand into my elbow and allows me to lead her down the stairs and into the elevator. She earns a few cursory glances on her way past, and I level all of them with a pointed look.

Anyone who looks at her ends up cowering in a corner.

I smirk and lead her down the stairs of the building and into the black SUV parked next to the curb. Ernesto is wearing a suit and looking very pleased with himself as we get into the car. When he pulls away from the curb, Isabella settles into my side and brings her head to rest against my chest, over the hammering of my heart.

With a frown, I wrap my arm around her shoulders and exhale. "There's nothing to be nervous about, dove. We've been to galas before."

Isabella snorts. "And we don't exactly have the best track record when it comes to them."

I plunge my fingers through her hair and massage her scalp. "Yes, but our dear old mayor isn't going to come after me in public. Not if he wants to make sure none of this leads back to him."

Isabella leans back to look at me, and a furrow appears between her brows. "You sound awfully sure. Is there something I should know?"

One hand falls from her waist down to her ass, and I squeeze. "It's nothing to trouble yourself with, dove. Try and have a good time tonight."

Isabella gives me a dubious look and settles back into my side. I play with her hair for a while longer and ignore the molten hot desire racing through me. When Ernesto pulls up outside the hotel where the gala is being held, reporters are lined up on either side of the red carpet, being held back by a team of uniformed security men and women.

Cameras click away steadily, and there's already a loud cacophony of voices, barely muted beyond the car's windows. I glance over at Isabella, who has squared her shoulders and lifted her chin like a soldier headed to war. I bring her hand up to my lips and press a kiss there. She gives me a pleading look, and I'm tempted to oblige.

Circling the block a few times can't hurt.

As soon as the thought crosses my mind, I spot Tristan and Paul standing side by side in their crisp dark suits and wearing identical tight expressions. With a growl, I get out of the car and hold my hand out to Isabella. Immediately, the cameras shift toward us, and I feel her resist the urge to shrink into my side. We glide down the red carpet and are stopped in the doorway. I glance over my shoulders at Tristan and the others, and they hurry over to us.

Suddenly, we're being led away through a side door, with a few of the same uniformed men and women I saw earlier forming a half-circle around us. We earn a few curious looks, and I grip Isabella's hand tighter. She laces her fingers through mine and doesn't say a word. Tristan and Paul are on either side of us, studying the path that we're taking.

After taking a series of twists and turns, we are brought to a stop outside a large empty room with chairs piled up on either side of us. Without warning, we are shoved in, and I swivel around, the gun already in my hand, only to find the door slammed shut in my face. Tristan and I launch ourselves at the door, but it won't budge. Paul murmurs something to Isabella, but I can barely hear anything above the dull roaring in my ears.

What the fuck now?

Can't we have one fucking night to ourselves?

I take a few steps back and turn to face Isabella. "I'm going to get us out of here, dove. This is just our new friend trying to flex and show us how powerful he is."

Even from a distance, Hughes is a threat.

I want to wrap my hands around his throat and squeeze until his eyes bulge and he loses the color in his face. When I get out of here, I'm going to make it my personal mission to hunt him down and teach him the meaning of the Blackthorne name.

Tristan and Paul try the other doors in the room while I hold Bella to me and rub her arms. She is shivering and hasn't said a word since we left the car. By the time I get her to calm down, the doors to the room fly open, and a few stern-looking men step in, all of them with broad shoulders, muscles, and guns tucked into the waist of their pants.

I step in front of Isabella and point a finger at the guy in the center. "Has the mayor sent us another gift already? I'm flattered that he thinks so highly of me."

The bald-headed man I'm facing tilts his head to the side and raises an eyebrow. "I've heard a lot about you, Mr. Blackthorne, but I can't say I'm impressed. It's quite a mess you've made for yourself and all because of her."

I let out a warning growl. "I'd watch the next words that come out of your mouth if I were you."

"The Natoris were right," he continues, as if he hasn't heard me. "The city is ripe for the taking but not without a little assurance first."

"You take one more step, and it'll be your last." I point my gun directly at him and level him with a pointed look. "It's a shame to ruin these expensive shoes, but it's a price I'm willing to pay."

The man nods, and the doors behind us burst open, allowing a few more men in. I wheel around to reach for Isabella, but she's snatched away from me and held at gunpoint. Another man holds a knife up to her long, slender neck, and her eyes grow wide as saucers.

The bald-headed man takes a step forward and shoves a hand into his pocket. "Let's try this again, Blackthorne, because I don't think you understood me the first time. You're going to give us all your contacts and all the information that you've gathered over the years."

I lower my gun and scoff. "And why the fuck would I do that?"

The man shoots the men in the back a look, and one of them cocks the gun pointed at Isabella. She lets out a low whimper, and it pierces through my heart. I straighten my back, shove my free hand into my pocket, and press my lips together.

"We know your little whore is the key. If you don't give us what we want, we're not going to be the only ones coming after her. I believe you know the Philips family, too."

"I'm going to enjoy making you pay," I tell him, pausing to offer him a grim smile. "Every last one of you is going to pay."

The bald man stares at me for a long time.

Silence stretches between us.

Then Isabella is knocked to her knees, and the gun is pressed to the back of her head. She refuses to lower her head until her attacker hits her on the back of the head, and I see red. Tristan and Paul shoot me quick looks, but I don't hold their gazes.

I'm going to personally hunt down every last one of them.

Isabella's attacker hits her again, this time across the side of her face. A bruise is already forming there, so I dig my nails into my palms. "You're wasting your time."

Isabella gives me a wounded look. "Carter, please. Don't tell them anything."

She is slapped again, hard enough to have her crumble into a heap on the floor. I stop breathing when she doesn't get back up right away. Then she sits up, blood and spittle forming on the side of her mouth, and gives the man behind her a withering look. When she draws her head back and spits at his feet, he advances on her and kicks her in the stomach.

Isabella doubles over and lets out a low hiss of pain. "He's not going to tell you anything. Go to hell."

The bald-headed man steps forward. "I can see why you like her. She's feisty. Maybe we'll take her with us when we leave."

I have the gun pointed at his head before I know what I'm doing. "Back the fuck off."

The man doesn't bat an eye as he signals to the other men. Isabella is tossed around like some sort of rag doll, with the men taking turns kicking and hitting her. It takes everything in me not to launch myself at them, taking as many of the bastards down as I can. It's the look in Isabella's eyes that stops me. That and the fact that I have several guns pointed at me.

I'd be a pin cushion before I got close enough to make any difference.

Everyone in the room knows it.

One of the men moves to rip Isabella's dress, and the door flies open, Blackthorne men steadily pouring through them. I disarm the men closest to me and throw myself at their leader. We land on the floor with a thud, and fists fly as we grapple for control. Once we roll to a stop, he kicks me away and staggers off. I can only see red until Tristan places a hand on my arm and yells into my ear.

The room sharpens into focus, and I see Paul on the floor with Isabella, trying to rouse her. I march over to them, scoop her into my arms, and let her head fall against my chest. She is covered in blood, and her breathing is steady but uneven. Rage and fear claw their way through me as we get into the backseat of the SUV, and Ernesto speeds through the streets of the city.

A gurney is waiting for us outside the double doors of the emergency room. I'm out of the car before Ernesto brings it to a complete halt, and the tires screech against the asphalt. I set Isabella down, but her hand is still in mine until we push through the doors. The smell of disinfectant hits me first, followed closely by the sound of beeping monitors.

Tristan materializes next to me. "What do you need us to do?"

"Give those guys a taste of their own medicine," I hiss under my breath. "I want the Philipses and the Natoris to know exactly who they're dealing with. Take fucking Donahue with you."

Because I'm not leaving Bella's side for a second.

And it's time our alliance with Rich fucking Donahue came in handy.

Chapter Twenty-Nine

Isabella

"Carter, what's happening?" I'm flipped onto my side, and I feel a breeze on my behind. Then I hear the sound of fabric being ripped, and goosebumps break out across my flesh. I'm pushed onto my back, but I can't make out much, save for the vague outline of doctors and nurses in scrubs coming in and out of my field of vision.

I try to sit up straight, but someone pushes me back.

So I stare at the ceiling and try to push back against the nausea threatening to overtake me. I press my lips together, take a deep, shuddering breath, and squeeze my eyes shut. Reluctantly, I pry my eyes open when I hear something being wheeled in and feel a pair of gloves pinching my skin together. When the needle touches my skin, my eyes fly open, and I scramble up.

The cold syringe pierces my skin, and I hiss. "I don't want that."

"It's going to be okay, dove," Carter says from the doorway, where he's standing with his arms folded over his chest with two large nurses in front of him, blocking him from moving any farther into the room. "I'm right here."

I swallow, and a thin sheen of sweat breaks out over my forehead. "Are you okay?"

Carter nods and doesn't say anything else.

This time, when I'm pushed back down onto the hospital bed, I don't fight them. Instead, I study the pale blue walls on either side of me and attempt not to gag at the metallic smell of blood. It isn't until I glance down at myself that I realize I still have specks of my own blood smeared over my bare skin. As soon as I glance back up and meet Carter's gaze, I swallow back the protest.

One by one, the doctors trickle out of the room, leaving me alone with a single blonde-haired nurse who adjusts the IV drip in my arm and checks something on the monitor. She writes something down on a clipboard and glances over at Carter, who is standing opposite me, a look of cold fury etched onto his face. After adjusting the IV drip again, she tucks the blanket around me and scurries away. The door clicks shut behind her, and Carter sits on the edge of the bed and gathers me to him.

He shudders, and I feel it through his entire body. "I'm sorry. I should've given them what they wanted."

I throw my arms around his shoulders and wince. "They wouldn't have stopped, Carter. You and I both know that. At least this way, the Blackthorne family hasn't lost everything they've worked to build."

Carter draws back to look at me, and his bright eyes are full of rage and anguish. "You're what matters to me, Isabella. Everyone else can go fuck themselves."

I touch his face. "You've worked hard to build your empire. I'm not going to let you throw it away."

Not when he's already risked a lot to be with me.

The scars on my body are proof of every hoop and hurdle, but seeing them doesn't make it any easier. Nor does seeing the pain and unease in the depth of Carter's eyes. Wave after wave of worry rolls off of him, and I can see him bite back his spiral in the tight way he holds himself and the way he keeps glancing over at the door.

I can't escape the feeling that he'd rather be prowling the streets and stalking the people who did this.

With a sigh, I push the thought away and settle back against the bed. Carter lies next to me, and I tuck myself into his side, not wanting to be separated again. Out of the corner of my eye, I spot something underneath the bed, and I realize it's the tattered remains of my beautiful dress.

"I'll get you another one," Carter tells me, pausing to squeeze my shoulders. "Tristan and the others are making sure those people who took us are taken care of."

"How many more dead bodies before this stops, Carter?"

Carter places his thumb and index finger underneath my chin and lifts it up, so I'm looking directly into his eyes. "I've never made what I do a secret, dove. Nor will I. You asked me to be honest with you, so I am, and this is part of the territory."

I search his face. "He's not going to stop coming after us. Hughes isn't going to stop, Carter."

No matter the price to be paid.

And I'm afraid that Carter isn't going to stop either.

How did we manage to get away from one shark and run smack dab into another one?

With bigger teeth.

At least with the Laceys, Carter could play dirty. When it comes to the mayor, Carter has to be very, very careful of how he retaliates and when. Otherwise, those same cops who once looked out for him are going to end up slapping him in handcuffs.

Again.

I shiver at the thought, leading Carter to peel off his jacket and drape it over me. "I'm going to get you something to eat and drink. You need your energy."

Without waiting for a response, he presses the button for the nurse, and she returns, a harried expression on her face. "She's in a lot of pain. Can you up the dosage?"

The nurse tucks a pencil behind her ear and nods.

Carter lingers near the foot of the bed, his arms folded over his chest. A few minutes pass, and nothing happens. Then, I feel like I'm drifting on a cloud, and my head is light headed. I can't feel any part of my body when Carter leans in and presses a kiss to my forehead. He whispers something to the nurse, hands her a crumpled-up bill, and exits the room. She swims in and out of my field of vision before swinging the door open. I stretch out over the mattress and squeeze my eyes shut.

The door opens again, and I try to sit up, but my body feels heavier now.

Rich's familiar face appears, and he's saying something, but it's garbled, and I can't make out the words. He angles his body, glances over his shoulders, and leans in closer. Rich smells like sandalwood and lavender, and I barely have time to register how close he is before he presses his lips to mine. My entire body is slack, and I can't push him off.

What the hell is he doing?

And why is he doing this?

Carter is going to kill us both if he walks in.

Rich keeps his mouth pressed to mine, soft and sweet and unfamiliar, until I make low noises of distress. Finally, after what feels like an eternity, he draws back and tucks my hair behind my ear. He looks directly into my eyes, a half-smile on his face. Then he presses his mouth directly to my ear, and I don't like how his hot breath feels against my skin.

This is wrong.

"I'm going to get you out of here, Isabella," Rich whispers, his voice rising toward the end. "It's not going to be much longer, you'll see."

I struggle to focus, but I can't make out much because of the thick fog in my brain. When I blink, Rich is gone, and Carter stands in front of me, saying something in a soft voice. He drops a kiss on top of my head, pushes my hair out of my eyes, and gives me a grim smile. When he hands me a Styrofoam cup, I curl my fingers around it and inhale.

Carter's phone rings, slicing through the air. "I'll be right outside, dove."

I sip my scalding hot coffee and try to determine if I dreamt up the whole thing with Rich when another doctor comes in. He is tall and lean, with wisps of hair falling onto his forehead. Wordlessly, he snaps on a pair of latex gloves and rummages around for a syringe. Once he has it in his hand, I gulp and set the coffee down.

"Is that necessary?"

"I'm afraid it is. Your arm is swollen, and we're afraid that if we keep the contraceptive implant there, it's only going to become more infected." He advances and picks up my arm. "You'll just have to remember to get another one put in once the infection clears up."

I blink slowly. "Okay, doctor."

As soon as he's done, I sink lower into the mattress and give him a loopy smile. Then I flip onto my side and adjust the pillow underneath my neck, missing the feel of Carter's body against mine. I smell him before he comes into the room, and my body is all too aware of the thin hospital gown I have on. He runs a hand over my arm, gives me a quick kiss, and says something under his breath.

I try to smile, but my eyelids are growing too heavy.

Carter

"Paul better not move an inch, or he'll have me to answer to," I grumble between sips of my coffee. "You're supposed to be helping."

Tristan leans against the wall opposite the vending machine. "I'll go there in a minute. I just wanted to check on you."

I let out a low, humorless laugh. "I had to watch them beat her up, Tristan. How do you think I fucking feel?"

Like I want to burn the whole world down and watch it turn to ash and rubble.

It's only the thought of leaving Bella alone that keeps me glued to the hospital, never too far from her room.

But it doesn't change the fact that the rules are changing, and the world is closing in on all sides. First, with my own family, then with fucking Lilian, and now with the Natoris and Philipses joining forces. A part of me is still in disbelief and reeling from everything happening, but the other part of me is calm and collected, knowing exactly what I need to do in order to send out a message.

There is going to be hell to pay.

I'm going to make sure of it.

"She's a lot stronger than I gave her credit for," Tristan admits, pausing to push himself off the wall. He's got specks of dirt and blood on his neck and knuckles, but he makes no move to wipe them away. "You still sure you want to keep her in the middle of all this?"

I give Tristan an annoyed look. "Watch it. Tonight is not the night to test me."

Tristan studies my face. "You've thought about it, haven't you? Carter, you and I have known each other for a long time. I know what you're like when you're pushed past the breaking point."

I toss my cup into the nearest trash can and straighten my back. "Yes, I've considered walking away from all of it and building a life with Bella, turning over a new leaf, and all that bullshit."

Except I know it's not going to be that simple.

For the first time since meeting Isabella, I am considering it, though, for her sake.

"That's not what I meant." Tristan shakes his head, exasperation written all over his face. "You can marry her if you want, settle down, and all that bullshit as you call it, but I don't think walking away from the family business is going to help. They'll still come after you, and without the family, you won't be able to fend them off."

Goddamn it.

I hate it when Tristan is right.

"The only reason we're still around, the only reason the Blackthornes are worth anything, is because of you," Tristan adds in a quieter voice. "You and I both know that. You don't turn your back on family."

No matter what.

Without me, the Blackthornes won't survive for long, and Tristan isn't the only one who knows it.

I have to stay, but for a few brief minutes, as we stand across from each other, listening to the garbled voice over the speaker, I contemplate what it would be like to leave.

For the first time in my life, I wonder if I can build a life for myself that has nothing to do with the Blackthornes or the family business.

And I imagine it all with Isabella by my side.

I can picture it as clear as day.

But when Tristan clears his throat, bringing me back to the present with a jolt, I push all those thoughts away and give him a nod. He and I both know I'm not going to walk away from the empire I helped build, not if I can help it.

I'll just have to do a better job of keeping Bella safe.

For her sake and mine.

CHAPTER THIRTY

Isabella

I lick my dry lips. "Do you know where Carter is?"

The nurse in the room checks the IV drip and gives it a firm shake. Then she peers at it, her dark eyes giving nothing away. "I haven't seen Mr. Blackthorne in a few hours, Ms. Julis."

I sink back against the bed and twist a loose thread between my fingers. When she's done checking the drip, I look back at the dark-haired nurse with some silver in her hair and sigh. "Do you have any idea when I can leave?"

"Once you're done with the IV drip, I can ask them to prepare the discharge papers for you," she replies, pausing to write something down on the clipboard. "Are you sure you're feeling well enough? You can stay for another night if you like."

But I've already been here for three days, and I'm itching to go back home.

Back to the penthouse I share with Carter, where the world feels like a million miles away, and nothing bad can touch us. Slowly, I sit up straighter, the covers falling to my waist, and clear my throat. "Actually, I feel better. Can you get the discharge papers ready for me?"

I want to surprise Carter by showing up at his door.

Even though I have no idea how I'm going to do that yet.

The nurse nods, adjusts something in the IV drip, and takes a step back. Without responding, she leaves the room, and the door clicks shut behind her. As soon as I'm sure I'm alone, I get up and stretch my arms over my head, a yawn passing through my lips. When I'm done, I step into the bathroom, pausing to pick the bag up off the floor. Slowly, I set it down on the counter, unzip the flap, and let it fall open with a soft banging sound.

Carter has packed an assortment of things, including a set of racy lingerie that makes me blush.

With a smile, I hold them up to the mirror and imagine his hands all over me, making every inch of my body shiver in anticipation. Humming to myself, I step into the shower and wait for steam to fill the bathroom. When I come back out, I pat myself dry and rake my fingers through my hair. In the room, my phone is vibrating incessantly and falls onto the bed.

As soon as I pick it up, the world spins and falls into the background.

I perch on the edge of the bed and read the brief article about Carter and Lilian, and bile rises to the back of my throat. Frowning, I read the article one more time, tears pricking the back of my eyes. Then, I scroll through my contacts and dial Carter's number. It rings a few times before going straight to voicemail. Panic and fear bubble up within me as I try Carter a second and third time.

But he remains out of reach.

And I start to pace the room, wondering if the article is true.

I've already seen the picture of Carter in our playroom at the club, with Lilian scantily clad in my lingerie. Although I don't want to keep picturing it, I keep replaying the scene in my head, this time imagining the two of them on the couch in the corner, doing all sorts of things to each other while the lights are dim and soft music plays in the background.

The image is so upsetting that I find myself staggering into the bathroom to empty the contents of my stomach. When I'm done, I splash cold water on my face and gargle. Then, I grip the edge of the sink and count backward from twenty. As soon as I feel steady enough, I hoist my bag onto my shoulders and return to the room. My hands shake when I sign the discharge papers, and I avoid the nurse's gaze.

In the hallway, I don't see any of Carter's men.

So I hang my head low, weave in and out of the people rushing past in either direction, and make a beeline for the elevator. Outside, a brisk wind has started, and a heaviness settles in the center of my chest. I begin walking in the general direction of the penthouse when I hear a pair of footsteps behind me. Fear slams into me as I quicken my pace and round a corner.

The man races past me, and I breathe a sigh of relief.

It lasts until another man emerges from the shadows and advances on me. "You're right where Lilian said you'd be."

I stumble back and hold my arms up on either side of me. "Stay away from me. You have no idea who you're messing with. Carter Blackthorne is not going to be happy about this."

In the moonlight, I see the man's expression shift and turn pleased. "That's exactly why we're doing this. You've caused enough trouble as it is."

I duck into an alley and break into a sprint, my heart hammering uneasily the entire time. Once I reach the end of the alley, I throw myself at the wall and try to climb it, but I'm dragged away by the back of my hair. Little pinpricks of pain dance behind my eyelids. I throw my head back to disarm the man, and he hisses. I fall to the ground and scramble away from him, but his meaty hands close around my ankles.

"We have all sorts of plans for you, little bird," he says, his putrid breath in my ear. "You're going to be worth a lot of money."

I squirm and thrash against him, but it's no use.

My last thought before he places a rag over my mouth is of Carter and how the fuck he's meant to find me now.

Carter

"What the fuck do you mean she's gone?" Before the SUV comes to a complete stop, I push the door open and race up the stairs to the hospital, barely seeing anything around me. When I burst through the double doors, my hands clenched into fists at my side, several people nearby jump back as if I'm going to unleash my anger in their direction.

With the way I'm feeling, I'm not sure that I won't.

I'm vaguely aware of Ernesto hurrying after me and saying something in a low voice, but I can't make out a word he says. All I know is that I left for a few hours to take care of pressing business, and the next thing I know, one of my men is placing the call. As soon as I reach the hallway where Isabella's room is located, I make a beeline for the man in question.

He barely has time to straighten his back before I slam him against the wall hard enough to make his teeth rattle. "You had one fucking job, and you couldn't even manage that. Give me one good reason why I shouldn't end you right now."

He tries to stay something, but my hands are tight around his neck.

Tristan appears next to me and places a hand on my shoulders. "Boss—"

"Don't say another fucking word," I snap, without looking at my cousin. "Someone has to pay the price for this, so unless you're volunteering, I suggest you stay out of my way."

Tristan withdraws his hand so quickly it's as if he's been burned. Then he takes a few steps back, and I press down harder, seeing nothing but red in my field of vision. Eventually, when the man starts to sputter and marks blossom around his neck, I release my grip. The man crumples into a heap on the floor, and I push past him and into her room.

It's as if she was never there, except for the lingering scent of her perfume.

I tear the whole room apart, leaving the sheets and pillows in a complete state of disarray. I'm so consumed with rage that it takes the blonde-haired nurse coming in and making a low squeak of horror to pull me out of my rampage. With a growl, I brush past her and take the stairs to the bottom floor, the movement doing nothing to quench the worry and panic clawing their way inside of me.

Where the hell is Isabella?

And why didn't she come home?

By the time I reach the bottom floor, my phone won't stop vibrating. When I take it out and see the messages from Isabella, my stomach dips, and I feel worse. Outside, I punch a hole in the wall nearest the emergency room door, droplets of blood following me down the pavement and into the SUV. Ernesto puts the car in reverse and speeds in and out of traffic, charting a direct path to the penthouse. As soon as he pulls up outside, I rip off a piece of fabric and wrap it around my bleeding knuckles. In the elevator, it takes every ounce of self-control I have not to break the whole thing down.

The red-hot anger pulsing through me only intensifies when I step into the penthouse and find Lilian draped over the kitchen counter, barely wearing any clothes. Her blood-red lips form a surprised 'O' as she slides off the counter and saunters toward me.

"You're late. I expected you home a while ago."

I give her my most menacing look. "What the fuck are you doing here, Lilian? How did you even get in?"

She places a manicured nail against my chest and purrs. "Have you forgotten already, baby? I can be very persuasive when I want to be, remember?"

I push her hand away and growl. "Get the fuck out of my

house. Now."

Lilian tosses her dark hair over her shoulders and places both hands on her hips. "Is that any way to talk to the woman who cleaned your house and made you food?"

I wasn't in the mood to play house, especially not with fucking Lilian, of all people.

She has no idea how much control I'm exerting right now. Or how much I want to hurt her for all the pain and damage she's inflicted.

The world would be a better place without a journalist like Lilian fucking things up.

"What's the matter, baby?" Lilian bridges the distance between us and bats her eyes at me. "You look like you've got something on your mind."

I take Lilian's wrist in mine and drag her away in the direction of the door. Before I slam the door shut, I catch a brief glimpse of her stunned face. Then, I fish my phone out of my pocket and scroll through my contacts.

Rich Donahue answers on the fifth ring, his voice pitched low.

"Where the fuck are you?"

"I'm at an auction. I'm looking for my sister."

"I don't care what the fuck you do with your spare time, but Isabela is missing, and I need more men out looking for her."

"Fuck." The loud cacophony of voices disappears as Rich moves somewhere quieter. "I'll make a few phone calls and see what I can do."

"You better." I end the call without waiting for his response and throw my phone away. It crashes against the wall opposite me and breaks into a million little pieces. Then I grip the kitchen counter, throw my head back, and let out a loud, blood-curdling scream.

Whoever did this is going to wish they'd never been born.

Isabella

"I don't know how to thank you." I fidget in the backseat of the car and fold my hands in my lap. "I'll find a way to pay you back, Rich."

He meets my gaze in the rearview mirror and shakes his head. "Don't worry about it. I'm glad I was able to put my money to good use."

I shiver and try to push away the image of what could've happened.

If Rich hadn't shown up when he had and bid on me using all the money at his disposal, I have no idea what would've become of me. But I know it wouldn't have involved a hot meal, a clean shower, and being handed a pair of clean clothes.

Fuck.

Just the thought of what those men almost accomplished sends another tremor through me, and tears prick the back of my eyes. Hastily, I wipe them away and sit on my hands to hide my tremor. Outside the car, the world rushes past, barely distinguishable in the waning light of the moon. I swallow, bow my head, and squeeze my eyes shut.

"I go there sometimes to look for my sister," Rich says in a low voice. He refuses to meet my gaze in the rearview mirror, and I don't know why. "I know it's stupid, and I know my chances of finding her are slim, but I can't help myself."

Both eyes fly open, and I lean forward in my seat. "How long has it been since your sister has gone missing?"

"A few years." Rich's voice is thick with emotion when he says this. He turns the wheel and pulls onto a small, well-traveled path that leads through a cluster of trees. The path stops in front of a pair of wrought-iron gates where a large house sits, bathed in the silver glow of the moon. Wordlessly, Rich rolls the window down and twists sideways to punch a number into the screen.

The gate shudders to life, allowing us passage.

Once the car rolls to a stop, I push the door open and stumble out of the vehicle. I wince when my foot catches on something uneven, and I stumble forward. Rich hooks me by the waist and helps me right myself. In silence, he leads me through the front door and flicks the light on, revealing high-arched ceilings, a balcony with glass doors overlooking the woods, and an open-concept kitchen with modern appliances.

"I'm going to take a look at your wounds," Rich murmurs before disappearing through a door on the right. Through the slit, I make out a bathroom, catching a glimpse of a sink and a glass shower stall. Rich reappears with his hair in tufts on top of his head and a first aid kid. Slowly, he takes my hand and leads me to the couch.

I don't realize that I'm crying until he hands me a pack of tissues.

"I'm sorry." I blow my nose and wince when he touches a piece of cotton on my raw skin. "I don't know why I'm crying."

"Because what they did to you is horrible," Rich replies without looking up. With a surprising amount of tenderness, he cleans the wounds on both arms before looking up at me. "It's okay to be a mess right now, Isabella."

I sniff, another ripple of goosebumps breaking out across my skin. "When can I see Carter?"

"There's a storm coming, so I haven't been able to reach him," Rich replies. "I was able to call ahead while I waited for them to release you, so the house is stocked. Don't worry."

I swallow. "I'm going to be staying here?"

Rich picks up the dirty rags and the bucket full of blood-tinted water and walks away. "You don't have to see me if you don't want to. You're safe here, Isabella."

I curl my legs underneath me and run a hand over my face. "Thank you."

I hear the sound of running water and sink further against the couch. "I don't know who they were or how they found me, but they knew exactly how to get to me."

As if they'd been lying in wait, stalking me like prey.

I know Carter has a lot of enemies, but nothing like this has ever happened before.

And I'm a lot more rattled than I want Rich to know.

All I want is to curl up on the big bed next to Carter, tuck myself into his side, and fall asleep with my head pressed against his chest. Wave after wave of emotion builds within me, and I squeeze my eyes shut. When Rich returns to the living room, I force my eyes open and give him a weak smile.

"Did they hurt you?"

I shake my head. "Not like that. Thank God they didn't get the chance."

Rich looks relieved. "Good, why don't I make us something to eat? Any allergies I should know about?"

I stand up and sway a little on my feet. "I can help you."

Rich studies my face. "Why don't you keep me company while I cook?"

I breathe a sigh of relief. "I can handle that."

Gingerly, I follow him into the kitchen, where he pulls a bar stool out for me. I hop onto it, my legs dangling over the edge, and lean over the counter. "I'm sorry you couldn't find your sister tonight."

Rich opens and closes several cupboards. "I'll find her eventually. I just have to keep looking."

"She's lucky to have a brother like you," I whisper to his back. "Sometimes, I wonder what it would've been like to have siblings."

Rich spins around and sets down a pan and a pot. He fills up the kettle with water and takes some vegetables and a package of chicken out of the fridge. "I actually wanted to be an only child, but I honestly can't imagine my life without my sister."

"What's her name?"

"Lorna," Rich replies before averting his gaze. "I can't even remember what I said to her the last time we spoke, but I know it was something stupid."

"It won't be the last thing you say to her," I offer, forcing my lips into a smile. "With the kind of money and resources you have, I'm sure you'll be able to find her, and I'm pretty sure you could ask for more help now."

Although I have no idea if Carter would be willing to offer it, considering how thin he's spread.

Still, considering the kind of fate Rich just saved me from, I know it's the least Carter can do.

Rich chops up the vegetables and cracks open two eggs. He places all the ingredients in a bowl and spins around to face me, the whisk moving steadily in his hand. "Speaking of help, how are things going with Carter? The last time you spoke, you were... concerned."

I snort. "That's an understatement. That journalist won't stop coming after us."

"After you," Rich corrects apologetically. "She doesn't actually want to hurt Carter. It seems like she's just trying to lure him back or something."

I sit up straighter. "Carter is not going to fall for it. He knows better now."

Because I know what we have is real, in spite of the vicious voice inside of my head telling me otherwise. The last thing I want is to give Lilian that kind of power over us, to make her feel like she's gained even one inch. Yet, a part of me can't help but wonder what Carter is going to do while I'm gone.

Or *who* he's going to do.

As soon as the thought crosses my mind, I banish it and gesture to the bowl in Rich's hand. "Why don't I whisk, and you focus on the chicken?"

Rich smiles. "You've got it. I know this isn't how you want to spend your time, but as soon as the storm clears, I'll take you back to Carter."

I don't want to think about how long that will take.

Or the kind of damage I'll find when I do make it back home.

Instead, Rich and I sit down to eat, and the lights flicker off. By the light of a candle, we sit across from each other, fierce winds howling outside. When it starts to rain, Rich and I carry the dishes to the sink, and he washes them while I dry them. There is a low whistling sound outside as Rich leads me up the stairs a short while later.

He leaves me in the middle of a large room with a terrace, holding a pile of clean sheets and pillows. When I crawl into bed at night, I keep going over my stay in the hospital, but everything is hazy, like I'm looking at it through a dirty camera lens.

I know I can't trust my memory, especially not with the amount of drugs in my system.

Rich wasn't in my room professing his love for me; he couldn't have been. Not when he only wants to help me and stay in business with Carter. For his mom's sake.

By the time sleep comes for me, I'm convinced it was all the medication making me hallucinate.

In the morning, I wake to the of Carter. Will I be able to connect with him today? Hopeful that the storm has passed, I take a quick shower and get dressed. When I head downstairs, Rich has made eggs, pancakes, and coffee.

I spend the day wandering around the house and checking my phone for a signal.

On the fourth day, the storm starts to clear up, and I find Rich by the balcony, peering out at the sky. "It looks like we're finally going to catch a break."

I nod and shove my hands into my pockets. "Thank you."

Rich spins around to face me, and there's a strange twinkle in his eyes. "Isabella, there's something I want to tell you, but I'm not sure if I should. It's about the reporter, and this article—"

I hold my hand up. "Whatever it is, I'll deal with it when I go home."

Rich hesitates, then nods. "I'm sorry that you have to go through this. I know you've got Carter, but if you ever need anything... *anything* at all, I want you to know that you can come to me."

I nod and lapse into silence.

A few hours later, Tristan and Paul pull up in a car outside Rich's house. In silence, I get into the car and twist to watch Rich lingering in the doorway, a crestfallen expression on his face. I push the expression out of my mind, lean back, and promptly fall asleep. When I stir awake, I have no idea where I am or how long it's been since I left the Donahue house.

All I know is that Carter is carrying me in his arms, the familiar smell of him washing over me.

I stare at him, taking in the days' old stubble peppered across his chin and the dark bags under his eyes. He looks like he hasn't slept or eaten in days, and my heart twists inside my chest as he carries me into our bedroom and sets me down on the mattress. As soon as he does, I sit on my hind legs and throw my arms around him.

Carter stiffens but doesn't pull away. "You never should've left the hospital, dove."

"I know, Carter. I'm sorry..."

He draws back, and his face is haggard, his eyes bloodshot. "Take off your clothes, and don't move."

Without waiting for a response, he disappears out of the room, and I hear his feet walking down the hallway. With trembling fingers, I hurriedly take off my clothes and drape myself over the bed, my heart thumping unsteadily the entire time. Carter returns without his shirt on, a belt in one hand and a toy in the other. He ties my hands together, pulls me up to my feet, and runs a single finger down my backside.

I shiver in anticipation and fear.

When the belt connects to my skin, I make a low noise in the back of my throat. Carter draws the belt back and hits me again, harder this time.

"Don't ever leave me like that again." Carter's breath is hot in my ears, and my legs tremble, but I don't move. "What the fuck were you thinking by running off like that? What the hell were you thinking by sending me those messages, huh?"

I swallow. "I didn't mean anything, I—"

"Who told you that you can speak?" Carter hisses into my ear. "I'm not done talking yet, dove. It seems like I still have a few lessons to teach you."

He places a hand on my back and forces me to lean forward so my arms are braced against the mattress and my ass juts into the air. Then a finger darts between my wet folds, and he places the strange object there. Wave after wave of desire builds up within me. As soon as he removes his hand, my muscles clench, and I exhale.

I hear Carter licking his fingers, and it sends another jolt through me.

Carter shoves two fingers into my mouth and growls. "Taste yourself, dove. You taste even better than you did before."

My tongue darts out to lick his fingers.

He pushes his fingers in further and makes another guttural sound in the back of his throat. Abruptly, he spins me around and frames my face in his hands, his grip a little too rough against my skin. "When I tell you that I'm not going to leave you and that I don't want to be with another fucking woman, I expect you to believe me. Got it?"

My eyes widen, and I nod.

Carter's eyes darken as he releases my face and pushes me down until I'm at eye level with his waist. He kicks his pants away so his erection springs free. "Let's see you put that mouth to good use, dove."

I lick my dry lips, and my mouth parts. Carter doesn't wait for a response as he thrusts forward. I take him all the way in, so he's at the back of my throat. My fingers itch to touch him, to soothe the turbulent emotions away, but I know I can't.

Not in the way I want to.

228

Not yet.

First, Carter needs to assert his control, and I know that having me on my hands and knees in front of him, tied up on a whim, is what it's going to take to make him feel better. I run my tongue over him, sucking and moaning as I do. Carter eases out and slams back into me, his deep growling making my entire skin erupt into goosebumps.

A part of me loves unhinged Carter, the kind who would fuck me just as wildly and passionately in the middle of a restaurant as he would in our bedroom. I cling to that thought as Carter winds his fingers through my hair and presses hard, sending little pinpricks of pain through my scalp. Suddenly, I feel something between my legs, and the device comes alive.

I falter and stop moving.

Carter's grip returns to my head. "I didn't tell you to stop, did I?"

I shake my head and whimper.

The device between my legs sends little pulses through me, the kind to make my blood turn molten. Sweat forms on the back of my neck and slides in rivulets down my skin. I lower my bound hands and press down on them. Then I tilt my head back and look up at Carter's enraptured face.

It's the face of the man I love, and it is glorious.

Every last scarred and flawed inch of him.

He tilts his head forward, looking directly at me, and his eyes narrow slightly. Then he pulls me back up to my feet. When Carter presses his lips to mine, he kisses me so thoroughly and so savagely that it leaves a little bruise. With a growl, Carter spins me around and pushes me onto the bed. I fall, and he advances, pausing to tie my hands to the bed on either side of me.

Another thrill of anticipation races through me.

Carter's eyes move steadily over my face while he spreads my legs open and ties them on either side of the posts. After he's done, he gives them an experimental tug and climbs off the bed. He retrieves a remote off the ground and switches it off, causing the little vibrations between my legs to stop. A whimper falls from my lips before I can stop it.

I don't recognize the expression on Carter's face as he climbs back onto the bed and settles in between my legs. He positions himself at my entrance and looks down at me. "Tell me you won't leave me."

"I won't leave you, sir." I gasp when he thrusts into me and places his hands on either side of my head. I wriggle, eager and desperate, wanting to touch any single part of him but unable to. "I'm not going anywhere."

Carter eases and slams back into me this time, and the bed creaks underneath us. "Fuck, dove. Do you have any idea what you do to me? Or how ready I was to go to war for you?"

Tears prick the back of my eyes. "No, sir."

Carter gives a few more thrusts, and his breathing grows labored. "You need to stay where I can see you, where I can feel you and touch you. Understand?"

I give him a tight nod.

Carter buries his face in the crook of my neck and lets out a wounded sound. I shift and try to draw him closer, but I'm completely at his mercy. All I can do is stay there while he pumps in and out of me at a fierce and animal-like pace, like he's trying to outrun something. The force of my orgasm rips through me, leaving me panting and gasping for breath.

I lift my hips off the mattress, and Carter slaps my ass with his bare hand, sending another jolt through me. When I lower myself back onto the bed, I pant, and spots dance in my field of vision. Carter shifts and moves down so he's at eye level with my dripping wet sex.

I lose all sense of time and reason when his tongue darts into my center.

Over and over, it moves, and I meet each thrust with one of my own. Eventually, Carter sinks his fingers into my waist and pins me to the mattress, so I'm unable to do anything. Another orgasm washes over me, and I call out his name like a prayer. Carter quickly replaces his tongue, his movements quick and precise as he seeks his own release.

When it finally comes, he looks up at the ceiling and empties himself into me.

As soon as Carter unties me, I pull him to me and bury my face against his chest. "I'm sorry. I didn't mean to make you worried."

Carter's fingers glide over my bare back. "I have no idea how Donahue managed to get to you in time, but I'm glad he did."

I stir and look back at him. "I'm not going to leave you for him, Carter."

Carter doesn't meet my gaze, but his hand stops moving. He gets up, pulls his clothes back on, and leaves the room. I have the sheets pulled up to my chin when he returns with a tray of food. He watches me eat in silence until I'm too tired to keep my eyes open.

My last thought before I fall asleep is how much I want to comfort him.

Because what kind of chance do we have if Carter still thinks I'm going to leave him?

CHAPTER THIRTY-ONE

Carter

I pry one eye open, the banging in the back of my skull still continuing. When I peel myself away from Isabella, who makes a low whimpering noise in the back of her throat, I force my other eye open. Then I realize that the banging isn't in my head.

It's coming from somewhere in the house.

With a growl, I pick my shorts up off the floor, tug them on, and take the stairs two at a time. Tristan barely has time to react before I grab him by the scruff of his neck and yank him inside. Frowning, I keep my grip around his neck, even as my cousin squirms and tries to push me off him. But we both know I'm stronger and a lot more capable than he is.

"You better have a damn good reason for waking me up," I say, pausing to pull him closer so my bare teeth are inches away from his gaze. "I'm fucking waiting."

"Loosen your grip first," Tristan replies with a pointed look. "That's no way to treat family."

I growl and give Tristan a firm shake. "If you want a warm greeting, that can be fucking arranged."

Tristan holds both hands up. "Jesus, what's got you so on edge? I thought you'd be happy to have Isabella back."

I shove Tristan away and run a hand over my face. "You need to learn to mind your own fucking business. Not everything has to be up for discussion."

Or subject to every prying eye and busybody in the family.

Especially not Tristan, of all people.

Because I still haven't forgotten what he almost cost me.

Sometimes, when I look at him, I can still see Isabella's face, contorted in fear and worry. Then I see her ripped clothes and staunch refusal to turn on Tristan, the man who put her in harm's way to begin with. With a slight shake of my head, I fold my arms over my bare chest and give Tristan an angry look. He draws himself up to his full height and clears his throat.

I half-expect him to pull his phone out and show me Lilian's damn article.

The one that has me more rattled than I'd like to admit.

"I wanted to confirm the news myself before I came to you," Tristan begins in a strange voice. "The Natoris and Philipses have banned together."

"I know that already. Talk faster, or I'm going to have one less cousin in the family."

Tristian frowns. "I'm getting to that. I've had a few guys keep their noses pressed to the ground. They're not making it a secret that they're working together, and they're throwing the full force of their support behind the mayor."

I let my arms fall to my sides, and I clench them into fists. "We already suspected as much. Again, this better not be why you woke me up."

Or Tristan is going to go home to Sam with a lot more than a black eye.

"They're opening up businesses on every block," Tristan continues as if he hasn't heard me. "Everywhere that you have a gambling hall or a club, or any business that's a front for guns or drugs, they're opening up the exact same thing across the street, only bigger and flashier."

I dig my nails into my palms. "What the fuck did you just say?"

Tristan takes a step forward and gives me a solemn look. "They're trying to move in on our turf, Carter. I saw the signs, and I did some digging."

I spin around, pick up the item closest to me, and hurl it with all my might. The flowers fall into a watery puddle on the floor, and the vase crashes against the wall opposite me, sending shards of glass in every direction. I pick up another item, an empty bowl with some kind of sickly sweet-smelling stuff, and throw it as well, but it misses the wall by a few inches.

"They knew exactly what they were doing when they chose those spots." I spin around to face Tristan and try to think past the roaring in my ears and the tight knots in my stomach. "This is a challenge. They think that because they're in with the mayor, they can pull shit like this, and no one is going to stop them."

Tristan blows out a breath. "We can't go after them. We don't have those kinds of resources, and you know it."

I give Tristan a menacing look. "That's not what I want to hear."

"I know, but I'm telling you anyway, and you can snap at me if you want. Hell, you can even take a swing or two if it'll make you feel better, but when you're done, we need to figure out a plan."

As far as I'm concerned, there isn't going to be a plan.

First, the Natoris came after me at the mayor's party, then they kidnapped Isabella to get back at me, and now they're targeting my businesses. If it weren't for the mess with the rest of the family, I'd already be out the door and on the hunt for blood. Unfortunately, because of my strenuous position as the head of the Blackthorne family, I know I need to think this through.

No matter how much the rage is telling me otherwise.

I can already see myself dragging all of them out, one by one, and taking them somewhere remote to teach them a lesson. I want to drag it out, make them suffer, and toy with them a little first.

Fuck me.

It's like they have a spy in our midst, feeding information to their unholy alliance and letting them know the worst moments to strike.

Both families are out for my blood, and I'll be damned if I let them get a whiff of me or anyone else I care about.

And if it means having to wage war against them, so be it.

"We need to call a family meeting," I realize darkly. "There's only one thing we can do."

The Natoris and Philipses have no idea what they've walked into, and I have every intention of making sure they have firsthand experience of what it's like to cross a Blackthorne.

No matter what it costs me.

Isabella

Anita points the spatula at me and pauses to retie the apron around her waist. "Are you sure you don't want anything to eat? You're looking a little pale."

I shake my head and offer her a small smile. "I'm okay. I'm not really hungry."

Anita grunts and pulls her spatula back. She reaches for the pan on the stove and pushes the eggs around. "I can't blame you. Hunkering down for long periods of time will do that to a person."

It had been days since Carter received news of the invasion.

Days since he woke me up and instructed me to pack a bag before whisking me away to his aunt's. Since then, it's been a steady stream of people coming in and out of the Blackthorne mansion, many of whom I recognized as Carter's relatives, a few I didn't. All of them, without fail, wore identical grim expressions and acted like soldiers preparing for a big battle.

In a way, I suppose they were.

Carter isn't going to let what they're doing go, even if it means having to call in every favor and pour all his time and focus into bringing the rival families down.

Crossing him once was a mistake he hasn't overlooked.

Coming after him a second time is borderline suicide, and I know for a fact that Carter has spent the past few days dreaming about ways to make them pay. While seeing the violent and volatile side of Carter still makes me uneasy, I know it comes with the territory.

I've always known.

Still, it doesn't stop a shiver from racing up my spine when the door to the dining room opens, and I catch a glimpse of Carter at the head of the table, his arms on either side of him, and a look of cold and calculating fury on his face. Everyone gathered around the table looks uneasy, like Carter is a volcano about to erupt, capable of destroying everyone in his wake.

When Tristan comes out of the room, I snap to attention and try to hold his gaze. He brushes past me on his way into the living room and stops in front of Sam. She is sitting on the couch in a pair of shorts and a T-shirt, with her hair piled on top of her head and a book in her lap. Tristan bends down to scoop up the book and gives Sam a sweet smile.

Sam gives him a smile in return, which makes some of the knots in my stomach unfurl.

Over the past few days, Sam and I haven't spoken much, and I've barely seen her because she's been sequestered somewhere in the house with Tristan, but on the rare occasions when I do see her, I'm relieved. She looks far happier than I've ever seen her, and she and Tristan have a certain ease around each other, the kind I recognize all too well.

She's falling hard for Carter's cousin, and I don't have the heart to tell her to get herself out.

Not that I think it's going to do her any good.

I can tell by the tender way Tristan brushes his hand against hers that it's too late. She laces her fingers through his, and the look on her face makes me unable to look away. A moment later, Tristan hands her the book back and presses a kiss to her forehead. Then he saunters off, and Sam follows him with her eyes. When she twists her head to the side, and our gazes meet, I know I should be embarrassed that I got caught watching them.

But I can't help myself.

It warms my heart to know that something beautiful and warm can grow in the middle of all this chaos.

Sam snaps her book shut and wanders over to us. "Anita, can I help you with anything?"

Anita is standing near the stove, chopping up some vegetables. "I'm fine, dear. Why don't you make yourself comfortable?"

"You have a beautiful home," Sam offers before coming to a stop on the other side of the counter. "Tristan told me about it, but I had no idea it would look like this."

Antia offers Sam a smile over her shoulders. "You're welcome to come by any time."

Sam averts her gaze and glances over at me. Guilt flashes across her face as she shoves both hands into the pockets of her shorts. "Tristan told me about what happened at the hospital. I'm sorry you had to go through that."

I nod. "It's a good thing Rich was there when he was."

Sam searches my face. "Yeah, I guess so, but it's still a lot to handle. You've been through a lot of shit lately, Isabella."

And as usual, Sam can't understand why I'm putting myself through this because of Carter.

I don't want to keep explaining us to her, not if she's determined to misunderstand.

Anita says something, and Sam leans over the counter to hear her better. I catch a glimpse of her smooth, unblemished back, and I breathe a sigh of relief. When Sam follows my gaze and sees where I'm looking, she leans away and stands up straighter.

"Tristan isn't like that," Sam says without looking at me. "He doesn't play mind games, and he wouldn't ever hurt me like that."

I swallow. "I know this is hard for you to understand, but it's not like that between Carter and me either. He really does love me, and I love him."

"I know you think you do—"

"I do," I interrupt, with a little more force than necessary. "Every couple has a different dynamic."

A part of me is glad her relationship with Tristan is a lot more normal and a lot less topsy-turvy, but the other part of me can't help but feel isolated. She's only been in his orbit for a few weeks, and she already seems much healthier and happier without any of the bullshit I had to endure.

And none of the scars that I carry as a reminder of what we've been through.

The other part of me is shocked to realize I'm jealous.

Sam deserves to be happy, but I can't help but wonder why the universe is rewarding her and punishing me. A year ago, before my life turned into a battlefield, and I didn't have the messy and complicated but incredible love of a man like Carter, I had no idea what I was supposed to do with my life.

Or who I was supposed to be.

I know that without Carter, I would've slaved away as Jacob Lacey's receptionist, dreaming of a better life for myself as I struggled to support my father. Now, I have everything I can ever want but no freedom to enjoy it. Even the thought of going outside makes me uneasy, given the number of near misses—and not-so-near misses—I've experienced lately.

At least in my previous life, I wasn't kept in a gilded cage.

Sam sighs. "I'm sorry I said that. That was out of line. I know that

Carter loves you. I guess I'm still trying to wrap my head around it all."

I clear my throat. "I know. Look, things with Carter and I haven't always been good, but it's different now."

Because we understand each other and have walked through fire for each other.

There is very little Carter wouldn't do for me.

And I won't ever stop defending him or trying to see the best in him.

We're a perfect match in that way.

Sam's hand darts out, and it settles on my shoulders. "Why don't we sit down and watch something in the living room? I think they're going to be a while."

I look from her hand to her face, trying to gauge her sincerity. "Sure."

Slowly, Sam withdraws her hand and offers Anita another uncertain smile. Then she leads the way to the living room, taking up her previous spot on the brown leather couch. I sit down next to her, leaving a wide berth of space between us. When I tuck my legs underneath me, Sam pats the couch for the remote and fishes it out from between the cushions. The TV above the fireplace mantlepiece blares to life, and she hastily presses down on the volume button.

"Sorry, I'm still learning how things work around here," Sam mutters, mostly to herself. With a grunt, she presses another button, and it launches a streaming app. "There we go. What do you feel like watching?"

I twist to face Sam and shrug. "Whatever you want."

Something glistens on her finger, and my hand darts down, spotting the ring on her index finger that catches the light and gives off an array of colors. Sam shifts and leans forward, and it's only then that I realize why she looks different. When I met her, Sam was struggling to make ends meet like me, and everything from the way she dressed to the way she looked reflected that.

Now, she looks every inch the part of Tristan's girlfriend with her designer clothes, manicured nails, and expensive-looking jewelry. With a frown, I turn away from her and fix my gaze on the TV, trying to understand the story unfolding before me. Unfortunately, the harder I try to keep my attention focused on the present, the more my mind wanders.

Suddenly, I wonder how different my life would've been if I'd rejected Carter's advances.

Would I be happier?

Safer?

I know that I've never felt more loved, and it's nice not to have the crushing weight of hospital bills on my shoulders, but I'm also painfully aware of what I've had to give up in order to get here.

And sometimes, it leaves me with a bad taste in the back of my mouth.

Halfway through the movie, unable to bear the viciousness of the voice in my head, I get up and wander over to the kitchen. After pouring myself a generous amount of iced tea, I eye Sam over the rim, and she looks happy and in her element. I finish the rest of my drink and rinse my glass before setting it on the counter to dry. A short while later, the door to the dining room bursts open, and Carter steps out, a few men following in his wake.

He doesn't look at me as he yanks the front door open and steps out.

A few of the Blackthorne men stay behind, including Tristan. I run to the window, push the curtain aside, and study Carter, an intimidating figure with his sleeves rolled up to his elbows and his button-down shirt tucked into a pair of trousers. He spins around to face his men, and our eyes collide.

For a while, he holds my gaze, but I see nothing of the man I love.

All too soon, he wheels around and gets into the back of Ernesto's SUV. When it peels away from the asphalt, I let the curtain slide back into place and take a step back. I keep walking backward until my back hits the wall. My pulse is a low thrumming in my veins, and I feel the restlessness rise within me.

Like I'm some kind of caged animal desperate to gnaw off her own leg.

Without pausing to give it any more thought, I turn around, and after making sure no one is looking at me, I take the stairs to the basement two at a time. Once I reach the bottom, I flick the lights on. There are a few cobwebs in the corner and a damp smell that makes my stomach roll, but otherwise, the place is empty... abandoned. I shove my hands into my pockets and plunge further into the basement until I reach the back door I discovered months ago when I was left to my own devices.

A hand touches my back, and I scream and throw my head backward.

Sam's muffled grunt brings me back to the present with a jolt, and my heart is racing unsteadily when I wheel around to face her. "What are you doing? You scared the shit out of me."

"I saw you sneak down here." Sam touches the bridge of her nose and winces. "I think you might have bruised my nose, but at least it's not broken."

I grimace. "I'm sorry. With everything that's been happening lately... you startled me."

Sam gingerly runs a hand over her face. "In retrospect, I shouldn't have done that. I don't know what I was thinking. Sorry, I startled you."

I clear my throat. "It's okay."

Sam reaches into her pocket and pulls out a set of keys with a pink ball attached to them. "My car is parked around the back. I think you're going to need it."

I pause a little longer than necessary. "I don't know what you're talking about."

"You've got the same look on your face that I used to get when I first met you," Sam whispers without looking at me. "I remember thinking that I wish someone would tell you that you can leave."

I stiffen. "I'm not trying to leave."

"Not forever," Sam adds hastily. "Just for some fresh air and to get your bearings. I know that being cooped up can take its toll."

"It can," I agree after a lengthy pause. "But I also know that Carter will lose his mind if I sneak out again, and I don't know how safe it is."

"What he doesn't know can't hurt him," Sam tells me, her gaze finally flicking over to mine. "I'll cover for you. Just use the car to take you wherever you want to go and don't be gone for too long."

My hand darts out, and I pause halfway. "You're going to get in trouble."

"Not if they don't know it was me." Sam's lips lift into a half smile. "Go before I change my mind."

I throw my arms around her and squeeze, the smell of freesias wafting up my nostrils. "Thank you."

"I don't want to be a bad friend," Sam whispers before releasing me. "I'm doing the best I can here."

"We both are." I take the keys from her outstretched hand and wrench the door open. "I'll be back soon."

Without looking back, I dart into the backyard, pressing my body to the fence as I do. True to her word, I spot Sam through the windows. She walks over to Tristan, who is closer to the window, and drapes an arm over his shoulders. She steers him away from me, and I can hear her voice spill out. A moment later, I dart across the yard and onto the neighbor's lush green lawn. When I'm sure no one has noticed I'm gone, I circle to the back of the house, where Sam's car is waiting.

The grey Mustang purrs to life when I turn the keys in the ignition.

I pick up a pair of Sam's sunglasses and a scarf, and I throw it over my head. Then, I hunch down in my seat and take the familiar route away from the suburbs and toward the city. Cars and people rush past me in both directions. My phone feels heavy in my purse, and I keep glancing at it, half-expecting Carter to find a way to climb out of it and into the car.

Before I know it, I'm pulling into the hospital parking lot, a sleek grey building that I know far too well by now. I back into a spot, kill the engine, and hurry out. My movements are slow and jerky, each step filled with more guilt than the last. Once the double doors spring open, the smell of disinfectant hits me first, followed quickly by the overpowering stench of sweat and an underlying metallic odor that immediately makes the hairs on the back of my neck rise.

My shoes squeak loudly against the linoleum floors.

No one looks at me as I drift past, like a ghost, and make a beeline for the elevators. On the fourth floor, the elevator doors ping open, and I spill out, making my way down the familiar blue hallway. Nurses and doctors rush past me, their faces tight with concern. When I reach my father's room, I'm surprised to see a large woman there, pulling a sheet over the mattress and humming to herself. With a frown, I step back and glance at the numbered plaque outside the door.

She fluffs up the pillow, straightens her back, and makes a low, startled noise when she sees me. Hastily, she yanks her earphones out and smooths out the edges of her pink shirt. "I'm so sorry. I didn't see you there. Can I help you with something?"

"Yeah, I must have the wrong room. I guess you guys moved him or something. I'm looking for my father—Alan Julius. Do you know where he is?"

The woman shifts from one foot to the other. "Ms. Julus, they were trying to get a hold of you. Why don't I go get a doctor?"

She tries to scurry past me, but I block the exit and draw myself up to my full height. "Why don't you just tell me where he is? You're already here, and I really can't stay long."

Her eyes dart back and forth listlessly. "Ms. Julis, I really can't—"

"Look, I know you're trying to do your job, but you have no idea what I've been through the past few months. I really need to see my father, *please.*"

I'm ashamed that my voice cracks a little toward the end.

But I'm desperate for some normalcy, for some semblance of my previous life.

The woman softens and leads me to the bed. She gives me an apologetic smile. "I'll be right back with the doctor."

I'm looking out the window when a young-looking doctor with blonde hair comes in. He tucks a clipboard underneath his arm and clears his throat. "Ms. Julus, we did try to get a hold of you, but we couldn't. Why don't you sit down?"

I wrench my gaze away from the park across the street. "I'd rather stand."

He clasps his hands behind his back. "Ms. Julus, I'm sorry to have to be the one to tell you this, but your father passed away earlier this morning."

The doctor says something else, but I can't hear him.

It feels like I'm underwater, and the world is spinning wildly out of focus. I take a step back, making a low noise that I don't recognize as the ground rises up to meet me.

I lose consciousness when my head hits the cold, hard floor.

Chapter Thirty-Two

Carter

I land another punch to the guy's stomach, and he wheezes. "This would go a lot faster and a lot easier if you just tell me what you know."

The man, who is bleeding profusely now, lifts his head up and gives me a cold look. With a frown, I punch him again, choosing the spots that I know are going to hurt the most. The metallic smell of blood wafts up my nostrils, and his heavy, uneasy breathing echoes inside my head, but I don't care.

All I care about is finding a direct link to the Natoris and the Philipses.

And I know this guy is the key because he is manning one of their soon-to-be stores.

I have half a mind to drag his ass back inside and put two bullets in his head just to make a point. But I know that the satisfaction from that will be short-lived, and it won't solve my more immediate problem. Given how bold and audacious both families are becoming, I know the only way to resolve this is to deal with them personally.

The Natoris and the Philipses need to get the message from me directly.

Otherwise, they are never going to understand who they are dealing with.

Mayor Hughes has probably given them nothing but a bunch of pretty words and empty promises. As soon as I find them, I have every intention of making sure they know exactly what they've started. With a shake of my head, I pause, my knuckles throbbing, and give the guy another menacing look. Then I grab him by the scruff of his neck and hoist him off the ground.

He kicks his legs out, and his pitiful whimpers fill the dark, empty alley, but they have no effect on me.

Because when I look at him, I see everything I love, including Isabella, being threatened.

I wrap my fingers around his throat and squeeze. "I'm going to give you one more chance unless you want to die a slow and painful death."

The guy makes a gurgling sound and says nothing.

I shrug and press harder. "Just remember that when your blood and brains are scattered everywhere."

Abruptly, I release the guy, and he falls into a heap. He claws at his throat and gasps for breath when I take the gun out of the waistband of my pants and point it directly at him. His eyes widen, and he scrambles backward, fear plainly streaking across his face. Hastily, he throws both hands up in the air and backs up so his back is pressed against the wall.

"I'm not an unreasonable man," I tell him calmly. "You've got twenty seconds to pray to whatever God you believe in."

The man starts to cry, the tears falling freely down his face. I roll my shoulders and start counting backward. When I reach five, he throws himself at my feet and links his fingers together.

"I'll tell you what you want to know."

"Talk faster."

He straightens up and uses the back of his hand to wipe away the snot and blood. "They have a safe house not too far from here. I can send you the address."

I keep one hand on the gun, and the other reaches into my pocket. When I hand him the phone, I press my weapon to the side of his head. "Type it into the map, and if you try anything funny, I'm going after your family next."

His fingers tremble as he types in the address. After he hands it back to me, I send the address to Ernesto. Then I wait for the man to stop shaking before I pull him up to his feet. "At least try to die with some dignity."

Before he can respond, I aim the gun at the center of his forehead and pull the trigger. His mouth forms a surprised "O". Seconds later, he crumples into a heap on the ground, blood already pooling underneath him. I take a step back and let out a low whistle. Out of the shadows, a few members of my family emerge and begin to drag his body away.

That's one less loose end for me to take care of.

Outside Ernesto's SUV, I pause to wipe my bloodied knuckles. "Did you get the address?"

"It's nearby," Ernesto replies before holding the door open. "A few more Blackthornes are going to meet us there."

I nod. "Good."

In the car, I unscrew the cap from a bottle of water with my teeth and spit it out. Then I guzzle down the entire bottle, but my throat still feels dry.

I need something stronger, but I also want to stay focused for what's about to come next.

I can't afford to give them a single inch if I want my message to be clear.

I'm halfway through my second bottle when I fish my phone out of my pocket and call Tristan. He doesn't answer until the last ring, sounding breathless and a little irritated. "How's it going?"

"I've got an address. Going to check on it now. How are things on your end?"

"Fine."

"Tell Isabella I'll be home soon," I reply before switching the phone to my other ear. "In the meantime, she and Sam can order whatever they want and indulge however they want, my treat."

Tristan pauses, and his voice sounds strange. "Okay, sure. I'll let them know."

I see the building in the distance, and I hang up. Ernesto screeches to a halt, but I'm out of the car before he's come to a complete stop. I adjust the jacket around me and shove both hands into my pockets. Out of the corner of my eye, I see more and more of my men appear, emerging from the shadows and out of similar SUVs. All of them fall into step behind me as we climb the stairs.

We take down the two uniformed security guards before they realize what's happening.

Once we're inside the building, I take down two more men and catch one before he hits the floor. As soon as I make sure none of them have sounded the alarm, I exchange a grim look with the rest of the Blackthorne men. Blood pools underneath our feet and stains the carpets and the hardwood floors. Overhead, the chandeliers glisten and sparkle, casting tiny particles of light on the walls.

We pile into the elevator, and I tap my foot impatiently.

On the second floor, we exit and head straight for the Philipses' men. They barely have time to take out their guns before we've gunned down two more. One of them dives behind a table, and I do the same, waiting for the perfect moment to strike. The Blackthorne men have taken out a few more when I roll out from behind the table and reach for my knife.

It sails through the air and pierces a man's chest.

His hands fly to the wound, and he falls backward with a thud. Behind the closed door, I hear a crash and a loud cacophony of voices. Grimly, I pull my knife from the bleeding man's chest and give him a dismissive look. Then I wipe the blood on the carpet beneath his feet and squint at the flickering lights overhead. Suddenly, the lights flicker off, and I hear one of my men curse.

I dive behind the nearest table and flatten my back, heart hammering uneasily inside my chest.

Moments later, the door to the apartment bangs open, and more of the Philipses' and the Natoris' men pour out, all of them armed and thirsty for blood. I hear a clash of bodies and grunts. Then, a few more gunshots go off, and I struggle to make out anything in the darkness. Unfortunately, I can barely see more than two feet in front of me when I roll myself into a ball, away from the noise of the fighting.

When I jump to my feet, I realize, by the dim light of the moon, that I'm in the apartment.

A bullet goes sailing past my ear and nicks it.

I touch two fingers to my skin, and they come up wet and sticky. I fire a few shots into the dark and hear the familiar thumps. Half-blinded, I creep forward with my back pressed against the wall. I hear the heavy breathing seconds before I'm knocked to the ground. Spots dance in my field of vision as I jump back onto my feet and growl.

I can hear his despair, his desperation.

I close my fingers around my knife, and my hand darts out. I feel it sliding into his skin, and I grunt. Before the body hits the ground, the lights flicker back on. Little by little, my vision returns, and I recognize the men around me as my own. Still, there is a group of armed men forming a half-circle around the head of the Philips family.

His white skin glistens with sweat, and he looks a little green around the edges.

My hand itches with the urge to put a bullet between his eyes. "Give me one good reason why I shouldn't kill you right now."

"Because it's only going to make things worse," Floyd Philips responds before straightening his back. "You're a smart man, Carter. I know you're going to make the right decision."

I point my gun at him and raise an eyebrow. "I wasn't aware we were on a first-name basis, Floyd. How does your wife, Janine, feel about that?"

Floyd's eyes tighten around the edges. "The same way I imagine Isabella feels."

"Keep her fucking name out of your mouth," I snap, taking a step closer. I don't care that I have several guns pointed directly at me. All of them would be a little too happy to turn me into their pin cushion, but I'm not going to give them the satisfaction.

Even though I've never dealt with Floyd personally, I know he's not stupid.

Killing me is as good as announcing an all-out war on the Blackthornes.

They are, however, trying to take over our territory, not make an enemy of us.

"It seems we're at an impasse," Floyd continues, in the same annoying tone of voice. He gestures to his men, and a few of them step back, allowing him to move forward and giving me my first real glimpse of the man. He's a lot shorter than I expected, and his hair is almost completely gone. Still, there's no mistaking the tightness around his mouth or the powerful build underneath his custom-made suit.

Floyd Philips doesn't look like much.

But I'll be damned if I underestimate a man of his power and influence.

"You could let us walk out of here," Floyd suggests, leaving a wide berth of space between us. "You've made your point, Carter. Haven't you killed enough men for that?"

"This doesn't end until you crawl back into whatever fucking cave you crawled out of," I tell him with a frown. "If you know anything about the Blackthornes, it's that we don't kindly to threats or invaders."

Or being made fools of. And Floyd is treading on very thin and dangerous ice.

Not that I care.

I'd sooner put a bullet through his head than let him walk out of here, but I know I have to be smart—for my family and the sake of the Blackthorne empire.

And for Isabella above all else.

The shrill ringing of a phone interrupts whatever Floyd is about to say next. He takes his cell out of the pocket of his trousers and presses it to his ear. "This better be good."

A long moment passes, and Floyd's entire expression changes. "Visting her father at the hospital? So, you've got eyes on Isabella Julus right now, do you?"

Ice settles in my veins.

Goddamn it, Isabella. What have you done now?

Floyd ends the call and shoves his phone back into his pocket. He stands up straighter and gives me a pointed look. "You're going to let us go now; otherwise, you can kiss your little whore goodbye."

I clench my free hand into a fist. "Don't you fucking touch her."

"You're not in a position to call the shots around here."

"Or I can just shoot you right now. Then go after your men," I suggest, barely keeping myself from lunging at him and ripping him apart with my bare hands. "I like my plan better."

A flicker of fear moves over Floyd's face. "You could, but something tells me you won't. For the sake of your precious *Isabella*."

I cross over to him in a few strides, and before his men have any chance of reacting, I have my knife pressed to his throat. "One wrong move, and I'll end him."

All of them exchange panicked looks.

"You don't threaten me," I say into Floyd's ear. "Or my family. You got that, you piece of shit?"

Floyd swallows and says nothing. "My men have instructions to go after the girl if they don't hear back from me in ten minutes."

I spin Floyd around so he's looking at me directly. "I want you to look at me and see the murder in my eyes. If you ever come near my empire or anyone I love again, I'll make you beg for mercy."

Floyd's face pales, but he says nothing.

Slowly, I release Floyd, and he scurries away from me. When I hear him mutter something unflattering about Isabella underneath his breath, I tap his shoulder. He spins around, his eyebrows knitted together, and his head snaps back from the impact of my punch. My knuckles are sore, and blood drips down his nose and onto the hardwood floors beneath our feet, but I don't care.

I take a few steps back and give the other men a pointed look. "This isn't over."

Reluctantly, we back out of the room, keeping our eyes on them the entire time. We walk backward, guns still aimed at them, until we reach the elevator. In the elevator, I try dialing Tristan, but I can't get through to him. Cursing, I barely keep from throwing my phone against the wall. Instead, I nearly punch a hole in the elevator wall because I can only see red.

I can't tell if I'm madder at Floyd Philips or Isabella.

I'm dimly aware of getting back into Ernesto's SUV and the car speeding through traffic. It screeches and swerves, but I don't look up from my screen. I send Tristan one angry message after the other, but he's still not answering. Eventually, I hurl my phone at the window closest to me, and it bounces back and lands unharmed on the leather seat next to me.

After pouring myself a generous amount of whiskey, I press my face into the cool glass.

During the ride to the hospital, I picture all the ways I'm going to punish Isabella.

And it immediately sends red-hot desire racing through me. I grip my glass a little tighter than necessary and watch the world outside, a blur of shapes and colors that rush past the SUV. When the hospital looms in the distance, the large metal building bathed in the pale glow of the moon, my stomach clenches.

It lurches and dips when Ernesto screeches to a halt, and I hurry out of the car.

I push my way through the double doors and past the main desk, filled with men and women in uniform and a slew of phones that won't stop ringing. In the elevator, I have to dig my nails into my palms to keep from doing something stupid. When the doors ping open on the floor where Isabella's dad is being kept, I race out.

I shove my way past doctors and nurses in scrubs who give me angry looks on the way past.

None of it stops me until I reach the room. There, I find Isabella on the bed, with the cover drawn up to her chin and an IV drip in her vein. As soon as I register what I'm seeing, some of the anger leaves my body, and I duck my head outside, my eyes darting up and down the hallway. I gesture to a nurse in pink scrubs, and she hurries over, her ponytail swishing back and forth.

"What the fuck happened to my girlfriend? Why is she in a hospital bed, and why wasn't I informed?"

"Mr. Blackthorne, I have no idea why they didn't call you," she stutters as she takes a few steps back. "Ms. Julis came in, and she was really agitated and looking for her father. When she couldn't find him, the doctor was paged."

I take a menacing step toward the nurse, who shrinks back and presses against the wall. "Where the fuck is Alan Julis? Why was he moved without our knowledge?"

It's no wonder Isabella has lost consciousness.

He's the only family she has left, and not knowing where he is must've taken a toll on her. I soften toward Isabella as I drift closer to her side, and she stirs awake. When she sees me, her eyes widen and sharpen into focus. Then she bursts into tears and presses her forehead against my chest.

"What happened, dove? Give me a name, and I'll make them pay."

Isabella only cries harder. "You can't fix this, Carter. I know you want to, but you can't. No one can."

I draw back and frame her face in my hands. "You won't know unless you tell me. I take care of you, don't I? Tell me what happened, and I'll make it better."

Isabella's expression is crestfallen when she licks her dry lips. "I thought they moved him, then I thought maybe the Natoris or the Philipses got to him, but he... my father is..."

I grip her shoulders tighter. "Tell me."

"He's dead," Isabella says, her voice barely above a whisper. "He died this morning, and they couldn't get a hold of me because of my stupid cell service. He died alone, surrounded by strangers, and I wasn't there for him because of my goddamn phone."

I hold her tighter and run my fingers down the length of her back. "It's not your fault, dove. It's not like you knew this was going to happen."

Isabella shudders and pulls back to look at me. "I should've known. He's my father. After everything he's done for me... I just left him all alone in this hospital."

My chest gives an odd little twinge as I place my hand on either side of her shoulders. "You can't blame yourself—"

"Yes, I can fucking can." Isabella shoves my hands away and rips the IV out of her arm. Little droplets of blood spray the bed, and some of it lands on her nose. But she doesn't seem to care. Even with a hospital gown thrown over her clothes and her hair a wild mess on top of her head, she's still the most beautiful woman I've ever seen.

Like some kind of fierce avenging angel, ready to swoop down and teach the mortals a lesson.

I've never loved her more than in that moment. Nor have I ever been more worried about her.

Over the past few months, I've seen all kinds of sides to her, everything from hungry and frustrated to frightened and determined and wildly horny, but I've never seen Isabella like this. It's almost as if she's on the verge of combusting, intent on destroying everything in her path, and there's nothing I can do to help her.

Not a damn fucking thing.

I wish I could take away her pain.

But cancer isn't an enemy I can hunt down or bring to justice. No matter how much I want to.

"Do you have any idea how any of this feels?" She runs her fingers through her hair and lets out a low, wounded sound. "I dropped out of school to take care of him. He was my whole world, and without him, I... Now, he's gone, and I wasn't here. I should've been here."

"Dove—"

"*I should've been here*," Isabella repeats a little more forcefully. She runs a hand down her face, the top right corner of her eyes twitching. "I have no excuse for not being here, and his last memory of me is going to be me looking over my shoulder, waiting for the other shoe to drop."

I step out from behind the bed and approach Isabella slowly and carefully as if she's some kind of wounded animal. I have no idea how she will react to my proximity, or if she even wants it, but since I can't give her what she really craves, I know this is the next best thing.

Abruptly, she reaches for the nearest item, an empty vase, and hurls it at the wall. Isabella winces when it shatters on impact, sending shards of glass everywhere. She doesn't even seem to mind that some of it has nicked her, and now she's bleeding in several areas. With a frown, I cover the rest of the distance between us and place my arms around her.

She struggles and beats against my chest. "Let me go! I don't deserve to be comforted."

"I don't care if you think you don't because the truth is you do. After everything you've been through and everything you did to take care of your father. Do you have any idea how fucking lucky he was?"

Isabella shudders and goes limp against me. "No, he wasn't. *I* could've done better. Instead, I put him in danger, and I couldn't even be there to check on him."

I grip her shoulders tighter and pull back to look at her. "Listen to me, Isabella. *None* of this is your fault. Lacey was a piece of shit, and he's the one who used your father against you. Everyone else just took a page out of his book, and that's shitty, but that's hardly your fault. You were trying to make the best out of a bad situation."

Isabella searches my face, and her lower lip trembles. "He died alone, Carter."

"He wasn't alone," I maintain in a softer voice. "He *knew* you loved him. He felt it *every time* you were here, and I'm sure that he never once thought that you were doing a bad job."

Isabella sniffs, and hot tears slide down her cheeks, each one sending a twinge of pain straight through my core. "I don't know what I'm supposed to do now, Carter. He was the only family I had left, and I... I don't know what I'm meant to be doing."

"You're meant to grieve, dove," I tell her as gently as possible. "You're not supposed to have all the answers right now. You've barely even had a chance to process any of this."

Isabella's eyes widen. "I haven't told the hospital what I want to do... and the funeral arrangements. Am I even allowed to have a funeral?"

"What do you mean are you allowed? Of course, you're fucking allowed. We're going to give a funeral fit for a fucking king, and anyone who doesn't like that can go screw themselves."

Isabella uses the back of her hand to brush the tears away. "You said we're supposed to be hunkering down, not drawing attention to ourselves."

I pull her into my arms and bury my face in her hair. "There's certain protocol that needs to be followed, dove. When there's a death in warring families, a temporary cease-fire is called. It doesn't last long, but it'll be enough for your father."

She swallows. "But he… he wasn't family—"

"He was *your* family," I interrupt, with a little more force than necessary. "Which means he was *my* family, too. That's all that matters."

Isabella stirs and pulls back to look at me. "I'm sorry."

I raise an eyebrow. "What for?"

"For yelling at you and shoving you away earlier. I didn't mean to, I—"

I press a finger to her lips. "I'm not going to punish you for that, dove. You just lost your father. You're allowed a little leeway."

A flicker of surprise moves across Isabella's face. "Really?"

"Don't get too used to it. If the circumstances were different, I'd have you on my knee and that tight and sweet little ass of yours at my mercy."

She hiccups and swallows. "Thank you."

"Sit down. I'm going to go get us some food, and when I get back, you and I are going to have a serious talk about your habit of sneaking out."

Without waiting for a response, I spin on my heels and leave the room. In the cafeteria, I run into a few of my cousins, and they all nod in my general direction. After grabbing two sandwiches, a plastic container of salad, and a couple of sodas, I stuff them into a plastic bag. On my way back upstairs, I pass a floral shop, the sickly sweet smell of flowers making my stomach churn.

Exhaling, I step into the shop and make a vague hand gesture. "My girlfriend's father just died. I don't know what's appropriate for a case like this."

The red-haired woman behind the counter glances up and does a double take. She draws her bottom lip between her teeth and chews on it. A thoughtful expression crosses her face as she pushes her stool back and stands up. In silence, she prepares a bouquet of somber, darker-colored flowers and hands it to me. After paying, I step outside and catch the confused looks on my cousins' faces.

I don't blame them.

I have no idea what the fuck I'm doing either or how to help Isabella mourn her father properly.

Hell, I'm not even sure how much longer we can stay in the hospital without becoming prime targets for the Philipses and Natoris. But I know that I don't want to rush her through this.

Not after everything she's been through.

When I make it back to Isabella's room, she's washed her face and is perched on the edge of the bed. She is startled when she sees the flowers and keeps glancing from my face to the bouquet.

"Who are they for?"

"For you," I reply, thrusting them out in front of me. "You did tell me that you like flowers."

"I didn't think you were listening." Isabella buries her face and inhales, looking far more vulnerable and youthful than I've ever seen her. "You've never brought me flowers before."

"You deserve whatever the fuck your heart desires, dove," I tell her before taking a few steps back. I set the food down on the table and shove one hand into my pocket. Using my free hand, I make a vague hand gesture. "Look, I'm not good at the hearts and flowers thing. Even before the family business, it's just not the kind of person I am, but I want you to know you're not alone."

Isabella blinks and gives me a confused look. "What do you mean?"

"I can't bring your father back, dove," I continue in a whisper-soft voice. "And it's not because I don't want to. Believe me, if there was anything I could do, it would be done."

And I wouldn't hesitate either.

Isabella is worth everything I own and everything I'll ever own.

Isabella lowers the flowers and gives me a teary smile. "Thank you."

She slips her hand through mine and leads me out of the room. I drape an arm around her waist and use my other hand to hold the bag of food. In the elevator, she tucks herself into my side, and I press a kiss to the side of her head. Through the glass doors, I see Ernesto pacing, the SUV parked dangerously close to the curb, and lines of worry written all over his face.

His expression turns relieved when he sees us. "I was about to call in the cavalry."

"Take us to Anita's," I say without looking at him. In the car, Isabella snuggles up to me and promptly falls asleep. Ernesto holds my gaze in the rearview mirror and gives the flowers a pointed look. I shift so Isabella's head is in my lap, and she stretches her legs out on the rest of the seat.

"Her father passed away this morning," I whisper, pausing to brush her hair out of her face. "It's a good thing we got here when we did. If the Philipses or the Natoris had gotten a hold of her in this condition…"

"Poor thing." Ernest lets out a deep and heavy sigh. "May his soul rest in peace."

The rest of the car ride is spent in silence.

When we pull up outside Anita's house, Tristan is already waiting for me outside. He jumps to his feet when I come out, cradling Isabella against my chest. I give him a meaningful look on my way past, and he hangs his head in shame. Voices follow me up the stairs to my room, but I ignore them all. Once I set Isabella down on the mattress, I rummage through a dresser drawer and pull out the box.

Isabella stirs awake after I've slid the ring onto her finger. She gasps and scrambles to sit up. "What is this?"

"I've been thinking about this for a while. I didn't plan on asking you like this, dove, but I figured this is as good a moment as any."

Isabella's mouth moves, but no words come. Finally, she clears her throat and lifts her gaze up to mine. "Is this what I think it is?"

"You're not alone, dove." I take her hands in mine and look into her eyes. "I'm here, and I want to be your family."

And I never want her to feel alone again.

Not so long as I was alive.

Isabella's eyes fill with tears. "Carter, I... I love you. Of course, I want to marry you, but you know you don't have to ask me because of what I said earlier."

I shake my head. "That's not why I'm asking you. I want you to be my wife, Isabella Julis."

Isabella throws her arms around me and presses her forehead to mine. "In that case, I can't wait to be married to you, Carter Blackthorne."

CHAPTER THIRTY-THREE

Carter

"What the fuck do you want?" I fold my arms over my chest and give Tristan a menacing look. "Didn't I tell you that I don't want to be bothered?"

Tristan exhales and doesn't break our gaze. "I know what you said, but I figured you weren't being serious. You're the one who went after the Philipses and Natoris, remember?"

I growl. "What's your point?"

"You can't decide to start a war and leave before we've even begun to strategize." Tristan steps into the house and kicks the door shut behind him. "It doesn't work like that, Carter. You have to finish what you started. You're the fucking head of the Blackthorne family, and you need to act like it."

I have Tristan shoved against the wall before the words finish leaving his lips. Then I draw my hand back and land a punch to my cousin's jaw. He doesn't flinch, and he doesn't even acknowledge the hit, but I do see the tears burning in his eyes, and it gives me a slight sense of satisfaction. With a small noise of disgust, I shove Tristan away and take a step back.

"I am the head of the Blackthorne family, and I don't answer to you."

Tristan rubbed his jaw. "No, but you do answer to the rest of the family, or have you forgotten about them? They need you, Carter."

"Not as much as Isabella needs me," I respond coldly. "Or have you forgotten that she's just lost her father?"

She's spent the past week curled up on the bed, reliving old memories and crying to herself. No matter what I do, I can't seem to pull her out of her misery, and I know that all my usual tactics won't work. Not when it comes to grief. Isabella needs to be able to mourn her father properly, and I want to give her all of that and more.

I want to be the one to pull her out of the dark hole she's crawled into.

Isabella has already pulled me out of the darkness once, so it's the least I can do. Without her, I still would've been the same man obsessing over finding a replacement for Brooke and taking my anger out on anyone and everyone who got in my way.

Before her, there was plenty I felt I had to do to atone for failing. Now, I'm determined not to make the same mistakes.

I refuse.

But I need Tristan and everyone else to back the fuck off before I give them something else to worry about. In spite of their insistence, all their pleas have fallen on deaf ears. Tristan has been handling things in my stead, and I know my cousin is more than up to the task. While I know it isn't fair to my family to leave them hanging in their hour of need, I also know they can handle themselves.

Isabella, on the other hand, has no one else.

And I'll be damned if I let that drive her into the arms of Donahue or anyone else.

She is mine, and she has everything she needs right here, and I'm going to do whatever I need to do in order to make sure she knows it.

Tristan shakes his head. "I haven't forgotten, Carter, but—"

"Then you have no reason to be here." I walk over to the front door and wrench it open. "I told you to hold down the fort while I take care of things here. So do your fucking job and, while you're at it, make sure Lilian doesn't bother either of us, or you're going to have another problem on your hands."

Without waiting for a response, I slam the door shut in his face and hurry up the stairs. Isabella is still sleeping when I enter the room and linger in the doorway. I watch the even rise and fall of her chest and the vulnerable look on her face, and some of the ice in my veins softens. With a smile, I enter the room and rummage through the drawer.

I'm tying Isabella's arms up on either side of her when she stirs awake. She blinks, her hair a tangled mess around her face, and the color in her cheeks is heightened. "What's going on?"

"Shh, just enjoy, dove. You don't have to do anything else," I murmur into her skin. Slowly, I toss away the nightgown I've peeled off her body. When I throw it over my shoulders, Isabella shifts, and her eyes soften again. I kneel on the bed in front of her and dig my nails into her waist.

"I'm the only one who can make you feel this good, dove," I whisper as I press hot, open-mouthed kisses across her thighs. I kiss my way up to her center and push her legs open. "When you're with me, nothing else matters. Not the sadness, not the war, and not that fucking useless journalist, do you understand?"

Isabella swallows and nods.

I pinch her soft skin between my fingers. "I can't hear you."

Isabella clears her throat, but it still comes out sounding husky and hoarse. "Yes, sir."

With a smirk, I lower my head so it's at eye level with her dripping wet center. I lick a path up, and she bucks underneath me, her hips rising off the mattress. Frowning, I give her leg a firm slap, and she jolts at the contact. Before she can say anything, I use two fingers to push aside her wet folds and bury my tongue into her pussy.

Isabella starts moaning my name and pulling against her restraints.

I know she wants to feel closer to me, to run her fingers over my skin, but I need her at my mercy.

Because I want her to understand what we have between us.

She needs to see that our bond is unbreakable and that even in her darkest hour, I'm not going anywhere.

I worship Isabella with my tongue, pushing her closer and closer to the edge of oblivion. She tries to wrap her legs around my head, but I stop my movements. When I pull back to give her a pointed look, she is panting, and her mouth is half open. I twitch with the urge to bury myself in her.

To give us both the release we so desperately need.

But I know it's too soon.

She can't find her release, not yet. Not until I've chased away the shadows in her eyes and made her forget about everything outside that door. I tug on her restraints and make them tighter, smiling at her little hiss of pain. Then, I lower myself back onto the mattress and bury my head in between her legs. She tastes fantastic, a strange mixture of sweet and sour that has the blood roaring in my veins.

I don't know how much longer I can wait, especially when she's begging me now.

I love hearing the filthy things she's telling me.

And I love that she adds a "sir" to the end of every sentence, with a moan that makes me plunge my tongue in further. Once Isabella crawls closer to the edge of release, I stop and kiss her. I kiss her thoroughly, letting her taste herself on my tongue. When I bite down on her bottom lip, she whimpers, and I taste her blood. Then I bury my head in her neck, and I press hot kisses there.

I wait until some of the haze of desire clears, and I undo her restraints.

Isabella is staring at the ceiling and panting, a slight furrow between her brows.

I hoist her up and set her down on a chair I've pulled out. After giving her another searing kiss, during which she tries to deepen it, I step back. She watches me through hooded eyes as I pull her back to her feet. I am impatient and eager as I tie her hands to the back of the chair so her back is facing me, and she's on all fours and entirely at my mercy.

"I want to see you."

I slap her ass. "Don't forget who's in charge here, dove. I'm the one who gets to call the shots."

Isabella whimpers and twists her head to face me. I push her head back to the front and step out of my boxers. Quickly and with a little more impatience than usual, I rummage through the drawer and pull out a toy. Isabella is dripping wet and muttering to herself when I return. As soon as I insert the toy between her legs, she jerks.

"What is that?"

I press my mouth to her ear, and she shivers. "Relax and enjoy."

She rocks back and forth against the toy, eager for more friction, and I touch myself. I move my fingers up and down my cock steadily, already eager for the feel of her mouth wrapped around my center. Isabella's entire body shakes as her orgasm rips through her, and she cries out. I don't wait for her to catch her breath when I remove the toy and position myself behind her.

In one quick thrust, I am inside of her.

I thrust in further, filling her all the way to the hilt.

Isabella wriggles and tries to take more of me. "Please, Carter. *Please*."

I place my hands on her back and ease out. "That's not my name."

"Please, sir," Isabella begs breathlessly. "I need you."

I slam back into her. "How much do you need me?"

"More than anything," Isabella gasps out. "I need you to fuck me, sir."

I continue to ease in and out of her, building up momentum. I picture myself fucking away the memory of Donahue and any other men who's ever laid hands on her. Then I see myself fucking away her pain and all the hurt she's feeling because of the Lilian situation.

Suddenly, I am moving with uncontrolled abandon, her walls clenching around me and the sweet smell of her wafting up my nostrils. Isabella meets each thrust with one of her own, and I am no longer surprised by her appetite, by her endless desire for me.

Because I know it doesn't compare to mine.

I need to brand her, to claim every last part of her, so everyone knows that we belong to each other.

When I sink my nails into her hips, Isabella throws her head back and moans. She wriggles her hips sideways until I grip her harder. "Didn't I say that I'm the one calling the shots?"

"But I'm so close…"

"Hold it," I growl into her ear. The blood is still roaring in my ears, but they're also ringing now, and I know I can't hold on for much longer. Abruptly, I untie Isabella, and she twists her arms over her head. With a grunt, I keep her bent over the chair and ram into her.

Repeatedly.

And with so much force that I feel like the chair is going to break.

She winds her fingers through my hair and tugs. Dual waves of pain and pleasure ricochet through me.

I pin her arms behind her back. "You're mine, dove. I am not going to lose you to anyone or anything else. Do you understand?"

"Fuck, Carter. Fuck."

"Don't come yet." I use my free hand to slap her ass again, hard enough to leave a mark. "Don't fucking come until I tell you to."

I give a few more quick thrusts and sink my teeth into her neck. I hear her sharp intake of breath, and her entire body shivers and explodes, the force of her orgasm ripping through her. She pants and writhes against me, and soon, my own release follows, and I can only see white. When I come down from my high, Isabella is curled against me and humming contentedly.

I drape an arm around her and whisper into her ear. "I know you miss your dad. If there was anything I could do to bring him back or take the pain away, you know I fucking would."

Isabella tilts her head back and looks up at me. "I know you would."

I press a kiss to her forehead and linger.

It isn't long before she drifts off to sleep and starts making low whimpering noises. Reluctantly, I slip out of bed and bend over to pick up my clothes. After getting dressed, I glance at Isabella's sleeping form over my shoulders, and something in my chest tightens. In nothing but the sheets and my ring on her finger, she is the most alluring sight I've ever seen.

And I want to climb back into bed and forget about reality.

But I have a fucking war to worry about.

And a journalist who needs to be taken care of.

Isabella

I sit up, my heart hammering unsteadily against my chest, and feel for Carter in the darkness. When I discover he's not next to me, I throw myself back onto the mattress and bring a hand to my forehead. Then I run a hand over my face and blow out a breath. My breathing is still labored and uneven when I pick up my phone and see the message from Carter.

Briefly, I consider going over to Anita's, but I know I'm not ready to face her yet.

I'm not ready to face anyone or anything.

Instead, I just want to stay in our room where I can sit in silence and miss my father. The aching hole in my chest feels vast and endless, especially when I scroll through the pictures on my phone and find the last picture my father and I took together. It was a year after he was admitted to the hospital, and in the picture, he was smiling, his hair parted to the side, and his bright eyes full of humor and hope. I don't even recognize the me sitting next to him in a wrinkled shirt, with her hair pulled back and dark circles under her eyes.

It's the last picture I have of the two of us, and it makes tears spring to my eyes.

Because I still have no idea how I got here. Or why it had to happen to my dad, of all people.

He didn't deserve to die alone in a hospital bed.

Before I know it, I wrap my arms around myself and let the tears fall freely, not knowing what else to do with myself. Through my blurred vision, I trace the picture on my phone and try to imagine something different. Finally, I think of my father in heaven, watching over me, with my mom by his side.

Together, the two of them are happy and at peace.

The thought eases some of the knots in my stomach, and my lungs no longer burn when I sit up straighter. Slowly, I push my hair out of my face and swing my legs over the side of the bed. Naked, I walk into the bathroom and set the phone down on the counter. In the mirror, I avoid looking at myself directly while I wait for the water to heat up. Once steam fills the bathroom, I pull the curtain aside and step in, soft music filling the silence around me.

My tears mix with the water as I place my hands on either side of the shower wall and lower my head.

I don't hear Carter come in since I'm so lost in my own grief. I don't feel him until he gets into the shower, his lean and muscled body pressing against mine. Wordlessly, he takes the bar of soap out of my hands and runs it over my flushed skin. I go still as he moves his hand slowly, languidly, as if we have all the time in the world. When he spins me around, he has a strange glimmer in his eyes, and my chest is bursting with emotion.

I throw my arms around him and kiss Carter with all my might.

Like I'm trying to lose myself in him. Like I wouldn't mind drowning in him.

He drops the bar of soap and digs his fingers into my waist. When he tugs on my lower lip, my breath hitches in my throat, and I lean further into his touch. Without warning, Carter spins me around so my chest and stomach are pressed against the cool tile walls. He uses his mouth to move over my skin, leaving a trail of goosebumps in his wake.

"Carter," I whisper, my voice catching toward the end. "I—"

"Shh," Carter whispers into my ear. "Let me take care of you, dove."

One hand stays on my hips, and the other moves to the front, quickly sliding down to my drenched center. He pushes one finger in my pussy and then another, and I'm already gushing wet. Carter makes a low growling sound in the back of his throat and begins to move.

Wave after wave of pleasure builds up within me. I swallow and squeeze my eyes shut. I feel every inch of him pressed against me, invading my space, my thoughts, and my heart.

But I don't mind.

I don't mind one bit.

Especially when he positions himself behind me and rubs in slow, circular motions. I twist my arms behind my back and try to grab a fistful of his hair. Using his free hand, he pins my arms over my head and makes another low noise that reverberates inside my head.

Fuck.

How is it that he's able to read me so well?

How is it that he's able to make me feel so many things at once?

I barely have time to finish my last thought before Carter thrusts into me, and I moan. Carter's fingers have moved to press against my clit, slowly circling the aching nub and sending wave after wave of molten-hot desire racing through me. My vision turns white when he eases out and slams back into me, earning a little gasp of delight.

"Nothing else matters," Carter murmurs in a deep and husky voice. "Do you understand me?"

"Yes," I murmur, twisting my head to look back at him. His hair is flattened by the water, and the hunger on his face is unmistakable, but it's the look in his eyes that nearly has me coming undone.

Carter is never vulnerable. But I know that everything is changing between us, and he's trying to show me what I do to him.

The kind of effect I have on him.

The thought makes me feel powerful and terrified all at once. As if I could have that kind of influence over Carter Blackthorne, of all people.

With a smirk, Carter brushes his lips against mine and thrusts again, deeper this time. Another whimper falls from my lips, and I turn my head back around. He keeps me pinned to the wall while he has his way with me, taking and giving with so much ferocity and sensuality that it brings tears to my eyes. When the force of my orgasm rips through me, and I cry out, I realize I never want it to end.

I don't ever want to be apart from Carter.

Wordlessly, he spins me around and helps me set one leg up on the edge of the tub. He pushes my breasts together and eases into me. Then he lowers his head and takes one nipple between his teeth. I have my head thrown back, and my fingers are tightly wound through his hair when another orgasm builds. Carter moves onto the other nipple, sucking and biting as if his life depends on it, and I fall.

I fall so hard that I feel my soul leave my body.

Once I return, I realize my breathing is labored, and my legs are still shaking. I feel something warm between my legs and glance down to find Carter kneeling in front of me. Using his tongue, he shakes his head back and forth. I dig my fingers into his shoulders and try to remember how to breathe.

How to exist without Carter inside of me.

And all over me.

His intoxicating smell, a mixture of leather and sandalwood cologne, wafts up my nostrils. I inhale, and my fingers move from his shoulders to the back of his neck. They wind themselves through his hair, and I hold on to him for dear life. Just as I'm about to fall again, Carter removes his mouth and thrusts his fingers between my wet folds.

Then he pulls me up and holds me to him.

In one quick move, he's inside of me again, and I fall, hurtling over the edge without a single care in the world.

All that matters is Carter.

All that will ever matter is him.

His own release follows soon after, and Carter crushes me to him as his entire body shakes. I squeeze my eyes shut and place a hand over his chest, over the erratic thumping of his heart. As soon as his breathing returns to normal, Carter sets me down with a surprising amount of gentleness. His eyes don't leave my face as he picks up the soap and runs it over my body.

I am still tingling when he switches off the water and bundles me up in a towel.

Without warning, he sweeps me into his arms. I place my head against his chest, still reeling and spinning. He sets me down on the bed, and I see the shopping bags lined up at the foot of the bed, a variety of shapes and colors. Raising an eyebrow, I sit back on my legs and give Carter an amused look.

"When did you have time to do all of this?"

"I made a few phone calls while I was at Anita's," Carter replies, pausing to pull on a pair of boxers with a snap. "They know what kind of clothes I like, and they know your sizes."

I secure the towel around my chest and crawl forward.

Every single item of clothing feels like butter between my fingers, and all of them are revealing in one way or another. I hold up a particular nightgown made of sheer pink lace and a matching thong and give Carter an incredulous look.

"What is this?"

Carter twists to face me and gives me a wicked grin. "I could show you how to try it on, but then I'd just rip it off again."

I blush. "I thought you didn't mind ripping my clothes off."

"I don't," Carter replies without missing a beat. "But I'd like to see you wear it at least once before I destroy it."

"Carter." I sigh and push the nightgown back into the bag. "You know I appreciate everything you're doing, but we've already been shopping twice this week."

"So?"

I make a vague hand gesture. "So… this is too much, and it's not like I have anywhere to wear a lot of these things."

Carter bends down to give me a searing kiss. "You can do whatever you want with the clothes, dove."

Between the shopping trips and the diners, it almost feels like Carter is a different person.

Underneath the surface, I know the broken, wounded, and angry man is still there, reeling from what almost happened when I snuck away to the hospital. Still, I appreciate that he's keeping him under lock and key.

For now.

But I know it won't be that way for long. Still, I appreciate him doing everything he can to make me forget about what I've lost. Of the kind of life I have to face without my father in the world.

On impulse, I glance down at my ring and admire how it catches the light. Carter sits on the bed next to me, rips off the towel, and pulls me to him. "If you don't like the ring, we can go get another one. I've made us dinner reservations."

I shake my head. "No, I love this."

Carter's hand traces a path down my back and pauses at my ass. He gives it a firm squeeze and exhales. "Good, because I want you to show it off at dinner tonight."

I lean back to look at him. "What's tonight?"

Carter stands up and gives me a smile that makes me forget my own name. "We're going out to dinner with my family to celebrate. I know you told me you're not ready to see anyone, but they all know that you need some time."

I swallow. "Okay."

"If it gets to be too much, I'll bring you right home," Carter promises with a shake of his head. "In the meantime, I have to go back to Anita's."

I nod, and a lump rises in my throat. "Okay."

"I think Tristan mentioned Sam wanting to check in with you. I'll see if she wants to come over." Carter gives me another kiss before pulling on the rest of his clothes. I watch him leave the room and then hear the front door close.

I am pulling on a pair of shorts and a T-shirt when the doorbell rings. In the peephole, I see Paul standing guard outside, and when he shifts to the side, I see Sam holding a shopping bag and looking uneasy.

I throw the door open and draw her in for a hug. "I'm really glad you're here."

"I didn't want to push, and I wanted to give you your space." Sam's arms come up around me, and she relaxes. "I'm so sorry about your dad, Isabella."

I sniff and pull back to look at her. "It's okay. At least he's not suffering anymore."

Sam steps into the house and kicks the door shut behind her. "Yeah, but you can still miss him."

I lead her into the kitchen and open the refrigerator to hide my tears. "I do, but I know he's better off."

Sam sighs. "You don't have to hide how you're feeling around me, Isabella. I know I haven't been a good friend to you, but this is all just… a lot, you know."

I reach for a bottle of wine and a container with cheese and salami. When I spin back around to face Sam, she is leaning against the kitchen counter, an apologetic look on her face. "Water under the bridge. Don't worry about it."

Sam's expression turns relieved. "Good. Um… Carter handed me this on my way out. He said to help you get ready for the celebration tonight."

I give her a small smile and pry the container open. "I'd like that."

Hours later, I am twisting to and fro and looking at myself in the full-length mirror in my bedroom. The blue dress shimmers and glides over my skin with every movement. It has a plunging V-neck that shows off my cleavage, and I've paired it with a simple gold necklace and a bracelet Carter left out for me. After helping me with my hair and makeup, Sam is back at Anita's, changing into her own outfit for the night.

Butterflies form in the center of my stomach when Carter materializes in the doorway to the bedroom, a handsome vision in his black suit, with the sleeves of his white button-down shirt featuring the black-rose cufflinks. With a lazy smile, he saunters into the room and pulls me to him. I tilt my head back to meet his gaze and give him a breathless smile.

"We have a problem, dove."

I frown. "What's wrong?"

"You look fucking amazing." Carter's eyes are moving steadily over me, leaving me feeling hot and bothered. "I don't think we can go out like this."

"Your family is waiting for us," I point out with a chuckle. "We can't be late to our own engagement celebration."

"Like hell, we can't." Carter hoists me up and sets me down on the dresser. He pushes the dress up so it's around my waist, revealing the lacy black underwear underneath. Carter palms me over the material, and I melt, turning into putty in his hands. I reach between us and cup him over the fabric of his trousers. He growls and pushes my hand away. I barely have time to register the zipper being undone and the familiar sound of cloth ripping before Carter is positioned at my entrance.

One hand grips the dresser underneath me, and the other flutters at my side.

I feel a strange sensation in my arm where the birth control implant is meant to be, but I ignore it.

Carter buries himself inside me, and my fingers dart underneath his shirt, moving over his bare skin.

An hour later, Carter and I walk into the restaurant holding hands. The restaurant is empty, except for the Blackthorne family, who are already eating and talking among themselves. As soon as she sees us, Anita lets out a whoop of approval and raises her glass to us. They all break out into applause, and color creeps up my neck and cheeks.

Tears prick the back of my eyes as Carter sits down first and pulls me into his lap.

I shift, the toy he placed between my legs making me feel particularly sensitive.

"Thank you all so much for coming tonight. We're sorry we're late."

Carter pushes my hair forward and presses a kiss to the back of my neck. "We had some unfinished business to take care of."

Underneath the table, he places his hand on my thigh and squeezes. I already miss him inside of me.

Throughout dinner, Carter doesn't stop finding excuses to touch me. Thankfully, the toy between my legs doesn't do anything, but I'm all too aware of how it feels against my bare skin and the feeling of Carter's erection through the bulge in his trousers.

I keep trying to focus on Carter's family, the glittering chandelier, and the soft strings of jazz music playing, but I can't.

All night, Carter is the only thing I can think about, and the fact that, someday soon, I'm going to become his wife.

Hours later, when I wake up in the middle of the night, Carter isn't in bed next to me. I roll over and see him sitting on a chair by the window, bathed in the pale glow of the moon. With a frown, I sit up and throw the covers off. Carter doesn't react or say anything until I climb onto his lap and bury my face in the crook of his neck.

He wraps an arm around me and continues to look out the

window. "You should go back to sleep, dove."

"I can't."

Carter twists to face me, his face half-hidden in the shadows. "I'll come to bed in a minute."

"Or we can just sit here," I whisper, fighting to keep the sleep out of my voice. "Is everything okay?"

Carter brushes my hair out of my face. "It's fine. There's nothing for you to worry about."

"But—"

Carter presses a finger to my lips. "You really need to learn to let things go, dove. When are you going to grow out of this habit?"

I shrug and study his face, committing his features to memory.

Carter removes his finger and gives me a pointed look. "I should punish you right now."

I wriggle against him. "Maybe you should."

Carter's expression tightens. "You lost your dad, dove. As much as I want to fuck the grief out of you, even I know it's not possible."

I curl up against him and exhale. "I wish you could."

Because as much as I'm enjoying being doted on and made to feel like the only woman in the world who matters, I know Carter can't keep this up.

Not with a war brewing outside his doorstep. And another civil war festering among the Blackthorne family itself.

I know I shouldn't be encouraging the shopping sprees and the dinners, but it gives me something to do and keeps me distracted. It's only been a week, and already I feel tired, more exhausted than I've ever been, and nothing is helping. Not the knowledge that Carter has this whole other side to him, not knowing that I've still got a job waiting for me, and definitely not the thought of planning a wedding.

If I'm being honest with myself, even Carter is barely keeping my demons at bay. But I don't have the heart to tell him that, not when he's trying so hard.

But all the shopping trips and the dinners in the world can't make up for what I lack.

We both know that.

So we sit there in silence, with Carter holding me while I cling to him. Eventually, when I drift off, he scoops me into his arms and carries me into the bed. When he pulls the covers over me, I don't let go of him. I mumble something in my sleep, and Carter inches closer to press his lips against my neck. I link my fingers behind his neck and play with the hair on his nape.

Carter pushes the straps of my nightgown down, allowing my breasts to spill forward. Then he nudges my legs apart and positions himself at my entrance.

We don't say anything as we move together, the bed dipping and creaking underneath us. I can hear my own uneven breathing, loud enough to fill the room. Carter digs his fingers into my hips and growls in the back of his throat. When my orgasm washes over me, I climb on top of Carter and straddle him. He thrusts in and out a few more times before his own release comes.

I fall beside him on the bed, and Carter pulls me to him, wrapping me securely in his arms.

In the morning, I'm too exhausted and spent to worry about the fact that Carter isn't in bed again.

Around midday, the door to the bedroom creaks open, and Carter comes in with a tray full of food. He is shirtless and only wearing a pair of shorts. In silence, I scarf down the eggs and toast before pulling the covers back up to my chin. My head feels heavy, and I refuse to leave the bed. Eventually, Carter exhales and mutters something to himself.

A short while later, after Carter leaves, Sam comes over, and she sits in bed with me.

We don't exchange a single word as she points the remote at the TV above the dresser and lowers the volume.

That night, when Carter comes home, he gathers me into his arms, and I bring my head to rest against his chest. The next few weeks are a blur of shopping trips and extravagant dinners at restaurants whose names I can't pronounce.

And Carter spends every free minute that he can with me.

Doting on me, buying me gifts, and worshipping me with his body.

I've heard the whispers in Anita's house, and I've seen the looks the other Blackthornes are giving him, but no one dares to utter a word. Still, I know there's a storm coming, and as usual, we're going to be right in the center when the worst of it hits.

For the umpteenth time since meeting Carter, I find myself praying that we emerge with as little damage as possible.

Because I have no idea how many more of these storms we can take.

Carter

"Orange looks good on you, Frances." I link my fingers over the table and lean forward to stare at the former mayor. "Sporting a new look, huh?"

Frances scowls and stares at me through his good eye, the right one swollen and drooping. "Cut the bullshit, Blackthorne. I know you had something to do with this."

I unlink my fingers and lean back against the metal chair. "I have no idea what you're talking about."

Frances is skinnier than when I last saw him, and I already know that his jumpsuit is hiding a wide array of bruises, many of them freshly inflicted.

And all it took was a few phone calls to the right people.

I'm not the forgiving type, and Frances knew that before going into business with me. Now that he's made his bed, he has to lie in, and I will gladly shove him into it if he hesitates.

"What are you even doing here? I didn't take you for the type to gloat." Frances gives me a look that's meant to intimidate, but all it does is highlight how pathetic he is. Underneath the dim florescent lightning, in the middle of a prison with similarly dressed inmates, he's a far cry from the once-powerful man running the city.

I can't believe I ever thought it was a good idea to back him up. Weaselly little shit.

Still, the fact that Frances has somehow survived, with a few lives to boot, could be used to my advantage. Which is why, against my family's advice, I had Ernest drive me out here and wait by the door.

Being inside Sing Sing prison isn't as unnerving as I thought it would be. Not when I know the police can't do anything to me... yet.

But with the clock ticking on our war with the Philipses and the Natoris and Lilian still pestering me with the impending release of her article, I know I'm playing with fire.

"I have a way for you to make things up to me," I tell Frances before slowly sitting up straighter and giving him a bored look. "You're not as stupid as people think you are, so I know you're not going to turn me down. Not without hearing what I have to say."

Frances pulls his mouth back to reveal a row of teeth. "I'm not making any more deals with you, Blackthorne. You're fucking poison."

"Oh, I think you'll want to hear what I have to say before you throw it in my face."

"How well is that bitch blowing you anyway? Does she still have you by the balls?"

I'm across the table, with my hands around his neck, before the words finish leaving his mouth. Frances sputters and glances at the guards, who take one step in my direction. With one look between my face and Ernesto's, they back off and return to their duties.

279

As if nothing out of the ordinary is transpiring.

"You're lucky I'm feeling generous today," I hiss before giving him another firm shake. "Otherwise, these guards would be cleaning your remains off the floor."

Frances wheezes, and his face turns red.

I squeeze him for a while longer, taking a grim sense of satisfaction from the colors playing out over his face. It isn't long before I smell the sweat and the fear lingering in the air. Abruptly, I release Frances and drape an arm over the back of my chair. Frances' hands move to his neck and the finger-shaped bruise already forming there.

His fellow inmates are going to have a field day with him tonight. I only wish I could be there to see it myself.

Frances clears his throat several times, and when he speaks, his voice is hoarse. "I see your negotiating skills haven't improved."

"I see you're still a conniving two-timing piece of shit, but who's keeping score."

Frances rubs his neck, annoyance flickering across his face. "What do you want?"

"I want Lilian McCoy's head on a platter, and before you think of playing dumb and denying that you even know her, I've got pictures of the two of you screwing."

Frances presses his lips together and says nothing.

I fish my phone out of my pocket and scroll through it. Then, I set it down between us and maximize the screen. "I'm thinking of having a few of them framed and sent to your family. Which one do you prefer?"

"Fuck you."

"I like the one where she's on your desk, next to the picture of your wife." I gesture to the phone and offer Frances a slow, unperturbed grin. "That one's really special... and classy too. How do you think she'd feel if I sent a few to the tabloids? You're still pretty famous, you know."

Frances curses me in a language I don't understand.

I pick my phone up off the table and tuck it away. "Now that I have your attention, we can get down to some serious business. You're going to tell me everything that you know about Lilian McCoy, or these pictures are going to be the least of your problems."

Frances holds my gaze and doesn't look away. "If I do this for you, you have to do something for me."

"Why would I want to help you?" I only want to put his face through a wall.

"Because you want to find this whore badly enough that you're willing to work with me. I'll tell you where she works. Hell, I'll even give you her last known address, but in return, you have to recover everything she has on me."

I snort. "I don't know why I ever thought you had the balls to be mayor."

"When I ended things, she took some files from my office, including some sensitive documents," Frances continues as if he hasn't heard me. "I want them back."

"Planning your re-election already? That's ambitious."

"Help me, and I'll help you." Frances sets his hands down on the table, his eyes never leaving my face. "I know you're not an unreasonable man, Carter. You want to find her more than I want those files. Do this for me and offer me protection in jail, and you've got yourself a deal."

I raise an eyebrow. "And why in the hell would I trust you?"

"You don't have much of a choice here, do you? It all depends on how badly you want to find Lilian McCoy."

"You're a fucking class act, Frances." I stand up and unfasten the first button on my jacket. "Consider it done, but if you screw me over again, prison time will seem like a walk in the park compared to what I'll do to you."

Frances mouths something to me and sits up straighter. "You'll get the rest of the information when I know I'm safe."

Without waiting for a response, I spin around and walk out of the visiting room. The guard who opens the door glances over at Frances and back at me. "It's a pleasure to see you as always, Mr. Blackthorne."

I nod and look over at Ernesto.

A quick look passes between us as we step outside and are led through a series of dirty-looking hallways. Outside, the same guard who spoke to me pushes a large door open with a creak. Ernesto drapes an arm over the man's shoulders and draws him away underneath a spot of shade and away from the prying eyes of the cameras.

Out of the corner of my eye, I see Ernesto hand over a wad of cash and whisper something into the guard's ear. Then the guard plasters a shit-eating grin on his face as he walks away. The door slams shut behind him, and I shove a hand into my pocket. In the SUV, Ernesto turns up the AC and backs away from the curb.

He kicks up dust and gravel as he drives away. "Are you sure it's a good idea to get into bed with him again, boss?"

"Fuck no. But for now, we need to let him think we need him more than he needs us." I take my phone out and scroll through it until I stop at Tristan's name.

"How did it go?" Tristan asks after he answers my call.

"He's got a lot of balls. I'll give him that. I've already brokered a deal with some of the prison guards so they can keep an eye on him. In a few more days, I want you to come and visit our dear old friend and remind him that he owes us."

"I knew it wouldn't take long to get him to squeal. Fucking rat."

"He might hate Lilian as much as I do." I switch the phone to my other ear. "By the way, you and Sam are coming over for dinner tonight. Isabella has been trying out these new recipes online, and she needs some guinea pigs."

"I wouldn't miss it," Tristian replies with an exhale. "Should I bring some plastic bags, just in case it doesn't go well?"

"If you feel the need to throw up, do it outside and without her seeing you," I snap before I end the call. With that, I shove the phone back into my pocket and press my head against the window. The world outside rushes past in a blur of shapes and colors.

When I get home, Isabella is in the kitchen in an apron tied over a pair of shorts and a tank top that exposes her midriff.

She spends the next hour dancing away from me and trying to swat my hands away.

My patience is growing thin, my hunger for her even stronger, but I'm glad to see that twinkle in her eyes again. Even if I know she has an uphill battle ahead of her before she feels normal again. Despite my impatience and my exasperation, I'm determined not to make it harder.

I will not take this away from her. Isabella deserves to grieve in whatever way she sees fit.

During dinner, she sits pressed against me, her eyes darting eagerly between Sam and Tristan, who are nice enough not to comment on the food. Underneath the table, I stroke her bare skin until my hand rides up and darts between her legs. She shoots me a dirty look and presses her legs together. I smirk and try to focus on my watery soup.

A few days later, I'm still thinking of how it felt to sneak into the study downstairs and bend Isabella over my desk while Sam and Tristan waited for us in the living room. I can still taste her on my tongue and feel her body pressed against mine when Ernest pulls to a stop outside a cluster of old buildings in a run-down part of town.

I adjust the jacket over my gun and push the door open. "Let's take care of our pest problem once and for all, shall we?"

Wordlessly, Ernesto gets out of the driver's seat and follows me. There are broken shards of glass on the pavement and an abandoned warehouse on the opposite side of the street. I feel several pairs of eyes on us, but no one says anything when Ernesto pries the front door open, and we go in. It is pitch black, and it takes a few seconds for my eyes to adjust.

My fingers curl around my gun as I creep forward.

Ernesto's loud breathing is somewhere ahead of me. He kicks the door to his right in, and we call out. When we step in, the lights flick on, and I'm blinded by the spots in my field of vision. Slowly, my vision clears and sharpens into focus. However, rather than seeing Lilian seated at a desk or on her couch in whatever scantily clad outfit she owns, I recognize a few members of the Philips family seated at the kitchen counter.

Two of them are on Lilian's old couch, their guns pointed directly at us.

Fuck.

How the hell do Ernesto and I keep finding ourselves in these situations? And why am I not surprised that Lilian is somehow involved with my enemies?

I've always known she was trouble, but this might just take the cake.

I'm feeling less and less guilty about what I might have to do to shut her up.

Gerald Philips uncrosses his ankles and stands up, pushing his chair back with a screech. "I really hoped it wouldn't come to this, Carter, but you've left us no choice."

I point my gun directly at him. "I'm not surprised Lilian is working for you. What's that saying about like calling to like? She's a piece of shit, and so are you."

Gerald cocks his head to the side and studies me. "You know, underneath all that anger and hostility, I know there's a sharp mind in there."

"You're not my type, Philips." I undo the safety and keep my gun aimed at the Philips family's right-hand man. "I'd save your sad attempts at dirty talk for your whores. I'm sure they'll appreciate it a lot more."

Gerlad shoves his hand into the pocket of his pants. "I can see I'm going to need to spell out the math for you, Blackthorne. You're outnumbered."

I offer him a grim smile. "And I can see that you need a quick recap. I like my odds here."

Especially because I know backup is on the way.

Ernesto made sure of it the second we stepped in through those doors and realized the lights were off.

Geral throws his head back and laughs. "I've heard you were delusional and drunk on power, but this is a lot worse than I thought. The great fucking Carter Blackthorne... It's almost a shame to kill you."

"I can't say that I feel the same." I fire my gun at one of the men in the background, and he slumps to the floor, the life immediately draining out of him. "That was a warning shot in case it wasn't obvious. I won't miss the next time."

Gerald scoffs. "You're not going to shoot me."

I glance between his men and at Ernesto over my shoulder. Another quick look passes between us. I pretend to lower my gun and shoot Gerald in the foot. There is chaos as he yells and hops on his uninjured foot. Ernesto presses his back against mine as they try to tackle us to the ground. Between the two of us, we fight as many of them off with our bare hands.

A few of them are on the receiving end of our bullets.

More and more of them pour out, and I hear the screech of tires outside. Rich materializes in the doorway, with a swarm of men behind him. He wastes no time in picking up the nearest gun and firing it. I'm almost impressed with the way he doesn't hesitate. Then I pause to wipe away the blood using the back of my hand. Donahue's men aren't as polished as I'd like, and they need to learn a thing or two about finesse, but they manage to hold their own.

Gerald is ushered away out a back door, with only two of his men to guard him.

Through the window, I see their car peel away and wait till it turns into a speck on the horizon. Once it does, I wheel around to face

Rich. "We need to move quickly. How fast can you make sure your men take over the buildings they left behind?"

Rich folds his arms over his chest. "How fast can yours?"

"They're already on the way," I reply, pausing to use a rug to wipe off my bloodied knuckles. "If your men make it there before mine do, you can have your pick."

Rich does a double take, a furrow appearing between his brows. "What did you just say?"

"I know the value of a good ally." I tuck my gun away and roll up the sleeves of my shirt. "As a thank you for helping the Blackthornes double their business, you get half of the spoils."

Rich barely manages to hide his surprise. "I don't know what to say."

As I brush past him, I pause to place a hand on his shoulders. "Don't fuck this up, Donahue, or else you'll have me to answer to."

With that, I brush past him and step outside.

On the streets, several more Blackthorne men are arriving. They all look relieved to see me, and a few even exchange surprised looks when Rich emerges, his own men in tow. I wait until I'm in the SUV before I take my anger out on the passenger seat of the car. I punch it a few times while Ernesto drives us through the streets of the city, not daring to say a word.

"Goddamn it. How the hell did Lilian manage to get their protection? What the hell did she offer them?"

Ernesto meets my gaze in the rearview mirror. "My guess is she promised to ruin you if she couldn't have you."

"Fucking bitch." I run my fingers through my hair. "I need to find her and kill that article before she finds out that Isabella and I are engaged. Otherwise, nothing is going to stop her from posting it."

And I have no idea how bad the damage is going to be.

From what little I've been able to glean, Lilian is not holding back any punches.

She's gunning for my family and me, and she's not exactly making a secret of it.

When I get home, I find Isabella working on a few sketches in the study. Even though I'm dirty, sweaty, and covered in blood that isn't my own, Isabella doesn't say anything. Wordlessly, she leads me upstairs and helps me strip out of my clothes. In the shower, she scrubs every inch of my skin twice until the water swirling beneath our feet is filthy.

I can't stop thinking about the fact that I might lose her.

In the morning, Tristan and I are out on the docks when we run into Rich and a few of his men. He doesn't look happy to see us, and when I approach him, more and more of his men emerge from the shadows.

Unease settles in the center of my stomach as I glance around. "What's going on here?"

"I really was hoping to avoid all this." Rich makes a vague hand gesture. "I'm sure you've realized by now that there's not enough room in this city for more than one powerful family."

I frown. "I'm well aware of that."

Was Rich unhappy with the business I gave him? Was he trying to shake me down for more?

I take a step forward and offer Rich an encouraging smile. "I'm sure we can talk about this—"

Rich holds his hand up and bridges the gap between us. "I don't think so."

Without warning, he draws his hand back and punches me squarely in the face. I spit out a mouthful of blood at his feet and throw myself at him. Rich and I fall onto the uneven ground, kicking up dust and dirt as we roll around. I manage to get in a few more punches before I'm being pulled to my feet.

Two of Rich's men hold me back. A third lands a kick to my stomach. I don't hiss or cry out because I don't want to give him the satisfaction.

Why hadn't I listened to my gut with this guy?

Jesus fucking Christ. Of course, he's working with the Philipses and the Natoris.

Rich uses the back of his hand to wipe the blood away. Then he strolls over to where they're holding me. Another one of his men forces me to my knees so I'm looking up at Rich. Gone is the shy and indecisive man who approached me, and in his place is a man with a cold gleam in his eyes and a calculating smirk that fills me with more dread than I'd like to acknowledge. Now, he looks just like his brother, Jacob.

He better not touch a hair on Isabella's head.

"Fucking Rich Donahue. I should've known you couldn't be trusted as an ally."

Rich shrugs and studies me. "I only pretended to be your ally so I could get close enough to you to determine what kind of threat you really were. I know all about you, Carter, and I'd heard enough from my brother to know that going after you wasn't the way to take you down."

My blood turns to ice. "What the fuck are you talking about?"

"Honestly, it was too easy slipping the new families information about you so they could target you. Even the mayor was a lot more susceptible than I thought he'd be. You'd think he would know better."

"You son of a bitch." I lunge at Rich, but at the last second, someone pushes a taser against my back, and my whole body jerks. I crumple into a heap, but all I see is red.

"It was a little too easy," Rich continues as if I hadn't interrupted him. "They were all too willing to do my dirty work for me and expose you, but now that you've taken care of them, I guess I'll have to find another way."

I give him the dirtiest look possible and say nothing.

"I have to admit I expected something a lot more dramatic," Rich says with a frown. "I expected more from *the* Carter Blackthorne, but I'll have to get over my disappointment."

"Fuck you. When I get out of here, I'm going to rip you apart with my bare hands," I inform him with a lift of my chin. "There won't be a single place in this city that you can hide."

"Unless I have Isabella," Rich replies with a smile that makes me sick to my stomach. "She's the real key, isn't she? I've been watching the two of you, Carter, and I have to say… I get it now."

I struggle against my captors, and they kick me again. "Touch her, and you'll wish you were never born."

Rich's expression turns thoughtful. "Violence really is all you know, isn't it? You and I both know that Isabella deserves better, and when I get rid of you, it won't take me long to make her see that."

In one quick move, they tase me again, and Rich draws me to my feet. He shoves a knife into my stomach, and little droplets of blood stain the ground beneath my feet. Still, I stagger forward and knock Rich onto the ground. I'm on top of him, throwing one punch after another, when I hear a few more cars arrive. Rich's men freeze when they see the familiar Blackthorne crest surround them.

Rich slides out from under me and crawls away. "This isn't over, Blackthorne. We're just getting started."

I chase Rich until spots dance in my field of vision, and pain shoots through my body, the adrenaline from the fight quickly losing effect. Without an injury, he's a lot faster than I am, and he jumps into a black SUV waiting for him at the end of the docks. Then the vehicle screeches away, and I limp to a halt. Suddenly, Ernesto and Tristan are on either side of me, murmuring something I can't make out.

When I realize I'm on the ground looking up at the sky, I frown. "What's happening?"

"We'll take you to a hospital."

I shoot up. "He's going to try and take Isabella. Where the fuck is she?"

"She's at Anita's," Tristan replies before draping one arm over his shoulders. Ernesto does the same with my other arm, so I'm being pulled away. "She's fine. Paul is keeping a close eye on her, and so is Anita."

"I have to find her."

Tristan and Ernesto tuck me into the back of the SUV, where I stain the seats and the floor. "This is going to be a bitch to clean."

Tristan exchanges a quick look with Ernesto before getting into the passenger seat. "That's not the only bad thing to happen today. Do you remember that article Lilian threatened to publish?"

I groan, sweat forming on my forehead and down my back. "Don't fucking tell me that she posted it."

"About twenty minutes ago. One thousand hits and counting," Tristan replies with a grimace. "I'm working on having it taken down, but I thought you'd want to know so you don't have any more surprises."

When we hit a speedbump, I hiss in pain and try not to think of what Isabella's going to say.

I need to get home as soon as possible.

Chapter Thirty-Four

Isabella

"Thanks for coming with me, by the way. I know it's short notice…"

Sam looks up from her phone and nods. "Yeah, of course. I wasn't going to let you go on your own. Carter does know you're here, right?"

"I did tell him a few times, and I messaged him, but he hasn't responded." I link my fingers over my lap and swing my legs back and forth. "But he's got a lot on his mind lately."

And after weeks of hovering and doting, a part of me is relieved he's getting back into his old habits.

Because I know we can't stay in our bubble forever.

No matter how badly I want to.

Still, I miss Carter with a fierceness that surprises me, and while I'm glad that Sam and I are reconnecting again, another part of me can't help but feel like Carter should be here. He should be the one sitting across from me while I sit on the exam table, waiting to hear back from the doctor about my test results. After an entire week of feeling sick, I know that I need to get to the bottom of what's happening.

Contrary to what Carter believes, I can't stay home forever.

"Yeah, things have been intense," Sam agrees, with a sigh. "I honestly can't believe how quickly things are escalating with the Philipses and the Natoris."

I swallow. "Has Tristan told you what's been happening?"

I hate feeling like I'm using Sam, but since my father's death, Carter has kept me even more out of the loop than usual. While I appreciated it at first, I know firsthand how dangerous it can be to have secrets, the kinds that fester and spread like poison.

I'm determined to make sure Carter and I don't repeat the same mistakes.

Sam drops her phone into her purse and stands up. "No, but I don't ask to be honest. I figure the less I know, the better."

I tilt my head to the side and study her. "Yeah, I guess you're right."

But I know Carter and I aren't like that.

We never can be.

Sam straightens her back and opens her mouth just as the door to the exam room opens, revealing a young red-haired woman wearing flats and carrying a clipboard. She offers us both a small smile and snaps on her latex gloves. Then she lifts the clipboard to her face and skims over the information. When she's done, she steps closer and motions for me to face the front of the room.

"Sorry to keep you waiting, Isabella. I'm Dr. Munroe." The doctor presses two fingers against my wrist, the smile never leaving her face. "So, according to your chart, you've been feeling sick lately?"

I nod and keep my arm held out. "Yeah, nausea, vomiting, bloated stomach, and I've been feeling very tired lately even though I'm getting a lot of sleep."

Dr. Munroe releases my wrist and unwinds the stethoscope from around her neck. She presses it against my back, the cool metal harsh against my flushed skin. "Take a deep breath for me, please. How about breathlessness?"

"Yeah, I've been feeling that too." I inhale, and when she signals, I release my breath. "And I've been getting these bizarre food cravings."

The doctor nods and removes her stethoscope. She jots something down on the clipboard. "I assume you're active sexually?"

A flush rises over my neck and stains my cheeks. "I am, but I had a birth control implant put in a while ago."

She writes something else down. "Alright, I'm just going to take a blood sample so we can rule out a few things."

With that, she sets her clipboard down on the desk and takes my arm in hers. She pats my skin for a while until she finally spots a vein. Then she opens a drawer and rips open a pack of brand-new syringes. When she looks back at me, she gestures for me to clench my hand into a fist.

I look over at Sam, who has drifted closer to the exam bed. She takes my free hand in hers and gives me a reassuring smile. "You're doing great."

There is a stinging sensation, and I inhale sharply.

A few short minutes later, Dr. Munroe moves away, and I hear the gloves being snapped off. I look back at her, and she's holding a vial with my blood. She presses a piece of cotton to the wound and motions for me to keep it there. "I can have the tests ready for you in half an hour, but you'll have to pay extra."

I look at Sam and then back at her. "Sure."

"Okay, you can wait here till then." Dr. Munroe gives me another smile and steps out, the door clicking shut behind her. Sam holds my hand for a while longer, then she releases it and wanders over to the window.

I lean back against the exam table and stare at the ceiling.

I don't realize I've drifted off until the doctor returns, a folder in her hand and a furrow between her brows. "Okay, your test results are back. Why don't we move to the consultation room so you're more comfortable."

We follow the doctor to her office as Sam and I share concerned glances.

Dr. Munroe sits behind a desk and sets the folder down. Slowly, I move forward and sink into the seat opposite her. Wordlessly, Sam takes the chair across from me and takes both of my hands in hers.

"So, you mentioned that you had a birth control implant placed, right?"

I sit up straighter and frown. "Yeah, why?"

"According to your medical files, it was removed because you had to go into surgery."

I have a vague memory of being told about the implant by a young-looking doctor with dark eyes.

But I don't remember anything else.

Dr. Munroe closes the folder and links her fingers together. "You're pregnant, Isabella. The good news is that it's still early enough that you can make the decision not to keep the baby."

I grip Sam's hand tighter. "I… I can't be pregnant."

The doctor reaches into her drawer and pulls out a pamphlet. "Why don't you go over these? Here's my card as well. Call me if you have any questions, and be sure to schedule a follow-up appointment with your obstetrician. Congratulations."

She pushes her chair back with a screech and gets up.

My ears are ringing, and my stomach is in knots.

Sam is the one to lead me into the blue-colored hallway, past nurses and doctors in scrubs. I'm vaguely aware of monitors beeping in the background and the smell of disinfectant following us out into the emergency waiting area. There is a flurry of activity as a few stretchers are rolled past, and loud voices call out for the doctor.

Suddenly, I'm outside, and Sam is helping me get into her car.

The seatbelt snaps into place, and the door clicks shut behind me. Sam hurries around to the driver's side and reaches for her belt. After checking the mirrors, she starts the car and backs out of her parking spot. After she merges onto the main road, she glances over at me and waves a hand in front of my face.

"Are you okay? Do you want me to pinch you or something?"

I blink, and the world tilts back into focus, revealing Sam's AC whirring in the background and a blur of trees and buildings rushing past me beyond the car windows. With a frown, I sit up straighter and run a hand over my face. Then my hand drops to my stomach, and I stare at it in disbelief.

How the hell did this happen?

"I can be there when you tell Carter," Sam says in a strange voice. "I'm guessing by your reaction that you didn't plan any of this, but that's fine. I'm right here, no matter what you decide."

A lump rises in the back of my throat. "I don't know what I'm supposed to do."

"I think you've still got time before it's too late." Sam places both hands on the wheel and rolls her shoulders. "You've got options, Isabella."

I glance up at Sam, and my throat is dry. "What if I want to keep the baby?"

Sam glances over sharply, then drags her gaze back to the empty road ahead. "Are you serious?"

I hold my arm more firmly over my stomach and blow out a breath. "I don't know, but I think I am. Sam, I… I can't get rid of my baby."

Because I can't imagine it. And I don't want to think about giving my baby up for adoption.

The thought of having a part of Carter and me out there in the world doesn't sit well with me. Not if it means not having the baby in our lives.

A swell of emotion rises and grows in my chest. "Look, I know it's crazy, but since my dad died, you know how hard it's been. I've been feeling really lonely and isolated, and I don't want to feel like Carter is my only family."

Sam's grip on the steering wheel tightens. "I understand that, Isabella. I do, but what about Carter? How's he going to feel about this? They're in the middle of a civil war, and there's the bullshit with that journalist…"

I push my hair out of my face. "I know, but this could be exactly what we both need to help us focus on what really matters."

In the distance, Anita's house looms, bathed in the glow of the late afternoon sun. On either side of us, mansions race past, and Sam hasn't looked at me once.

Not since we got into the car.

She probably thinks I've lost my mind. And I'm not sure that I haven't.

I can't bring a baby into this world, can I?

Sam eases her foot off the gas and circles to the back of Anita's house. There, she brings the car to a stop and lets the engine idle for a few more seconds. "I want to be supportive, Isabella. I do, but I think you need to think this through. A baby is a lot of responsibility. It's a tiny person that you need to take care of and feed."

I frown. "I know."

Sam switches off the engine and twists so she's facing me directly. "Isabella, please don't look at me like that. I'm not trying to be the bad guy here, but you can't raise a baby in this world. And I know that somewhere deep down inside of you, you know it too."

I unbuckle my seatbelt and let it slide back into place. "Things are different now. Carter is different."

Since the incident outside the hospital, Carter has been keeping a closer eye on me and making sure I feel safer and more secure. While a part of that has included having to keep tabs on me at all times, I know it's for my good.

I need to know that Carter can protect and take care of me. And he's been nothing short of amazing the past few weeks. I don't have any reason to doubt him, not when I've seen, time and again, how strong and powerful he is.

Carter will protect us, I'm sure of it.

Still, Sam's words stay with me as we get out of the car and go into the house. Anita is in the kitchen cooking, and a few Blackthorne men are on the front porch. I swing the refrigerator door open and smile when Paul comes in, acting like he hadn't been shadowing us the entire visit to the hospital and back. When I find a container with some cheese and Italian sliced meats in it, I take it out.

Anita kicks Paul out of the kitchen and spins around to face us. "So, how was the doctor's appointment?"

I pry the lid open and sniff. "It was fine. Yeah, nothing to worry about."

Not unless Carter loses his shit, but I'm determined not to think about that. Or about the fact that Sam is right.

Instead, I focus on making myself a sandwich. Anita makes small talk while Sam and I move around the kitchen, helping her take out pots and pans and chop vegetables. Once we're done, I pour myself a large glass of iced tea and take a bottle of water upstairs. In the doorway to our room, I pause and glance around. When I glance over my shoulder, Sam is hovering near one of the guest rooms.

We exchange a quick look, but she doesn't say anything.

"I'm just going to lie down for a bit before we meet up with the ladies," I tell her with a wave. "Can you make sure I'm awake in like an hour?"

Sam nods and folds her arms over her chest.

The door clicks shut behind me, and I kick off my shoes. I crawl between the sheets and down all the iced tea in one gulp. When I'm done, I use the back of my hand to wipe my mouth. Then I pull the covers up to my chin, bringing one arm up behind my head and using the other to cup my stomach.

It feels strange to know that there is life growing inside of me.

Before I drift off to sleep, I think I feel a flutter, and it sends another wave of emotion through me.

Sometime later, when Sam comes into the room and gently shakes me awake, I am deep in the throes of sleep. Slowly, I sit up, push my hair out of my face, and give Sam a sleepy smile. Then I stagger out of bed and into the adjoining bathroom, splashing cold water on my face. Through the slit in the door, I see Sam adjust the covers on the bed and smooth out the wrinkles.

She's a good friend, and I'm glad to have her back in my life. But she doesn't understand things with Carter, and she's never going to.

Dating Tristan isn't going to change that.

With a slight shake of my head, I peel my clothes off and leave them in a pile on the floor. I wait for the water to heat up, and I'm examining myself in the mirror when steam fills the bathroom. Once it does, I pull back the curtain and stand under the shower head, letting the water swirl at my feet.

Am I making this decision for the right reasons? Can I even raise a baby in this world? What is that even going to look like?

A million more questions race through my mind while I lather up some soap and scrub my skin. I'm wondering how the logistics of raising a baby are going to work, safety-wise, when I run my fingers through my hair. As soon as I'm done rinsing the shampoo out, I spend a few more minutes under the water, enjoying how it feels against my flushed skin.

When I come out, Sam isn't in the room anymore, but she's helped me choose an outfit.

I change into my jeans and a loose, flowery top, then drag a comb through my hair before blowing it dry. After using deodorant and spritzing on some perfume, I shove my feet into a pair of sneakers. Sam is waiting for me in a similar outfit at the foot of the stairs, and she smiles when she sees me. In silence, we make our way outside to the car parked next to the curb.

Paul is the one who drives us to the mall to meet up with our neighbors.

They're already there when we arrive, and they have several shopping bags in hand. Sam and I offer them a smile, and she stays close while we wander through the air-conditioned mall, moving from one shop to the next. Now and again, I spot Paul and another of the Blackthorne men trailing a few feet behind us. When we go into a perfume store, I see the two of them linger outside and fold their arms over their chests.

Are they going to be the ones protecting the baby and me? Can Carter even spare them like that when the family's in the middle of a war?

I barely interact with the other ladies, so Sam keeps up a steady stream of conversation, gushing over nail polish, clothes, and everything in between. Now and again, I feign just enough interest so our new friends don't get upset, but I can't muster up any kind of enthusiasm.

Not for this, at least. Not when I keep thinking about how I'm going to tell Carter.

A part of me imagines a moonlight dinner and handing him a shirt or a mug with the news. But the other part of me knows that's incredibly cheesy and conventional, and I can't picture Carter wearing a shirt that announces the news.

I can't even see myself handing it to him.

Frowning, I follow Sam and the other women through the rest of the mall. Halfway through our excursion, when I begin to sweat, Sam insists on taking me to the food court. She waves the rest of the women away and returns with a smoothie. I finish it all and straighten my legs out in front of me. When I stretch my arms up over my head, I notice that Sam is watching me.

"What?"

Sam shrugs and sips her drink. "I haven't said anything."

"I have thought about what you said," I tell her before letting my hands fall to my sides. "And I think it's going to be fine. It will take some adjusting, but that's the case for every new parent."

Carter and I aren't the only people in the world who are going to have to make some changes.

Nor will we be the last.

Sam takes another long sip of her drink. "So, you've decided you're going to tell Carter?"

"Yes."

"How come you didn't have another implant?"

I sit up straighter. "Honestly? I think I must have been pretty out of it when the doctor told me; otherwise, I would've remembered."

Because as happy and excited as I am about the baby, I wouldn't do this on purpose. I'm not looking to entrap Carter, not when we have an entire future planned, first with the wedding and now this.

I'm going to have a family again.

The thoughts bring tears to my eyes, and I try to hide them behind my phone screen. Sam and I are getting ready to get up when our new friends return, wearing identical expressions of concern. Wordlessly, they pull more chairs out and form a circle around the table.

As soon as they do, I take one look at their faces and stiffen. "What's wrong? Did something happen?"

Mary Jane, who is sitting closer to me, takes her phone out of her pocket. After a quick look at the others, she clears her throat. "We don't know if you've seen the article yet, but we thought you'd want to know."

I glance from one woman to the other, but no one wants to meet my gaze.

Suddenly, I'm afraid that Lilian has done something stupid and irreparable.

Out of the corner of my eye, I see Sam rummaging through her purse. She takes her phone out, and her eyes widen. Then she lowers her head, and her finger moves quickly. I wait for her to look up at me, and when she does, I wish she hadn't.

It's written all over her face.

My heart is pounding against my ears when I speak. "How bad is it?"

"It's bad," Sam replies with a shake of her head. "We should probably get going."

One by one, the ladies stand up and take their chairs back. Sam moves to help me, but I wave her away. In a daze, Sam and I find Paul and return to the car. In the backseat, I have to resist the urge to take out my phone and see the damage for myself. Although I hate being kept in the dark and not knowing what's being said, I also know that I don't want Paul to see my reaction.

And I don't want to break down in front of Sam. Not again.

I need to be strong, and I need to keep it together until I get home.

In silence, Paul pulls up outside Anita's house. Sam gets out first and spins around to face me. I don't meet her gaze and offer her a grim smile instead. Then I walk up the steps of my own house and fish the keys out of my pocket. I don't realize I'm trembling until it takes a few tries to get the door open. When I hear the familiar click, I breathe a sigh of relief and push the door open the rest of the way.

My purse falls to the floor with a clatter, and I kick the door shut.

I roll up the sleeves of my shirt and wander into the living room. There, I sink onto the couch, prop my feet up on the coffee table and inhale. On the count of five, I exhale and reach for my phone. It doesn't take me long to find the article in question.

Still, I hover over the link and wonder if I should wait for Carter.

He hasn't responded to any of my texts, and he hasn't called.

Either he hasn't seen the article yet, or he isn't worried about the fallback.

Reluctantly, I drum my fingers against my knee and turn the matter over and over in my head. A few moments later, I square my shoulders and set my phone down. After retrieving my laptop from the office, I set it down on the coffee table and open the lid, finding and quickly clicking on the link before I can change my mind.

I see her name first, Lilian McCoy, and it sends little bursts of anger through me.

She wastes no time in introducing Carter in the harshest light possible. I settle back against the couch, set the laptop down on my lap, and continue reading. In the article, she talks about everything from Carter's suspected mob ties to his connection to the old mayor to the slew of dead bodies he leaves in his wake.

The more I read, the worse I feel.

I drape an arm over my stomach and force myself to continue.

And it only gets worse because Lilian isn't just attacking Carter on a professional level. She's also done her homework and has gone above and beyond in securing witness statements detailing Carter's particular tastes in the bedroom and his preference for curvy brunettes. I taste bile in the back of my throat, but I swallow past it and keep reading.

When I reach the part where she mentions me, I jolt upright and push the laptop away.

I'm bent over the toilet in the guest bathroom before I know what I'm doing.

Everything I've eaten that day comes back up, making my eyes water and my lungs burn. When I'm sure there's nothing left in my stomach, I lean back and rip off a piece of toilet paper. I wipe my mouth, and on shaky legs, I stand up. Using the counter, I hoist myself up and grip the sink as if my life depended on it.

I wonder if it's the only thing keeping me from collapsing.

Or if it's the thought of the baby growing inside of me.

All I know is that I manage to splash cold water on my face and pat it dry. Somehow, I make it back into the living room, but rather than going back to the laptop, I go into the kitchen. I fill up the kettle, make myself some chamomile tea, and take it back to the living room.

I ignore the warning voices in my head and tuck my legs underneath me.

Despite my better judgment, I continue to read.

It feels unnerving to learn all this about Carter, to have names and lists of all the people he's hurt and all the women he's slept with. Like I have an unfair advantage by getting a peek into his past.

Each word that I read and each name that I see sends a fresh wave of anxiety through me. When I finish reading the article, I've bitten through half of my nails. Despite knowing it won't get better, I read it again, and I begin to give faces to the names.

Suddenly, I can't stop picturing all the horrible things Carter has done. Or all the women he's screwed to get Brooke out of his system.

Until a few months ago, I was one of them, and I know I can't escape that. As much as I want to leave the past behind and forget how Carter and I came to be in the first place, I know I can't. No amount of wishful thinking or praying is going to change the truth.

Or the reality of what we have to face.

But a part of me can't hide from the fact that I've been in denial. Since meeting Carter, I've come up with one excuse after another and jumped from one justification to the next, all to convince myself that he's a good person. After months of trying to convince myself that Carter isn't the monster everyone makes him out to be, it's more than a little unsettling to know that the truth is a lot more complicated.

To be forced to face it sends me reeling.

What if Sam is right? How can I bring a baby into the world, into *this* world, knowing full well the danger the baby will face?

It's bad enough that Carter's enemies target me and make kidnapping and torturing me a sport. Horror and revulsion fill me as I realize what they might do to the baby. To *our* baby.

This baby is half-Carter's, whether he likes it or not, and from the moment the baby is born, he will have a target on his head. Once he's out in the world, there'll be very little I can do to protect the baby from the people gunning for him, short of taking him and disappearing altogether.

But I can't do that to Carter, can I?

I push the laptop away and reach for my phone. Sam answers on the second ring, her voice muffled and breathless. "Have you seen the article?"

I stand up and run my fingers through my hair. "Sam, what the fuck am I going to do? I can't bring a baby into this world. Seeing that article has driven the point home for me. I know Carter has been doing a better job of protecting me, of keeping his enemies away, but a baby isn't the same."

Sam exhales, and I hear a door opening and then closing. "Of course, it isn't the same."

I glance down at my stomach and swallow. "A baby is small and helpless, and he's going to need me to protect him, to make the tough decisions that I don't want to make."

"Yes."

I sink into the couch and squeeze my eyes shut. "What the hell am I going to do, Sam? I can't leave Carter…"

"Can't or won't?"

"Does it matter? I don't want to. I love him. We're engaged. We're supposed to be getting married."

Sam sighs. "Look, I know this isn't what you want to hear, but there's a reason you called me. It's because you want someone to tell you the words you don't want to admit to yourself."

My eyes fly open, and I clutch the phone tighter. "Which are?"

"You know you can't bring a baby into Carter's world," Sam whispers, her voice catching toward the end. "I know it sucks, and I know you two have been through a lot together. I'm not saying you don't love him, Isabella… but you do have to ask yourself if love is going to be enough for the baby."

Because it's not just me anymore.

I'm a grown-ass woman who knows what I've signed up for with Carter. But my baby hasn't made that decision, and I can't make it for him.

I *won't*.

I scrub a hand over my face. "I need to think."

Without waiting for a response, I hang up and carry the laptop with me upstairs. I take the stairs two at a time, barely registering anything around me until I reach our bedroom. There, I set the laptop down and clear the browser history. Then I take a suitcase out from under the bed and unzip it. When it's open, I start throwing things into the bag haphazardly without realizing I'm crying.

I sniff and throw more clothes into the bag.

Halfway through packing, I perch on the edge of the bed and bury my face in my hands. The tears come more freely now, and my shoulders shake, but it's like a dam has burst, and I can't stop.

I'm not even sure I want to.

Because I know that I have to make the right decision for my baby, but I don't want to leave Carter.

He's my home and the only man I've ever loved.

Even if I had somewhere else to go, which I don't, I can't imagine leaving my beautiful, broken man behind.

Once the tears begin to subside, I drape an arm over my stomach and sink onto the floor. "What are we going to do, little bean? I already love you so much."

And I can't bear the thought of someone hurting my baby.

"Mommy is going to figure it out," I whisper, pausing to stroke my stomach. My eyes dart listlessly around the room until they settle on the dresser and the music box on top of it. Slowly, I rise to my feet, pick the music box up, and wind it.

Soft music fills the room and eases away some of the sorrow and ache.

"You know, my mother had a music box like this," I murmur, my gaze dropping back down to my stomach. "Every night, she used to wind it up and set it to play. We'd dance around the room together until we were breathless. And sometimes, my dad would join us and twirl my mom around."

My lips lift into a half smile. "You would've loved your grandpa, Bean. And he would've loved you so much."

I stop talking when I realize I'm crying and miss my father with a fierceness and ferocity that surprises me. Reluctantly, I sit back down on the bed and place the music box in the middle of the bag. I'm in the bathroom washing my face when I hear the front door open. Carter's familiar footsteps fill the house as he races up the stairs.

In the doorway to the bathroom, I meet him, and my eyes widen when I see the blood all over his shirt and notice his pale, ashen color. "What happened? Are you okay?"

"I'm fine. Someone jumped me at the docks and managed to stab me. Tristan took me to the hospital to get stitched up." Carter folds his arms over his chest and studies me. "Why is there a bag on the bed?"

My heart misses a beat. "I... well, I thought we could take a vacation. You have been telling me that you're going to whisk me away somewhere. Don't tell me you're going to go back on your word."

Carter's expression shifts and softens. "Yeah, we can go on vacation, but we won't be able to go anytime soon."

"Is this because of whoever attacked you?" I take Carter's hand and pull him back into the room. Then I make him sit down on the chair by the dresser and lift his shirt. He has an angry red welt in the middle of his stomach, with gauze covering the worst of it, including the stitches.

Bile rises in the back of my throat as I kneel in front of him and touch two fingers to his skin. "This looks pretty deep. I hope you got a good look at whoever did this."

Carter stiffens. "I did, and believe me, they're going to pay."

I remove my fingers and glance up at his face. "Was it that new family or their allies?"

Carter presses his lips together and doesn't say anything.

I stand up and clasp my hands behind my back. "I thought we agreed we weren't going to keep secrets from each other anymore."

Carter stands up and pulls his shirt back down. "I'm not keeping things from you, dove. And if I am, it's for your own good."

"Don't do that."

"Do what?"

"Act like I can't handle things." I throw my hands up and make a vague hand gesture. "I'm a lot stronger than you think I am. I can handle a lot, okay?"

Carter advances on me with a strange glint in his eyes. "Have you seen the article?"

Without breaking our gaze, I tilt my head back to look at him. "What article?"

Carter blows out a breath. "It's nothing important. Just don't read anything that comes out about me or you. There's a lot of shit in the press right now."

I force my lips up into a half smile. "What else is new?"

Carter bridges the distance between us and crushes me to him. "You do know that I wouldn't let anything happen to you, right? I'll kill anyone who lays a fucking hand on you, dove."

"I know."

Carter pulls back to look at me, and I can see the hunger written in his eyes. He points at the bed, and I obey. After stripping out of my clothes, I drape myself over the bed and watch him. Wordlessly, Carter pulls off his shirt and his pants and leaves them in a heap on the floor. Then he rummages through the dresser drawer and pulls out two sets of handcuffs.

He motions for me to hold my arms out on either side of me. "You're going to do exactly as I say, dove. And you're going to like it too."

"Are you sure you should be exerting that much effort after you've been stabbed?"

Carter flips me over and gives my ass a firm smack. "Didn't I say that you're going to do what I say? No interruptions, no objections and no questions."

"But—"

He gives me another firmer slap, and I swallow back the rest of my protest. When I'm quiet, Carter flips me back over and secures the handcuffs on either side of the bed. He gives them a firm tug and leans forward to press his lips to mine. His kisses are different, searing and demanding, like he's trying to make me forget something.

But it feels like he wants himself to forget, too. I know it has something to do with the article, but I'm too afraid to ask. Because I know if I bring it up, I can't take it back.

Neither of us can.

So I kiss Carter back with as much emotion as I can, wanting to drive his demons away and assure him, in whatever way I can, that I'm still his. Carter pushes the suitcase away, and it falls to the floor with a clatter, sending my things flying in every direction.

I don't have to make the decision about our baby now.

There's still time.

That's what I keep telling myself as Carter draws back and disappears. When he comes back into the room, he's got a feather in one hand and a glass with a few ice cubes in it. He crawls forward, and I realize he's holding a blindfold. After securing it around my head, I hear his mouth parting, and then the ice cube is being pressed against my flushed skin.

Goosebumps break out across every inch of me, and I shiver. Not being able to see Carter is only making this more erotic.

He uses his mouth to move the ice cube down the slope of my chest and over my stomach. Then he stops over my waistline and begins to pepper the area with hot, open-mouthed kisses. I lift my hips off the mattress, eager for more friction.

Carter pushes me down. "You're meant to be a good and obedient little dove. Remember what happens when you don't listen to me."

I tug on my restraints. "I think I need reminding, Carter. Please remind me."

In one quick move, he undoes the handcuffs, and my hands fall to my sides. Carter removes the blindfold, but before I can process anything else, he drapes me over his lap so my ass faces upward. I brace my elbows on either side of me and twist to face him. He is stroking me with a look of fierce concentration on his face. His fingers move over the tender skin, tracing the spots where the marks have mostly faded.

Wordlessly, he reaches into a bedside drawer and pulls out a belt. When it hits my skin, I don't flinch, and I don't look away.

Carter holds my gaze as he hits my behind again, a little harder than the last time. The skin is bruised and tender to the touch. He throws the belt away and hoists me, so my back is pressed against the headboard. My vision sharpens as he re-cuffs one hand and spreads my legs open. Using the feather, he trails a path down my stomach and stops at my center.

"Touch yourself, dove," Carter says in a deep and husky voice. "I want to see you please yourself."

I whimper. "I want you to touch me."

"So impatient today." Carter makes a low noise in the back of his throat and crawls up so we're at eye level. He rubs himself against me, and my breath hits my throat. I try to shift, to move closer to him, but I can't.

Carter remains frustratingly out of my reach.

He continues to rub himself against me, sending little pinpricks of frustration through me. But Carter continues to ignore my whimpers, and when I realize I'm getting nowhere, I sigh. Slowly, I drop my free hand between us and trace a path down to my heated core. I stroke myself using one finger, then two before I plunge three fingers between my wet folds.

It isn't long before I'm moaning and chanting Carter's name.

He stops rubbing himself against me and sits back on his legs.

Carter watches me so intently with so much hunger that I think I'm going to explode. I arch my back, and my fingers move faster as if chasing something I can't see. I squeeze my eyes shut and imagine Carter on top of me, ramming into me with wild and unrelenting abandon. Then the image shifts, and I see Carter on his hands and knees with his head between my legs.

I can almost feel his tongue on me.

Driving me wild and pushing me past the brink of insanity.

I climb higher and higher until abruptly, Carter takes my wrist between his hands. He ties up my other hand, and both my eyes fly open. I'm panting and half-crazed with impatience. Through hooded eyes, I give him an incredulous look and blow away an errant lock of hair.

"I like you like this, dove," Carter tells me with a wicked smile. "Then again, I like you in every way. On your hands and knees in front of me, with your ass hanging in the air. There are so many positions to try."

I squirm and lick my dry lips. "Carter."

"You know what I like most?" Carter is on top of me now, inches away from my center. I try to shift, but it's no use.

I'm completely at his mercy. The thought alone nearly has me coming undone.

"I like it when you beg when you're half-blinded by your desire for me that you'll say anything and do anything." Carter grips the back of my neck, sending dual waves of pain and pleasure through me. He holds my gaze and thrusts into me. "Like this. You like it rough, don't you, dove?"

I swallow and nod.

Carter eases out and slams back into me. "Louder. I want the whole neighborhood to hear you scream."

I focus on my breathing and the beautiful man before me. "Yes."

Carter stops moving inside of me and stays still. "Yes, what?"

"Yes, I love it when you fuck me like this." I breathe, the words pouring out of me in a rush. "I love being at your mercy, and I love it when you drive me wild."

Carter starts thrusting again, with practiced ease, each movement sending shocks through my system. "What else?"

"I love it when you play with me and make me feel like I'm the only woman in the world." My chest is tight now, and I feel a familiar rush building within me, growing stronger and stronger. "Fuck, Carter. Yeah, just like that."

He digs his nails into my hips and sinks his teeth into my neck.

I throw my head back and let out a deep, throaty groan. "Carter, I... I... oh, God."

Carter draws back to look at me and places his hands on either side of the headboard. "God has nothing to do with this, dove. Only I do. I'm the only one who can ever make you feel this good. Don't you ever forget it? You're mine."

"I'm yours," I repeat, in a daze. "I'll always be yours."

Carter's fingers dart to my clit, and with a few quick flicks, my entire body jerks and spasms. The force of my orgasm rips through me as I ride out my high. He throws his head back and gives a few more deep thrusts. I'm still staring at the ceiling, trying to draw air into my lungs when Carter's release comes. For a while, he stays still and doesn't move, so much so that I begin to wonder if he's fallen asleep.

I force both eyes open and wriggle underneath him.

A heartbeat later, Carter unlocks my wrists, and they fall to my sides. With a sigh, I wind my fingers through his hair, and he pressed his forehead to mine. Then I place my hand on his chest, over the pounding of his heart, and try to hear past the pounding in my ears.

I want us to always feel this way, to always feel this close. As if nothing in this world can come between us.

To my surprise, Carter doesn't move right away, nor does he shift away from my touch. On the contrary, he leans into it, and as his breathing evens out, I wonder if I should say something. I debate whether or not to tell him about the article in the spirit of ensuring there are no secrets between us.

But as soon as I open my mouth, the words won't come. Because I know what'll happen if Carter knows I know.

He'll double down on hunting down Lilian just to make sure the article doesn't hurt me anymore. And I know he has more important things to worry about than my pride and my ego.

The last thing I need is to find out that Lilian's name has been added to Carter's list of collateral damage. With a sigh, I release the back of Carter's neck and fall backward onto the mattress. He shifts, and I catch the myriad of emotions on his face before he stamps them out. With a smirk, he stands up and pulls on his boxers. He glances over his shoulder at me, which sends a jolt of electricity straight through me.

How am I ever going to leave this man? How am I supposed to walk away from the only man I've ever loved?

A lump rises in the back of my throat as I sit up and draw the covers up to my chest. Wordlessly, Carter ducks into the bathroom. A moment later, I hear the sound of running water. Reluctantly, I lower the sheet and swing my legs over the side of the bed. After flipping the suitcase onto its back, I pick my clothes up off the floor and re-fold them.

In a daze, I set them back in the bag, pausing to run my fingers over the edge of the music box.

When I'm done, some of the knots in my stomach have unfurled, and everything doesn't feel as bad as it did before.

How can it be when I'm still buzzing. When it feels as if every inch of me is thoroughly satiated.

Pushing away all negative thoughts, I step into the bathroom and pull the curtain aside. Carter is underneath the shower head, hair matted to his side and an expectant smile on his face. My heart does an odd little somersault as I step in, and Carter pulls me to him. His lips find mine, and I melt into his embrace. When he spins me around and presses my back against the wall, I want to melt into a puddle at his feet.

I want to be in his arms forever.

He places one arm on either side of me, caging me to him, and I don't mind. I wish I knew how to stay here with him so nothing and no one can come in between us.

A sigh falls from my lips, and Carter draws back. In silence, he reaches for the bar of soap and lathers it up. He picks up the loofa and scrubs my skin, so I'm spotless and hungry for him. Once he's done, I take the other loofa and the bar of soap and return the favor. I linger while I clean his body, admiring his lean muscles, the tautness of his stomach, and his strong, powerful shoulders.

When I reach his chest, Carter makes a low growling sound and hoists me off my feet.

This time, when he kisses me, I know he's trying to run away from something.

We stand there for the longest time, kissing until the need for air becomes too great.

Abruptly, Carter releases me and switches off the water. Then he hoists me over his shoulders and carries me into the bedroom. He returns with a towel, and I wrap it around my waist. I sit back on my legs and watch as he dries himself off, completely and utterly mesmerized by him. Once Carter is done, he pulls on a pair of pants and a button-down shirt.

Through hooded eyes, I continue to watch him. Until he leans forward and gives me another earth-shattering kiss. I move to deepen the kiss, and he growls.

"Where are you going?"

"I have a meeting at Anita's." Carter bites on my lower lip. "Come with me, dove. You can keep me company and sit on my lap."

I choke back a laugh. "I have a feeling you wouldn't get a lot of work finished that way."

Carter pulls back and gives me a knowing smirk. "I'd get plenty of work finished, dove. Don't underestimate me."

I shake my head. "Never."

Carter gives me one last look before he disappears. I listen for the sound of the door opening and closing. As soon as it does, I fall back against the mattress and bring one arm over my head. The other cups my stomach. I count backward from ten and wait for the fluttering in my chest to abate.

What am I supposed to do now?

I can't possibly leave Carter.

Carter

"How did she take the news?" Tristan pushes himself off the wall and takes a step in my direction. "I imagine she wants to hunt Lilian down herself."

I shrug. "She would if she'd read the article."

Tristan raises an eyebrow. "How has she not seen it yet? It's all over the news and social media."

"I don't need you to tell me," I snap with a pointed look in Tristan's direction. "Are you going to contribute something useful, or are we just going to stand out here and waste time?"

Tristan opens his mouth and slams it shut.

I climb up the steps of the front porch and push past him. As soon as I step into Anita's, the loud voices of my family hit me first, followed by the distinct smell of tomato sauce and soup. I venture further into the house and find everyone gathered around the kitchen counter. A few of the Blackthornes are on their phones, their eyebrows knotted together.

Others are whispering among themselves.

All of them straighten when they see me, and conversation trails off.

I don't look at anyone as I make a beeline for the counter and pull out one of the chairs. The screeching sound echoes in the house, but no one moves or even acknowledges it. I sit down, link my fingers together, and glance around the room.

"I know you've all seen the article by now. Somebody better have a fucking solution for this."

A murmur of unease rises through the crowd.

"And why the fuck is Lilian still running around? She was meant to be taken care of weeks ago."

"I went back to see Frances today," Tristan replies, with a quick look around the room. "He's given us the locations of a few more addresses and known associates. Paul is following up on that information."

But it's obvious he hasn't found anything, or Tristan would've told me by now.

I clench my hands into fists at my side and stand up. "This is not the news I want. We don't need any more scrutiny, not with the new mayor breathing down our necks."

Especially because I have no idea what kind of information Lilian has armed him with.

And now that Donahue has shown his true colors, we can't afford a war on all fronts—not without allies and more resources.

Fuck.

How many of them already know about Donahue's backstabbing? How many of them saw it coming?

I swing my gaze over to Tristan, who is leaning against a wall with his arms folded over his chest. "What's going on with the Philipses and the Natoris?"

"They're still recovering from our last hit," Tristian replies, with a lift of his chin. "We won't have anything to worry about for a while. They need to re-group."

I give my cousin a tight nod. "Fucking finally. We need more news like this. What about Donahue? I want his fucking his head on a platter."

And I want to serve it to my entire family… and Isabella.

There's nothing I hate more than a rat who gets away.

Imagining what I'll do when I see him is the only thing keeping me from prowling the streets and hunting him down myself. That and the fact that I need to find a solution to my more immediate problem.

Lilian fucking McCoy.

I should've known she was more trouble than she was worth, and I should've taken care of it when I had the chance. Any restraint I have is growing less and less by the day.

With a slight shake of my head, I stand up straighter and allow my gaze to sweep over the room. "Call our contacts in the press. Get me someone on the phone who knows how to kill this story. Now."

Everyone erupts into a frenzy of activity except for Tristan, who drifts closer to me. He waits until everyone else is occupied or gone before he leans against the counter opposite me. "What about a press release?"

"I've already spoken to Mitch. He's looking for the legal repercussions of the article and trying to determine if a press conference will do more damage than good."

"And the mayor?"

"Are you just going to stand there stating the fucking obvious? I don't need a play-by-play, Tristan. I already know what's at stake."

And I know that containing this isn't going to be easy. Between Lilian, the warring families, and now Donahue, we have our hands full. For the first time in a long time, I don't know where the hell I'm supposed to start.

All I know is that I regret leaving Isabella in bed to come here.

I'm tempted to go back home, crawl into bed, and pull Isabella to me. I want the smell and feel of her to wash over me and keep everything else at bay.

But I know now isn't the time to lose my focus. If we have any hope of fighting this off, the Blackthorne family needs every last part of me to be aware and present. And ready to bury our enemies.

It's what I'm good at.

It's one of the many reasons why I was chosen as the head of the Blackthorne family. After another brief pause, I unclench my hands and take my phone out of my pocket. "When you're done, we have something else to take care of."

"Got somewhere else you got to be?"

I give Tristan a cold look. "We know where Lilian is working. It's high time I visited her boss and let him know who he's dealing with."

Tristan and I exchange a look as he pushes himself off the counter. "I'm ready whenever you are."

CHAPTER THIRTY-FIVE

Isabella

"Sam, please don't look at me like that." I pick up another item of clothing and put it away. "I know what we talked about, and I know what we said…"

Sam sighs and sinks into the chair by the bedroom window. "I just don't understand what changed."

"Nothing changed. I just decided to give Carter the benefit of the doubt. He's been keeping me safe, so I know he'll keep the baby safe, too."

He has to.

What other choice does he have? Unless he doesn't want the baby to begin with.

Shit.

I've been trying not to wonder what would happen if he refuses to take responsibility and decides he doesn't want to be a father after all. A part of me pictures Carter sweeping me into his arms and kissing me senseless when I tell him. The other part of me imagines Carter's angry face as he moves away from me and paces.

I'm terrified to realize that I have no idea which way this is going to go. Or if I'm even going to be allowed to stay here if Carter decides he doesn't want a baby.

Does he love me enough to keep me around? Or is he going to find an excuse to cast me out?

"Isabella, I'm asking you to reconsider, please." Sam sits up straighter and links her fingers together. "I'm not telling you to keep it a secret from him or even leave him. I'm just asking that you go into hiding until the baby is older."

I pick up another item of clothing and pause with my hand in the air. "Raise the baby on my own?"

Sam exhales. "Look, I don't want to be the one to say this, but it's not like Carter is going to be able to help you even if you do stay, and that's assuming he wants the baby to begin with. What if he tells you to put him up for adoption or something?"

I drop the dress and wheel around to face Sam. "He wouldn't."

Would he? I wish I knew for certain, but even I know Sam has a point.

Carter is the kind of man who is used to getting his way, and there's nothing he dislikes as much as being rejected or disobeyed.

What if I defy Carter and keep the baby? Will it mean the end of us?

Sam untucks her legs and stands up. "I'm not saying he will or won't. I honestly have no fucking clue. That man is a mystery to me, so I won't pretend to understand him. But I think I know enough about you to know that you will not be able to live with it."

I dig my nails into my palms. "What do you mean?"

"I mean, you've got a big heart, Isabella. Too big for any of this shit, and you love Carter too much to demand anything from him, even things he rightfully owes you."

"He doesn't owe me anything."

Sam throws her arms up and comes to a stop a few feet away. Her eyes settle on my face, and a furrow appears between her brows. "Babe, Carter owes you a lot. He dragged you into this mess to begin with, knowing full well what it would mean for you and your life."

"It's not like he forced any of this on me. I chose this life, Sam."

And I would choose it all over again for the chance to be with Carter.

I have very few regrets in that regard.

"Yes, but you chose it without knowing what it meant. It's okay to admit that, Isabella. Even I don't know what most of this means. But you and I… we're different. We're grown-ups. Right or wrong, our decisions are ours to make."

I suck in a harsh breath. "Are you telling me I'm making the wrong decision for my baby? I wouldn't endanger him or her like that."

I already love my baby more than I thought was possible.

Over the last few weeks, as Carter has prepared himself to go to war with the warring families, Lilian, and everyone in between, I've spent my time online, reading about mothers and babies and all of the things I need to do to ensure the baby's arrival is as smooth and painless as possible.

But none of the websites included advice on how to deal with the mob banging on my doorstep. Or getting bloodstains out of the carpets. And none of them will.

Sam takes both of my hands in hers, and her expression softens. "Isabella, I know you wouldn't. I don't mean it like that. I just want to make sure you've thought about this because it sounds to me like you chickened out."

I wrench my hands away and give Sam a wounded look. "That's a mean thing to say."

"It's not. You're an emotional person, and you tend to make decisions based on your heart, not your head." Sam gives a slight shake of her head, and her expression turns apologetic. "I'm not saying that's necessarily a bad thing, but in this case, you need all the help you can get."

I blink back the tears. "I'm trying, Sam. You have no idea how hard all of this has been."

Or how much I wish I could go visit my father, have him throw his arm around me, and stroke my hair. Suddenly, I'd give anything to have him with me, feel his body shielding mine, and hear his deep voice soothe all my fears. He would've known exactly what to do.

But nothing I say or do is going to bring him back, no matter how badly I want it to be true.

"I know all this is hard. I can't even imagine what this must be like, but you need to be honest with yourself, Isabella. Starting with the article. Carter doesn't know that you know, does he?"

I swallow and shake my head. "When he came home, and I saw his wound and the panic in his eyes, I... I just couldn't do that to him."

Not when it meant having that information between us. And giving the article more power than it already has.

Lilian is using her information like a weapon to force us apart, and I'll be damned if I let her get away with it. Carter and I have been through too much to let one power-hungry, lustful journalist get in the way.

Sam grimaces. "I get it, but he will find out sooner or later. You can't keep it a secret forever, and you need to figure out how you're going to tell him about the baby."

I nod, but the tears are still burning the back of my eyes. "I know."

Because as much as I want to protect and give us time to process everything, I can't let these secrets fester between us. They've done too much damage already.

I clear my throat. "Do you have any idea who betrayed the Blackthornes? Carter won't tell me what happened at the docks."

Sam shakes her head. "Tristan won't tell me either, but it must be serious."

"They should go to Donahue for help," I murmur, pausing to push my hair out of my face. Although I haven't seen him since he rescued me from being trafficked, Rich has been on my mind. Now and again, I wonder if he's had any luck finding his sister, and I feel the urge to reach out to him and make sure he's okay.

But I know it's going to do more harm than good. Carter is too jealous of Rich for us to ever be friends. The mere mention of his name sends Carter into a dark place, and I know it's the last thing he needs.

Still, I wish I could talk to someone who understood, who isn't going to judge or try to point me in one direction or the other.

Sam is trying, but no amount of effort is going to change the fact that she can't relate.

Sam's phone rings, and she fishes it out of her pocket. "I should get going. Are you going to be okay?"

I nod and give her a small smile. "I'm going to unpack the rest of the bag and take a bath."

"Maybe work on some of the designs as well. You haven't done that in a while." Sam puts her phone away and gives me a pointed look. "I'm here if you need me."

Without waiting for a response, Sam spins around and exits the room. When she's gone, I finish unpacking the rest of the bag and reach for the music box. I run my fingers over the edge, slowly, delicately, as if it's the most precious thing in the world. Then I set it down in the middle of the dresser and wind up the tiny ballerina.

I hum along to the music as I strip out my clothes.

In the bath, I submerge my body beneath the bubbles and listen to the sound of running water. When I turn it off, I'm plunged into silence and left at the mercy of my thoughts. Rolling my shoulders, I drape my arms on either side of me and frown. I have my head tilted back, and I'm singing to myself when Carter comes in, wearing a grim expression.

Without changing out of his clothes, he gets into the bathtub with me, causing some of the water to slosh over. He stretches his legs out on either side of me and presses me to him. His clothes are dirty and smell like sweat, but I don't mind, especially when he wraps his arms around me and presses a kiss to the back of my head.

Carter is usually never this sweet or tender. Not that he doesn't have his moments, but they are too few and far between for my liking.

Since discovering this side of him, I have tried to bring more and more of it to the surface.

I twist an arm over my head and wind my fingers through his hair. "What happened? Are you okay?"

Carter nods and releases a deep breath. "We haven't been able to have the bad press completely killed."

"Didn't you say that your lawyer is taking care of it?"

"Mitch has his work cut out for him," Carter replies in a strange voice. "There's a lot of shit happening. But he's good. I know he'll come through. I just hope it isn't too late."

I twist to face Carter, but he pushes my head forward. "Don't shut me out, Carter. We talked about this."

Carter runs his hands over my bare skin. "I know, but there isn't much to say, dove. War is a necessary evil, but it's still one I try to avoid."

"I thought the Philipses and Natoris were still recuperating from the last attack."

"They were." Carter exhales and plays with the hair on the nape of my neck. "But they've had a little help from other allies, and now they're back like the fucking cockroaches they are."

"What about Donahue? Can't he help?"

Carter shifts and presses a kiss to the back of my neck. "The Blackthorns need to do this on their own."

"What about Frances? Didn't you mention that you have some kind of deal?"

"So far, we've held up our end of the bargain, but Lilian has proven to be a lot more resourceful than I gave her credit for."

I wriggle away from Carter and move to the other end of the tub so I can face him. He is watching me intently as if I have all the answers in the world. "What can I do to help?"

Carter's expression tightens. "You are not going anywhere near this war, dove. You've already fought enough, and you've been dragged into too much of this shit. Don't ask me about this again."

I move my arms and pull some of the bubbles closer so they're covering my chest. "Carter, you know you can ask me for a lot of things, but you can't ask me to stay out of this. I'm already in it."

Carter frowns. "That's not the same thing, and you know it. There's a big difference between you being forced to deal with this shit and walking right into it."

I grip the edges of the tub and give Carter a frustrated look. "Don't split hairs, please."

Carter shakes his head and gets out of the tub, causing more water to slosh over. I watch his back as he stands over the sink and grips the edge. "I don't know why you're being so fucking difficult."

I frown and sink lower into the water. "I'm not trying to be—"

Carter spins around to face me, and his face is etched in cold fury. "Do you have any idea the kind of things I do for you? What I have to do to keep us safe? To keep you safe? If you knew, you'd be on your knees every night instead of this bullshit."

Abruptly, I stand up, and I don't care that more of the water spills over and drowns the bathroom floor. I cross my arms over my chest and give Carter a pointed look. "That's not fair. I never asked you to do any of those things."

"I don't do them because you fucking asked me, dove. I do them because that's what a man is supposed to do for the woman he loves, and you're my goddamn fiancée."

"Exactly. *You* pointed it out yourself. *I'm your goddamn fiancée.* You need to start acting like it. I'm not some prize to be kept or tucked away when you want to take it out and show it off. I'm a human being."

Carter's hands clench into fists. "You think I don't fucking know that?"

I slide one leg over the tub, then the other, and bridge the distance between us. Carter doesn't move away from me or react when I wrap my arms around his neck and look up so I meet his gaze directly. Instead, he continues to stand there, as stiff as a statue, his breathing harsh and uneven.

I wind my fingers through his hair and breathe out. "Carter, I am not trying to push you away or make your life harder. I know you have a lot to deal with, but I don't want to be pushed away."

And I have no idea how much longer I can take him icing me out.

In the beginning, when my dad first died, I didn't mind because it gave me the chance I needed to process and grieve. While I know that I'm going to miss my dad for the rest of my life, and the pain of not having him around is never going to go away, I also know that I can't live in it forever.

I can't dwell on it for the remainder of my life. Not with a baby growing inside of me. And not when I'm trying to fight for a future for Carter and me.

The only chance we have is if we work through the hardship together, side by side, like we're meant to. Otherwise, we might as well throw in the towel right now and call it a day.

But I can't imagine doing that, not where Carter is involved, and I know he'd rather die than give up on me.

On us.

Reaching Carter has become more challenging since this whole business with the Philipses and the Natoris, and I know a large part of that is because of me. I should've pushed harder.

I shouldn't have retreated into my shell in order to shut out the outside world. While a part of me appreciates the time I was given away from everything happening, the other part regrets the price I've had to pay. Rather than finding everything the same, I realize that the world is quickly moving on without me.

And if I don't catch up, I'm going to be left behind… by Carter and everyone else. I'm not going to let that happen, not if I can help it.

CHAPTER THIRTY-SIX

Isabella

Carter's hands move to his back, and he unlocks my fingers. Then he steps out of my arms and disappears into the bedroom, where I hear him muttering and shoving things away. Hastily, I snatch a towel from behind the bathroom door and secure it around my chest. Once I do, I nearly lose my footing and go sprawling, face first, onto the floor. At the last second, I catch myself and collide with Carter's powerful chest. His hands immediately move to my waist to steady me.

I tilt my head back, and the rest of the words die on my lips. Carter has already come a long way, and I can already see how difficult this is for him. How much it's hurting him to keep me away.

In his own way, he's trying to protect me by keeping me as far away as possible from the debris and chaos. Considering everything I've faced over the past few months, especially as Carter and I have gotten closer, I understand his reasoning.

But I know there has to be another way.

These can't be our only two options. I refuse to believe that.

Carter keeps his arms around my waist as his eyes move over me, drinking in every inch of me. "You are not being pushed away, dove. I am fucking doing everything within my power to protect you and make sure you don't get kidnapped again."

I nod. "I know that, but part of that means letting me in. It means telling me what's on your mind so you don't have to go through any of this alone."

Carter exhales and presses his forehead to mine. "I'm not the hearts and feelings type, Isabella. You've always known this about me. Don't ask me to be something I'm not."

Nor would I.

I fell in love with Carter because of his strength, loyalty to the people he loves, and willingness to do what needs to be done. Even getting his hands dirty.

With Carter, I feel something I've never felt before.

I feel safe.

Safer than I've felt in years, despite the chaotic and messy life I've been dragged into and Carter's endless slew of enemies who are willing to play dirty and go to whatever lengths they need to in order to win. While I know that Carter doesn't have the moral high ground, not by any stretch of the imagination, I at least know that he does have some boundaries.

Carter would never go after their families. No matter how far they pushed him.

Knowing that gives me some comfort, making me feel like he might accept our baby after all. Over the past few days, I've been trying to work up the nerve to tell him. Unfortunately, the harder I try to find the courage to tell him the truth, the more complicated it gets.

Because I know this isn't the right time.

With everything going on, there's never going to be a right time.

When Carter pulls away to look at me, I take his hand and lead him to the bed. Despite his insistence on maintaining control over every aspect of his life, including where I'm involved, Carter doesn't protest. He doesn't even protest when I push him onto the bed and climb onto his lap. In silence, he wraps his arms around my waist and tilts his head back to look up at me.

"I love you, Carter Blackthorne. I know you know that, but I need you to believe it." I place a hand over his chest and look into his eyes. "Whenever things get tough, whenever they get to be too much, I want you to remember that. Remember me and what we're fighting for."

Carter makes a low noise in the back of his throat. In one quick move, he shifts me so I'm on the mattress, and he's on top of me. He lowers his head to kiss me, and it feels different, sweeter, like he's trying to make me understand something he can't put into words.

It makes butterflies erupt in my stomach. My entire body feels on fire like I'm going to burn from the inside out. But I don't care, not as long Carter is the one who is fanning the flames.

He and I could burn together, and it wouldn't matter.

I kiss him back with just as much fervor and just as much passion. However, when I move to deepen the kiss and link my legs around his waist, he stops. Reluctantly, he wrenches his lips away and looks down at me as if he's trying to commit me to memory. I give him a confused look and wriggle against him.

"What's happening? Why did you stop?"

Carter frames my face in his hands and says nothing. "War is coming, dove. I've done my best to avoid it, but I don't have a choice anymore. It's not just going to be against the Philipses and the Natoris. It's against the mayor too. He's a fucking snake, but he's a lot more resourceful than I gave him credit for."

"Can't you ask the Donahues to help?"

Carter frowns. "No."

I sit up on my elbows and huff. "Why not? Rich has already proven his worth more than once. Please don't tell me it's about those stupid pictures that were posted of us. He doesn't mean anything to me, Carter. You know that."

Carter's expression darkens as he leans back and scowls. "We are not talking about Rich fucking Donahue anymore."

"Carter, don't be stubborn. You need his help, his resources—"

"I said we're not talking about him anymore," Carter replies, his voice rising toward the end. "I'm not discussing this anymore, dove. You need to stop pushing."

I open my mouth to protest, see the look on his face, and slam it shut. I don't want to keep having the same argument.

With a sigh, I fall back against the mattress, and Carter curls up against me. He sleeps on his side, so he's facing me, and I let my eyes move over every inch of him.

Like I'm trying to carve his features into my brain. I want him committed to my memory and engraved on my heart.

"I was thinking about the wedding," I whisper, pausing to link my fingers together. "How would you feel about somewhere tropical? I can't remember the last time I went to the beach."

"Whatever you want, dove."

I frown. "You get some input, too. It's your wedding."

Carter shrugs and flips onto his back. He places a hand behind his head and stares up at the ceiling. "I honestly don't give a shit where we get married, as long as we do."

"Oh."

"I don't want you to worry about the expenses or anything like that," Carter continues, not hearing the disappointment in my voice. "But don't expect me to be a hands-on type of groom. Tristan will get me there in one piece."

"Were you expecting to get there in several pieces?"

Carter twists his head to look at me and gives me a blank look. "Your humor needs some work, dove."

"I know, but you're not allowed to get blown up or cut up into pieces or whatever, okay? You make sure you come back to me, Carter."

Otherwise, I'm going to have to hunt down his enemies myself. And I don't know the first thing about revenge or making people play.

But I'm all too sure that if anything happens to Carter, his family will be more than happy to help me.

"You and I are going to get married soon," I add in a lighter voice. "And who knows, maybe we'll even start our own family."

I watch his face carefully, but his expression doesn't change when I say the words.

"I know we've never talked about it before, but I do want to have kids someday," I continue, my voice rising a little toward the end. Pausing, I clear my throat and ignore the nervous fluttering in the center of my stomach. "I think you'd make a great dad, for what it's worth."

Carter snorts and doesn't look over at me. "Your sense of humor isn't going to improve if you make jokes like that, dove."

I swallow. "What if I'm not kidding? What if I do want us to become parents?"

Carter flips onto his side to face me, a furrow between his brows. "I honestly can't tell if you're serious or trying to keep my mind off things."

"A little of both?"

"You'd make a fucking amazing mother, dove," Carter tells me with a half-smile. "I don't doubt that, but I don't know the first thing about being a father, and at this point, I think it's too late for me. I'm set in my ways."

"You could learn."

Carter places his hands on my waist and draws me closer. "I could, but why in the fuck would I want to? I enjoy having you all to myself. It's not like we can raise a baby in this environment anyway."

My heart drops at his words, but I try not to let it show on my face. Carter has no idea why I'm asking. As far as he's concerned, I'm just making small talk in an effort to keep his mind off things.

And I'm not even succeeding.

I'm overcome with the urge to tell him the truth and let the chips fall where they may. Until he opens his mouth and speaks again.

"Besides, you've got the implant, so there's no chance you're getting pregnant. We've got bigger things to focus on, dove."

My eyes flick down to my arm, and sweat forms on the back of my neck. "What if the implant wasn't there anymore? Not on purpose, obviously, but what if it was removed because of some kind of accident?"

Carter's hands move to my back, and he helps me out of the towel. When I'm naked in front of him, he runs his fingers over my skin, tracing something I can't see. "I don't deal in hypotheticals, dove. Neither should you."

I study his face and fall silent. It's too late for me to tell him now anyway. The moment has passed.

But I can't help but mourn it as it passes.

Chapter Thirty-Seven

Isabella

"Speaking of bigger things to focus on, tomorrow you and Tristan are going to the mansion in the woods," Carter states, clearly changing the subject away from children.

I lean back and stare at Carter incredulously. "What? Why?"

"Because I have a war to win, and I can't do that if I know you're not safe."

"I can stay at Anita's," I offer, my mind racing to come up with possibilities. "Or I can stay in a hotel or something. I don't want to go to the mansion alone."

Especially because the last time we were there, we were attacked. An image of the man's inert body springs to mind, and I shudder.

"I don't want to go there, Carter. Please."

"It's the only place safe enough and remote enough, dove," Carter replies with a little more force than necessary. "Tristan is going to be with you, and I'll see if we can spare anyone else."

With the war, I know that leaving Tristan with me is difficult enough. I don't want them to be stretched thin.

Not on my account.

"I don't need anyone else," I tell him in a small voice. "I just want to stay here and wait for you."

"It's not possible, dove. Everyone who isn't in the war is going into hiding, including you. Anita is going to be in a safe house not too far from where you are."

"Can't she come with me?"

Carter shakes his head. "It's not safe to have the two of you in the same place in case security is breached. But I've made sure you're as safe as can be."

My stomach fills with knots, and unease races up my spine. "What if they break in again? Tristan can't save me by himself."

Carter stares at me for the longest time.

Wordlessly, he gets up and rummages through a drawer. When he swings his gaze back to mine, he's holding a small gun in his hand. He takes both of my hands and closes them around the sleek and cold metal. Ice settles in my veins.

"I don't want this." I try to give it back to him, but Carter moves out of reach. "Carter, seriously. Just take this back. I'm not going to use it."

"You shouldn't have any reason to use it. This is for my own peace of mind, dove," Carter responds before taking a few more steps away. "Tristan will show you how to use it. You need to make sure you keep it on you at all times, put it under your pillow or something. But always make sure you have the safety on."

My hands begin to tremble, and tears pour out of my eyes. "Carter, please. I don't like this. I don't want the gun, and I don't want to go to a safe house. There's got to be something else I can do, somewhere else I can go."

Carter remains unmoved. "I need to keep you safe, dove. This is the only way to do that. You trust me, don't you?"

I nod through my tears. "I do, but this has nothing to do with trusting you."

It has everything to do with the outside world coming for me. Again. Whenever Carter and I are apart, bad things happen, and I'm not looking to test my luck. Not now, of all times.

Carter kneels in front of me, and his eyes move over my face. "You have to trust me, dove. When this war is over, I will come for you. In the meantime, Tristan is going to keep you safe."

I stare at Carter until the tears stop. Until some of the knots in my stomach unfurl, and some of the ice in my veins melts.

When he takes the gun out of my hands and places it on the dresser, I'm only too relieved to hand it over. Then he pulls me to my feet, and I let him. His hands drop to my waist, and Carter kisses me like he's been starving or I'm the air he needs to breathe.

Like he's been wandering the desert for a thousand days.

I kiss him back like he's the only thing keeping me tethered to the ground, and I need him to keep from disappearing. Carter makes a low growling sound in the back of his throat, and I tilt my head to the side. He nips on my lower lip, and my mouth parts, allowing him access. His tongue darts in and begins a sensual battle for dominance.

His fingers dig into my back, and wave after wave of pleasure rises within me.

I moan when Carter keeps a hand on my waist as the other darts up to cup my breast. He flicks one nipple and then the other until they're both as hard as pebbles. With a growling sound that sends shivers breaking out across my skin, he pushes them together.

Molten-hot desire continues to build within me.

Carter wrenches his lips away and presses hot, open-mouthed kisses over my jaw and down my neck. His mouth, that searing, hot, capable mouth of his, traces a path down the slope of my chest. He stops when he reaches my waist and looks up at me. I'm trembling by now, and I've got a thin sheen of sweat on my forehead.

None of it seems to matter.

All that matters is the man lowering himself onto the floor in front of me and spreading my legs apart. I fall backward onto the bed, the breath whooshing out of me. Carter pauses to hoist me up and tie my hands together. Wordlessly, he kneels back down in front of me and buries his head between my thighs. Slowly, he kisses a path along the inside of my thighs, driving me more and more crazy.

I think I might explode if I don't feel his tongue between my wet folds. Or his hands playing with my breasts.

Every part of me aches for him and yearns for him in a way that still surprises me.

Carter's hands move up, and he grips my hips. He rubs his head against my center, the days' old stubble sending little pinpricks of desire through my veins. Then, his tongue darts out and licks a path down the center. I jolt, and my body lurches forward. Carter pinches my skin, and I sit up straighter, spots dancing in my field of vision.

His tongue darts sideways, lapping up my already gushing juices.

I swallow and try to keep my gaze fixed on him. "That feels so good, Carter."

He makes a low noise and runs his tongue back and forth. Over and over, he brings me close to the edge of oblivion and stops. Finally, he reaches between us and pushes me so my back collides with the mattress. I'm staring up at the ceiling when Carter stops devouring me and stands up. His eyes stay on my face as he pushes his boxers down and reaches for one of his toys.

With a smirk, he places it between my wet folds and pulls me to my feet.

When he gives my ass a firm slap, dual waves of pain and pleasure ricochet through me. Carter kisses me again, and I melt against him. Without deepening the kiss, he spins me around so I'm on my hands and knees, my ass hanging in the air. His hands move to the front, and he does something to the device, so it comes to life.

It starts vibrating, and I almost collapse against the mattress.

The tiny device inside me sends little bursts of energy through me, so

I press my lips together. Carter strokes my behind and rubs himself against me. I whimper and try to bridge the distance between us, but Carter is determined not to give me what I want.

He wants to drag this on for as long as possible.

And I want him to.

But I also want him inside of me, filling every inch of me, so I can't tell where he begins and I end.

In one quick move, Carter pulls the toy out, thrusts inside me, and groans. "Fuck, how are you always so tight, dove?"

I grind against him and gasp. "You're so big, Carter. And you feel so good."

Carter's hands dart between us, and he pinches my nipples between his fingers. He thrusts in and out of me at an even pace while continuing to roll them between his fingers. I'm panting and sweating. I call out his name when Carter slams into me again. This time, he holds himself absolutely still as he fills me to the hilt.

I wriggle, but he slaps my ass hard.

I know it's going to leave a mark, but I don't care. I want him to mark me, to leave an imprint of himself on my skin.

A part of me wants the whole world to know what we have, how unshakeable it is.

As soon as the thought leaves my mind, Carter straightens his back and grips my waist. He keeps me in place while he thrusts in and out. I hear a low clicking sound, and the device inside me starts making low vibrating sounds. All my senses are invaded at once, and it takes everything I have not to collapse onto the mattress in a heap of pleasure.

I don't even know how I'm holding myself upright.

With an exhale, I press my lips together and focus on the headboard.

The bed dips and creaks underneath us, and Carter strokes my back. My skin is flushed and eager and tingling, but Carter still won't give me what I want. He is torturing me, one practiced and eased thrust at a time, and there isn't a single thing I can do.

Except let him have his way with me.

My stomach does odd little somersaults when Carter brings his head to rest against my back. His mouth parts, and he presses kisses there, sending shivers racing through me. I tug on my restraints, but it's no use.

Whatever Carter has planned, I'm going to have to follow his every order.

His every whim and desire.

"Don't even think about coming yet, dove," Carter whispers into my ear. "We've got all night, and I plan on making every second count."

I cry out when he rams into me again.

"You're going to be screaming my name, and you're going to be sore that you're not going to be able to walk straight for days," Carter says, punctuating each word with a thrust harder than the last one. My muscles contract and expand, and sweat forms on the back of my neck and down the sides of my face. When I'm covered in sweat and nearing my release, Carter stops, and I whimper. He pushes me forward so I'm on my stomach. I twist my head to face him, and Carter helps me so I'm curled up sideways on the bed.

Then he presses his lean and powerful body against mine and buries himself inside me.

I rock back and forth against him, the swell of emotion within my chest growing.

He presses my breasts together and uses his free hand to stroke my center. I move my legs further apart and marvel at how everything feels. From the way his fingers glide over my skin like I'm made of glass to the way his cock feels inside of me, like its sole purpose is to shatter me.

To break me.

I have no idea how much longer I can hold on, but I'm not surprised when tears prick the back of my eyes.

What Carter and I have is transcendent; it makes the earth move and shatter.

I want to cling to it for as long as possible, so I squeeze my legs together and stop moving against Carter. He digs his nails into my waist and sinks his teeth into my neck. A jolt of electricity rises through me as Carter throws a leg over me and pins me against the mattress. Both of his hands move to my chest until my breasts are tender, my nipples as hard as pebbles.

Still, it's not enough for him.

Carter rams in and out of me like a wild animal that both surprises and excites me. I try to match his energy, but my heart is galloping wildly in my chest. I can barely hear past the pounding in my ears, but when I realize I'm breathing heavily and Carter hasn't broken a sweat, my stomach dips.

He is still sucking on my skin, and I'm sure it's going to leave a mark.

At this point, my entire body feels like Carter's canvas, a work of art to be admired by only the two of us. I lean into his touch and shudder. Carter's hands fall to my waist, and he grips it hard. Then he removes his mouth and buries his face against my hair. His breathing is hot against my skin, and it's sending more and more butterflies to my stomach.

My breath quickens, my muscles clench, and my entire body explodes.

I writhe and spasm, falling as the force of my orgasm rips through me. Carter doesn't stop moving inside me, doesn't stop dominating my body with his. Spots dance in my field of vision, and I think I'm going to shatter into a million pieces. Then I come back down to my body to feel Carter's fingers inside me.

A tremor still moves through my body when he flips me onto my back.

My vision is still hazy, the thick and heavy fog of desire settling around me as Carter positions himself on top of me. He drapes my legs over his shoulders and thrusts into me. I gasp at the impact, at how it feels to be so exposed and so vulnerable, but I don't care anymore. Especially when Carter starts moving, his pace slow and measured, like we have all the time in the world.

I link my fingers together and moan. "Carter, Carter."

"Keep saying my name like that, and I'll push you up against the wall and fuck you until you can't speak," Carter warns in a deep and husky voice. "Do you want me to punish you, dove? Is that what you want?"

I barely manage a nod.

Suddenly, Carter tugs me to my feet and pulls me to the wall. I am facing the wall when Carter lifts my arms on either side of me. I feel something brush against my skin, and then Carter ties my feet together. When I twist to face him, he has retrieved his belt from the dresser drawer. I don't look away as he rubs his fingers over it and brings it down against my skin.

I jolt at the impact.

He whips me again, the hunger on his face growing more and more animated. "I'm the one in control here, dove. You answer to me. You submit only to me."

I swallow and press my lips together.

He kicks my legs further apart and tosses the belt away. His hand connects with my bare skin, and he starts to stroke me. I lean my head against the wall and ignore the pounding in my chest. Carter nudges my legs further apart and positions himself at my behind. I brace myself when he pins my arms against the wall and thrusts in.

Every part of my body comes alive. I'm tingling and brimming with sensation.

He groans and grunts against me, and I fall again. My lungs burn with effort while I struggle to keep myself upright. Using one hand, Carter keeps my arms pinned together, and he uses his other hand to wind his fingers through my hair. He tugs my head back, exposing my neck to his mouth. He latches onto it and presses hot, open-mouthed kisses there.

Then he sinks his teeth there, over the previous mark, and I'm sure he's drawn blood.

But I don't care. I want his ferocity, his single-mindedness, his determination. I want all of it, all of him, all the time.

Carter removes his teeth and gives my hair a firm tug, sending little pinpricks of pain through my scalp. I tilt my head back and release a deep, shaky breath. Carter continues to thrust in and out of me. Abruptly, he stops and moves me to the bed, where my knees give out, and I fall onto the mattress. Carter climbs on top of me, never once breaking our contact.

I listen to his heavy breathing, to the bed creaking and groaning underneath it, and I think my heart can't possibly feel more full.

Or more alive.

Until Carter buries his head between my shoulder blades, and I come undone again. I am floating and drifting on clouds as I try to remember how to breathe. Carter gives a few more quick thrusts, and his own release follows. I feel warmth pool between my legs and exhale. A short while later, Carter releases my restraints and pulls me against him. I bring my head to rest against his chest and go limp.

"I think you've killed me," I murmur, a pleasant tingling sensation racing through me. "Not that I mind, but it is definitely going to be hard to function after this."

Carter runs a hand down the length of my back and pauses at my ass.

Still sore and tender, he gives it a firm squeeze, and I yelp. "No, you feel alive to me. That means I haven't quite done my job properly, have I, dove?"

I lift hooded eyes up to his. "What do you mean?"

Carter tilts his head to look down at me. "I promised that you wouldn't be able to walk for days. I think I can do better."

I shake my head. "Are you kidding? I can barely breathe. My entire body is sore. You've definitely done your job, Carter. Unless you want me to be stuck in this bed."

Carter's answering smile is wicked. "That is definitely something I want to see."

My lips lift into a half smile. "It can be arranged."

Carter captures my hand in his. "I know what you're trying to do, dove. You're hoping I'll fuck you hard enough that I won't be able to leave in the morning."

"Am I that obvious?"

Carter presses a kiss to the inside of my wrist. "Yes, and as much as I'd love to be buried in that tight and sweet little pussy of yours all night, we can't."

I throw a leg over him and use my fingers to trace a path down his chest. "Are you sure I can't convince you otherwise?"

Knowing I'm going to be separated from Carter, regardless of the duration, makes me want him even more. The fire inside me has yet to be quenched, and I don't know how to tell him. Carter prides himself on his virility and mastery in the bedroom. Anything less than that is unacceptable, but I also know that he's right.

In the morning, before he heads over to Anita's, Carter has to take me to the safe house.

This will be our last night together for God knows how long.

I want to make every moment last, but I also want to savor how he feels pressed against me, his arm around my shoulders, and the smell of him wafting up my nostrils.

I wish I could freeze this moment and keep us here.

"You've become very persuasive, dove." Carter's voice pitches low, and his eyes blaze with emotion. Still, he captures my other hand in his and pins me to the mattress. When he straddles me, my heart misses a few beats and starts thumping erratically. He bends down to kiss me, and I forget how to exist.

All too soon, he pulls back and collapses onto the mattress with a groan. "You're too irresistible, dove. I'll need to sleep in another room if

I'm going to be well-rested for tomorrow."

"I'll behave," I murmur, pausing to leave a few inches of space between us. "Don't go."

"It's not you I'm worried about." Carter pulls me to him and buries his face in my hair. "You're inside of me, dove. Every last part of me. You're in my veins, in my lungs, and everywhere else, too. I couldn't escape you even if I wanted to."

I wrap my arms around his shoulders and inhale. "I can't escape you either, Carter. And I don't want to."

No matter where this life takes us or what the future holds. I belong here… with Carter.

My decision is made, so I lean back and press my lips to his. He growls into my mouth and climbs on top of me again. This time, I wriggle and squeeze my breasts together. The look on Carter's face is almost enough to make me take it back.

Almost, but not quite enough.

With a smile, I roll my nipples between my fingers and study his reaction. His eyes are tight around the edges, but there's no mistaking the hunger and desperation in his eyes.

I hope it's mirrored in my own.

For the rest of the night, Carter and I explored each other with frenzied impatience, the kind that takes my breath away. At the crack of dawn, when the first rays of gray light peek out from below the horizon, I fall backward onto the mattress, exhausted and spent. Moments later, Carter tucks me into his side, and I curl into him, sleep already calling to me. Through sleep-filled eyes, I study Carter until I can't keep my eyes open anymore.

When sleep beckons, I succumb, the smell of Carter still on my skin.

Chapter Thirty-Eight

Isabella

In my dreams, I'm in a field of grass with a bright sun overhead. There's nothing but blue clouds overhead and only an empty stretch of land for miles on end. I'm barefoot, lying on my back and staring up at the sky, with Carter stretched out next to me. When I twist to face him, Carter disappears before my eyes, and I jump to my feet.

I see him standing at the edge of the field, but no matter how fast or how far I run, I can't reach him.

His hand is still held out, but he won't move closer... no matter how much I beg him to.

Our fingers are inches away when I'm jolted back and thrown to my knees, the bare fabric of the dress I'm wearing not protecting me from the fall. Pain radiates in my limbs and behind my eyelids, but none of it matters. Not when I'm this close.

I reach for Carter again, and he gives me a sad smile before disappearing. I pound on the ground, call out his name, and cry.

When my eyes fly open, I realize I'm drenched in sweat and shaking. Carter sits across from me, one leg tucked underneath him and the other planted firmly on the ground. He's got both arms around my shoulders and a panicked expression on his face.

Little by little, my surroundings tilt and sharpen into focus.

I'm still in our bedroom, but Carter is dressed in a pair of dark trousers and a button-down shirt. There are droplets of water in his hair and on the sides of his face. He holds both of my hands in his, and some of the tension on his face melts when I lift tear-stained eyes up to his. Carter squeezes my hand and offers me a grim smile.

"I'm okay," I whisper unconvincingly. I pause to clear my throat and try again. "It was just a bad dream."

One I hope never comes to fruition.

Carter says nothing as he draws me to my feet and takes me into the bathroom. There, he helps me out of my nightgown, which clings to my body and is soaked in sweat. He balls it up and tosses it into the hamper. Then he switches on the water and watches me while we wait.

In silence, I shift from one foot to the other.

Once enough steam has filled the bathroom, Carter hoists me up and sets me down under the shower spray. Wordlessly, he adjusts the pressure and the temperature. His lips tip into a ghost of a smile as he leans forward and presses a quick to my lips. When he's gone, I sag against the wall and try not to replay the dream in my head.

It's just a dream, after all. It doesn't have to mean anything.

When I come out, Carter has laid out some clothes for me, and I spot my suitcase from the corner of my eye. On top of the suitcase is a smaller bag with a few toiletries and the music box. I smile and change into my jeans and t-shirt, and I'm in the middle of lacing up my shoes when Carter comes in with a tray of food. He doesn't say a single word as I eat the omelet, linger over the yogurt cup, and then finish all the orange juice.

"Tristan and Sam are waiting downstairs."

I swallow and rise to my feet. "Already? I thought Tristan was going to meet us there."

"Sam is here to say goodbye. She's going to be staying with her family up north," Carter replies without looking at me. "Tristan is here to take you to the safe house. It's not safe for me to be the one to drive you there."

My stomach drops, and I can't find the words.

Until Carter leads me downstairs, and the sight of Sam makes me burst into tears. She pulls me in for a hug and strokes my back. When I finally stop, she pulls back and gives me a tight smile. "I got you a burner phone, and it's got my number on it. Call me anytime, okay?"

My throat closes up, so I nod.

Carter wraps his arms around me from behind. I lean into his touch and press my lips together. I am blinking back tears when I give Sam another hug, and Tristan ushers her outside. Through the glass, I see Sam get into her car and Tristan linger in the window. The two of them embrace, and Sam drives off, turning into a speck on the horizon.

For a long moment, Tristan stands in the middle of the driveway, staring at the space Sam occupied. With a shake of his head, he gets into the car and places both hands on the wheel. I twist to face Carter, but I can't keep my lower lip from trembling.

"You could still drop me off. There's time, right?"

Carter's expression is solemn. "When it's safe, I'll come and get you. I promise this will be over soon, dove. Stay close to Tristan. Don't leave the mansion, and don't try to contact me. Tristan will give you updates whenever he can."

I cling to Carter and refuse to let go.

In the end, he has to carry me out of the house, and I spot the note I left by the door out of the corner of my eye. He sets me down in the passenger seat and pulls the seatbelt over, and it clicks into place. Even though Carter doesn't say anything, his emotions are written all over his face.

But he has to be strong for both of us. Because if he breaks down, I won't ever be able to leave him.

I bridge the distance between us to kiss him and pull back. "I'll see you soon."

"I'll see you soon," Carter echoes in a strange voice. He steps back, slams the door shut, and raps on the roof of the car. I press my fingers to the glass and keep my eyes fixed on him. With the early morning sun slanted behind him, he looks like the loneliest man in the world.

Especially as we drive away. He gets smaller and smaller, and I twist in my seat and stare at Carter until we round the corner.

Even then, I don't turn around because I don't want Tristan to see how hard this is for me. To his credit, he keeps both hands on the wheel and doesn't say a thing. The entire ride, I curl in on myself and press my face against the glass. When the mansion materializes in the distance, my stomach clenches, and I feel like throwing up.

Already, I feel like this place is a prison, gilded and luxurious but meant to keep me trapped.

And away from all the things I love.

Carter

"We can't go after their business, not directly at least. They'll see us coming." I trace the blueprints in front of me and glance up at the slew of familiar faces gathered around Anita's dining room table. It feels strange not to have her here, the familiar sound of banging and the smell of her cooking lingering in her air.

And I hate that Isabella isn't somewhere in the house, waiting for me.

But I also know it's better for them to be far away.

I can't trust the Philipses or the Natoris not to attack Anita's house. Already, they've proven to be cunning and resourceful, completely disregarding any kind of courtesy between our families. Instead, they've doubled down on their efforts to expand their business and take the city by force.

I'm already impatient to show them exactly what I'm made of. What we—the Blackthornes—are made of.

Everyone around the dining room table is committed to seeing this through, and every last one of them has proven themselves loyal and true to the cause. When I look over at Paul and see him straighten his back, I return my attention to the blueprints.

"We've got intel about their safe houses and a few places where they conduct their operations," I continue. "We're going to split up into groups. We hit them fast, and we hit them hard, leaving no time for them to recover."

"What about the Donahues? They're already moving in on the docks."

"Rich Donahue is a prick, and I've underestimated him. I won't be making that mistake again. He's going to be my problem, but we need to take care of the Philipses and the Natoris first."

Because they are the more immediate problem.

Focusing my attention on Rich is personal and won't get me where I need to be.

Eliminating the Philipses and the Natoris, however, remains my priority.

Once I'm done with them, I'm going to make sure Rich and his men bathe in their blood. Throughout the day, more and more Blackthorne men show up, many of them arriving from out of the country. Considering the number of people we're meant to fight and the severity of the threat, I've called in all reinforcements.

Even the Blackthornes who've expressed their doubts are here.

Despite our issues, we are all united under a common banner, a common enemy.

And we won't rest until our enemy's legs are cut off and thrown to the wolves. In the afternoon, I send out the first group to target one of the Philipses' warehouses. Since it's one of the lesser-known ones, my men are able to break in easily and set the whole place on fire. In the distance, I watch as black smoke forms and rises to the sky. Then I take a few pictures and tuck my phone away.

Next, we target another one of their warehouses, a bigger one with more security out front.

I take most of the guards out without breaking a sweat, and as I step over the trail of dead bodies, I'm filled with a grim sense of satisfaction. Inside, it's all too easy to lay claim to the merchandise: bags and bags of unattended drugs and guns. Once we're done loading up the vans, I give the signal, and the whole place goes up in flames.

By nightfall, we've received more than our fair share of threats from the Philipses and the Natoris.

War is finally on our doorstep, and I welcome it with open arms.

I know how to navigate this terrain; it's as familiar to me as the back of my hand, and it's not the first time I've had to fight for my family.

But it is the first time I've had something precious on the line.

Each person I kill, each name I cross off the list, is one less threat, and I tell myself that I'm making the world a safer and better place for Isabella.

During my first night without her, I sleep on the couch at Anita's, and my monster lies awake while I toss and turn, the smell of blood still lingering in my nostrils. I ache for Isabella's touch, for the sound of her voice in my ear, and her even breathing reverberating inside my head.

She's the only one who can calm my demons—the only one I'll let close enough to try.

But I can't have her anywhere near this, not when I know the bodies are just going to pile up. In the morning, when the early morning sun pours in through the open curtain, I'm already awake. I am pouring myself a cup of coffee in the kitchen when Paul bursts in, his hair in tufts on top of his head and a wild look in his eyes.

I eye him over the rim. "This better be important."

"I looked into that thing you told me about." Paul drifts closer and runs a hand through his hair. "It took me a while to be able to find out the truth because Rich isn't his birth name. Our guy on the inside was more than willing to help after Rich had his girlfriend killed."

I take a long sip of my freshly brewed coffee, and it's suddenly cold and flavorless. "Having someone from within the Philips ranks is useful. Did he say anything else?"

Paul pulls a folder from behind his back and tosses it onto the counter. "They're keeping a close eye on him, so he's gone radio silent for now."

I frown. "Fuck. We need to keep him happy. Find a way to get him what he needs, and what the fuck do you mean Rich isn't his birth name?"

"It's his middle name," Paul explains, with a vague hand gesture to indicate the folder. "That's why it took a while to find out. This folder has some of the plans Rich has in mind when he takes over."

"And his sister?" I set the mug down on the counter, some of the liquid sloshing over. Pulling the folder closer, I flip it open, and the ringing in my ears grows louder. "Have you found anything about her?"

"There's no sister," Paul replies, with a shake of his head. "I pulled in a few favors, and I had them check. There's no record of Nathan Rich Donahue having a sister."

I clench my hands into fists. "Not even a half-sister?"

"Only Jacob," Paul confirms, pausing to run a hand over his face. "There's something else too. The guy's mom isn't sick. She never was. She works for some mobster in Vegas."

"Fuck." I swing my fist, and it connects with the nearest wall. A sharp pain shoots up my arm, but I ignore it and punch the wall again, needing to let my frustration out on something. "That lying motherfucking piece of shit. Is there anything he said that's true?"

How in the hell did I not look into any of this? How had I let myself be blinded by my need for an ally?

I'm usually a lot better at digging into people's pasts and dragging out skeletons they left buried in the most obscure of places.

IVY BLACK AND RAVEN SCOTT

Rich fucking Donahue shouldn't have been an exception. I'm going to rip his head off with my bare hands when I get a hold of him.

"He and Jacob didn't get along. That much is true. There was some kind of bitter rivalry, and their father encouraged it, thinking it would make the boys tougher."

"Put out some feelers." I stop punching the wall and spin around to face Paul, letting my bloody hand fall limply to my side. "Offer a reward for anyone who knows anything about the whereabouts of Rich Donahue. God only knows what that son of a bitch is planning."

Or how long he's been waiting in the wings to swoop in. Jacob's death gave him the excuse he needed to step out of the shadows and into the limelight. And like an idiot, I've been paving the way and clearing all obstacles for him.

Goddamn Donahues.

I give Paul a pointed look, and he scurries out of the kitchen. Through the window, I watch him stagger and stumble down the driveway before getting into the car. Once he's gone, I call Tristan and tap my feet impatiently. I'm debating whether or not to drive over to the safehouse myself when Tristan picks up, sounding disoriented and confused.

"It can't be over already."

"You need to keep a close eye out. Fucking Rich lied about everything. This means he's going to gun for Isabella."

Tristan's exhale is sharp. "How much bullshit are we talking about?"

"I don't have proof yet, but I'm guessing he was behind the kidnapping at the hospital and everything else. I'm going to fucking bury him myself."

Already, I'm imagining how to do it. Because I want it to be slow and painful.

I want Rich to beg and plead for his life, and I want to watch as he comes undone in front of me, completely and utterly at my mercy.

"Shit." Tristan's voice is softer when he speaks. "She needs to know,

Carter. She likes and trusts the guy. I can't believe you still haven't told her."

"Isabella has been betrayed by enough people in her life. I'm not going to tell her one more person wants to use her."

"Carter—"

"When this is over, I'll decide when and if I tell her," I snap, my breath coming out in short, shallow gasps. "Your job is to fucking keep her safe, not play shrink. You got that?"

A long moment passes.

"Got it."

As soon as Tristan hangs up, I hurl the phone across the room and watch as it misses the wall and bounces onto the floor. I storm to where it sits, pick it up, and debate crushing it in my hand, but I know it won't do me any good.

Not when I'll be picturing Rich the whole time.

An hour later, I'm in the front seat of the SUV, with Ernesto sitting next to me and a tense Paul in the backseat. Although he spent the last hour trying to gather more information, all his contacts have nothing else to add, and I can't spare him because of the war we're waging.

Fucking Rich is going to have to wait till I'm ready for him.

With that in mind, the car screeches to a halt a few blocks away from another warehouse. The Philips men are already waiting for us, and both sides of the street are empty. Almost abandoned.

I duck behind the SUV, take out my gun, and fire blindly.

Smoke fills the air, and the sound of gunshots rings in my ear when I step out. I fire off a few more rounds, the blood pounding steadily against my ears. We take out a few more men, only pausing to drag the bodies back inside. Once we're done, Paul and I snap a few pictures, and I keep them on file.

I can't seek out Mayor Hughes yet, but the file I'm preparing for him should be enough. Any man with a lick of common sense would run in the opposite direction.

Despite his ambition and greed, the mayor doesn't strike me as the self-sacrificing type. On the contrary, I fully expect him to flee in the opposite direction, leaving his new allies to fend for himself. Little by little, I'm going to cut off all his options until he's left to stand on his own two feet.

Then and only then will I go after him myself.

On the fourth day, Paul has found an in with the press, and the article has been taken down. We barely have a chance to rejoice when we get the news that our businesses are being attacked. I run out the door, with Ernesto and Paul following close behind. Under the cover of night, another battle breaks out, leaving a slew of dead bodies on both sides.

I taste blood on my tongue, and my ears are ringing when the gunshots stop.

That night, I'm suddenly glad that I sent Isabella away.

War is a messy business, and I can tell it's going to take a lot more than a few planned strikes and the threat of blackmail to stop my enemies.

While I was distracted, they've gotten bolder and bigger. But I'm not the kind of man who makes the same mistakes twice.

Chapter Thirty-Nine

Isabella

"Tristan, come on." I link my fingers together and frown. "It's just a walk."

"I'm sorry, Isabella, but Carter will have my head on a pike if I let you out." Tristan shakes his head and shifts to block the door. "There's a gym downstairs. Why don't you use one of the treadmills?"

I throw my hands up in the air. "I don't want a treadmill. I want fresh air."

"Why don't you go out into the garden?"

With its barbed wire fence and large trees and bushes obscuring us from view, the garden isn't much better. Knowing that we've been cooped up here, away from everything, doesn't help, nor does the knowledge that I've been away from Carter for a while.

We've never been apart for this long. And it's making me angsty and restless and keeping me up late into the night.

Only the thought of the life growing inside of me gives me any kind of incentive to do anything. Because I know that I need to stay healthy for our baby. Our baby needs me more than I need Carter.

I huff. "Fine, can you at least get in touch with that guy who delivers stuff? I need a few things from the pharmacy."

Tristan purses his lips together. "Write it down."

"Why don't I just carve it into the wall like other prisoners?" I grumble before shifting away from him. I feel Tristan stare at my back, but I don't acknowledge him. Instead, I step into the kitchen and rummage around for a pen and paper. After writing down a few things, including a few vitamins Sam recommended, I hand Tristan the paper.

He folds it and places it in his back pocket. "Anything else?"

"I'm going to be a little late for dinner, warden."

Without waiting for a response, I turn my back on him and hurry down the stairs to the basement. I flick the lights on and wait for my eyes to adjust. The pool is covered, and there is state-of-the-art equipment to work out on, but none of it feels impressive.

It feels cold and impersonal. And they're all covered in a thin layer of dust. I hate this place and everything it represents. It's not the haven Carter wishes it was, through no fault of his own.

Frowning, I find a clean rag and wipe down the treadmill. Then I power it on and bring my arms up on either side of me. While I walk, I wonder how much longer I'm going to be staying here.

And whether or not Carter is going to keep his promise.

News has been scarce, with Tristan only giving me the bare minimum regarding Carter. Not being able to see him is hard enough, but not being able to hear his voice is worse.

Still, I know it's for the best; otherwise, I'm going to sink further into my depression. My frown deepens as I change the speed on the treadmill and move faster as if I can outrun this place and everything it represents. An hour later, Tristan's footsteps reach me, and he emerges carrying a plastic bag in his hand.

He sets it down on the floor and straightens his back. "Any preferences for dinner?"

"I didn't know I had a choice in any of this."

Tristan runs a hand over his face. "I don't want to be here either, Isabella. Do you think I like knowing that I'm stuck babysitting while the rest of the Blackthornes are out there fighting for our future?"

I jab the stop button and wait for the treadmill to slow to a halt. "Then let's go back. We can both be useful, Tristan. You know that Carter needs me right now, and I know he needs you."

Tristan shakes his head. "Not as much as he needs you to be safe. I'm not going to make that mistake again, Isabella. Carter and I might have our differences, but I know how much he cares about you. I'm not taking you back."

I give him a blank look and press my lips together.

Tristan's expression hardens. "Look, I don't care if you sulk or pout or whatever it is that you want to do. I'm here to keep you safe."

"I'm not a child."

"I don't fucking care," Tristan snaps with a sweeping hand gesture. "We're both here whether we want to be or not, and it's because of Carter. So do with that what you will."

With that, he spins on his heels and leaves.

As soon as he does, I sink to my knees and draw my legs up to my chest. Tears stream down my face when I bring my back to rest against the wall and squeeze my eyes shut. I'm dashing away the tears and ignoring the damp smell that's making my stomach recoil when my phone rings.

Sam's number flashed across the screen. I let it ring for a while.

When I answer on the last ring, Sam sounds relieved. "I was beginning to worry."

"I'm not mad at Tristan, not really." I twirl a loose thread around my finger. "He's just following orders. I know that, but he doesn't have to be such a dick about it."

Because it reminds me too much of Carter and what I've left behind. I don't even know if Carter is coming back to me. And the thought keeps me up long into the early hours of the morning.

I can't eat, and I can't function.

And I hate that I'm locked up in my gilded cage while Carter is out there, fighting for the future of his family. While a part of me is proud of him for standing up for what he believes in, the other part wants this to be over.

I've never been so conflicted in my entire life.

"I hate to be the bearer of bad news—"

"I know it doesn't end with this war," I interrupt, pausing to run a hand over my face. "I know this is just part of the life that Carter leads, but I can still hope for some peace, can't I?"

Sam sighs. "Or you can ask Carter to walk away."

"Walk away from the mob life?" I pull the phone away from my ear and snort. When I press it against my ear again, I'm filled with amusement and disbelief. "Have you met the guy? It's like so deeply ingrained in his personality, I don't think he knows how to function like a normal human being."

Carter's been the head of the Blackthorne family for a long time. So long that I doubt he remembers what it's like to be an average guy.

I don't think he would know how to function in the real world, where his biggest problems would be traffic, taxes, and keeping up with the rising cost of living. The more I think about it, the more ridiculous I feel.

Carter can't have a nine-to-five job and come home to me at the end of the day so we can watch movies and talk about our days. As hard as I try to picture him in a suit, with a briefcase, a boss, and a regular salary, I can't. Since the moment I laid eyes on him, I've known Carter was different, ruled over by ambition and single-minded determination.

It's what has gotten him this far. It's one of the many reasons I love him, in spite of the darkness. And I don't want to think about what would happen to the Blackthornes if he walked away.

What would become of Tristan, Anita, Paul, and the others? Would they even survive without Carter in their corner?

As scared and worried as I am, I know I can't condemn his family to that life, not without carrying that guilt around. Carter loves me enough to consider it. Hell, he might even agree to walk away for a time, but I don't want him to resent me for making him walk away from his empire and his own blood.

Like it or not, the Blackthorne empire is part of the package deal.

Sam murmurs something in the background, and I hear a door click shut. "You could always ask. You've got nothing to lose, right?"

I shake my head. "I've got everything to lose. If Carter feels like I'm having doubts about him or us, he's going to fly into a rage. And he needs to stay focused. One problem at a time."

"Aren't you having doubts though? Isn't that what this is about?"

I stretch my legs out in front of me and blow out a breath. "I don't know, but I do know that being here isn't good for my mental health. It's driving me crazy, Sam. I don't know how much more of this I can take."

Or how much longer I can remain at the mercy of the vicious voices in my head. The ones telling me that Carter might not come back to me after all.

What if when he's done, he realizes that I'm too much of a hassle?

I don't fit into his world. I've never fit in, and a part of me will always wonder if he could find someone better suited. Especially in my current condition.

"Please tell me you at least told him about the baby," Sam whispers after a lengthy pause. "I don't know how much longer I can keep it a secret."

"I left him a note."

"A note? Why didn't you just tell him?"

"I kept trying, but I couldn't find the words. Anyway, he'll see the note when this is all over, and then we can talk about it."

"I hope you know what you're doing."

I do, too.

Because right now, I'm just trying to keep my head above water to survive.

CHAPTER FORTY

Carter

I slam my hands against the table hard enough to make it rattle. "What the fuck do you mean our man on the inside has disappeared?"

Paul winces and takes a step back. "I've tried all the usual methods to contact him, but nothing."

I sweep everything off the table, and a few cups shatter, sending shards in every direction. Abruptly, I push myself away from the table and begin to curse.

How in the hell are they still one step ahead of me? Even with a man on the inside, feeding us information about their next moves?

Without him, we're going to have to go in blind, and I don't like our odds. I don't fucking like them one bit. We're already drawing too much attention to ourselves, and with the police in the mayor's back pocket, I know they're circling us.

How long is it going to be before they come knocking?

The only thing keeping them at bay is the knowledge of what'll happen if they target us directly. While the police might be in the mayor's back pocket and on his payroll, I know the chief of police isn't stupid enough to go after me directly.

Or any of my men.

Because he knows the Blackthornes have ties beyond the borders of the city. Unless he wants fire and brimstone to rain down on his precious city, the chief of police is going to keep turning a blind eye and find excuses to let me off the hook.

Even as the pile of dead bodies grows.

I've already lost too many of my men to consider this a sweeping victory.

Right now, we just barely have the upper hand, but I know it won't be long until our enemies throw something else at us. I've spent all week fending off attacks from the Philipses and the Natoris, just barely keeping them at bay. As for our dear mayor, I haven't seen hide nor hair of him, and I know exactly why.

When push comes to shove, Mayor Hughes is a fucking coward. This might be the only good thing he's ever done for me.

And I know that he's hunkering down in his fortress and waiting to see who emerges victorious. When the smoke clears, and he's left to clean up the debris, Mayor Hughes will be free to claim victory for himself and clean up the city for his constituents. After that, it'll be a matter of allying himself with the winner.

Fucking asshole.

I should've taken care of all of them before this spiraled out of control.

When I spin around to face Paul, he's eyeing me warily, and his hands are clenched into fists at his side. "Find me another man on the inside. I don't care what it takes, and I don't care how much it costs. We need to stay ahead of them."

And I need to know what Rich is planning next. Because a man like that doesn't just disappear.

As soon as Paul leaves the room, I fish my phone out of my pocket and dial Tristan. He answers on the second ring, and I hear Isabella's voice in the background.

It soothes some of the anger pumping through my veins. "Has

anything happened? Are you safe?"

Tristan pauses. "We're safe. Isabella wants to talk to you."

Before I can protest, her voice comes on, and I have to press my head against the nearest wall. "You have no idea how much I fucking miss you, dove."

"Carter, I miss you too. When am I coming home?"

"I don't know yet. There's still a lot of shit that needs to be taken care of, and I don't want you here until it's safe."

Isabella exhales, and I hear her footsteps. Moments later, I hear a door open and close. When her voice comes back on, it's clearer than before and filled with sadness. "I wish you were here."

"Just pretend that I am," I tell her in a husky voice. "Pretend I'm behind you right now, running my fingers over your soft skin and kissing the back of your neck."

Isabella's sigh is full of longing and yearning. "I can feel you."

"Can you feel me pressing myself against your back? Can you feel how much I miss you?"

Isabella makes a low noise, and it's all I can do not to snatch my keys off the counter and race to her. I imagine pressing on the gas and speeding past all the traffic lights and all the traffic until she's in my arms. Then, I see myself kicking down the front door and taking her into my arms.

I need to feel her.

I need to taste her.

"Imagine me tying your hands together," I continue in a thick voice. "Are you imagining it?"

"Yes." Isabella's voice is low, breathless, and full of hunger. "I'm imagining myself pressed against the wall in your study, completely naked, while you stand behind me."

I release a harsh breath. "I had no idea you were so good at this, dove. What other hidden talents do you have?"

Isabella lets out a low moan. "You could come over here and find out."

I groan. "Don't tempt me, dove. I want to bend you over and fuck you so badly."

Before she can respond, the door to the dining room opens, and Paul emerges. I wheel around to face him and give him an angry look. A few more men linger in the background, all of them waiting for our next plan of action. With a frown, I stand up straighter and clear my throat.

"We'll finish this later, dove. Enjoy yourself for me."

Without waiting for a response, I hang up and shove the phone into my pocket. In silence, I motion for everyone to spread out, and they take up their usual spots around the dining room table. For the rest of the afternoon, we discuss one plan after the next, trying to find a way out of the labyrinth that's been created.

Without someone feeding us information, I'm all too aware of our blind spots.

Because of our consistent barrage of attacks, the Philipses and Natoris have closed in on themselves and hunkered down. Every warehouse and every safehouse they have is now heavily guarded, leaving us with fewer areas to attack. A part of me races to find a solution and think of a way to draw them out.

Another part of me wonders if it might be time to broker a treaty.

Before disappearing, Paul's inside man was convinced they were going to reach out to discuss the terms of surrender on the condition that we stop attacking them. Unfortunately, in the two days since, there's been nothing but silence. They've even stopped going after my businesses directly.

I have no idea what they're planning, but I know it can't be good. How can it possibly be?

"Since they haven't reached out to discuss a truce, we're going to keep hitting them," I announce, pausing to let my eyes sweep over the room. "We're going to keep attacking for every Blackthorne man who has given his life for this war because those sons of bitches need to learn who they're messing with."

Blackthorne isn't just a name. It's a reputation, and I'm not going to rest till the streets of the city are soaked with their blood.

After reviewing a few more details, I gesture to Paul, who waits until everyone leaves. "We need to find fucking Donahue. Even if we manage to beat the Philipses and the Natoris, it won't mean anything unless every last threat is taken care of."

Paul nods. "Do you want me to increase the bounty?"

I shove my hands into my pockets. "Change the terms of the bounty. Make sure that every hitman out there knows that Rich Donahue is wanted dead or alive."

Isabella

"I know you're cheating." I throw my cards onto the table and fold my arms over my chest. "I just haven't figured out how you're doing it. But I'm going to kick your ass when I find out."

Tristan lifts the beer bottle up to his lips. "I'm not cheating, Isabella. You've got a terrible poker face."

"I do not," I insist with a shake of my head. "You've just had more practice."

Tristan takes a long swig of his beer and sets it on the table between us. "I keep trying to teach you, but I don't think going fish is your thing."

"Maybe Texas hold 'em or something."

Tristan snorts. "Are you trying to stroke my ego or something? Whatever you want, the answer is no."

I push my chair back with a screech. "I honestly don't know how Sam can stand to be around you. You're a pain in the ass."

"It's exactly why she likes me," Tristan replies with a quick grin. "Can you get me another bottle?"

I step into the kitchen and roll my eyes. After retrieving the bottle of beer from the fridge, I grab the pitcher of iced tea. Then I pour myself a generous amount and eye Tristan over the rim. He has his chair pushed back, his gun on the table, and is scrolling through his phone. From where I'm standing, I can see the security camera footage.

Tristan has everything set to maximum security. It doesn't make me feel safer. If anything, it makes me feel more trapped.

"You could stop staring and ask me what you want to know," Tristan says without looking up. "This is a state-of-the-art security system. Carter had it installed after the last time we were here. The barbed wire, too. It's electric and programmed to render anyone useless."

"How do you turn it off?"

"Biometric scan, fingerprint, and voice recognition. The works." Tristan places the phone down and looks up at me. "You and the baby are as safe as you're going to be, Isabella. You don't have anything to worry about."

I choke on my drink and sputter. "What the hell are you talking about?"

"I know you're pregnant." Tristan holds his hand out, and I bridge the distance between us. After handing him the bottle, I lower myself into the chair across from him.

"Did you think I wouldn't notice the throwing up, the weird food cravings, and the vitamins you ordered?"

"I thought you'd give me a little privacy," I grumble, mostly to myself. "Or are you going to be hovering over everything I do?"

Tristan has the good sense to look apologetic. "I got worried when I noticed how often you were throwing up. Then I watched you and put two and two together. I take it Carter doesn't know?"

I take a long sip of my iced tea. "I left him a note. He should find out when he goes home."

"He's been spending all his time at Anita's," Tristan replies between sips of his drink. "I don't think he can stand to be in the house without you there."

"That makes two of us." I sit up straighter and set my glass down. Then, I link my fingers together and clear my throat. "Have you told him yet?"

"No, and I'm not going to. It's not my business."

"You didn't seem to have a problem getting involved before."

Tristain winces. "Fair enough. I know I fucked up, Isabella. I'm not going to do that again. For the record, I didn't have anything against you. I just didn't like how Carter acted around you."

"And now?"

Tristan exhales. "Now, I know you're here to stay, so I might as well make peace with it."

It's not the ringing endorsement I'm hoping for, but it's the most I'm going to get from Tristan.

For now.

I can't expect anything else, given our history.

Tristan takes a long sip of his drink and sets it down. "For what it's worth, I think that is one lucky kid. You're both going to be great parents."

I raise an eyebrow. "So, you think Carter will want to be a part of the baby's life?"

Tristan pauses, and his expression turns thoughtful. "It's hard to say, but yeah. I think he will, and it's going to make him more insufferable."

His words ignite a spark of hope inside of me.

And the warm feeling stays as I climb up the stairs and turn in for the night.

CHAPTER FORTY-ONE

Carter

I hoist the enemy up the scruff of his neck and pull my lips back to reveal my teeth. "Where did the Natoris go into hiding?"

The man with a bloodied and bruised face presses his lips together and doesn't say anything.

I punch him again, aiming for the wound in his stomach. He wheezes, and his blood pours down the sides of his face and his nose. Still, he won't say a word. He's a lot harder to crack than I thought he would be.

All the Philips and Natori men are. It makes me wonder what they do to traitors.

By now, our inside man is probably long dead, his body dumped in a shallow grave somewhere.

Pausing to roll my shoulders, I release the guy and give him another menacing look. He crumples into a heap at my feet, covered in his urine, sweat, and blood, but he still doesn't beg for mercy. With a frown, I drag him back up to his feet and take him outside to the alley, where Paul and the others have a few more men lined up against the wall.

All of them lift their heads up and say nothing.

I point a gun at the back of the man's head and force him to his knees. "Any last words?"

"Fuck you, Carter Blackthorne."

"I was hoping for something more original than that." I aim the gun and fire, bits of blood and brain matter flying in every direction. Then I kick the man away and gesture to Paul, who drags another shorter man to his feet. He sputters and cries and pleads.

It only makes me angrier.

I take care of him, too, and more of our captives flinch.

When I reach the fifth person, I'm growing impatient, the anger burning through me becoming almost impossible to ignore. I cock my gun and get ready to shoot when the man surrenders. With a grim smile, I pull him to his feet and shove him to Paul. Paul drags him away, and I clean the blood off my knuckles.

That night, I'm in the shower when Paul gets the news.

A short while later, Ernesto is driving me to a press conference in a secure location, where a lot of my men are lying in wait. When I get there, a swarm of reports is already lined up outside. The security team I've hired for the night keeps them at bay, but everyone is on edge. While I know that holding a press conference to help clear my name isn't the way to go about it, I also know that it's important.

I need public opinion to be in my favor. Especially where Mayor Hughes is concerned. And I want to rub my freedom and influence in his face.

Ernesto pulls up next to the curb and grips the steering wheel tighter. "Are you sure you want to do this, boss?"

"They're going to try and shoot me in full view of the press. It's going to drum up a lot of sympathy and outrage because even criminals deserve their day in court," I tell Ernesto without looking at him. "This is all going according to plan."

Ernesto twists to face me. "And if they don't try to shoot you?"

"Then I'll give the press something to think about." I flash Ernesto a grim smile and push the door open. "Stay close and stay in touch with Tristan."

I shove one hand into my pocket, and two of the security team flank me. I climb up the stairs toward the mayor's office, lit up by the pale glow of the moon, and stop when I reach the landing. With a smile, I spin around to face everyone and give them a half-wave. A makeshift podium has already been set up, so I step behind it, the smile never leaving my face.

Out of the corner of my eye, I see Ernesto and a few others hovering on the edge of the crowd.

The crowd goes still and quiet.

"Good evening, and thank you all for coming here tonight." I tap the microphone and lean into it. "I know everyone is busy, so I'm going to get straight to the point. A lot of things have been said about me in the press, and I want you all to know that none of it is true."

Cameras start flashing, and a few reporters lean forward to get closer to the podium.

"As you all know, I ran for mayor and lost. Because of his inability to accept my standing in the community, Mayor Hughes has launched a personal attack against me. I have been nothing but gracious and kind, but I cannot let these accusations hold any longer. I will no longer stand by and allow the mayor to drag my name and the names of the people I love through the mud."

A loud cacophony of voices rises as everyone tries to be heard over each other.

Spots dance in my field of vision.

I search for Ernesto in the crowd and nod. The lights go out, and I take a step back. One of my hired men, a man who bears a passing resemblance to me from a distance, steps forward and takes my place at the podium. Quickly and using the cover of darkness, I creep away and meet Ernesto in the side street. Almost on cue, shots ring out, and the gathering crowd erupts into chaos.

A scream rises through the air as the lights come back on.

My man is on the ground, blood staining his shirt and a strained look on his face. Ernesto pushes me against the SUV and glances around. A few more gunshots are fired, slicing through the air, and the crowd of reporters starts scrambling to get away. A few members of the hired security team lurch forward and pull my double to his feet.

He staggers and stops to look over his shoulder at the press.

Cameras are still flashing, and phones are being taken out.

Everything is a blur of sounds and voices as I jump into the backseat of the SUV and flatten myself against the floor. Ernesto gets into the car and speeds off, weaving in and out of traffic while I talk to Tristan. When we make it to another safe house, one not too far from Anita's house, Ernesto skids to a halt, his heavy breathing filling the air.

I scramble out of the back of the car and run a hand through my hair. "That went better than expected. The mayor is not going to know what fucking hit him."

I only wish I could be there to see his reaction in person.

But I know I can't risk something like that, not when I need everyone else to think I've been seriously injured. Lulled into a false sense of security, my enemies are going to start growing lax and careless, and it's exactly what I need to find their Achilles' heel.

And drive the stake right through their heart.

I can almost taste the victory now.

Ernesto gets out of the car, his hand flying to the gun at his waist. "How long do you think they'll buy it for?"

"If the hospital does its fucking job right, long enough for me to end this war," I reply with a quick glance around the empty street. Slowly, Ernesto and I walk across the front lawn with overgrown weeds and dead grass. At the front door, Ernesto stops to pull the key from his pocket.

I close my fingers around my gun and peer into the darkness. "With the exception of you and Paul, everyone else needs to lay low."

Ernesto doesn't say anything and follows me inside.

In the semi-darkness, I creep forward. The only sound other than my own breathing is Ernesto's. He is somewhere to my right, and I can feel his fear and uncertainty. When I reach the window, I rip the curtain open and stop, allowing moonlight to pour in and cast tiny particles of light on the hardwood floors.

In silence, Ernesto opens the rest of the curtains, giving the entire place a soft and eerie glow.

Without looking at him, I set up the security system using facial recognition and a biometric scan. Then I flick on the main light and slam the door shut. Once the system is up and running, I clap my hands together and give the place a once-over. With two rooms, an old couch with a large sheet draped over it, and a small fireplace covered in dust, this is one of the older Blackthorne safe houses.

It's not the one I want to be in. Not with Isabella in the Blackthorne's manor.

I miss her more than I want to. More than I care to admit it.

My fingers itch to reach for the phone, but I know I can't contact her. Not with my enemies on high alert. They are going to be circling everyone I know or care about in search of the truth.

And they need to think I'm down for the count.

As far as the Natoris and the Philipses are concerned, I've been shot by one of their men and am currently being treated at the hospital. While a part of me knows it's a little risky to let them think they have the upper hand, another part of me knows what happens next.

They're going to go after me at the hospital. Which is why I need to lay low and plot the next phase of my plan.

Meanwhile, the rest of the Blackthornes need to play the part of the grieving and shocked family; otherwise, we don't stand a chance in hell.

After doing a thorough sweep of the safe house, Ernesto returns, some of the tension draining from his face. He sets his gun down on the kitchen counter and runs a hand over his face. "They're going to figure out it's not you once they get close enough."

"By then, this should all be over." I fish my phone out of my pocket and send Tristan an encrypted message, something only he can decipher in case he's looking at the news online. The last thing I need is Tristan or Isabella to buy into the report that I've been injured.

The rest of the world, on the other hand, should be eating out of the palm of my hands.

Ernesto takes his other phone out, a secure line he keeps for emergencies, and boots it up. Once it starts, he raises an eyebrow and twists the screen in my direction. "You're trending, boss."

"And that's how you fucking strike." I give him a grim smile and sit down on one of the stools. "Hughes is going to be pissed he didn't think of it."

Now that I've drummed up sympathy on a political scale, I know Hughes is going to be screwed.

How can he explain allowing this to happen on his watch?

He's meant to be a gracious winner. Instead, my press conference casts him in the worst light—as someone who can't handle competition and will do anything to eliminate the enemy.

Fucking Hughes had it coming.

"What about Donahue? Tell me there's news about the son of a bitch." I put my phone down on the counter and keep my gun next to it. As my eyes dart around the room, I try to keep my mind from racing, knowing I need to focus on my next problem.

Rich needs to be eliminated.

While waiting for the Natoris and Philipses to turn their backs, I finally have some time to go after Donahue myself, and I'm buzzing with impatience.

Ernesto shakes his head. "Every single one of our contacts has gone dark. There's talk about them being too afraid of being dragged into this war."

I scowl. "Fucking cowards. Up the price of the bounty."

Ernesto gives me a pointed look. "Are you sure that's a good idea? Won't it look strange that the Blackthornes are increasing the bounty for Donahue when the head of the family is lying in a hospital bed?"

I'm out of my seat and giving Ernesto my most menacing look. "If I want your opinion, I'll fucking ask for it. Just do what you're told."

Otherwise, we are going to have a problem on our hands.

Confined in a space together isn't how I want to plot the next phase of my plan, but I know that Ernesto means well. And I can't stay in a safe house by myself, not if I hope to stay one step ahead of the enemy. Ernesto, Paul, and I need to take turns watching the house until it's safe for me to go back out into the world.

With a frown, I head to the nearest bathroom and slam the door shut.

I can taste the anger and feel it pump through my veins. So I rip off my clothes and throw them into a heap on the tile floor.

In the shower, I think of Isabella, of her soft, sensual mouth and the way her skin tastes in the morning. I picture her in the bathroom with me, stark naked and already wet for me. Then I bring my head to rest against the wall and clench my hands into fists.

I see her with her hair matted to her forehead and a shy smile etched onto her features.

Goddamn it.

Am I having withdrawal symptoms?

It's been ten days since I last laid eyes on her, and in that time, although I've had my hands full, I've been riled up and filled with too much pent-up frustration. Whenever I think of her, I'm filled with the urge to drive to the mansion, kick the door down, and bend her over the nearest surface.

But I know I can't do that yet.

Steam fills the room as I touch myself and imagine Isabella's fingers instead. I see her on her knees in front of me, then pressed between me and the wall. My movements grow faster and more impatient. I press my lips together, and when I finally picture myself buried deep inside of Isabella, I explode.

I wait until my body is no longer jerking and shaking before I clean myself off.

After wrapping a towel around myself, I go into the bathroom and pull the bag out from under the bed. When I go back to the main room, Ernesto is watching the security feed on his camera, a furrow between his brows. "There's a few other people on the street."

I wave his comment away and rummage through the fridge. "The place was swept and secured before we got here. We need to preserve our energy for those fucking bastards."

Ernesto sets his phone down and nods. "Okay."

A short while later, Paul knocks on the backdoor, three consecutive knocks, and a low whistle. I check the feed for a few moments before unlocking the door. His hair is matted to his forehead, and he smells like sweat, but Tristan's brother is a sight for sore eyes.

He gives me a grim smile when he kicks the door shut behind him. "It worked. I wanted to wait long enough to make sure the Natoris and Philipses bought it. Rumor has it they're already planning how to break into the hospital to kill you."

"Make sure the others put up a good fight," I instruct before sliding the lock into place and ensuring the rest of the security system is secure. "To the outside world, it needs to look like I'm the one who's been compromised."

"Consider it done, boss."

"What about that inside man of yours?"

"He's re-surfaced. When he thought they were onto him, he had to lay low, but he's back and ready to help."

"You better make damn fucking sure that he hasn't turned on us, or it's going to be your head on a silver platter."

Paul nods. "Of course."

"Donahue needs to find out the news. It's the only way he'll come out of hiding."

And a man like Donahue, who has been playing the long game all along, will want to make sure of the news himself. With all his grand plans and all his scheming, he's not going to leave it up to chance or the rumor mill. Word of my incapacitation should be enough to have him racing back to the city.

And then I'll make sure he has the kind of welcome he deserves. The welcome I've been planning for three weeks.

"I'll reach out to the press and see if we can leak some information about your current state." Paul takes out his phone and presses his lips together. "How bad do you want it to be?"

"Rich should think that I'm on my fucking deathbed."

CHAPTER FORTY-TWO

Isabella

"You need to stay off the internet," Tristan warns. "There's a lot of shit out there right now."

I untuck my legs, pull my phone away, and look over at him. "Is there something I need to worry about?"

"Carter is fine, but he has to lay low for a few days."

Fear settles in the center of my stomach and claws through me. "What happened?"

Tristan grimaces. "The less you know, the better. He's fine, Isabella. He just won't be reaching out until the next phase of his plan is in motion."

I swallow. "Please tell me it's going to be the last phase."

Tristan exhales. "It should be."

I cross over to Tristan and link my fingers together. "I need you to tell me what's going on, please. I can't live like this."

Floating from one room to the next, trapped in this too-large house, with my innermost fears and insecurities chipping away at me. I'm going to go crazy if I don't find out what's happening.

I need to know more than the fact that Carter is safe. I want to hear it from his own lips, but I know I'm out of luck.

Tristan has spent the past few days muttering into the phone and staying awake. On the few occasions I've seen him asleep, he is on the couch or at the kitchen counter, his head at an awkward angle, and several guns near him. I know that being here with me is hard for him, but I also know that he's not going to let Carter down.

Not again.

Tristan and I have a strange sort of understanding between us now. And we are bound together by our desire to survive the silence and being kept on the outside.

"It shouldn't be much longer, Isabella," Tristan tells me without meeting my gaze. "Why don't you give Sam a call? I know she'd love to hear from you."

I give Tristan one last pleading look, but he is unmoved.

Huffing, I go down to the basement and flick the lights on. Unable to think of anything else to do with my time, I spent hours last night cleaning every surface till it sparkled and gleamed. Without the dust and dirt, I'm able to appreciate the space better, and I can almost see why Carter included it in the design.

In the morning, the entire place is flooded in sunlight, and it's got a generous view of the backyard, with its lush green lawn and large sycamore trees. With a sigh, I take my burner out of my pocket and dial Sam's number. It rings for so long that I think she isn't going to answer.

On the last ring, she picks up, though she sounds breathless. "Hey."

"I was beginning to think you weren't going to answer."

"No, sorry. I've been spending a lot of time with my family. I haven't seen them in years, so I thought it would be a good chance for me to catch up."

I sit down on the last step and fix my gaze on a random spot on the wall. "I thought you had a good relationship with them."

"Most of them," Sam replies, and then I hear a door clicking shut behind her. "Some shit went down between us when my dad left us, and my mom died. For a while there, it seemed like a lot of them thought that

I did it."

I frown. "Why would they think you killed your mom?"

"They thought my mom had money," Sam replies in a strange voice. "It took them a long time to figure out that I didn't steal it, and that I didn't kill her. Too long, if I'm being honest."

"Fuck. I'm sorry, Sam."

"I'm better off," Sam responds in a quieter voice. "But I have kept my distance because I didn't want to get hurt again."

I twirl a lock of hair between my fingers. "I get that. It's their loss."

"Damn right. So, have you thought of baby names yet?"

I drape an arm over my stomach, and in spite of my situation, I smile. "Yeah, I was thinking of—"

Suddenly, I'm interrupted by the sound of muffled voices and a loud popping sound. Then I hear a heavy thud and a frantic voice calling out to me. The hairs on the back of my neck rise, and I jump to my feet. I reach for the gun tucked into my pocket, and my hand grows sweaty as I hold it.

Shit. Have we been compromised?

"I think someone broke in," I whisper, barely able to hear anything over the pounding of my ears. "Do you have a way to reach Carter?"

"I can reach Anita. She'll figure out how to get a message to Carter. Isabella, don't do anything stupid."

"I have to help Tristan. Get a message to Carter and stay safe." Without waiting for a response, I hang up and shove my phone into my other pocket. I'm trembling when I come out of the basement and see the spatters of blood on the floor.

The blood roars in my ears as I follow the trail and find Tristan on his stomach, his breathing shallow and uneven. Leaving the gun in my pocket, I drop to my knees beside him and press two fingers to his neck. "I'm going to call for help."

Tristan says something, but it's garbled and indistinguishable.

I lower my head and struggle to make out what he's saying. "You should conserve your strength."

"I've already called for help." I'm on my feet and wheeling around before I know what's happening. Rich steps out of the shadows, his hair sticking up on top of his head and a few bruises already forming on his face. He holds his hands up on either side of him and gives me a grim look.

"It's okay, Isabella. Carter sent me. He suspected that security had been breached, and since I was nearby, I knew I could get to you first."

Bile rises in the back of my throat. "What happened?"

Rich gestures to Tristan's outside man, lying in a crumpled heap on the kitchen floor, his blood forming a puddle around him. "He betrayed you for money."

I blow out a ragged breath. "We need to call Carter." I grab Tristan's phone from his pocket and rush to dial Carter's number.

Rich bridges the distance between us and takes the phone out of my hand before I even press the first number. "You're not going to be able to reach him. He has to go underground. That's why he sent me. We need to get out of here, Isabella. How fast can you pack your things?"

"I'm just going to need a few minutes." I move toward the stairs and pause to glance at Rich over my shoulders. "How will Carter know where we are?"

"I'll leave him a note," Rich replies, pausing to take a few steps back. He kneels down beside Tristan and says something into his ear.

"We need to move quickly. The sooner we leave, the sooner Tristan can get the help he needs," he says, gesturing for me to hurry.

I hesitate on the landing. "We shouldn't leave him behind."

Rich stands up. "I'm sorry, Isabella, but we can't take him. He's been seriously injured. It's a good thing I came along when I did; otherwise, you'd be hurt, too."

I am panting when I reach the top of the stairs.

All I can think about is Tristan bleeding out downstairs. I can't stop myself from shaking as I pack up the few items I have with me into the suitcase. Once I'm done, I cast a quick glance around the room, and my eyes linger on the music box. Hastily, I stuff it into the bag before darting into the en-suite bathroom and splashing some cold water on my face. Quietly, I pull my phone out of my pocket. It takes me a few tries to be able to send a message to Sam. I wait till I'm sure it's gone through before returning to the bedroom.

I walk toward the bed and am zipping up my bag when Rich appears in the doorway.

It's then that I notice the cut over his right eye. His clothes are rumpled, and he's got a strange gleam in his eyes, but I'm still thankful to see him.

And I'm relieved Carter was able to reach out to him before going dark.

Rich grabs my bag and picks up my phone, which I left lying on the bed. *Stupid.* I should have put it back in my pocket.

Holding my sweater out, he smirks and tucks my phone away. "Let's go. We've already stayed too long."

"Are you sure it's safe for us to go on the run?" I follow Rich down the stairs and spot Tristan lying on the couch, his face almost completely devoid of color, clutching his wound. In the doorway, I dart back to Tristan and give his hand a firm squeeze. "You're going to be okay. We'll see each other soon."

Tristan's eyes widen, and he looks distressed. He struggles to speak, but I don't understand what he's saying.

But before I can ask him to repeat his words, Rich ushers me outside and toward his car, hidden behind a row of bushes. He pauses in front of the car, tosses my bag into the back, and gestures to me to get in.

I pause and glance up at Rich's face.

"What did you say happened again?"

Rich gives me an annoyed look. "I was nearby, checking on something for Carter, when he called me because he got a tip. As soon as I found out, I rushed over. The guy who's been helping you with food and supplies wouldn't let me pass, and that's when I realized he was working with the enemy."

Ice settles in my veins. "So, you killed him?"

Rich glances down both sides of the empty street and back at me. "We really don't have time for this. We should already be driving away. Let's discuss this later."

"I want to know why you killed him."

Rich runs a hand over his face. "Are you being serious right now? Just get in the damn car before you get us both killed."

My earlier unease returns tenfold, and I realize why. I have a sinking feeling that Rich is lying to me, but I can't prove it.

And for the life of me, I can't figure out why.

"What I'm trying to understand is why Carter would call you and not Tristan. It doesn't make sense." Why would Carter trust Rich over his own cousin?

Carter and Tristan have had their differences, but when push comes to shove, I know those two have each other's backs. And after the weeks we've spent together, I know that Tristan and I have come to an understanding of sorts. None of this makes sense.

Rich steps forward and holds his hands out in an obviously calming gesture. "You're exhausted, and you're paranoid. Let's get in the car and talk about it at the safehouse."

I shake my head. "I want to talk to Carter. Right now."

Rich frowns. "Isabella," he growls, his impatience clearly on the rise.

I pull my gun from the pocket of my sweater and point it at Rich with trembling hands. "Was I not being clear?"

Rich glances between the gun and my face. "Put the gun down, Isabella. We both know you're not going to shoot me."

I remove the safety and ignore the sweat forming on the back of my neck and sliding down the side of my face. "You have no idea what I would do to protect the people I love."

Rich raises an eyebrow. "You're bluffing. You know how I know? Because you're not like him, Isabella, and that's why the two of you are never going to have a future together. You know that as well as I do."

"Stop talking."

"You know that if you stay with him, you're going to have to become like him, and you don't want that."

"Call Carter. Now."

Because I am definitely not getting into a car with Rich. I have a sinking feeling that Rich is the "bad press" Carter has been dealing with for weeks, and I hate not knowing for sure.

Rich reaches into the pocket of his jacket, adopting a placating expression. "Why don't you just calm down, okay? There's no reason you and I can't reach an agreement."

Before the words completely leave his lips, he launches himself at me. Startled, I drop the gun and fall backward with a thud. Pain blossoms behind my eyelids as I struggle to push Rich off. He has a crazed look in his eyes as he tries to yank me to my feet.

I struggle and squirm. "Get off of me, you asshole."

"I just need to get you away from him, and you'll be able to see the truth." Rich hoists me up and pins my arms behind my back. I writhe and scream, biting him when he covers my mouth. Panicked, I throw my head back, forcing him to loosen his grip. He grunts as I scramble away from him and fumble for the gun.

Before I know what's happening, Rich launches himself at me again.

We both struggle for control of the gun. He turns it around and points it at me. My eyes widen as I work to push it away. Then, a shot rings out, and I squeeze my eyes shut.

When I don't feel any pain, my eyes fly open, and I glance down at myself. Then, I look at Rich.

Rich's eyes are wide open as he glances down at the stain on his shirt. With a wheeze, he falls backward, blood quickly pooling around him. I drop the gun and scramble away, unable to control my shaking. Without stopping to check if he's still breathing, I pat Rich's pockets for the car keys and fish them out.

In a daze, I get into the car and start the ignition.

When I'm far enough away, I realize I'm crying and shaking.

I pull over to the side of the road, stumble out of the car, and empty the contents of my stomach. Over and over, I relieve the scene in my head while my stomach continues to recoil. When I have nothing else to retch, I lean against the car and squeeze my eyes shut.

My heart is racing, and a headache is quickly forming in the back of my skull.

Horror and fear rise within me as my eyes fly open, and I see the blood on my shirt and hands. Using all my energy, I stagger to my feet and open the trunk of the car. After changing out of my stained shirt, I scrub my fingers raw.

It isn't until I'm back behind the wheel of the car that I realize what I've done. Carter's life has finally caught up to me. I've become the thing I fear the most. I'm just like the rest of them.

A murderer.

And I have no one to blame but myself for not getting out sooner. I drape an arm over my stomach and use the other to grip the steering wheel.

What the hell am I going to do now?

Carter

Before the car comes to a complete halt, I push the door open and run up to the front gate. I'm growling and cursing while I wait for the security system to complete the biometric scan. As soon as it's done, I'm racing up the front steps, Isabella's note burning a hole in my back pocket.

I still can't believe I almost missed the note she left me at home before she went to the manor with Tristan. I'm angry that she didn't tell me about it, but I'll deal with that later.

I kick the door open before I come to a complete stop.

It slams backward with a loud cracking sound. I step in, my gun already in my hands, and glance around. When I see the pool of blood on the floor, my heart misses a beat. "Isabella! It's me."

When I don't hear anything, my stomach forms tight knots, and I think I've forgotten how to breathe.

I find a body in the kitchen, his gaze wide and unseeing. Pausing to check his pulse, I step over him and call out again, louder this time. Then I hear a gurgling sound and something like a wheeze. My heart races as I make a beeline for the living room and come to a complete halt.

Tristan is lying on the couch, one hand on his side and the other dangling lifelessly on the floor. When he recognizes me, his eyes widen, but nothing comes out of his mouth. I'm on my hands and knees and gently cradling him by the back of the head. He wheezes something and coughs.

I place my ear next to his mouth and pause. The next words out of Tristan's lips don't surprise me.

If anything, they make the red-hot anger pulsing through me burn hotter. Quickly, I dash into the kitchen and grab the linen tablecloth, tearing it into strips.

"How the hell did Rich get in here?"

Tristan tilts his head in the direction of the body and sways a little.

Ernesto helps me tie the fabric around his waist to staunch the bleeding, but it quickly turns red. "Does he know who took her?"

I make a low noise in the back of my throat, and the vase on the table nearby goes crashing to the ground as I rear back in anger. "Who else would it fucking be? Of course, Rich would go after her."

It makes sense that Rich thought it would be safe to take Isabella.

But I still can't quite believe he has her, so I leave Ernesto and race up the stairs. I kick down every door in the house until I'm standing in the room she stays in. It still smells like her, like flowers and honey, making my stomach dip. I pull out every single drawer and punch the mirror above the dresser repeatedly.

She can't be gone. I refuse to believe it. Not when the contents of her letter are still weighing heavily on me.

I've spent the two-hour drive here reading and re-reading Isabella's note, scarcely able to believe that she didn't tell me the news herself.

Why didn't she tell me in person? Why did I have to wait till I got home to find her note next to the front door?

And if it hadn't been for the fact that I needed more ammunition, I wouldn't have seen the note at all. With a growl, I kick a few more drawers aside and step over the shards of glass on the floor. Ernesto doesn't look surprised when he finds me standing in the middle of a room that looks like a tornado ripped through it.

He motions to me and then follows me downstairs.

"He can't have gotten far. I want that fucking bastard on his hands and knees in front of me."

"Without knowing where his safe house is, he could be anywhere."

When I reach the landing, I swivel to face Ernesto. "I don't fucking care if he's in Antarctica. I want Rich fucking Donahue, and I don't want excuses."

Knowing Rich, he wouldn't have gotten far, not when he wanted to gloat. And lord it over me.

It's only a matter of time before I hear from him, or at least that's what I'm hoping. Because a man like Rich doesn't strike me as the type to relish a quiet victory.

I never should've kept his betrayal a secret.

Tristan says something while Ernesto is tending to his wounds. I spin around to face him and study his face intently. Finally, Ernesto hands him a pen and paper. When I read the words he's written down, the sick feeling in the center of my stomach intensifies.

I'm going to find Rich Donahue and kill him with my bare hands.

Then I'm going to bring Isabella and our baby home if it's the last thing I do.

YOUR FREE GIFTS

Wow we hope we've satisfied your romance itch… for now. If you've enjoyed reading about these alpha males, please take a minute to leave a review.

Are you craving for more dark mafia romance stories? Don't forget to claim your FREE exclusive access to the prequel by joining our VIP newsletter.

You'll also be the first to hear about upcoming new releases, giveaways, future discounts, and much more.

Click here to sign up and get your FREE access to The Umarova Crime Family Series Prequel now! https://BookHip.com/JAJXVPR

See you on the inside,
Ivy Black and Raven Scott

Printed in Great Britain
by Amazon